INTRODUCTION

The agents of Delta Underground Operatives have one critical mission: Keep magic secret. Humans are not ready to know that the creatures from their dreams are real. They're even less prepared to fight the monsters from their nightmares.

When the gods were killed, Alder Shaw—the sole surviving demi-god—established DUO to protect the status quo, solve the mystery of the gods' fates, and safeguard the Puddle, the last reservoir of divine magic. Aided by twin witches Maven and Moxie, Shaw paired up beings of magic who resonated with each other. In tandem with the Puddle, these individuals now enjoy access to a second set of abilities, making them tough to beat.

These beings are the agents of DUO.

Following are the case files of DUO agents:

ACCESS RESTRICTED
File Codename: Hunter's Curse

INTRODUCTION

Agents: Eryn & Larcen
All information is for Your Eyes Only

PROLOGUE

Eryn

POISONED ARROWS SLICED out of the smoke.

I reared back as a shaft whizzed past my cheek, my hair swirling into a twist above my head. A face followed it—pinched, angular, thin lips peeled back into a snarl—and I yanked the bladed fan from my belt as the drow roared a battle cry.

The pointed tines of the fan caught the downward sweep of a crescent sword, snapped closed, and I solidified my shoulder into crystal and rammed into the drow's sternum, knocking him and his sword aside. The dark elf recovered, pivoting and slashing at my head. The poisoned blade passed right through my eyes. At least, it would have if I hadn't caught an air current and swept out of the way.

"Damn sprite," the drow hissed.

My eyes sharpened into diamonds, and I gave him a disapproving look. "I'm an ariel, you cave-skulking, cobweb-

1

munching barbarian. I'd even accept the term air elemental, but—"

I drifted on the wind, out of reach, as the drow slashed at my chest. The air current lifted me higher than I'd planned, and a shift in the winds blew the smoke away.

The valley of the night wisps was burning. Button mushrooms that radiated a pearlescent light shriveled under the heat, and ash lifted from the willows that guarded the valley, scorched black by the fires. The moon well was crushed, spilling milky-white liquid to soak into the grass, and the air seemed to visibly thin, as if dozens of protective veils were being torn away and leaving only one still intact. Everywhere, innocent night wisps winked out of existence, glowing bright purple one moment and snuffed out like candle flames the next. Their shrieks, shrill as the whistle of a boiling tea kettle, were drowned out by the snarling flames.

Their home was being devoured, and it was all my fault.

For a heartbeat, my world stilled, desperation turning to rage as the dark elves flooded into the valley like army ants.

Then I felt it: a wasp's sting as a poisoned arrow passed through my foot. My body convulsed, solidifying into crystal without my permission. I plummeted towards the ground, glass moments away from shattering into glittering shards. The white feathers of my armor fluttered into my face, lashing me to stay awake.

Wrenching my arm even as it stiffened, I sent a blast of wind from my bladed fan. It threw the archer who'd shot me high into the sky, his form disappearing into the smoldering trees, and sent me into the arms of a sentry willow. The whip-like branches were still alive enough to mesh into a net, and they guided me to the ground. I tumbled out of their embrace, fluttering to a halt into the dirt.

I was already frantically trying to relax into my ethereal

form, but the poison had me in its grip. I'd freed only my right arm up to the elbow when the drow with the crescent sword loomed over me. His white hair hung in soot-streaked dreads over his dark face, his violet eyes gleaming with battle lust.

"You've failed, guardian," he gloated. "This valley is ours, and the night wisps will be—"

The drow screamed as I plunged my bladed fan into his foot. It skewered him to the spot, and even as he shifted back to angle a stab into my heart that would shatter me into a thousand pieces, my body relaxed. I hadn't been named guardian solely for my prowess with the bladed fans. I had the Steorra bloodline, the essence of stars and Ancient kings, and no poisoned arrow kept me prisoner for long.

I rolled away from the stab, abandoning my bladed fan and pulling its twin from my belt. The starlight metal tines flashed like moonlight as the fan snapped open. The drow shaded his eyes from the blinding light with a hiss. I still didn't have complete control over my body, and my feet made loud, stomping sounds as I ran over the ground instead of soared. Ducking under the swipe of his sword, I pulled the fan from his foot as I flipped away, slinging dark blood in an arc across the grass. It sizzled on contact, white wisps of steam escaping towards the night sky like ghosts. Like the wisps his kind had attacked and slain.

I whipped around, murderous intent in my eyes. The smile that normally adorned my face was nowhere to be seen. The drow's sneer faltered on his thin lips. My body returned to its misty transparency, and I swept one fan in front of me and then the other, conjuring a cutting wind. The magic of my people tingled like an electric current down into my fingertips.

It shot me like a lightning strike through the air.

I landed on the other side of the drow, fans dripping dark blood. The trampled grass hissed with every droplet. Then there was a creak, like that of a rusty door opening, and the drow's head tumbled off his shoulders. His dreadlocks scattered from his severed head like withered seagrass, and his body slumped first to its knees and then to its chest, the chainmail armor ringing like jingling coins.

Snapping my wrists, I flicked the blood from my bladed fans and looked for my next target. I could kill them all and it would never avenge the massacre I'd failed to prevent. This valley was supposed to be secret, and they'd broken its defenses as easily as if cracking an egg. I coughed as the wind shifted, smothering me in the smoke of the dead once again.

The gray clouds swirled as another drow appeared. A circlet of black iron trapped his white locks against his head; no doubt the general of this slaughter.

I raised my fans with a scream.

"Please," the drow hissed. "Take them."

Startled, I realized he cradled a milkweed pod the size of an overgrown gourd in his hands. I would've decapitated him just like the other drow, but then he would've dropped the pod, and the night wisps inside would've been lost.

"How did you—"

"There's no time." He twisted his head, his pointy ears registering the nearby shouts. I'd heard them too. "Take it."

"This is some sort of trick," I said, but I felt my bladed fans lowering. He was unarmed—or rather, that wicked-looking blade was sheathed at his side—and despite him being a drow, he actually sounded sincere.

"I cannot take them myself. You're a guardian ariel, are you not?"

I blinked in surprise. Drow were our natural enemies. They skulked in caves while we soared the sky. Their world was darkness, ours was celestial light. They never referred to us by our given name, only by the derogatory name "sprite."

"Please." His violet eyes pleaded with me. I'd never think a dark elf was pretty, but those violet eyes were flecked with gold, and the effect was mesmerizing. "They're the last."

I snapped one fan shut and shoved it into my belt. I extended a hand, keeping the other poised to slash him clean across the neck. He hesitated for a moment, knowing he'd have to get close to my bladed fan, but then he gently transferred the milkweed pod into my care. I cradled it as I would my own offspring.

Backing away and keeping my fan between us, I glanced down at the pod. Its dark-brown surface was as smooth and supple as calf leather, veined with lines that pulsed with a faint purple glow. It was whole, intact, the unborn wisps safe and healthy.

"Why are you doing this?" I asked, looking up.

The drow was gone, and the shouting was getting closer.

I replaced my fan into my belt and held onto the pod with both hands, fearful I'd drop it.

This valley was lost, but these few could be saved.

They had to be.

CHAPTER ONE

Eryn

THIS WAS the last dawn of my life, and even as I watched the sun break through the clouds and herald a new day, I knew it was a lie. Nothing this beautiful could mean death. Right?

"It's sunrise, Guardian Eryn," a voice behind me prompted gently. Gentle Ciri. She was risking her standing within the hierarchy by requesting to be part of my escort.

"She is guardian no more," a second voice corrected, this one also female. Shara, bitter as the north wind. "She is exile. In accordance to the law, you have one hour after dawn to vacate the temple, or you will be—"

"Turned to stone and buried away from the air forever, I know," I interrupted cheerfully.

"The Windless Place hasn't had another statue in millennia," Shara sneered. "Just think. No light, no wind, nothing but the earth pulling you deeper—"

"And no Sharas to weigh us down with their depressing

monologues." I beamed a smile at her. "Sounds quite restful, doesn't it?"

"Eryn," Ciri began.

I flung up my hand, silencing any other opinions, and spent another precious second memorizing a view I would never see again. I'd seen every morning from this balcony for the last two hundred years, and they were not about to ruin my last one. The view was impeccable from the Temple of the Sky, a haven forged of sun gold atop the clouds that shrouded a sky spire mountain. Celestial light was untainted up here, as was the air, and I'd never know such purity again. Being a guardian of this sacred place was all I'd ever wanted to be, and now—

"Three hundred and forty-nine years," I muttered, turning away from the balcony. "Wasted."

I was young for an ariel—an air elemental, as the humans and fascinari liked to called us—and there weren't that many of us around since the Ancients left, so my kin would mourn me even as they condemned me. Well, except Shara.

She was large for an ariel, tinted silver where the rest of us were as pale as the morning mist. Shara lacked the quintessential sunny disposition and scowled more than smiled.

I wouldn't miss her.

"Just look on the bright side," she sneered as I floated past. "We'll always remember you here, exile. The cautionary tale we'll tell our offspring."

"You? Have offspring?" I said, genuinely surprised. "What a horrid idea."

Ciri choked back a laugh.

Smiling, I flew to my bed where the night wisps—my adopted offspring—were congregating in a downy huddle on the celestial silver sheets, readying for sleep. They looked like glowing, purple dust motes, if dust motes were the size of quail eggs. They'd grown well these past ten years. If these few could survive another attack, they'd even grow to the size of walnuts or even plums. They were the last of their kind, but now that they could fend for themselves and colonize a new valley, I was no longer needed.

By anyone.

The biggest one, Nef, rose from her sleepy siblings, drifting on an unseen current. She'd fought off the pull of sleep—night wisps were solely nocturnal—to say goodbye. I cupped her in my hands and lowered my face until I felt the softest touch against my forehead. Night wisps this young couldn't speak, but they could relay emotions through touch. I tried not to focus on the sad ones.

"I'll miss you too," I whispered, setting her back down with the others.

The night wisps stirred drowsily at my touch, and I felt the currents of contentment, happiness, security, and peace ripple across my fingertips. Another wisp, this one paler than the others—Lox—was roused enough to consciousness that he drifted into my hand.

Shara lunged forward, slapping my wrist away. "That is enough!"

Her fingers brushed against Lox, and for the briefest second we were all connected. I saw a flash of something dark before Lox tumbled out of my hand and into the mass of the glowing purple bodies of his siblings.

"What the—"

"You've spoiled them long enough." Shara flew into my face, and I immediately backed up.

Ariels didn't like their space being invaded by others of our kind. It led to essence blending, and it could take weeks to purify yourself after an encounter. It was how our kind dueled, the essence of the one with the stronger will prevailing. My hand reached for my bladed fan.

Shara's silver-tinted eyes gleamed. "Do it, exile. Give me an excuse."

Clenching my jaw, I released the fan and forced myself to smile. I was baring my teeth, actually, and it had the desired unnerving effect.

Shara straightened.

"You should've never let them sleep with you in that bed," she said. "Now they'll never leave it."

"Lucky for me, I don't give a gnat's fart what you think," I replied cheerily. "And they deserved whatever comfort I could give them."

"You didn't need to coddle them."

"They lost their entire race in a single night," I snapped at her, finally losing my patience. The smile was still on my face, but my eyes had hardened into cut crystal. "There are fifty-seven of them left. Fifty-seven reasons why I wasn't banished immediately. If they wanted to eat lychees for breakfast instead of nectar, I would've served it up on a sun-gold platter for them and then dusted each and every one of them with Luna moth powder to fight through the indigestion."

The night wisps began to swirl, sensing my agitation. I immediately released the hold on my anger, letting it dissipate, fearful they'd feel the anxiety and sadness welling up within me. I wanted their last memory of me to be of happiness, not an echo of the time we'd first met.

"Eryn," Ciri prompted again, this time with worry in her voice.

She didn't use the honorific this time, but neither did she call me "exile" like Shara was so fond of doing.

I was risking eternal imprisonment in stone if I didn't hurry. "Make sure you turn the starlight metal lamps on at night," I told no one in particular. "They need the extra light." With one last look at my darling night wisps, I flew towards the moon gate door.

Shara blocked my path, her bladed fan in her hand. It wasn't open—yet—but the fact that it was out of her belt was threat enough. She smirked, tapping the fan against her thigh. "You take nothing with you."

Staring her right in the eye, I drew the bladed fans from my braided belt and dropped them unceremoniously to the floor. Then I shucked my belt and sloughed out of my feather armor. The white plumes fell like wilted lily petals to the ground. Only guardians and the elders had the strength to wear clothes made of celestial silver silk or albino ostrich feathers. Naked, my body automatically morphed into a more modest and androgynous presentation.

With a gust of wind that made Shara stumble, I swirled to the moon gate, pausing to take a glance at the room that had been mine for over two hundred years. Our Ancient ancestors had refined sunlight into sun gold, a metal as delicate as spun sugar but as tough as corded steel. It absorbed the sunlight during the day, radiating a brilliant yellow light, and glowed amber in the evening. Spiraling sun-gold pillars supported a vaulted ceiling, and pale moonlight streaked with gray composed the floor. White curtains spun from starlight and celestial silver fluttered at the windows and balcony, the breeze gentle yet persistent.

The Temple of the Sky was never without wind.

The night wisps are safe, I told myself for the hundredth time that morning. *They're safe. You can diminish now.*

"Having second thoughts?" Shara snickered. "It's too late for that."

"Just because no one's survived on their own before doesn't mean you won't," Ciri reassured me.

"I still have a few more minutes, right?" I asked.

"Seven," Shara smirked. "You'll never make it to the front gate in time now."

"Plenty of time." I solidified my fist from mist into crystal and punched Shara across her smirking face with all the power of a hurricane. She sailed across the room and crashed into a pillar, dissipating into a flurry of sparkling specks. Her bladed fan and feather armor slumped to the floor, empty. I brushed my hands off as if shedding dust or dirt and sucked in a deep, satisfied breath. "Now, I can leave."

Flashing past a slowly reforming Shara, I dove off the edge of the balcony and plummeted down to the ground.

"Eryn," Ciri screamed, clutching the railing lest she follow me over.

The tower was a blur of sun gold beside me, the ground with its mosaic tiles of colored sky glass rushing up to meet me. Moments before my body would be dashed into a heap of glitter against the tiles, I banked, whooshing past scholars on their way to the archive tower and scattering their star charts and scrolls. Laughing, I blitzed through the fountain in the center of the temple, splashing the guardians as they practiced their forms with their bladed fans. I'd forgotten how much easier it was to fly without armor. I was faster, lighter, almost reckless with the joy of flight. It was the only joy I had left.

The slant in the sundial ticked to the first hour past dawn just as I landed at the base of the temple stairs. My heels were a hair's breadth away from the first sun-gold step, but I technically wasn't inside the temple grounds. Behind me, the temple rose as a beacon of light, and before me, the path of paved white bricks snaked off into a dark forest.

"That was close," a wry voice commented.

I turned around, my hair swirling into a twist above my head. The ariel before me wore a nine-point crown of starlight metal on his head, his hair cropped short so it swirled around

12

his shoulders in an unseen current. A robe of celestial silver silk covered him from neck to ankle, the shoulders and sleeves adorned with stardust. I should've bowed, but I no longer belonged here, so I lifted my chin in response.

"K-King Erysson!" Ciri panted, sailing down the stairs. Shara was not too far behind her, glowering and still trying to adjust her armor. "She was escorted—"

"Looks like she brought herself here to me."

I shrugged. "They tried."

Erysson's colorless eyes flicked to Shara, who still hadn't completely reformed from being scattered against the pillar. Half her face drooped down past her neck, and her right arm trailed behind her in a six-foot-long tendril. "Indeed."

I beamed a smile at him, batting my eyes prettily.

His expression, which had been wry interest before, turned formal. "Guardian Eryn, you are forthwith stripped of your title and banished from the Temple of the Sky, never to enter its halls again on penalty of being imprisoned in stone and buried in the heart of a mountain, never to feel the air on your flesh again."

I didn't nod, I didn't blink, I didn't think. If I had done any of those things, the reality of my banishment would've crushed me into stardust right then in there. The only thing I could do was stare King Erysson in the eye. He stared back at me, each of us rooted to the spot. He hovered on the first step of the temple stairs, me on the white brick, less than a hand's breadth between us, yet a world apart.

"Take care of them, Father," I told him. Nef, Kin, little Lox, all fifty-seven of the adolescent wisps no longer had my protection, such as it'd been.

Pain flickered across his eyes as he turned away. "They're no longer your concern."

Ciri inclined her head as the king floated up the stairs, then she raised her gaze to meet mine. "Don't worry, Eryn, I'll take good—"

"Junior Guardian Ciri," the king roared. "You will not speak to the exile!"

She shriveled under the power of his voice, and even Shara stiffened. Ciri dropped into a puddle of glistening specks on the stairs, prostrating herself before her king. She didn't reform until after he'd gone, giving me a terrified glance.

I sucked in a deep breath and mouthed, *"Easy breezy."*

Ciri gave me a tremulous smile, then remembered her duty and pointed to the world beyond.

Turning, I faced the dark forest at the end of the white-brick road and clenched my misty hands into fists. This was my future now. My life's goal, gone. Lost, I felt a sudden panic well within me, and my strangled cry shook the leaves of the nearest trees like a storm wind.

My cry was choked off as a floating white cloud appeared from the forest. A man—a human man!—dressed in a three-piece suit stepped off the cloud as if were a raft and not vapor, his caramel-leather shoes clicking on the bricks. The cloud waited behind him like an obedient pet, and he put his hands on his hips, arching back and sucking in a deep lungful of air.

It was probably the purest air he'd ever inhaled.

When he exhaled, he opened his eyes and smiled warmly at me. "And you must be Eryn. I'm—"

"Peregrin Alder Shaw," I said immediately. How he knew my name was a mystery, but it was irrelevant at this point. The fact that he was standing at the edge of the Temple of the Sky was the real feat. I wondered if his being a druid and a demi-god had anything to do with it.

"So you've heard of me. And it's just 'Alder Shaw.'"

"There might be a scroll or two about you." And not just about him, but of his company too. Delta Underground

Operatives, or as we ariels liked to call it, Assassin's Academy. It was a place where the magically gifted became assassins for the greater good. No ariel had ever been recruited before.

He rubbed his hands together. "This makes the next bit easier, then. I—"

"What *is* that thing?" I interrupted, pointing to the cloud. It hadn't lost its shape, nor had it floated away.

"Oh. That." Alder flashed a smile. "Just something my magitech geniuses whipped up back at HQ. Safer than portaling. Besides, how else was I going to get way up here?"

"Huh."

"So, I assume you know why I'm here?"

"Training for the next Ironman competition? That's the only reason a demi-god would have to be at this altitude."

"Not the only reason." He looked pointedly right at me.

A smile of disbelief split my face. "You're not serious."

"You've got something better lined up?"

"No ariel would ever become an assassin."

He cocked his head to the side. "Ariel?"

Guess this guy didn't know everything. "It's what we call ourselves. Sounds much more musical than your human term 'air elemental.' And the answer's no. We're protectors."

"And that's what you'll be doing. Each assignment protects the world from those who would seek to exploit or destroy it."

He sounded rehearsed, like a used car salesman. Yet something in his eyes told me he was sincere.

Alder took a step forward, and I would've flown backwards had the steps of the temple not been at my very heels.

"I know why you're here," he said softly. "I was alerted of your... impending exile years ago. I'm offering you a chance to protect those who have no one else. For you to guard against those who would hurt them. Those night wisps will eventually need to colonize a new valley. Wouldn't you like to be a part of keeping them safe?"

My heart leapt into my throat, and I swayed, hardly daring to hope.

Alder stretched out his hand, his face kind and warm, the face you'd give a wounded animal to tell it you were a friend. "You're exceptional, Eryn, and DUO can give you the tools to prevent such a catastrophe from ever happening again. Don't you owe it to them to try?"

Fifty-seven of the night wisps were alive because of me—well, not *just* me—but legions of them were dead for the same reason. Their blood stained my hands down to my very essence. Alder was right. I *did* owe them. I would never stop owing them.

Swallowing, I nodded, and took hold of his hand. He jumped at my cooler touch, just as a jolt of heat from him zinged up my arm. Smiling softly, Alder swept his hand through the air, gesturing to his cloud... ship. I joined him, floating just above the cloud, not convinced I should touch it just yet.

With a snap of his fingers, the cloud floated away, leaving my old life—my home—behind.

CHAPTER TWO

Larcen

BAREFOOT, I padded forward with the same silence as a shadowcat. They didn't have those here in the human realm, and a good thing too, since humans would've been usurped from their position at the top of the food chain overnight. They prowled the Night Lands, sometimes delving into the caves of Drozvega if they were hungry and desperate enough to take on a drow.

My ears twitched, sensing microvibrations to the left. I turned, white hair swishing across my shoulder. The spray of a waterfall splattering against a vine leaf. Nothing. I prowled forward, the silver links of my chain dagger slithering down my arm like a friendly snake to slip my blade into my hand.

This training room had been designed just like the caves of my home: vaulted ceilings; pillars that spiraled like twisted roots; mushrooms and creeping vines and thin waterfalls that all glowed with bioluminescent light. Alder Shaw had created it specifically for me, though he'd welcomed anyone else to use it if they so desired. Not many did.

I listened for my opponent's heartbeat. I normally fought against projections, so sparring against a real opponent was a treat. Timmeron had sparred with me here once or twice, but he was a wood elf and didn't care for the subterranean dark. And since he'd partnered up, I hadn't seen much of him.

The scimitar was a slashing crescent moon through the darkness.

My own blade blocked it with a ring, and I whirled, lashing out with the chain dart. The eight-inch dart resembled a silver stake, but thinner, meaner, like a crucifixion nail. A length of chain connected it to my dagger, and it struck like a scorpion's stinger. There was no impact, no flesh for it to bury into, so I recalled the dart. It zinged into my left hand as I tightened my grip on the dagger in my right.

A shadow loomed from above. The spry bastard had climbed the pillar, using the inherent ability of a drow to blend into his environment. No wonder my dart had hit nothing. The shadow dropped, and a dark elf landed in front of me, slashing with his scimitar. His eyes, purple flecked with gold, sparkled with delight. Uncle Malcan only had two great loves in his life, and one of them was fighting.

His scimitar slashed at my chest, and I backflipped out of range, kicking it aside.

My feet hadn't even hit the ground before my chain dart arrowed out of my hand.

Malcan slashed it aside, the dart burying into the stone floor. I stomped on the chain, freeing the dart, and yanked. Malcan caught it before it could return and started reeling me in like a hooked marlin.

"That's the problem with chain weapons," he laughed as I struggled against him. "Someone catches it and you're done for. Might as well be handing your weapon over on a silver platter."

A flick of my wrist, and the dagger released from the chain. Malcan had pulled me in close, and I'd let him, pretending he had me at a disadvantage. Most elves, regardless of race, were as lean as willow branches, but Malcan was built like an oak, and he was going to use his extra weight to crush me.

"Ten years away and you've already forgotten how to fight," he sneered.

My dagger flashed, and a dark line appeared on his cheek, just under the scar that already marred his skin. "Says the drow with blood on his face."

Malcan shoved me away and pressed his palm against his cheek. He rubbed the blood away on his thigh. "Hn, first blood. Well, I supposed you haven't forgotten everything I've taught you. But you still gave me your weapon!"

The chain dart speared me through the chest.

At least, it would have had I not melted into the shadows. The dart hit nothing but air as I reappeared directly behind him, sliding the curve of my dagger around his throat in a perfect fit.

Malcan immediately stilled, lowering his scimitar until the tip *tinged* against the stone floor. "Damn that shadow-walker ability to the scorpion pits and back."

"Jealous." Smirking, I lowered my blade and stepped back.

"You're damn right I am." Malcan whirled around and threw my dart at me.

It was a petulant throw and I caught it easily, letting the chain slide through my hand until it came to the end so I could reattach it to my dagger. Pressing my thumb against the scorpion engraving on the dagger's blade, I held the blade steady as the chain slithered into the hilt, connecting dagger and dart into a seamless unit. It was magic, of course, something the magitech twins had modified to make it adaptable to this human realm. They were brilliant like that, not that any drow would ever admit it to their faces.

"If you'd used actually used your gift earlier, you would've had me a few moves back," Malcan said, giving me a judgmental look.

"And ended the fight too quickly. That'd be boring."

"Drow always go for the fastest victory; it's how we rack up obscene kill counts." Malcan flashed me a wicked grin before turning serious again. "So what is it? What's bothering you that you let a drow seven hundred years your senior almost get the drop on you?"

I rolled my eyes with a snort. "You didn't, for one thing, and it's pathetic, really, and I don't want to talk about it."

"Ah, the gnomes."

"When isn't it the gnomes?" They'd been the bane of my existence ever since I'd won them in a game of backgammon. A little poison pill that had come along with the deed to the plant nursery, no thanks to that bloodsucking bastard of a vampire. The gnomes would grow you the best of whatever you'd like— grain, fruit, veg, herbs, or flowers—but an old curse made them impossible to please, impossible to kill, and impossible to get rid of—unless you tricked someone else into taking over. I'd been desperate eight years ago, and that old vampire at Midnight Crossings had seen me coming from a mile away.

"A shadowcat doesn't concern itself with the opinions of mice, nephew."

Easy for you to say.

"Especially not you. The average drow can manipulate light refraction enough to blend into his environment, but you, you can disappear entirely." Malcan gripped my shoulders. "Why are you wasting away here? Shadow-walking is the rarest ability of our bloodline. You should be with me, Larcen. What you could do—"

The smirk vanished from my face. "Did Father send you? Is that why you're here? To welcome me back with an invitation?"

"I came because I'm lonely and I miss my nephew."

I snorted again, but Uncle Malcan's teasing smile was effective in transforming my anger into mild annoyance. "You always were such a sap."

"And you never judged me for it." Malcan sheathed his scimitar and slung his arm around my shoulders. "I am asking you back, Larcen, but not back to my brother. It's not a true invitation to return to the home cave, but I can get him to agree to anything." Then he touched one of the scars on his cheeks. "Well, almost anything. But I want you with me. I'm on the verge of something magnificent, something you can help me with if you were to use that special sight of yours."

He knew better than to say what I was aloud. Mine was a rare profession, something you couldn't just learn. You had to be born with the predisposition, just like your had to be born a shadow-walker.

I gave him a sideways glance, trying to determine if he was serious. Uncle Malcan rarely took anything seriously, unless it was fighting or his job. He was the only ambassador in Drozvega, but the whispers said it was just his way of spying on everyone else with an invitation.

Malcan released my shoulders, turning to look me right in the eye. "Scorpions and spiders, it's like looking into a mirror when I look at you. We're alike in more ways than one, Larcen. We don't... fit drow society."

He wasn't wrong there. Mine was by choice—mostly—but Malcan was definitely the white sheep of the family.

"I've made my choice, Uncle," I answered quietly. If anyone could get me to come back, it would be him. But without an invitation from the king, I would be shot on sight, regardless of being his one and only son.

"Yes, a flower shop in Savannah. How... invigorating."

"It's a plant nursery, actually. With the best—"

"Roses south of the Mason-Dixon Line. I know. Your mother tells me all the time. Whatever that means." Malcan shook his head with a sigh. His white hair, braided back from his face in our traditional warrior style, whispered over his dark skin. Disappointment flickered across his eyes, but then his lips crooked up into a lopsided smile, and he clapped my shoulder. "Well, if you ever reconsider, you know how to contact me."

Spider webs. Unlike that fat thing camping out in the corner of my herb greenhouse, Malcan had his little arachnid friend clinging to the back of his right ear.

The faint teal light of the glow worms clinging to the ceiling started to pulse.

"And that would be the boss man," I said.

"Considerate of him not to just throw open the door." Malcan withdrew a pair of sunglasses from a pouch on his belt and slipped them on. "Oh, and before you go. Here."

He pressed a sealed packet into my hand: mushroom spores.

"Don't tell your father," he said, giving me a wink.

I snorted. I hadn't spoken to my father in over a decade. I slipped the packet into my vest. "Would you be able to deliver this?" I withdrew a wax-sealed letter from my vest pocket, somewhat damp from the sparring. The ink letters that spelled *Elvera* were starting to bleed.

Without a word, Malcan put it in his own pocket, placing a finger against his lips.

I stuffed my feet into boots at the door and slipped some sunglasses onto my own face. Just before I opened the door, I gave the cut on Malcan's cheek a wary look. "Sorry about your face. Do you want something to heal it before you go back? DUO's got all sorts of healing stuff here."

Malcan gave me a brief, close-lipped smile. "It's barely anything, and it'll heal without a scar. Unlike the last two times I was cut on the face." Twin, sickle-shaped scars marred either side of what most would consider a handsome face. They were thick, raised, and no amount of healing salve would ever erase them. Drow needed to know he'd challenged another and been defeated. Twice.

I glanced down at his hand, the one wrapped in bandages. It hadn't impeded his grip on his scimitar, but it had started to seep. "And that?"

He gave my shoulder a shove. "Quit mothering me, nephew, or I might think you've gone soft."

I yanked open the door, choking back a crass reply. I wasn't expecting to see the director of DUO on the opposite side of the door, just one of his errand boys, but it was, in fact, Peregrin Alder Shaw. He looked composed in his striped shirt and three-piece suit—though the jacket must be in his office—except for his eyes. They were delighted.

I never thought he'd look at me with anything but chastising sternness since the topiary incident, and here he was... excited.

"Your partner has arrived," he announced.

I just blinked, too stunned for words. I'd been recruited ten years ago, and after spending two years at headquarters just waiting around, I'd left to forge a new life in Savannah. The heat and trees dripping with mossy tendrils reminded me of home. I came back to HQ every couple of months to check in and train, but after six years of that, I really hadn't expected the Puddle, the Council, the director—or whoever was pulling the strings around here—to finally find me a partner. I'd only stuck around this long because I didn't want to go home to Drozvega. And now...

"You can always back out," Malcan whispered in my ear.

Alder Shaw gave him a narrow-eyed look. It wasn't necessary. My mind had been made up years ago on the battlefield, my blades soaked in innocent blood.

"Should I change clothes?" I asked.

Alder shook his head. "You'll find that your partner doesn't hold much stock in physical appearance, and you've waited long enough, haven't you?"

"Yes." I turned to my uncle. "Want to come?"

"I wouldn't miss it. Maybe the Spider Queen will bless you with an orc or a yeti, you know, something respectable from a berserker class."

That overgrown arachnid can keep her blessings.

We followed Alder down the hallway, and the people bustling to and fro gave us a wide berth, but it wasn't because we were with the director. Drow, dark elves, whatever you wanted to call us, had a bad reputation, if well earned. I wasn't here to change their minds about my kind, so I didn't go out of my way to correct the more egregious of their assumptions. Let them think of me as a fanatic killing machine. It got them scurrying out of my way like frightened rabbits, and it always kept the champagne stocked in the cafeteria.

Alder led the way out of the training tunnels and to the portal that transported us from HQ to the auxiliary office located in downtown Salt Lake City, Utah. Nicknamed the Hub for its resemblance of a wagon wheel—though those in Drozvega would call a great hall—it was a massive rotunda crowned with a glass dome and hallways that spoked away deeper into the facility. In the middle of the recessed floor was a wide fountain, and boxwood topiaries reached for the dome's sunlight from terra-cotta urns.

I immediately scanned the area, searching for those who

didn't belong. My attention narrowed on a cluster of new faces by the fountain: two humans, a dwarf, a naiad, and a—

"Sprite," Malcan hissed.

There were no words an ariel couldn't hear. Her face, once sculpted from mist, hardened into crystal and snapped in our direction, her colorless eyes widening. "*You*," she screamed.

CHAPTER THREE

Larcen

"You have no iron circlet in your hair, but it's you," the ariel screeched.

The newcomers around her shrieked as she summoned wind, blasting her across the rotunda. The water in the fountain froze with her passage, the pipes groaning under the pressure. One of them burst, jettisoning a stream of water like a geyser towards the glass dome ceiling. It sprayed the air with fine droplets, so fine they almost obscured the ariel.

Almost.

I batted her diamond-hard fist away from my face, landing a strike to her shoulder that sent her careening into the nearest topiary. She dissolved from crystal to mist faster than I could blink, reforming on the other side of the glistening boxwood leaves.

How was she doing that? I'd never seen an ariel phase between mist and crystal at will before.

"Stop," I shouted above the screams and gushing water. I shoved a panicked bystander out of the way as I advanced, drawing the scorpion blade. My thumb hovered above the scorpion icon, but I didn't press the release button, hoping I wouldn't have to unleash the chain dagger.

"You can't reason with a spite, Larcen," Malcan spat, drawing his scimitar. "You just put them in the ground."

There was a ripping sound, and the topiary was cleaved in two from the power of the ariel's wind crescent. She floated through the gap between the bowing halves, her misty form positively glittering with fury. "The night wisp valley. Decimated. Because of you!"

She spun, unleashing a flurry of wind crescents.

She didn't have a fan to help direct her attacks, so they went a little wide, but they were still sharp enough to slice through wood and stone. I melted into the shadows of an urn, reappearing across the rotunda in the shadow of a twisting boxwood just in time to see a portion of the fountain slough off like a shedding scale. Water poured out of the basin like storm surge.

The ariel whizzed here and there through the air like an angry horsefly, her shape hardening and dissolving instantly as she passed in and out of the water spray. She didn't avoid the water like her kin always had, but she had to be solid under the spray, lest the water interfere with her mist-like body and prevent her from reforming. It was an ariel's only weakness.

Something Malcan was going to exploit.

"Here, you miserable sprite," the dark elf shouted, waving his scimitar. "I'll bury you in the dirt just like your—"

The ariel screamed, the sound reverberating off the domed ceiling and making the water droplets shudder in midair. She dove, hands outstretched like eagle talons. They glinted like cut crystal just before she struck, but I'd already released the scorpion blade.

28

The chain dart coiled around her wrist, clinking against her crystalline body like a teaspoon against a champagne flute.

I yanked, and the ariel soared through the air into the water fountain. I pounced, seizing the ariel and forcing her head under the water. Any other ariel would've dissolved into stardust now, but she was as solid as stone in the water, yet I could feel her neck giving as my fingers crushed.

"That's it, nephew," Malcan said, sloshing through the water. "Hold her steady and I'll finish her off."

"Back off," I snapped.

"This isn't the battlefield, Larcen. We can share this kill."

The ariel thrashed, shouting or screaming under the water and releasing a screen of bubbles that obscured her face. I kept my hands tight, half afraid she'd vanish.

"I said back off," I snarled at Malcan. When he clicked his tongue at me in disgust and moved away, I turned back to the ariel. "Yield!"

Her colorless eyes narrowed and her fist went straight for my face. I swerved to the side, narrowing missing the wind crescent. Behind me there was a sickening snap, and I glanced to see the top six feet of a swirl-shaped topiary crash to the tile floor. It hit the terra-cotta urn steadying the rest of the artistic hedge, the pottery shattering under the impact and scattering shards across the floor like skittering cockroaches. The wounded topiary groaned, swaying as its roots were no longer supported by the urn. Like a felled giant, it swayed until gravity claimed it. The topiary crashed across the tundra, smashing the fountain's spire to ruin.

I melted into the shadows, taking the ariel with me, and when we reappeared a safe distance away, she was screaming in terror. Shadow-walking could have that effect on those not used to it. Not many creatures had ever experienced all-consuming darkness, and it could be... disorienting.

I released my grip on her throat as she calmed, but I kept the chain dart wrapped around her wrist, the poisoned tip inches away from her heart. Unlike my uncle, I didn't want to kill her, but I didn't want to get decapitated by one of her wind crescents either.

"That. Is. Enough!" Alder Shaw boomed.

His caramel-leather shoes clicked against the stone floor and down the stairs until they sloshed through the water. They stopped at the edge of my vision, and I dared a glance up into his face.

"My. *Topiaries*," he hissed. "Again. Really?"

I swallowed thickly. Alder Shaw had given me a chance, more than one, and as much as I didn't care for the thoughts of others, this druid's opinion mattered to me. "It wasn't my fau—"

"Haven't they seen enough degradation?" His hard eyes flicked to the ariel. "And you. You were told no fighting."

"But he killed—"

"Take a look around, Eryn. You're in DUO. Everyone here has killed before."

The ariel shook her head, her hair clinking like wind teasing a crystal chandelier. "Not like him. Not like *him*."

"Well you'll have to come to grips with that real fast." Alder straightened, giving his trousers a little tug the way he did when he was getting ready to give someone some bad news. "Eryn, Larcen. Meet your new partners. Congratulations, you've just become DUO's next team."

~

"THEM? *PARTNERS*?" Malcan seethed. "Do you have any idea who that drow elf is?"

Alder Shaw's face was a firm as granite. "I do. And you'll take your hand off me now, Ambassador Nightblood, or see my hospitality revoked."

Malcan released his fist, and Alder swiped his shirt free of wrinkles.

I looked down at the bewildered ariel and saw my own dumbfounded expression reflected in her colorless eyes. In a daze, I eased my grip on the dart and slowly unwound the chain from her wrist.

"Don't release her, you fool," Malcan snapped.

"You don't give the orders around here," Alder said, taking a step forward. It placed him square into the path of a spurting pipe. "Hang it all. Nadia! Do something, would you?"

The naiad peeled away from the irritated bystanders—all of which had weapons drawn or magic summoned, ready to protect themselves from becoming collateral damage—and gave a sweep of her willow-like arm. The water from the ruined fountain ebbed until it was just a trickle.

My attention returned to the ariel trapped beneath me as she cleared her throat. She arched an eyebrow. "Well? Finish up."

I didn't care for her bossy tone, but I finished unwinding the chain from her wrist. Free, she soared out from under me and floated by Alder's shoulder. I rose, pressing the scorpion icon on the dagger's hilt, and replaced the blade in its clasp on my thigh. The eyes of hundreds watched me, and I knew without returning their gazes that I'd destroyed whatever reputation I'd built.

Drow were nothing but bigoted killing machines who fought without thought to others. The broken fountain, the ruined topiaries, and the frightened looks of the DUO staff proved it. A shadowcat didn't concern itself with the opinions of mice, as Uncle Malcan would say, but I had to work with these people, especially now that I had a—

"Partner?" the ariel shrilled.

For someone so upset I didn't see why she was smiling. A nervous tic?

"Alder, you told me you—"

"Had someone who could match your magic. And Larcen Nightblood does."

"In what world?"

"Exactly!" Malcan added.

Alder clapped his hands slowly. "Look at you two, mortal enemies and you've found some common ground. I'm so proud."

I grabbed my uncle's shoulder and yanked him back before he could run his scimitar through the druid's gut. "Enough, Uncle. You are not bound to this ariel. I am."

The ariel actually gasped in surprise. I suppose she would; my declaration was pretty radical for a dark elf.

"Over my dead body," Malcan said.

"If I still bowed to the crown of Drozvega, perhaps, but I'm pledged to DUO now. You can stay for the ceremony, or you can leave."

"I'll not watch you disgrace your ancestors by bonding with that... that—"

"Say 'sprite' again," the ariel said, flashing a savage smile.

"That failure of a night wisp guardian," Malcan said instead.

The ariel's scream knocked Malcan onto his back and slid him across the recessed floor until he shored up against the steps on the other side. His white hair lashed his face as his dark cheeks rippled like the surface of a pond after a stone has skipped across. The force of her scream snapped his head back.

I jabbed the poisoned dart into the ariel's gut as hard as I could.

She gasped, her mist-like body crystallizing without her permission. Alder caught her as she fell so she wouldn't break against the slick stone. He flashed me a wild look, and I mouthed, *"Sorry"* before running over to my uncle. My boots echoed across the silent rotunda as they splashed through the water.

Malcan's eyes were bloodshot as he glared up at me and slapped my outstretched hand aside. He got to his feet and rolled his head on his neck a few times before he realized there was blood trickling out of the corner of his mouth. "Well, I can't say I agree, and your father... If you were in a self-imposed exile before, you'll be officially banished when I return to Drozvega."

I nodded once.

Malcan clicked his tongue against the back of his teeth in his characteristic show of disapproval. Then he jerked his chin towards Alder and the ariel, who was transforming slowly back into mist limb by limb.

Spider bites, how is that possible without the antidote?

"At least you know where your loyalty still lies," Malcan said, patting his stomach. "That was a good thrust, by the way." He sniffed, looking around at all the faces in the room. "Looks like I've outstayed my welcome. Best be off. Despite this... setback, my offer still stands. Come join me whenever you want. I'd love to spend more time with my favorite nephew."

"I'm your only nephew."

"Not for long. Your sister's pregnant."

Uncle Malcan didn't elaborate, instead turning on his heel and marching down one of the six hallways that led away from the central hub. DUO security staff—a pair of towering orcs—fell in step behind him, no doubt to escort him out.

When I turned to face Alder, the ariel was hovering directly behind me. A crazed smile jumped onto her face a second before she sucker-punched me across the jaw. "You stabbed me!"

I staggered back a step, shaking the black spots from my vision. I hadn't been hit in a very long time, and certainly not by something that could land such a powerful punch while smiling like one of those human Miss America contestants. Baring my teeth at her, I snarled, "Yeah? Well you were going to kill my uncle!"

"You think I give a gnat's fart about what happens to a drow?"

"You should. Apparently the magical powers that be thought you were only fit to be partnered with a drow, so what does that say about you?"

The ariel gasped in outrage. She gasped again when Alder seized her ear. Faster than a night heron plucking a minnow from a pond, he'd snatched my ear as well.

"If you keep bickering, I'll treat you like the children you are. Honestly, a thousand years between the two of you and you act like this." Alder twisted his hands, wrenching our ears. "My office. *Now*."

CHAPTER FOUR

Eryn

ALDER REMOVED the carefully pruned bonsai from its place on his desk into a nearby cabinet, giving the dark elf a judgmental look the entire time, pressing the door firmly until the latch clicked into place. Apparently he wasn't concerned about the welfare of the sparrows nibbling seeds from a bowl on the windowsill. When the bonsai was secure, he sat down at his desk and steepled his fingers together like a disapproving headmaster.

I'd seen such a look before on the astrology master's face when she'd caught me doodling instead of studying my star charts. In a world dominated by the sky, you needed to learn the stars so you could find your way home. I hadn't paid her much mind; it was impossible not to see the Temple of the Sky burning like a second sun above the cloud line, day or night.

The dark elf sat down in a chair, obviously having been in this office before, but still respectful enough to sit up straight and look contrite. I didn't believe it for a second. Genocidal mass murderers were never contrite.

I didn't sit, of course, and hovered over by the window with the sparrows instead. There was a nice breeze coming down from the mountains, and since I hadn't had any celestial nectar to drink since leaving the temple, the pollen drifting in on that wind would have to suffice.

"Eryn, I would appreciate it if you'd come over here so I don't have to look in two places when I reprimand you both," Alder said.

"He started it."

The dark elf spared me a condescending glance. "I believe the security tapes will prove that I was the one provoked."

"You started it when you invaded the night wisp valley!"

"I don't need to explain the orders of my king."

"Then why give me the night wisp pod?"

Alder turned to the dark elf, eyebrows raised in interest. "That was you? The Council knew you were involved, of course, but not that..."

The dark elf pursed his lips into a thin line and refused to answer either of us.

"And you want me to partner up with that?" I cried. "You might as well chain me to a grindstone. It'd have the same range of emotion but at least it wouldn't glare at me every time I breathed."

The drow narrowed his violet eyes. I'd never forgotten them, not even after ten years. Violet flecked with gold, as if someone had accidentally dropped glitter on amethysts.

"Do you even have lungs?" he asked. "Or do you breathe through your skin like a nematode?"

I flew into his face, my hands hardening at my sides. "Did you just call me an earthworm?"

"If the shoe fits."

Alder cleared his throat warningly.

My teeth hardened into crystal as I clenched them, but I returned to my seat. Well, the air above my seat.

I didn't have anywhere else to go, and ariels didn't do well on their own. We were social creatures, the butterflies of the mythical realm, and due to our physical nature, we survived longer in flocks. Or armor. But I'd given up both when I left home. DUO was my only chance. And then there was another chance to protect the night wisps.

"Are we going to have a problem here?" Alder said.

The drow looked at him like he'd grown an extra head. Of course there was a problem here. Partnering a drow with an ariel was the equivalent of putting a viper into a canary's cage and asking them to become friends.

"I'm sorry," I said, giving him the benefit of the doubt with a smile, "but I'm still getting used to human mannerisms. Was that question rhetorical? Or are you seriously asking if I have a problem with that cobweb-munching, shadow-skulking, sadistic—"

The drow drummed his fingers on his strange double-bladed weapon, fingernails clinking against the metal. The message not to continue this line of insult was very clear, but I chose to ignore him.

"—rat-roasting, conceited, mildew-encrusted mudpie of a—"

"My hygiene is impeccable," the dark elf finally exploded.

"—caveman?" I finished.

"Enough!" Alder sliced his hand through the air and would've knocked the bonsai over had it not already been secreted away in that cabinet. He knocked over a cup of pens instead. "*I* didn't choose to pair you. The Puddle did. It sees something in you that I clearly don't, so we're all in the same boat of 'what in the veritable hell is going on?' I would appreciate a little grace on each of your parts as we work through this."

"I'm not working with that."

The drow pointed to his chest. "*Him.*"

"Debatable."

He scoffed, looking resolutely away from me as if he was concerned he'd lower his social standing by entertaining my presence any longer. I coughed, and a wind sprang up and lashed his warrior braid into his face. Like that other drow I'd battled in the Hub, he wore his fine white hair long on top and shaved on the sides. It was plaited into a fishbone braid away from his face, letting his sharp cheekbones and even sharper ears stand out. A vest left his arms as bare as his feet, his exposed skin a lacework of threadlike white lines. Scars?

"Eryn," Alder chastised. Then he scrubbed his face with his hands. "Look. No one is forcing you into this arrangement, but you both have limited options. The Puddle has chosen you, but you have to choose it too. Both of you have rare bloodline abilities that make you exceptionally powerful. Eryn, your Steorra ancestry enables you to change your density from mist to crystal and back again with just a thought. Larcen, you're a shadow-walker. I'm not sure if that is the reason the Puddle has decided to pair you, but regardless, its magic can only enhance your own. Together, if you don't kill each other, you can be one of the strongest teams DUO has ever seen. You can use that gift to move forward, and with some time, maybe even heal old wounds."

The dark elf sent me a sideways glance at the same time I looked at him. What wounds could that iron-wearing prince have?

"You both know why you're here. Whether you choose to stay is up to you."

"I'm staying," the dark elf answered immediately.

I stared at him, shocked. Was his past so horrid he'd over-look being bound to his mortal enemy for the rest of our immortal lives? His past was his business, but his future was mine. Alder was wrong. DUO wasn't my only choice. I'd ruin this dark elf and bring him to justice in front of my father. My kin would welcome me back as a guardian and I could have my old life back, my dream job. And I'd do it all with a smile on my face.

I sent another puff of air, this one blowing the hair back out of the dark elf's face, settling it back across his broad shoulders. He sent me another sideways look, distrust and curiosity brewing like a storm in his face.

"Sign me up," I said cheerfully.

CHAPTER FIVE

Larcen

THE DAMAGE to the Hub's lobby had all been restored by the time we returned. Those were the perks of having fascinari in your employ, and an environment where they could perform magic without being persecuted or at risk of exposing our world to the common variety of pitchfork-and-torch-waving Homo sapiens.

We drow didn't necessarily look down on humans—their weapons technology was incredible, if blunt—but we did find them a little classless for our tastes. My opinion of them hadn't changed much since my time in Savannah, often lowering in that diverse environment, but this was the world I'd chosen to live in. I gave a long sigh that would've rivaled the apathy of my supermodel cousins and stepped up to the newly repaired fountain.

"Usually these binding ceremonies take place in the Puddle," Alder said, "but given your... concerns, Eryn, we'll perform it here. This is very unorthodox, you understand, as the Puddle is more than its name suggests. It is the essence of the gods, and it's unclear how it will react, even when handled by its caretaker. So, of course, I thought it'd be best if the Hub was evacuated."

"Smart," the ariel said brightly. Her attention abruptly shifted to the glass dome and the stars above. "Ooo. Is that Jupiter? And in Sagittarius, no less." She gave me an assessing look, as if she were a Westminster Dog Show judge having second thoughts.

"And?" I prompted. "Don't tell me you're one of those horoscope floozies." Humans had polluted the art of astrology so thoroughly that it was just spider scat at this point, but to the older races, like the centaurs and elves and—*shudder*—ariels, it was still as reliable as science. For those who could still interpret the stars, of course.

She gave me an imperious, patronizing look. "Sagittarius is considered by many to be the luckiest of zodiac signs. And Jupiter is known as a force of good fortune. Seems like this partnership might not be as doomed as I thought." The ariel gazed up at the stars again. "Although, I have been wrong once before."

I snorted. "Only once?"

"Indeed. About you, no less."

She soared past me without elaborating, clearly lost in thought.

"Well, let's hope for the former, shall we?" Alder said, rubbing his hands together. "Now no two ceremonies are the same, so I can't coach you in any way of what to expect, except you must be willing. That's the only thing that matters."

I nodded. I knew I was willing, just maybe not for the reasons the Puddle wanted. I didn't know what kind of sixth sense it had, but it couldn't know I was going to use its power to destroy the Spider Queen's sanctum or it never would've picked me. That labyrinth of tunnels with its veins of pulsing green light, poison dripping from the walls, enslaving—

"Well, then," Alder said, "if you'd just step over here, away from the topiaries, Larcen, thank you. Eryn? Not so close to the fountain, that's good. Larcen, your hand, please."

I stretched out my hand, palm upward, and Alder dropped two gold coins into it, each emblazoned with the Delta Underground Operatives crest.

"You'll need to literally flip a coin to activate the Puddle's power," Alder explained, "and once activated, you must channel that power into you. Coins specific to your bond will be fashioned from these, and you must keep them on your person at all times. Dualcasters sometimes wear them like cufflinks or necklaces, and one team had them fashioned into wedding rings... which turned out quite poorly in the end since they're divorced now. Just adds a little more proof to the saying not to mix business with pleasure. I don't think I, or the Human-Fascinari Resources Department, need to worry about that with either of you, I daresay."

The ariel looked like she was about to vomit, and I glared at the director as if I were trying to flay his skin from his flesh with only my eyes.

Alder cleared his throat, loosening his tie. "Well, shall we? Eryn, take his hand."

"No one said anything about touching him."

"You think I want you to touch me?" I demanded.

"You're a drow. Who knows what goes on in that perverse little mole brain of yours?"

"Children," Alder snapped. "I doubt you'd be so immature if you were in a room filled with your peers. If you cannot have any respect for each other, then have respect for me and my office!"

I bared my teeth at the ariel and thrust my hand out. She

flicked her swirling mist hair over her shoulder with a "hmph" and then slapped a diamond-hard hand against mine, grating the gold coins into my palm. My fingers wrapped around her crystal ones and clenched. Drow were natural rock climbers with incredible grip strength, and the ariel gritted her teeth, her perpetual smile turning into a snarl.

"Wonderful," Alder said, producing a vial from his pocket. He flipped the latch, and the rubber seal popped as he flicked the stopper back with his thumb. "Hold on."

The druid sprinkled a shimmering quicksilver over our joined hands and jumped back.

White light exploded from our hands. It was like a star being born, bleaching the Hub of color and sound and all sensations. Nothing else existed except the ariel and me, and even then I wasn't sure I wasn't a pile of atoms already. Then a sound like a storm surge driven by hurricane winds roared in my ears. A burst of power threatened to tear us apart, the coins between our hands growing impossibly hot. For a moment, I wanted to let go. As darkling youths, we drow would dare each other to see who could hold the chunks of molten rock tossed up by the magma rivers the longest. This was nothing like that.

You have to be willing.

I was willing. Willing to do whatever it took to destroy the Spider Queen's sanctum.

I had to have access to the Puddle.

With a shout, I clamped my free hand over the ariel's, pinning hers between mine. She mimicked me, a scream tearing from her throat. It was piercing, like the cry of a falcon, and it cut through the roar of the Puddle's power in my ears. The wind tore at us, trying to force us apart, but I just squeezed tighter, working my hand up her arm until I reached the crook of her elbow. Mirroring me, she pulled me closer as I dragged her forward, each of us too stubborn to let go.

The power was screaming at us, shrieking like a sky full of seabirds. I got my arm around her shoulders, and she lodged our clenched fists against her chest as her other hand seized my belt. The coins grew hot, seeping golden light through the seams in our fingers.

Suddenly the heat vanished, the coins cool as if their warmth had been a figment of my imagination. The roar of the Puddle's power and the blinding light evaporated, leaving nothing but a dome full of nighttime stars above us, and a naked woman as white as starlight in my arms.

We were on the granite floor, having collapsed sometime during the ceremony, both of us panting with exertion.

Since when could air elementals pant?

This woman was Eryn, but she wasn't at the same time. Ariels, born of mist, could morph their bodies to resemble any shape, but her damn Steorra bloodline allowed her body to harden into a matrix that resembled cut crystal. However, this was something else. She was unmistakably herself, and unmistakably a woman of flesh and blood. White skin, as flawless as marble but with the warmth of living flesh, replaced her mist-like form, and white hair as fine as spider silk poured over her shoulders and sluiced down to her thighs.

"S-Selena?" I whispered.

Blinking, the ariel lifted wide eyes the same delicate green of the palest jade to meet mine.

She gasped at what she saw reflected in my eyes and touched a hand to her blush-pink lips. An actual hand. She looked down at her fingers in shock, then at the rest of her.

"Gnat farts," she shrieked. "Why do I have a body? And why in the Underrealm am I naked?"

CHAPTER SIX

Eryn

"Sirius, Canopus, Rigel Kentaurus," I muttered, pacing back and forth. My bare feet slapped against the granite floor, a hard sound that was like a nail being driven through my skull. An entirely preposterous idea, since no nail could ever do such a thing when my flesh was celestial mist, or at least, it had been. I slapped my hands against my ears and continued my emotional breakdown. "Arcturus, Vega, Ca—"

"Eryn, why are you reciting star names?" Alder Shaw asked, screening his eyes with a hand. "Perhaps you'd prefer to put on some clothes?"

"They're not just stars," I said, plastering a maniacal grin on my face so I wouldn't cry. "They're the brightest stars in the sky. I once flew among them, but now"—I gestured to my legs, those white, fleshy stems that rooted me to the ground—"explain to me how I'll be able to do that!"

"Changes can happen during the binding ceremony, it's true, but—"

"Changes? I don't see *him* suffering from any changes!" I slapped my hand against my throat, wondering why it was starting to hurt. I used to be able to scream storm winds without so much as a tickle, so why was shouting irritating it? "*Capella, Rigel...*"

The drow was staring at me, completely unchanged except for the gold bracelet-and-coin that dangled from his right wrist. I had a matching one around my own fleshy wrist, the coin slapping against my palm with every pacing step.

"Something wrong with your eyes?" I shrilled.

The dark elf blinked, finally startled out of his stupefied stare. Abruptly he turned his attention to the domed ceiling.

I pulled at my hair, my *real* hair, and continued to pace. "Stars above, I feel so heavy. How do you *live* like this? Procyon, Achemar—"

"There will obviously be an adjustment period," Alder said. "Which you can begin after you put on some clothes—"

I walked straight up to the director of DUO and poked him in the chest. "—*and Betelgeuse!*"

Alder wet his lips and then pursed them. He shrugged out of his suit jacket and held it out for me. I'd worn clothes before—or armor, rather—but this beige tweed was different. It wore me down liked I'd just bathed in mud.

"There will be advantages and disadvantages to your bonding which will affect you magically and physically," he said, "but there is no way to predict them. We only know it's some sort of bleed-over ability. For instance, if either of you had bonded to a shifter, you may have received enhanced vision or smell."

"That would've been nice to know *before* that ordeal," Larcen said, crossing his arms over his chest in a fashion I was quickly figuring out was his go-to move to express disgust, anger, and possibly pleasure.

For once, I actually agreed with him. But what did this caveman have to complain about? "You have no right to be indignant. You still look like you!"

"Eryn." The director of DUO cupped my cheeks, smearing the first tear I'd ever shed away from my skin with his thumb. His hands felt so *warm*. "The Puddle wouldn't have chosen you if you couldn't do this. Larcen has lived in this world longer than you have. Go with him to Savannah. Adjust. He will help you. When you're ready, we'll put you to work. Alright?"

One of the most helpful things about being an ariel was the ability to detect a lie. While humans relied on facial tics with varying degrees of success, ariels could determine through microvibrations in spoken words with unimpeachable accuracy if words were true or false.

Alder Shaw, the director of DUO, with complete conviction, believed a dark elf could help me.

I bowed my head in submission.

"I'll scramble the jet tonight. You'll be okay, Eryn. Now, a few things to discuss before you go. Larcen, come here." Alder took Larcen's forearm in one hand and my hand in the other one. Lifting them upward, he drew our attention to the twin coins that dangled from our wrists. "These are your dualcaster coins. Your tangible connection to the Puddle, the source of your new magic. Its power will fortify you against the villains you will face. But a word of caution, it is a primordial power, left over from the gods. It has both light and darkness, and just as it can enable you to accomplish great things, it can exact a great toll."

"What kind of toll?" the dark elf demanded.

"The effects are specific to the user, but there will be a warning when you reach the threshold. It will be your choice whether or not to heed it. Now, this power can be very destructive if you're not prepared to use it, and while practicing is not entirely practical, you must train your minds and bodies to improve your endurance. That means working together."

The dark elf and I flinched in unison. Even after we'd agreed to be partners, just the words "working together" were enough to stimulate revulsion. I could never *work with* that murdering caveman, but I could definitely work at discovering why he and his kin had slaughtered the night wisps. Even a blind bat could discern it was not a raid for resources.

"And how do we activate this Puddle?" the dark elf asked.

"That's the easy part," Alder replied. "You flip your coins."

"Excuse me?"

"Flip your coins. But you have to do it together. Should one of you use your coin without your partner's consent, the Puddle will still activate, but it will claim your partner's life." Alder paused, staring at the floor as he swallowed hard, collecting himself. "And since this Puddle is a primordial source of magic, the death will not be swift. It will be slow, agonizing, and…"

"Just don't do it," I said, adding a brightness to my voice I didn't feel.

Alder cleared his throat, finally looking at us again. "Exactly."

Larcen fiddled with his coin, his upper lip curled in disgust or disdain or something else equally unpleasant. "Any other side effects we should know about?"

"During the joining ceremony, some of your innate powers or abilities transferred to each other. Think of it as a signing bonus."

"And that's a bad thing?" I asked. As much as I didn't want anything to do with this drow, gaining additional powers didn't seem like a drawback to me. There might be a learning curve, but I was over three hundred years old. I could learn pretty quick.

Alder shook his head. "No, but sometimes—most times—as I mentioned before, there's a drawback."

"Like how I got a *body*," I said, glaring at the dark elf. My smile sharpened into a cutting sickle of white. If only it could cut him.

"You're welcome," Larcen sniffed.

"You think I wanted this?" I shrilled.

"Eryn, calm down," Alder said, giving Larcen a you're-not-helping look. "Power is all about balance, am I right? And nature will always enforce that balance. For instance, about twenty years ago we had a vegan druid—who could speak to animals, just like me—join with a jaguar shifter. He gained the shifter's enhanced senses—vision, hearing, smell, the works—*but* he also gained his partner's insatiable desire for meat."

Larcen barked out a laugh.

Alder crossed his arms over his chest and gave the drow a disapproving look. "He was able to curb his cravings, eventually, but not until after severe emotional and moral stress."

"What's a vegan?" I asked.

"That's not important," Alder said, placing his hands on my shoulders and looking me in the eye. "What's important is that these drawbacks can be mitigated. Even resolved through adaptation. You gained a body, yes, which I understand to an ariel might be a terrifying thing."

An anchor to the ground? You have no idea.

"*But*, it can be an advantage if you learn to use it. Which is why I want you to go with Larcen to Savannah and train. Get to know each other. *Trust* each other."

Larcen snorted.

Alder poked him in the chest. "You agreed to this, Larcen Nightblood. She is your ward now, just as you are hers."

The dark elf sobered, his violet eyes hardening. He gave Alder a nod and turned to look down at me. The drow stood a full head taller than me, except when I straightened my spine. Then my feet lifted off the ground, and I floated in midair, meeting his eye with a triumphant smile. I might have a body, but I could still fly. I would've thanked Selena for that mercy, except the goddess was probably one of the reasons we had the Puddle in the first place, and I was still sore about being trapped by flesh.

The dark elf's eyes narrowed at the challenge, but his voice was calm and firm. "Eryn. Let's go home."

I STARED out of the porthole window and rolled my eyes for what had to be the thousandth time. "A jet," I muttered. "A jet with cream leather seats and sparkling wine and—Gnat farts! I'm an ariel and I'm flying *through the air* in a jet. If I wasn't already disowned, this would've sealed my fate for sure."

"There's a lot of irony in DUO, that's for sure," a peppy voice said.

I looked up from the patchwork farmland at the woman standing in the aisle. After Alder Shaw had given us the bare-bones version of what I assumed was a lengthy lecture about the Puddle—I was still waiting for a moment to actually process that information—he had introduced us to the magitech twins. The perky one who stood before me was Maven Clarke, and her sister Moxie sat closer to the front of the jet with Larcen.

Apparently the two were the brainiac geniuses behind all the crafty inventions the dualcasters used, as well as the head cura-tors of all magical artifacts the dualcasters might find scattered around the world. Born in Barbados, Maven and Moxie had learned everything the islands had to offer and more—including Trinidadian Shango and Haitian Vodou—furthering their education at MIT. Alder Shaw had told me that as if it'd meant something important, so I only assumed this "MIT" was some sort of prestigious advanced learning center. The twins were sponges for everything mystical, magical, and technical, and while it seemed Maven was the kind of sponge that released her knowledge in a wrung-out flood, Moxie let hers sedately drip.

From the look on Maven's face, she wasn't here to give me the run-down on her latest invention. There was a glint in her brown eyes that made me equally excited and afraid. She bent over, placing her hands on her knees, and lowered her voice to a whisper as if she was sharing a secret.

"There is a whole closet of goodies back there," she said, biting her lower lip as she contained a white smile. "We keep it stocked so the dualcasters can always dress for whatever mission they're on, or get fresh clothes if something should happen to them."

"Does that happen often? Dualcasters losing their clothes?"

"Oh, you never know sometimes. Rosa got hers caught on fire last month, Dimitri got his mostly gnawed off by some sort of chupacabra-like thing, and well, any shapeshifter is bound to have a wardrobe malfunction. But *you*, you've never worn clothes, have you?"

I shook my head. "Just feather armor."

"This is going to be so exciting." Maven grabbed my hand and hauled me out of the leather seat. It was unnerving that people could just grab my hand and not pass right through it. "Moxie, Larcen, stop whatever you're doing. We're going to have a fashion show!"

"Maven," her sister said, looking over the rim of her glasses, "I'm trying to get at least one half of this new team up to speed with the latest communication tech and—"

"There'll be plenty of time for that! The flight's three hours long."

"I'm also prepping for when we pick up the team in Charlestown."

"Three. Hours. Long." Maven pushed me behind a curtain and snapped her fingers at her twin, indicating the two seats closest to the rear of the plane. "We've never had an air elemental join DUO before, so we are quite literally making history. So you're going to get yourself a Mauby or a rum punch—"

"I drink tea, Maven."

"—and sit your fine booty down in this seat over here, and try to have just a smidgeon of fun. You too, Larcen. Be like a bunny and hop to."

Maven whirled around, her black hair swishing across her shoulders as the smile spread wider across her face. It was almost manic. She snapped the curtain shut behind us. "Now let's you and I take a look-see, yeah? That frumpy smock simply won't do."

"Okay, okay, okay." Maven hurried away as I retreated into the walk-in closet, the curtain swishing behind her as she entered the main cabin to join Moxie and the drow. "We're ready for you when you are," she called.

"I went with a classic daiquiri," Moxie told her sister. Her voice was drier than a desert. "Hope that's okay."

"Ooo! Look at you sashaying out of your comfort zone."

"This is a special occasion. Of sorts." There was a click and a hiss of a pop can opening. "Here's another one of those Java Monster energy drinks you're so fond of."

"Shiny, thanks. Larcen, you okay over there? Need another drink? What about food? I don't know how a drow could manage it, but you're looking rather pale."

"I'm fine."

I felt heavy in this new body, so I picked the lightest garment I could find to try on as my first attempt at assimilation. I shucked the smock Alder had given me as a replacement to his jacket, balling it up and kicking it into the corner of the walk-in closet. The dress I'd chosen was form-fitting in the bust but loose everywhere else, gauzy, and almost as light as my feather armor had been. It had this wonderful way of swishing against the tops of my thighs as I twirled, and I began to think that having a human body might not be so bad after all. I would have preferred the dress to be white, but it was as red as a cardinal. I lifted my hair and wiggled so the dress hung correctly before I swept the curtain aside.

"How do you like my dress?" I asked.

The drow spewed his champagne all over the carpet.

Moxie blinked wide eyes from behind her wingtip glasses, and Maven's sculpted eyebrows had flown off her face.

Moxie cleared her throat and straightened her cardigan with a little tug, looking everywhere but at me. "I'm sorry, did you call that a dress?"

"Eryn," Maven began slowly. "That's a baby doll. That's lingerie."

"Why do you even have that back there?" the drow sputtered.

"We don't censor or discriminate how our operatives get their jobs done," Maven told him crisply.

"So... this isn't normal, everyday wear?" I asked, confused.

"I guess it depends on what profession you're in," Moxie said.

Maven slapped her twin on the arm and lurched out of her seat, hurrying me behind the curtain. "Eryn, um, *most* people don't wear that unless they're, um, getting ready for horizontal mambo time. Well, I guess it doesn't necessarily have to be *horizontal*, but—"

"Why don't we leave the birds and the bees talk for HFR, Maven," Moxie called. "I have tech stuff to do if this fashion show catastrophe has concluded."

"We're not done yet," Maven barked. She turned back to me, forcing a smile. "Why don't you let me just preview what else you've picked out?"

I nodded, and, according to Maven, I'd apparently also picked out a lacy bodystocking, a sheer robe, and a satin slip. She threw it all into the corner opposite my smock and handed me the only remaining piece I'd selected. She helped me dress and smacked the curtain aside with a very proud, "Ta-da!"

"Great, she figured out what a sundress was," Moxie said, plucking the umbrella out of her glass and downing the rest of her daiquiri. "You look perfectly presentable, Eryn. Can I get back to work now, Maven?"

"You are the worst," her sister hissed. Then she turned to me, beaming a smile and clapping. "Absolutely lovely, Eryn. Well done." She leaned over and patted the drow on his arm to get his attention. "When you take her out shopping in Savannah, make sure she gets stuff like this."

"Me? Take her shopping?"

"She's your partner now, Larcen," Maven said tartly. "And you'll take her shopping."

"Why can't she just take clothes from the plane?"

"Because if she took every silk sundress from here, DUO would have to replace them, and such expenses come out of your own pocket, Larcen Nightblood, not the company's."

"I don't get paid enough to buy silk," he grumbled.

"I'm sure you'll figure it out," Moxie told the drow. "Now, let's enjoy the perks of this private plane with some more champagne, caviar, and some of our newest inventions. See, Maven? I know how to have a little fun."

CHAPTER SEVEN

Larcen

"Oʜ, Master Larcen, thank the slop bucket you're back. You won't believe what—"

"Not now, Rumple," I said, tossing the chrome briefcase Moxie had given me onto a vacant potting table. "Any web messages?"

"The spider's been quiet, sir."

"Spider bites," I cursed. I hadn't heard anything from Elvera in weeks and had resorted to passing her letters through my uncle. It was... pathetic.

I hurried down the aisle between the hoyas and the orchids, sucking in a deep, calming breath. The humidity of Savannah Belle Floral Emporium was a welcome sensation after the dry heat of Utah. The irrigation drips reminded me of the subterranean rivers, and the smell of greenery that permeated anything was reminiscent of the bioluminescent mushroom groves. "That case goes down the chute, and I'm not to be dis—"

"Master Larcen! Who is this?" Rumple squealed.

"Short version: Eryn, my dualcaster partner. Get her whatever she needs."

"But, sir, that's gnome work. I'm not a butler, I'm a foreman and a p—"

I reached the steel door that led to the walk-in refrigerator where we stored wedding arrangements and gripped the handle to hide the shaking in my hand. "And I'll be back in a moment. I'm to be left alone, Rumple." I yanked open the steel door and shut it behind me before I could hear any more protests. When it wasn't opened from the outside—Eryn might've been nosy enough to follow me—I walked to the end of the aisle of grated shelves to the only plant that perpetually lived in the walk-in.

Midnight vine.

It grew out of an enormous cube-shaped pot that was completely covered in spikes. They were nastier than locust thorns, making it impossible to lift the two-hundred-pound pot with bare hands, and they were sharp enough to saw clean through ratchet straps. The vine itself didn't require a trellis, preferring to coil its fat tendrils like a nest of Burmese pythons within the confines of its pot. Unless the flower arrangements contained peonies, nothing was put on the shelves nearest to the vine lest it be viciously attacked, and Rumple and the gnomes avoided it like a mouse avoided a bobcat den.

The black vines slithered at my approach, unwrapping and revealing a wide black mouth lined with yellow, tooth-like hairs. Humans might liken this plant to a Venus flytrap, but this carnivorous beastie could actually hunt if it wanted to. Its mouth snapped open, flashing me with a cardinal-red maw. Syrup-like sap dangled from the barbs within its mouth, glistening like dew. Wiggling its black vines like arms, the plant snapped its jaws at me, beckoning me closer with a high-pitched whine.

"Sorry, Drosera. No snacks. You know you get fed after."

The midnight vine deflated, clacking its jaws. With a mournful keen, the plant thrust its tendrils over the rim of its pot, suctioning against the ground like the tentacles of an octopus. Then with no visible strain whatsoever, it slid itself and its pot about a yard to the right, revealing a staircase in the floor.

A sauna-like breath exhaled from the floor, wrapping me in delicious humidity.

"I'll be quick," I told the vine, and I wasn't joking. The tremors in my fingers had increased.

Drosera repositioned itself over the opening as I trotted down the stairs, the motion-activated lights snapping on with gentle *fooms*. I hurried to the workbench and pulled a packet with a sterilized syringe out of the center drawer. Forcing myself to stay calm even as my fingers twitched, I yanked open the door to the small incubator that squatted on the bench and extracted a small vial of black liquid. I tore open the syringe package and thrust the needle into the vial. As the syringe filled, I wrapped a tourniquet around my arm and swabbed the crook of my elbow with alcohol.

The syringe plunged into my vein, and the black liquid flooded into my blood.

The relief was instantaneous.

I sagged onto a stool and watched the skin on the back of my hand visibly darken, and the tremors vanished from my fingers. The hunger that always gnawed on the edges of my stomach abated, at least until the effects of the elixir started to wear off.

After cleaning the syringe and sealing it in another package to autoclave with its kin later, I pulled out my logbook and marked the date and time. My last injection had only lasted fifteen days. When I'd first left Drozvega ten years ago, I hadn't had to take my first injection until I'd spent a year in the human realm. I ran a hand over my warrior braid with a resigned sigh. I needed to find a permanent solution, and quick.

Ha. You've been telling yourself that for years now, Cen.

Well I really mean it now.

How you gonna do that with an ariel floating about all up in your business?

I'll figure it out.

I pushed away from the workbench, throwing the spent vial into the trash can, and turned to the growing trays that lined the opposite wall. Four shelves tall, each with their own grow lights, they supported hundreds if not thousands of Drozvegan mushrooms. Inkcaps.

The largest were the size of grapefruits, their gills a dark violet or brilliant orange or iridescent green. Bioluminescent yellow freckles marred their otherwise flawless black caps. The smallest were no larger than buttons, nestling like chicks under the canopies of their bigger siblings. I gave the fattest ones a gentle flick of my finger and harvested those that released a shower of black spores.

Carrying them upside down, I brought them to the workbench and prepped them for the centrifuge. As the next batch of elixir spun, I replaced a burnt-out grow light and inoculated a new tray with the spores Malcan had given me. As I'd painstakingly learned, it took every species of inkcap to create the perfect concoction of nutrients I was missing. As a child, I'd only seen the ones with the violet gills. Uncle Malcan had found the rest.

When the centrifuge was done, I extracted the black liquid, strained it, and aliquoted it into individual vials. The precipitate was spread out on a dehydrator tray to dry out for me to powder down into Night Dust. Inkcap mushroom powder was to drow as alcohol was to humans, an inhibitor-reducer when ingested. But to anyone not a drow, the powder was much more intense, giving the user a fit of the giggles and hallucinations and psychedelic color shows. It was the whole reason behind the topiary incident, actually.

My work done, I cleaned the bench with alcohol and went to the chest freezer by the stairs. I extracted a whole chicken and trotted up the stairs, rapping my knuckles against the bottom of Drosera's pot.

The vine obediently slid itself to the right, vine arms wriggling with excitement. It smacked it leathery jaws, sap dripping like drool from the corners of its maw.

"Close the door, Drosera," I reminded.

The pot practically flew across the floor, sealing the hidden workroom away and trapping in the heat. I tossed the frozen chicken into the midnight vine's maw, the strong jaws snapping shut like an alligator's. It whined when I turned away, begging for more.

"One visit, one chicken," I said over my shoulder. "You don't want to get so fat you can't move your pot."

The carnivorous plant let out an indignant squeal, wrapping its tendrils around its stalk as if crossing its arms.

I emerged from the walk-in as Drosera sulked, expecting to find the nursey as I'd left it with all the gnomes singing and going about their work, but instead I found Rumple trussed up like a suckling pig ready for the oven and the ariel in the midst of the bickering gnomes. Marigold was even waving a miniature garden hoe.

"What happened?" I demanded.

The gnomes spun, facing me with all the anger their little bodies could muster.

"I tried to tell you," Rumple squealed. "They unionized while you were gone. This is a revolt!"

I glared at the ariel, knowing this wasn't her fault, but no doubt she'd helped incite things along against "the man" because Rumple hadn't been hog-tied when I'd gone into the walk-in.

She gave me one of her smiles, that mask that hid what she was really thinking. "I didn't know you had a talking pig working for you. How progressive. Oh, and the gnomes want an espresso machine."

CHAPTER EIGHT

Eryn

"THEY DON'T DRINK COFFEE," the drow said flatly, crossing his arms over his chest and making his biceps bulge.

What was that, some sort of intimidation technique? I smiled even wider, hiding my irritation.

"No, but it makes foamed milk," the gnome with the pointy yellow hat said. We'd just recently met, and the charming young man—he was only eighty-five years old—had introduced himself as Cornelius. "We like the mouth-feel!"

"Yeah, and stop buying off-brand Oreos," Marigold piped up, waving her miniature garden hoe. "We can taste the difference."

The drow swept a hand wide, gesturing to vast forest of greenery under the polytunnel. "You're letting these plants die because you want foamed milk and Oreos?"

"And we want more fruit variety at breakfast," another gnome said. "Cantaloupe and honeydew melon aren't always in season, you know. You're being stingy!"

The drow pinched the bridge of his nose between thumb and forefinger and let out a frustrated sigh. "Need I remind you, if you don't work, there is no money to pay for the things you want. Besides, I just got you all that pottery throwing station last month. Savannah Belle Floral Emporium cannot continue to pay for such a lavish lifestyle."

"Says who?" Cornelius climbed the trunk of a yellow hibiscus and ran down to the edge of the row, holding onto the twisted vine of a hoya as he sniffed the drow's face. Larcen snapped his pointy teeth at the gnome, and Cornelius yelped with a shudder. Retreating to the safety of the terra-cotta pots, he thrust an accusing finger at his employer. "Just as I thought. Champagne and caviar on his breath!"

The assembled gnomes gasped.

"You won't pay twenty-one cents an ounce for Oreos, but you'll pony up ninety dollars an ounce for caviar? Insufferable!" Cornelius crowed, only his yellow pointy cap visible above the hoya pots.

Fascinated, I watched the dozens of gnomes in their gardening overalls and multicolored hats stampede the dark elf like a bunch of feral cats.

The drow took a step back as if to run, but he was only slipping into a fighting stance, violet eyes glinting. Just as someone lobbed a miniature trowel at him, the dark elf dissolved. A shadow-like presence in his exact shape replaced him, and the trowel sailed right through his calf. It clattered harmlessly against the cement on the opposite side of him, and then the shadow's violet eyes gleamed like twin stars, narrowing in on the trowel-lobbing gnome. He lunged with a shadow-like hand as the gnomes screamed.

"Stop," I shouted as I soared over the ground, throwing up a hand.

The gnomes suddenly blurred. I was abruptly seeing double,

as there were twice as many gnomes as there were a second ago. But they were staticky, like a mirage, yet the vision was convincing enough to make Shadow-Larcen straighten in surprise. The gnomes were just as confused as he was, shying away from their doppelgängers with panicked shrieks. They broke off the attack, scattering like cockroaches and wailing as their mimics chased their heels.

"Retreat," Cornelius shouted, his yellow hat bobbing between the hoya plants. "You've not seen the last of us! We won't be intimidated!"

I lurched to a halt so I wouldn't trample them, barreling into Larcen as he materialized.

The two of us tumbled to the ground, shoring up against the basin of a water fountain. At least we hadn't tangled up in the patio furniture display. Groaning, I lifted my head up off the drow's chest and found a stone frog gazing impassively down from its perch on the rim. It croaked and hopped into the fountain.

"Ugh, get off," Larcen said. "You're wrinkling my clothes."

"What did you do?" I demanded, scrambling to my feet.

"I don't know!"

"Well that's about as helpful as a bag full of bees."

"I could ask you the same thing."

"You went all magic-freaky first."

Larcen flipped onto his feet and brushed the cement crumbs from his clothes. "This is spider silk. Completely one of a kind..." His voice trailed off as he examined his hands. "I... I just *willed*..."

"Yes?" I prompted.

He glared at me. "I don't know how to explain it! It was different from shadow-walking. I didn't want to disappear, I just wanted to... evade. The gnomes are as vicious as mudcrab spiders if they go after your ankles."

"So you... dissolved into shadow." I looked down at my own hands, foreign yet familiar. "You phased at will. That's my blood-line ability."

He ran a hand over his warrior braid. "I guess so." Then he gave me a suspicious look. "And what did *you* do?"

It was my turn to become tongue-tied. "I was just trying to protect them. Maybe... draw your attention away from them somehow? I don't know. It felt a bit like when I conjure wind, but I had more control over it. Like I could manipulate it into—"

"An illusion." The drow's eyes widened. "It's an inherent trait in all drow. We can bend light and shadow to a small extent to make ourselves blend in with our surroundings. You took it one step further."

At the same time, we took a large step away from each other, distrust and fear mirrored in our eyes. We had just made our greatest enemies more powerful. His hand went to the hook on his belt for his scorpion blade, and my own hand went to my hip, but there was no bladed fan there. I would have to remedy that, and quickly.

But, I reminded myself, I had to earn this caveman's trust. Otherwise he'd never divulge just what had happened all those years ago in the night wisp valley. That valley had been a secret, known only to a few ariels, and sacred to the goddess Lena. She had ascended to the sky with her sister, but it was still our sworn duty to protect her wisps. Without that information, I couldn't return to the Temple of the Sky and regain my rightful position as a guardian.

"Um, excuse me," a voice said. "A little help here? They don't call it hog-tying for nothing, and it's massively uncomfortable."

We craned around and found the pig on his back, trotters up and lashed together with gardening twine. The gnomes had even secured it to the bronze collar around his neck. Rumple gave a pitiful snort.

I hurried past the wary drow and rolled the black pig onto his side. If I got in good with the dark elf's subordinates, maybe he'd eventually warm to me. I'd gain his trust and extract that information out of him like sap from a maple tree. Ariels didn't believe in torture, or any unwarranted violence, but we didn't need to. If anyone could make themselves endearing to even the most cantankerous of fascinari, it was an ariel. No one could resist our bubbly personalities for long. I'd wiggle my way into that caveman's heart and then destroy him. A smile crept to my lips, and it wasn't even a fake one.

"I don't need your help, ariel," Larcen said, crouching down and grabbing one set of flailing limbs.

"You might not, but I do," Rumple snorted.

"There, there," I said, petting the pig's bristly head. "You'll be right as rain in a moment."

"Ah," the pig sighed. "A woman's touch. You should consider keeping her around, Master Larcen."

"Out of the question." A little *snick-snick* of his scorpion blade, and the hog was free. Larcen replaced his scorpion blade in its holder with a faint *clink*. "We're not hiring."

I helped Rumple as he heaved himself up.

"Well, you might be the owner of this fine floral establishment, but I am your general manager and official gnome wrangler, sir. Hiring falls in my jurisdiction."

Larcen's eyes narrowed. "Oh does it."

"A-and, after I review the books, payroll might be able to accommodate another employee. I'm sure *you* would appreciate another set of hands that weren't pint-sized or actual trotters when you're delivering wedding arrangements. S-sir."

"Hn." The dark elf turned and started to make his way to the big wooden desk by the walk-in. "Speaking of the books..."

"You'll find them all in order, Master Larcen." The pig lifted his nose and trotted confidently after the dark elf. He looked over his round shoulder at me, giving a jerk of his jowls to encourage me to keep up. "The website's been updated as you've requested, and we're supposed to get that delivery of coffee mug and planter pot merch this evening. Despite not having thumbs, without me, this whole place would fall apart."

"I'd say this place has fallen apart if the gnomes are unionizing," the dark elf said as he dropped into the leather rolly chair behind the counter. "I supposed that means I should fire you."

"No," Rumple protested. "Where would I go? It's not like Indeed.com hires a lot of talking pigs."

"There's always Beauregard's Processing on the south side of town."

The pig gasped. "Take that back."

"I'll take it back when those gnomes fall in line. I lead, they follow. That's their job description. And yours too."

"It *would* be if they weren't curs—"

"What was that?" the drow asked sharply.

"Nothing!" Rumple sniffled, or snorted—it was kind of hard to tell—turned on his trotters, and walked briskly down the aisle. "Cornelius," he called, "a word, if you please?"

I crossed my arms over my chest, wrinkling my sundress. "That wasn't very nice."

"Leadership doesn't have to be nice."

"It's better if it is."

"Listen here, ariel, this is my business, and I'll run it as I see fit. You're just a guest here until you can find some other useful employment."

"Well, I guess I'll leave you to your snobbery and just take myself on a tour. You know, something *you* should've done when we first got here instead of disappearing into a walk-in refrigerator. Honestly, where are your manners?"

He didn't seem bothered by my barbs, and I wasn't about to

spend one more minute with him if I didn't have to. I would "adjust," as Alder called it, better without him. I jumped, expecting the air to catch me, and it did, but only for a moment. I sank back to the ground. Panicked, I tried again and again, and I returned to the earth as if I was lashed by an invisible three-foot tether.

"Something wrong with take-off?" the dark elf sneered.

"This isn't happening, this isn't happening," I whispered, pulling on my hair. "I'm an ariel. I belong in the air! I—"

I cried out in pain as a growl ripped from my midsection. Something inside me twisted, clenching my insides and churning like a boiling soup pot. I doubled over when the growl sounded again, a panicked yelp tearing from my throat, the resulting wind shattering the nearest terra-cotta urn. The yellow hibiscus slumped as its soil spilled onto the cement.

The drow, who had been laughing, lurched up from his seat to steady the plant. He got it situated into a new pot, and then the smug mirth returned to his face.

"What?" I demanded, more angry than afraid now. "What is wrong with me?"

"You're too weak to fly," he answered.

"I know that. Why? Do I have a parasite or something inside me? What is making all that noise? And why does it hurt so bad?"

"You're hungry," he said. "That growling you're hearing is your stomach."

My face fell. "A stomach? You mean... I have a digestive tract now?"

The drow nodded. "Comes with the body."

"No," I wailed, dropping to my knees. "Do you have any idea what this means?"

He shook his head.

"I'm just like you now."

His lifted a skeptical eyebrow as he crossed his arms over his chest. "I doubt that. How so?"

"Give me a few hours and I'll be just as full of crap as you are."

Larcen's violet eyes drilled into me, and it was then and there that I decided I would ingratiate myself with him tomorrow. I still had a few centuries of name-calling and grudges to unload first.

CHAPTER NINE

Larcen

I DIDN'T SETTLE in Savannah for the food—which like all Southern fare in my opinion was one plate closer to a heart attack—nor for the hospitality, though the backhanded expressions like "bless your heart" reminded me fondly of home. I'd settled here for the pace. Things were done slower down here, probably because of the heat and humidity, and it allowed me time to find a solution to my little mushroom problem. In theory.

Though the country food here didn't meet the standard of even the most common table fare in Drozvega, there was one restaurant I made a habit of frequenting regularly, solely because they experimented with so many other local food sources beyond bacon-fat-smothered collard greens and cheddar grits, though those were also on the menu. Magnolia Kitchen had some Creole roots despite being so far away from

Louisiana and specialized in showcasing a new mushroom dish every week.

Abigail sauntered up to our table, a small white teakettle, mug, and an assortment of tea sachets on her tray just for me. She worked every day, and so I saw her every day. I sat in her section by the bay windows overlooking the street. Abigail was dark, like me, and wore her hair braided, though she had hundreds of them while I had just the one, and she decorated hers with gold thread. I'd have to tell my sisters about that style the next time I saw them.

Abigail didn't pester me with idle chatter, and I appreciated that. As she arranged the beverage service in front of me, careful not to knock the little vase of yellow daisies in the middle of the table, she said, "I already put the mushroom dish du jour in for you, hon."

I nodded, thumbing through the tea selection. Like always, the only one worth the hot water was the Lady Grey. They really needed to broaden their selection.

The waitress turned to Eryn, who hadn't even picked up her menu. She'd been too distracted by the restaurant's décor, especially the daisies, and, strangely, the condiment caddy. From the look on Abigail's face, Eryn was a distraction all by herself: paler than new-fallen snow, fine white hair that hung straighter than a plumb line, delicately boned as if she was half bird. Ethereal. No doubt half the locals who'd seen her on the street this morning had thought they'd seen a ghost.

But Abigail was an experienced veteran in the service industry and quickly smoothed her facial expression like she was ironing wrinkles from a sheet. "You want something to wet your whistle while you look over that menu, hon?"

The ariel gave me a panicked look. "I have a stomach *and* a whistle? What's a whistle?"

"Sweet tea," I told the waitress.

She sauntered off, her hips rolling with every step of her kitten heels.

"What *is* this?" Eryn asked, flapping the laminated menu from front to back to front again.

"A list of culinary delights, or so they'd have you believe," I said. "It's food. Pick something."

"But I don't even know what I like!"

"Then it won't matter what you decide."

"This is a nice place," Eryn said, abandoning the menu and looking around again. Seriously, she had the attention span of a butterfly. "Not that I've ever been to one of these—what do you call them?"

"Restaurants."

"A restaurants. Yes."

"No, no. *Restaurant.* Singular. 'Restaurants' is the plural."

"Oh. Well. Either way, never been. Never had to go to one. Celestial dew and sun pollen was all an ariel needed. And now" —she gripped her stomach as it growled again—"I feel terrible."

"Uh-huh." I wrung the tea from the spent packet out with my spoon and gave it a sip. It was no champagne, but it was drinkable.

"What are you getting?" she asked.

"Mushroom something or other."

She wrinkled her nose at me. "Yeesh, it's like pulling teeth with you. Now that I have real teeth I can fully appreciate that saying, and I must say, it's entirely accurate. You don't talk much, do you?"

"Not since meeting you."

"Hmph." The ariel turned her attention back to the condiment caddy and started riffling. Sugar packets, mustard, ketchup, hot sauce. She had to touch it all. Selecting the hot sauce, she carefully read the label. "'Slap Yo Grandma Hotter Than Hell Chipotle Pepper Sauce.' Stars above, how violent."

She uncapped it, squirted a little on her finger, and gave it a taste with a dart of her tongue.

I slumped my chin into my hand. "Seems we'll have to work on your table manners too. You can't just go around flicking your tongue out like a crystal lizard."

"I don't know why this would make me want to slap my grandmother," she said, setting the hot sauce aside. "Or anyone for that matter."

I tapped the menu. "Pick something."

Abigail returned with a perspiring glass of sweet tea, and the ariel gave her a beaming smile.

"I have a few questions," she said.

Of course you do.

"I don't see any pollen listed here," she said, lifting the menu as if asking for another one with different options.

Abigail cast a sideways glance at me. *Is she for real?*

I sighed over my teacup. *Yep.*

"Hon, if you're into those alternative lifestyle food choices, there's a spice shop down the street that sells jars of bee pollen. But here, what you see is what you get," the waitress replied.

"Oh." The ariel tried to hide her disappointment with another smile. "Well, what are the butterbeans like?"

"They're so good they'll make the gators jump for your garters."

"Oh! And the honey biscuits with lavender and lemon curd?"

"Bees'll chase you all the way home, hon."

"First my grandmother gets slapped, then gators are going to attack me, and now bees? Do you have a less violent menu available?"

I snatched the menu from the ariel's hands and thrust it at

the waitress. "Just get her whatever's closest to a sampler platter."

Abigail, clutching the menu to her stomach with pale-knuckled fingers as if she was afraid the ariel would ask for it back, quickly retreated to the kitchen with little clicks of her kitten heels.

"I wasn't done with that," Eryn said, fiddling with her straw. She gave the sweet tea an experimental sip and gagged. Quickly, she wiggled the plastic spout off the hot sauce bottle, shoved the straw in, and took a long, grateful swallow. "Ah, much better."

"Hn, you'd think someone who was used to eating celestial dew and sun pollen would prefer sweet things."

"I know, right?"

Abigail returned with our food, sliding the plates in front of us with hardly a clatter. She gave the ariel a mortified look, cleared her throat, and asked, "Can I get you two anything else?"

I shook my head.

The ariel flashed her a smile and gave a little wave with her bottle of hot sauce. "All good here."

"Well... enjoy."

I ignored the ariel as she gave everything on her platter an experimental poke and turned back to the plate in front of me. It was some sort of chicken stew with mushrooms, okra, and herbs. Chanterelle, porcini, chestnut, morel. I'd discovered a few years ago that I could prolong the effects of my elixir if I ate a diet high in the mushrooms of the human realm, but they were still lacking that essential nutrient I needed, whatever it was. Especially if I'd had to take an injection just fifteen days after the last one.

I hadn't been an alchemist when I'd lived in Drozvega, otherwise I might've discovered the cure decades ago. And it's not like I could trust anyone other than Malcan with what I was up to. I doubt even my uncle knew what I was truly doing with those mushroom spores, and no one with the mark of the Spider Queen on the back of his neck would even dare to think of removing himself from her service.

"So," the ariel said, giving the little ceramic cup of shrimp and grits a taste, "are we going to talk about what happened in the garden?"

"Plant nursery," I corrected.

She gave me a close-lipped smile, blinking those pale jade eyes. I'd grown up with three of the most vicious women Drozvega had ever seen. I knew what that kind of look meant. It was the kind of look my sister Lyrsa would've given me right before she threatened to gut me and skewer me on a spit.

"I think we should really explore these new abilities," she pressed. "And that means talking about them."

"Part of having good table manners is letting people eat in peace, you know."

"Animals eat. We *dine*. And part of dining involves conversation."

I let out a short sigh. "Alder said we would adapt to each other's powers. You can change the state of your being from solid to vapor. Now so can I. Done and done."

"How can you be so calm about that?" she asked, lurching forward.

I caught her teetering glass before it could sluice the table with sweet tea. "After you've lived a few centuries, not much surprises anymore." *After you've grown up in the service of the Spider Queen, you simply don't ask questions. You just accept.*

"Gnat farts. Well I've lived for a few centuries too and I *am* a wreck, if you have a modicum of decency to care."

"Fresh out."

She didn't seem to hear me, saying, "I have an actual diges-tive system now, no thanks to you, I'm sure, and this *body* that might as well be a cage—these must be some of the negative side effects Alder had warned us about—and what *advantage* do I get out of this arrangement? I can create illusions. So can one of those human magician hacks you find in Las Vegas."

I just blinked at her.

"I saw a poster advertisement on my way to the Hub. Apparently some fae like to go to the shows and poke fun at the performers. They call it 'amateur hour.' But that's not the point." She gestured to herself. "A body that lashes me to the earth, the one place that is death for an ariel. In exchange for creating illusions that aren't even that good. It's not fair!"

"Does that hurt?" I asked.

"Does what hurt?"

"Smiling like that. You just delivered that little temper tantrum while wearing a beauty pageant smile the whole time. Is your jaw hinged or something?"

"I think I liked it better when you didn't talk as much." Eryn gave a little sniff and turned her attention back to her sampler platter. "Stars above, what *is* this monstrosity?"

"That'd be a fried tenderloin."

"It's delicious!"

Between one blink and the next, the ariel, who had never had an ounce of solid food in her entire life, had polished off not only the fried pork tenderloin, but the shrimp and grits, the bacon-braised collard greens, the biscuit slathered in white sausage gravy, and the jalapeno creamed corn. She left the stewed apples and sweet tea alone, washing it all down with the rest of the hot sauce.

Even I was mildly impressed. "Woah."

"Do you think they have any more of that hot sauce?"

"You've had enough. How do you... feel?"

"Excellent," she said, beaming at me over her hot sauce bottle. Then her eyes narrowed in suspicion. "Why?"

"Well, you ate enough food to satisfy a lumberjack, and I'm just surprised—but only a little—that eating that much meat didn't leave you with an upset stomach."

The perpetual smile on her lips faltered. "I ate... meat?"

"Unless you know another way to make biscuits with *sausage* gravy and a fried tenderloin out of something other than pork. Not to mention the shrimp—sea meat—and bacon, which is the probably the best culinary discovery the humans have ever made."

"But, *meat*. As in an animal?"

"A pig, more precisely."

The ariel's pale face turned green.

I thrust my finger across the table at her, hissing, "Don't you *dare* get sick. I did not just drop twenty-five dollars on your Taste of the South platter for you to splatter it all over the sidewalk because you suddenly realized that delicious thing you just ate actually had a face at one point."

"I ate a pig," she wailed, causing the nearest diners to look over in alarm.

"And you loved it."

"I didn't mean to love it," she sobbed. "I didn't know! You, you tricked me. *You* ordered me the sampler platter."

I rolled my eyes. "And yes, I *force* fed you every bite. You never told me you were vegetarian."

"I'm an ariel! I protect the weak, the preyed-upon. That *includes* animals! Even the ones that roll around in mud."

"Consider me informed. So now that you've had your little moral dilemma and aren't dying of hunger anymore, we need to get back and train."

She glared at me, wiping the tears from her eyes with angry swipes of her napkin. "You mean you need to go back so you can handle the gnome uprising."

I ignored her and took a few bills from my wallet, tossing them onto the table and standing.

"Larcen—wait, can I call you Lar? Larc? Cen? Ceny? Larceny?"

I glared at her. She was just trying to get under my skin now because of that damn fried tenderloin.

"Which one do you prefer?"

"I'd rather you not address me at all."

She swept my preference aside with a pale hand. "You can't let something like the gnomes fester. Just like I'm not going to let this malicious subterfuge of my stomach fester. Larcen, I *forgive* you."

I grabbed her elbow and wrangled her out of the booth. "Come. On. And my business is no affair of yours."

"Yes it is. We're partners," she said, giving the skin on the back of my hand a vicious pinch to make me let go.

I drew the scorpion blade from its clip on my hip and waved the poisoned dart warningly in front of her nose. The scorpion insignia on the blade glowed, activating its camouflage. Any human watching us would see me waving a pen in front of her face instead of a chain dagger. "Don't make me use this."

"Pfft. I'm solid right now," she said, waving her pale hand in front of my face. "What's that gonna do? Make me more solid?"

I smacked her hand aside. "I'm game to find out if you are."

She stuck her tongue out at me. For an ariel over three hundred years old, she was shockingly immature, but maybe ariels were just like that. They were known to be the social butterflies of the magical realms, so I guess they couldn't take themselves too seriously. I jerked my head at the door. "Go."

"You know I'm right," she said, shoving open the door.

"Dualcaster partners, not business partners."

"Maybe we should be. I am an ariel after all. I know all about pollination. And I'm nicer. I'm sure the gnomes would prefer to work for me over you."

"They just met you."

"And yet you attract more bees with honey than tomcat piss."

"The expression is 'more than vinegar.'"

"Not where you're concerned," she said sweetly, skipping down the street.

CHAPTER TEN

Eryn

"The oppressor has returned! Scatter!"

The gnomes parted before Larcen like fish before a shark, their multicolored hats bobbing through the greenery as they scurried away to the opposite ends of the polytunnel.

"Oh, Master Larcen, thank the slop bucket you're back," Rumple cried.

"We would've been back sooner if *someone* hadn't gotten distracted in Forsyth Park."

I lifted my chin and soared past him—that's right, I was air-mobile again after that mortifying breakfast, although I was still solid flesh and blood—my hair fluttering in a white cirrus cloud behind me. "It's a park. I'm an ariel. I shouldn't have to explain myself. And what that poor beast was being subjected to was simply atrocious."

"What's this now?" Rumple asked, the bristles on his back rising. "What poor beast?"

"It was a dog, Rumple," the dark elf said. "Relax."

"That *dog* was being forced to perform at that human's command for money," I said. "*That* is indentured servitude!"

"Ooo, I like her," Cornelius said.

"The dog was fine, Eryn," Larcen said firmly. "He was even enjoying himself. And so was everyone else until you decided you needed to go on a crusade."

"You walk around collared and leashed and see how you like it," I bit back.

"Sounds kinky to me," a gnome whistled, stroking his chin-strap beard.

"Quiet, Roberto," Larcen snapped. "Now where's the fire? And who left open the compost chute again?" He diverted to a trapdoor in the center of the polytunnel, the only piece of floor that wasn't cement but a metal grate, kicking the prop aside and letting the grate clang flat. "If we have a customer fall in there, the lawsuit will be incredible."

"Oh sure, worry about the customers," a gnome's voice said from the cluster of hostas. "What if we slip inside? We're too small to climb out. We'll be digested immediately!"

"Then keep it shut when you're not using it," Larcen barked at the hostas.

"Digested?" I exclaimed.

Ignoring me, Larcen bent down and adjusted the bronze collar on the pig's neck. He smeared the grit away from the surface, making the inscriptions gleam with renewed vigor. "Is your collar malfunctioning again? Did a customer see you? I swear, I'm going to throttle that slimy fae swindler with my bare hands—"

"No, no, nothing like that," Rumple assured. "Your DUO communications device—it's been blinking for the last fifteen minutes."

"Spider bites. Why didn't you call me? Did you sit on your cell phone again?"

"No, but you know I always get the gnomes to punch the buttons for me. They're too small for my trotters. And well, with them mutinying... they ignored my pleas."

"*Cornelius*," Larcen roared.

"Why is DUO calling us already?" I floated over to the counter, hovering over the gem-like communications array. It was a lychee-sized sphere of what looked like garnet, reminiscent of a paper-weight or one of those knickknacks you see in souvenir stores. Frantically blinking, as if half a dozen fireflies were trapped inside, the gem cast crimson shadows all over the desk. "We've been dual-casters for less than a day. I thought we were going to be given time to adjust. I still haven't learned how to use the bathroom yet!"

Larcen waved his hand at me, shooing me away like a buzzing fly. Instead of banking away from his hand, I phased, and his hand smacked against my crystal ribs.

"*Ow*."

"Serves you right. Now how do we get this marble to stop blinking?"

"Communications array. If *someone* had been paying atten-tion to Moxie's instructions, you'd already know that answer." Larcen lowered his wrist and swiped his coin over the top of the sphere, as if disrupting an invisible ward. "It's linked to our coins so only *we* can access the messages. Less chance of compro-mising sensitive information that way."

I glanced down at my own coin that dangled on my wrist. I hadn't had the time to really examine it yet, and I wasn't given the opportunity now because an image projected from the array like a released spirit.

The red-tinted bust of Alder Shaw, in miniature, glared at us. "You both had better be thankful I can leave messages on this thing. When DUO calls, I expect at least one of you to answer it in a prompt fashion. Obviously this is a recording, so you will call the office back immediately."

His image narrowed into a thread and was sucked back into the marble.

"And how do we do that?" I asked.

Larcen placed his fingertip on the marble and gave it a spin in its cradle.

Moxie answered after a few rotations, and the marble jerked to a standstill as her eight-inch bust came into focus. She adjusted her wingtip glasses with a touch, a self-satisfied smile tugging at the corner of her mouth. "Looks like the prototype is working."

"Can I get my own marble?" I asked. "Larcen has been hogging this one and he won't let me stay here and—"

"He what?" Maven came into view, smooshing against her sister.

Moxie rolled her eyes and walked out of the frame. "I'm going to get the boss."

"Don't you worry, my little cinnamon roll, we'll get this straightened out," Maven assured me. It was hard for such an impish and sweet-looking face to turn menacing, but she managed it. "Larcen! Where is your sense of charity? Eryn has been in the human realm for less than two days and you're just going to dump her out on the streets like an unwanted kitten?"

"She is unwanted."

"Larcen," a new voice said flatly.

Maven vanished, and the director of DUO took her place. He obviously was on the opposite side of the country, and yet the temperature in the polytunnel seemed to drop a few degrees.

The dark elf straightened, like a soldier in front of a superior, and said nothing.

Alder Shaw gave him a narrow-eyed look and then turned

his attention to me. "Eryn, seems like you're back in the air. And not just a few feet above the ground either."

Indeed I was hovering horizontally five feet above the ground, my chin cupped in my hands, as if I were reclining on my stomach. I beamed a smile at him. "I had some Slap Yo Momma Hotter Than Hell hot sauce."

"That's... great." Then his voice flattened. "I shouldn't have to leave messages for you two."

We nodded in unison. There was no excuse, no reason for our tardiness. I hadn't known about the communications marble, but my ignorance was my own fault. I'd been too worried about figuring out what to do with this new body I found myself in instead of focusing on my new role as a dual-caster. Beside me, Larcen squared his shoulders. He'd let his frustration with me get the better of him and had left the marble behind when we'd gone to the diner; an amateurish mistake, and he was a seasoned warrior.

"It won't happen again," he said.

"I know it won't," Alder said.

"Can I still get my own marble?" I asked.

"This is a prototype, so there is only one until the twins make more. You'll have to share, and so you'll have to stay together."

Larcen ground his teeth.

Alder let the silence draw out as he glared at us. The warning was clear. *Get along.*

After an uncomfortable minute, he cleared his throat and continued, "I know I promised you time to adjust to your new lives and surroundings, but sometimes fate has a different agenda. You have your first assignment." He lifted a file folder, and suddenly his red-tinted image vanished and was replaced by a series of images.

"The Savannah History Museum?" Larcen extended a finger

and swiped through the images as if they were tangible objects. I hovered over his shoulder to get a better look.

"Despite its modest size, it is home to over ten thousand artifacts," Alder said. "And it seems someone wants this one."

I reached over Larcen's shoulder to swipe the images for myself, and shot right past it.

"Gently," Larcen admonished, returning to the correct image. "And stop hovering, you little bat."

I just chittered in his ear. I knew I had to play nice, but he was so insufferable I just couldn't help myself.

"*This* is the Zhu dagger," Alder told us sternly, and we stopped bickering, focusing on the picture of the artifact. "So named because the blade itself has a green tint, like that of bamboo. To be brief, it was fashioned in Asia millennia ago, spent a few centuries in the Middle East, was brought back to Europe during the Crusades, and then found its way to the United States when the French aided in its revolution."

"It doesn't say that on the that little history tag," I said, squinting at the placard beneath the dagger's display case.

"Not all history is remembered, Eryn."

"So why is it a target?" the dark elf asked.

"What history did get right—according to that little history tag, Eryn—is that the dagger brought whoever wielded it good luck in battle, lending credence to the myth that it was fashioned from dragon bone, probably a tooth. Unlike European dragons, who have a tendency to be vicious and greedy, Asian dragons have a reputation of humility and kindness. No doubt this was given to some worthy soul as a gift."

The images disappeared, replaced by Alder's red-tinted bust once again. "Magic can wax and wane in the human realm, as you know, and this dagger has lain dormant for quite some time. The dragon it came from must have died, taking its magic with it. However, the dagger can still *channel* magic."

"So it's a tool."

"With the potential to be a very powerful one."

"So why isn't it already locked up inside one of your vaults?" I asked.

"It was lost to us after the Civil War, just recently reemerging from a private collection after the latest owner passed. It was donated earlier this week; Moxie was already in negotiations with the museum."

"Stubborn," was all Moxie had to say.

"We have reason to believe someone will be making an attempt to steal it tonight," Alder said. "It's a new moon, which, as you know, is a very auspicious time to thieve."

"'Someone?'" Larcen leaned forward, bracing himself against the edge of the desk. "I wasn't an official dualcaster until last night, and you run a tight-lipped ship over there at headquarters, but even I've gleaned from the decade I've been here that it's never just 'someone.' It's always an occult group messing in things they don't understand or a creature whose loved one was killed by humans and seeks revenge."

"Or power-hungry genocidal murderers who destroy a valley of innocent night wisps for no good reason other than race dominance," I added.

Larcen didn't look at me, but his shoulders tightened, and the edge of the oak counter he gripped cracked under his hands. "There's always a name," he ground out.

Alder shook his head. "This time, there isn't. The Council has only provided us with a place and a time. Savannah History Museum. Midnight tonight. The dagger is important, but I would daresay finding out who wants to steal it is even more so. They're using a type of cloaking magic we've never seen before."

"And I hate it," Maven's voice added. "DUO is the only one who's supposed to have the fancy toys, and I don't like being upstaged. Avenge my honor!"

Alder nodded, clearly humoring her. "This type of magic shouldn't even exist, and if someone is using it to thieve artifacts such as the Zhu dagger, then the intent behind it can be nothing but nefarious. Which is why it has come across my desk. Which is why you, Larcen, in particular, have been selected for this mission."

I gave the dark elf a startled look, but then it transformed into a brittle smile that demanded answers.

He flicked a look at me from the corner of his eye and cleared his throat. "I'm a tracker."

"An elfin tracker, how cliché," I snipped.

"Of magic," he snapped.

"He's a spellhunter, more specifically," Alder clarified, though that didn't bring me any clarity whatsoever. "Honestly, Larcen, I should not be the one who is informing your partner about these kinds of details."

"Drow aren't the sharing type," he growled at Alder, then he turned to face me fully with a huff. "I'm a spellhunter. I can *see* spells, their influence, the strands of magic they leave behind, whatever you want to call it, and I can trace those tracks back to their source." He glared at Alder. "There, happy now?"

"If you can do that, what are you doing growing plants?"

He glared at me for even asking and turned back to the red image of Alder's bust. "Details on the assignment?" he prompted.

"All the information we have has been uploaded to your array, and everything you'll need for this mission should be in the briefcase. Retrieve the dagger, eliminate the thief. I'll expect notification immediately following the completion of your mission. Good luck."

"Wait," I cried as his image flickered. It solidified, Alder's eyebrows raised in mute question. "I'll need a weapon."

Alder just gave Larcen a cutting look, and his image vanished.

I stared at the garnet marble another second or two, hoping he'd reappear, but he didn't. I turned to the dark elf. "What was that all about?"

The drow let out the most world-weary sigh I'd ever heard, pushing himself away from the desk. "Come with me."

CHAPTER ELEVEN

Eryn

I HALF EXPECTED Larcen to divert to the walk-in just behind him, but he took me to another door with the sign "Employees Only" on the opposite side of the fountain. It opened to a small storeroom, neat and orderly, the gnome-sized ladders fashioned to the shelves to allow for easy access. As it banged shut behind me, I heard a secondary *fwap*, and realized there was a pig-sized cutout in the bottom of the door screened by strips of canvas.

"Keep up," Larcen said.

Hidden in the shadows of a shelf was another door, and I was beginning to think there was no end to this system of door-room-door-room. Door to the polytunnel, door to the walk-in, door to the storeroom, and-and-and. I was an ariel, and I was used to flying about wherever I pleased. The Temple of the Sky had no doors to speak of, just moon gates and arching windows to provide easy access. Even our archives with their precious star charts and histories weren't locked behind doors.

I followed Larcen into what could only be described as a barracks. Gnome-sized bunks were cut into the walls, all connected by those miniature ladders; there was a slop trough for Rumple; several couches all with split seams and leaking stuffing; cushions strewn across the rugs; a whole host of mini fridges lined up against the long wall like a bunch of town-houses. It was the only bare wall in the place, the rest of them painted to resemble a sunny English garden in full bloom. Cat trees, stripped of their carpeting and replaced with moss, were dotted around the room and connected by rope bridges and ziplines in a series more intricate than a spider's web.

I phased into mist, delighted I had the energy to do so, and passed through the ropes as easily as vapor. Larcen drew his scorpion blade and cut through one line with an irritated, "Told them to keep the walkway clear."

Then he glanced over his shoulder to make sure I wasn't dawdling. "Restroom is over there. Shower is over there, and you'll have to share with Rumple. The gnomes have their own drip irrigation line set up. Oh, and their pottery throwing station is in there, so watch your step."

"And my room?"

Ariels might be social butterflies, but we still preferred to have our own spaces to relax.

"Pick a bunk," he said, waving his hand at the wall of gnome-sized beds. "You can change your shape, can't you? I'm sure you'll find somewhere you can fit."

I just gave the back of his head a surly look as he disap-peared through yet another doorway. This one didn't have a door, per se, but it certainly had a shimmering forcefield. It looked like a sheet of rain, but without the noise.

I fluttered to a halt on the other side, giving it a wary glance.

"It won't force you to phase," the dark elf said. "It's just a deterrent."

"A deterrent for what?"

"Anyone who doesn't want to endure a slow and agonizing death. Come on."

Steeling my nerves, I flew through the forcefield fast, just in case. I felt... nothing. Just as I was about to flash Larcen a cheery smile, I saw what that forcefield had been shielding. Stairs. Stairs that led *down*.

"Oh no," I said, floating away. "This is where I draw the line. I don't go underground. Uh-uh."

"You want to prepare for this mission or not?"

"Absolutely. But outside. In the *air*."

"Where everyone can see us? I don't think so. Come on."

"Open your ears, you creepy crawly caveman, I don't do—ah!"

My body crystallized, the drow catching me before I could shatter against the floor. He replaced the poisoned scorpion blade on its hook, hoisted me into his arms, and trotted down the steps.

I fought through the panic of the crushing darkness, the stale air, the lack of light, focusing on my rage instead. I got my mouth to loosen up first. "There is no curse I could utter to convey how—"

Larcen shifted his hold and clamped a hand over my mouth. "Ah, finally."

I frantically worked on unlocking the crystal matrix, using the power of my Steorra bloodline to burn away the poison. Like sunlight sharpened through a magnifying glass, it liquified my core first, but Larcen was swift on his feet, arriving at the bottom of the winding stair before I could release my limbs.

The dungeon, for that's all it could be, was as dark as this drow's soul.

He set me on something soft yet firm and abandoned me for the only square of light in this vast underground. It was the terminal end of the compost chute, and it led straight into the mouth of the largest pitcher plant I had ever seen. The pitcher was large enough to swallow a man whole, its throat ribbed in purple and yellow, and spade-shaped purple leaves the size of unfurled umbrellas crowded around its base. It sat on a barrel-shaped pedestal, a wide tube with a pump attached extending from the base and disappearing into the wall behind it.

The dark elf padded forward silently on bare feet, having shucked his boots at the doorway, and approached the pitcher plant, crooning something low and unintelligible. Then, as if the pitcher plant were an affectionate pet, Larcen rubbed the plant's throat. "Give it up, Berthold."

The pitcher plant belched, expelling the chrome case Moxie had given us. Surprisingly, it was as clean and shiny as the day it'd been cast on the manufacturer's floor. Larcen caught it easily, giving the plant's massive belly another pat before striding away.

Pale light illuminated his path: bioluminescent vines that crawled along the ceiling. One vine extended, lowering a melon-sized bulb. The petals unfurled, revealing a fuchsia interior with dangling stamens like anglers' lures. Bright light surrounded the dark elf like a spotlight, reflecting sharply off the chrome case.

It also gave me plenty of light to see by; the firm-yet-yielding surface beneath me was a training mat that extended the entire length of the room. One wall had been converted into a weapons rack, containing various slashing and cutting things I had never seen before much less knew the names of. Behind the pitcher plant, a honeycomb lattice like a wine rack framed the wall. Almost all the cubbies were empty, but a few had bundles of what looked like rolled-up clothes. It was the strangest closet I'd ever seen.

Larcen was just unlatching the briefcase when I finally reassumed control over my body. I jumped into the air and screamed, a storm wind jettisoning from my throat. He jumped,

backflipping over the attack and landing with the most condescending look I'd seen on his face yet.

As I sucked in another breath, this time resolving not to
miss, Larcen's hand darted into the open case and yanked out
something white and familiar.

The storm wind died in my throat.

Momentarily distracted from my anger and panic—the
ceiling in this vast underground training room was incredibly
high, lessening my claustrophobia—I soared over the training
mat.

He dropped the object into my hands before I could get too
close, warily taking a step back.

My bladed fans. Even my belt of braided starlight threads
was in the case, the guardian insignia winking on the buckle: the
horn, the bow, and the sword intertwined as one. I lifted a fan
into the pale-pink light of the hanging plant bulb. Every nick
and scratch was familiar in their starlight metal, and a sheaf of
thin parchment nestled between two blades. I eased it out, lest it
become confetti, and read in the familiar handwriting, *For Eryn.*

I clutched the fans to my chest. "You had no right to keep
these from me," I snarled at the drow.

He snorted. "Like I was going to give you a weapon
voluntarily?"

CHAPTER TWELVE

Larcen

THERE WAS no security measure that could keep a shadow-walker out of anywhere he wanted to go, except for a laser grid. The Savannah History Museum didn't have one, so I slinked out of the shadows like I owned the place.

Doors meant nothing to an ariel, so she phased through the one behind me, hovering over my right shoulder like my own personal poltergeist. Though she had returned to flesh and blood, her white hair still had this strange ability to float around her like a cloud as if caught in an invisible air current. It only obeyed the laws of gravity when her feet were on the ground.

"We're on a stealth mission," I said under my breath, knowing her ears could hear anything. "Did you have to wear that dress?"

It was the silk sundress Maven had given her, white with tiny rosebuds—red Charlottes, if I wasn't mistaken—and it might've just as well been a "We're Here" neon sign. White liked to catch every available mote of light and reflect it like a mirror, especially in the dark. I knew she couldn't have done anything about her ethereal appearance—except tame her hair in a braid—but she could've worn something more appropriate.

"This is not my first guardian job, you know," she replied with a sniff. "And it's not like you offered me anything drab to wear."

Drab? My clothes were cut and tailored to fit me perfectly with craftmanship that would make any of the reigning fashion houses burst at the seams with envy. They were all navy blues, charcoals, and black, but they certainly weren't *drab*. And let an ariel wear one my damask vests? The Spider Queen sting me through the heart right now. I swallowed my indignation and focused on the big picture. "We're not guarding."

"We are until the thief shows himself. Or herself. Ooo! Do you think it's a lady thief? I hear they're a lot craftier than male thieves. She might even make this night a little interesting."

"Don't say that. You never want a job to be 'interesting.' You want it boring. Boring is better. And predictable. But it certainly won't be if the thief sees you first."

"Worry about your own look, caveman. Who wears sunglasses at night? Going for a boho-goth look with those leather pants and bare feet?"

I yanked the sunglasses off my face and nestled them in the V of my vest. I'd needed them for the occasional streetlamp outside, but in here, only soft LED lights illuminated some of the displays. Drow didn't need to wear shoes; our soles were tough and well-suited to gripping wet and dry surfaces alike. I only wore boots out in public, lest I draw any more attention than I already did with my dark skin and white warrior braid.

The ariel snickered, the sound akin to a musical chime, and

soared through the rooms, examining every one as I paced to the only one that mattered. The museum was housed in an old railroad passenger station from the mid-1800s, and I could smell the sweat of the laborers that lingered in the bricks. There was a train engine replica in the middle of the museum—scaled down, of course—and displays of Revolutionary War uniforms in individual cases. I expected to find the Zhu dagger in the "Savannah in the Civil War" exhibit, but the intel Alder provided us said it was in the rear of the museum with the quilt display. Apparently the previous owner had wrapped the dagger up in an exquisite quilt and hidden it all away in an old sea chest, and it was the only exhibit large enough to display everything.

There was only one point of entry into the quilt exhibit, which shared a space with a display dedicated to some woman who had organized a bunch of girls into scouts. So what? Come to Drozvega and you'll see a bunch of girls able to take down a swarm of mudcrab spiders before their seventh birthdays.

Even though there was only one doorway, it only mean that it was the most obvious choice to enter the room. If the thief had any magical ability, inherent or learned, there was a distinct possibility he could appear right in front of the dagger's display case and disappear just as quickly. I needed to be in room with the dagger.

The quilts weren't hanging from the ceiling as I expected, instead tacked to wooden frames and angled on a raised shelf along the perimeter of the room. Plenty of shadows to hide in. I slipped into the nearest one, reappearing in the darkness behind the frame of the quilt closest to the dagger's display. In position, I listened for the telltale whisper of the ariel's passage through the air and heard nothing. "Eryn," I hissed. "Eryn!"

Nothing.

Where was she?

Hissing my displeasure, I settled into a comfortable crouch behind the quilt to wait.

The coin dangling from my wrist suddenly felt like a grindstone. Drow were fairly independent creatures, but we came together to fight viciously for clan and king and that overgrown arachnid. I knew how to work with others, but this flighty little butterfly they'd anchored me to was something else. Herding snakes was easier.

I slipped my finger under the coin, angling it into the ambient light. The gold only shone with a mute flash, revealing a swirling design on each side, one raised, one recessed. It attached to the bracelet by a minuscule spindle, allowing the coin to spin at will, but the magic of the Puddle was discerning. I had to, with clear intent, flick the coin with my finger to activate the Puddle's power. But only with the ariel's consent, otherwise it would kill her. Alder had been very clear about that.

She would never agree to help me destroy the Spider Queen's sanctum, despite it being the home of her mortal enemies, so I would have to bide my time. I couldn't return home without an invitation, but I was working on that. Or rather, Elvera was working on that, or she should've been. Her family was high in the hierarchy, closeted followers of the twin moon goddesses just like my mother and me, and if we were going to free our people I would have to be in Drozvega with a cure. And if *I* came back, so did the ariel. Eryn had been willing to sacrifice herself to defend the night wisps, so she certainly wouldn't mind sacrificing herself for other innocents. And she wouldn't be alive to tell me otherwise.

I let the coin slip from my touch, unwilling to examine it further. I didn't want to tempt fate, or the Puddle, just yet.

With nothing else to do, and the ariel nowhere to be found, I let my mind slip into a meditative state and waited for the thief.

The thief was early, skulking into the exhibit at 11:55 p.m. Or maybe the clock on the wall was just running slow. A lot of magic relied on precise timing and preparation, especially if the practitioner was a human, and he certainly was. I could smell him as easily as if he were standing right in front of me instead of half an exhibit away. Sweat, silver filings, hair gel.

A magician.

But what kind? The chiseled arms and shoulders extending from his black tank top proved him well-muscled and trim like an acrobat, and there was a healthy if tacky glow to his skin, so he wasn't a dark mage. Practice dark magic long enough and a rot sets in. He could be a warlock, but he didn't move like one. Warlocks had a glide to them, as if they were rolling on an unseen cloud, not this cocksure swagger the thief presented as he strolled up to the display case. The silver I smelled on him could mean he was an alchemist, but athletic alchemists— unless they were elves—were rare, spending too much time in their laboratories and developing a paunch.

And the hair gel... What was up with that? And why was I smelling bubblegum?

Wait a minute...

This guy was a patsy.

The thief extracted a little pouch from his belt and with unnecessary flourish sprinkled the silvery contents all over the display case. Steam hissed, pressure sensors deactivated, alarms disengaged, and the thief took what looked like a bone splinter from another pouch on his belt and merry-as-you-please drew a circle against the glass, whistling the melody of Daft Punk's "Get Lucky." The bone splinter dissolved the plexiglass with an acid-like substance, and then the thief extracted the bubblegum he'd been chewing, stuck it against the circle, and used the suction to withdraw the glass. Another sprinkle of that silver glitter over the gum dissolved it instantly, leaving no trace of it nor the thief's saliva.

Okay, still a patsy... but a patsy with skills.

Still whistling, the thief extended his hand through the hole, gripped the dagger's hilt, and yanked.

The dagger refused to budge.

Curious, I remained in my hiding place, watching.

Cursing under his breath, the thief braced his gloved hand against the plexiglass display case and twisted his shoulders in an attempt to wrench the dagger free.

The dagger lifted from its mount, but the thief still couldn't pull it through the hole.

Inside the display case, the air suddenly condensed into mist, concealing the dagger and the thief's arm up to the elbow in white vapor.

The thief cursed. "No one said anything about magical wards."

But there weren't any. I would've been able to see those.

He braced his foot against the display pedestal and frantically searched the pouches on his belt for something that would help him. His fingers wiggled through a leather pouch, pinching red granules and flicking them at the vapor that roiled out of the circular hole.

"Let the unseen be seen," he cried.

The ariel materialized, either from his magic or just right on cue, her jade-green eyes bright and a crazed smile on her lips. Her white hair floated above her in a cloud-like haze, one hand on the dagger's sheath and her other hand clamped around the thief's wrist. "Surprise, suckah!"

The thief staggered back with a cry, but the ariel's grip was a diamond-like latch on his arm.

"Look, Larcen! I got him!" She looked at me right in eye, despite me being entirely shrouded in shadow, her smile instantly changing from crazed to proud delight. Like a young terrier who'd finally caught her first rat.

I shadow-walked into the darkness beside the display case, and the thief shrieked again. "See?" I told the ariel. "Boring is better. This guy's clearly just spider fodder with a few potions up his sleeves. Nothing nefarious about him. Strange, because—"

"I don't wear sleeves," the thief snarled. "I am the Great Billy Macon—"

"Ah! That's why I thought you looked so familiar," the ariel exclaimed. "I saw your poster for a magic show in Las Vegas. Larcen, this is the magician hack I was telling you about."

"*Hack?*" Billy's hand flashed to his belt and returned with a dark-silver knife.

The coating was an eerie iridescent yellow-green.

"Eryn!" I said.

"Wha—"

The magician slashed the dart across the back of Eryn's hand, and the ariel's diamond grip on his wrist turned to mist. Just like the poisoned darts of Drozvega, this knife forced the ariel to phase, but not necessarily into a crystalline structure. The poison leached up her mist-like hand and into her arm, the vapor condensing first into frost and then into crystal. She still had a diamond grip on the dagger's sheath, and the dagger blade disengaged with a click as she fell heavily to the floor.

The thief stumbled away and gave me a wild look. We stared at each other for a heartbeat, unsure if I was going to lunge after him or help my partner. It was all the time the thief needed. Billy threw something against the ground, and the exhibit erupted with a thunderous clap and a cloud of smoke.

Smoke powder, are you kidding me?

The concussive blast activated every alarm within the museum, and water burst from the overhead sprinklers. The smoke dispersed under the rain, and the Great Billy Macon was nowhere to be seen.

Eryn was still in a half-crystal, half-mist heap on the floor, her jade-like eyes bulging in disbelief, her mouth frozen in a surprised cry.

Without a second thought, I shadow-walked to the roof.

CHAPTER THIRTEEN

Eryn

I BURNED through the poison with the ferocity of a blazing sun and sprang into the air in a cloud of mist. "Why that cobweb-munching, cave-skulking—abandoning me like that!" I shot through the cracks in the ceiling, the vent, and the bricks in seconds and materialized as a floating woman above the rooftops of Savannah.

Panting, to my left.

I could hear it as loudly as if it was right beside me, cutting through the droning crickets and the whispers of the wind passing through the dripping Spanish moss. The dagger sheath still in my hand, I shot after the sound like an arrow.

The dark elf raced along the rooftops of the sleeping city, disappearing into shadows and reappearing farther down the street, and closing the gap between him and the thief at an incredible rate. And the Great Billy Macon, while just a Las Vegas magician, was moving at an inhuman speed.

I was still too far away for my bladed fan to be of any use, so I landed on the roof of a plantation-style home, braced myself, and let out a silent scream. The storm wind cut through the leaves of the nearest trees, racing through the humid air and slamming into the magician's shoulder.

Billy tumbled as I jumped into the air. He caught himself on a gutter before he could roll off the roof. Dangling from one hand, he plucked a vial from his belt and splashed the dark contents into his mouth.

"What was that?" I asked as I drew even with the dark elf.

"Vampire blood," Larcen replied, shadow-walking away and reappearing on the roof of the house two away from me. "Keep up."

I soared to the right, phasing just in time to avoid the broad canopy of a live oak tree, and swept around for a pincer maneuver. The enhanced Billy Macon launched into the air, landing on the roof half a street away, and disappeared in a blur.

The dark elf skidded to a halt, lifting his nose to scent the air. "I can still smell him."

"And I can still hear him," I said, flying past. "Now *you* keep up!"

Using our senses, we tracked Billy to the restaurant district at the edge of the river. Smart to retreat here, hoping the smells of crab boils and fry oil and the deep water itself would mask him. The barges were quiet at this time of night, only the ambient glow of security lights washing the riverfront in an orange light. It was a beautiful place, brick-lined and dotted with trees and walking paths, soured by the thief's presence. Above, the stars shone as bright and hard as pinpricks in the moonless sky. Billy had stopped on the flat roof of an old brownstone overlooking the black river, and he wasn't alone.

A lean, hooded figure waited for him, arms crossed over his chest and the hem of his cloak fluttering about his knees. He towered over Billy Macon, impatiently thrusting out his hand for the dagger as we crept forward.

"What is this?" a deep voice demanded.

"You wanted the dagger, so you got the dagger," Billy replied. "This damn sprite or something wouldn't let go, but you still got the business end of the blade. Now pay up."

We snuck forward; the dark elf was liquid shadow, sliding in and out of the darkness with the same silence as a snake slipping into water, and I drifted on the wind, lighter than a whisper. I knew my bright white hair would give me away, so I phased to my true mist-like form.

And realized I couldn't maintain it for long.

"Damn this body and its need for food," I hissed under my breath. Changing from mist to crystal used to be as effortless as thinking, but now that I was no longer sustained by celestial dew, there was a limit to how many times I could phase. My stomach, even in this mist-like form, growled a warning.

The hooded face wrenched in my direction.

Phasing into a floating woman, I yanked the bladed fan out of my belt just as he swept a recurve bow off his shoulder. He drew the bowstring back to his ear, and a shimmering green arrow magically appeared. Instead of firing at me, he cursed and swept the bow to his right and fired.

Larcen, who had used my growling stomach as a distraction, had appeared in the shadow Billy Macon had cast. He'd been poised to snap Billy's neck or at least put him in a headlock, and the green arrow hit him straight in the heart.

The dark elf slammed onto his back as the magical arrow slithered into his chest like a bolt of lightning, and between one blink and the next, Larcen disappeared. His clothes lay against the roof as if he had simply vanished.

"No!" I cried.

"Dude, that was awesome," Billy said, turning back to the archer. "What did you d—"

The magician's voice turned into a garbled cry as the archer rammed the Zhu dagger into his gut.

I landed on the roof, slashing with my bladed fans. The archer wrenched away from Billy and deflected with dagger and bow, but the starlight metal bit through it all. While I couldn't keep my body in its true form—whether mist or crystal—I discovered this new human flesh was a harmonious blend between the two. I was still light and fast, and I glided through the attacks as if I were water.

But I had never faced anyone like this hooded archer before. My attacks might be seamless, but he made fighting look like an art form. But I just needed one opening, and I was nothing but patient.

A kick to my chest was followed by a dagger swipe to my thighs and a spinning slash of the bow. I backflipped and ducked under the bow, catching the bowstring with my bladed fan. The string snapped, and the archer looked down at the dangling threads in a moment of disbelief. Then his grip tightened, the wood creaking under his fingers, and he attacked with a ferocity I hadn't anticipated. I took a soaring leap backwards and let out a silent scream. He threw up his arms, buffeting the storm wind with the bow, but the wood snapped under the blast. The two halves clattered against the roof as he slid back to the very edge.

Landing, I slapped both fans together, the wind arrow knocking the archer over the edge to plummet five stories to the brick walkway. I whooshed to a halt at the edge of the roof just in time to see the archer disappear into the shadows. They caught him as easily as a lake absorbs a raindrop, and he reappeared, unharmed, in the shadow of a tree on the opposite side of the street. I could tell from his posture that he was glaring up at me, and I sank into a fighting stance, challenging him.

The shadow-walker slipped into the shadows and vanished.

UGLY PURPLE VEINS like vines spread from the dagger wound in Billy Macon's gut. He was dead, white, foamy spittle ebbing from the corners of his mouth as his black eyes stared unseeing up at the moonless sky. He'd clawed at his wound until a paralysis had gripped him, contorting his limbs to resemble those of a squashed beetle.

Behind him, the bow I had cut in half was now two piles of smoking ash.

I gave the magician only a passing glance as I hurried over to Larcen's clothes. His disappearance frightened me more than the appearance of another shadow-walker or the thief's death. I knelt by his vacant vest and empty leather pants, fighting the panic that was forming a hard lump in my throat.

"Our first time as dualcasters and we haven't even dualcasted anything and my partner gets—"

The words died in my throat as I saw something move under the vest's left breast. It was a lump no bigger than a plum, and it was rooting around in his vest like a mouse.

"L-Larcen?" I lifted the damask silk and gave it a shake.

A goldfish bounced against the leather pants, flapping its red fins and gasping as its eyes bulged. A bracelet with a gold coin pendant, clearly having been shrunk to size, dangled around the fish like a necklace.

"Stars above." I gave the struggling goldfish a shaky laugh as I picked it up by its tail. "Well, this night turned rather interesting, didn't it, Larcen?"

CHAPTER FOURTEEN

Eryn

WHEN ALDER SHAW'S garnet-red bust appeared from the marble at two o'clock in the morning, looking not the least bit groggy, he didn't get a chance to speak.

"We have a very serious problem," I said, baring my teeth in a bright smile.

Alder Shaw's eyes narrowed, like he was peering. "All I see is a coffee mug that says 'Grow, Dammit' on the side."

"Oh, right." I set the mug down and flicked my fingers, creating an air pocket that encased the contents of the mug and drew them up for the director's inspection.

Alder eyed the swirling ball of water and the goldfish inside, visibly starting when he caught sight of the dualcaster coin dangling from the goldfish's neck. "*Larcen?*"

The goldfish let out a stream of bubbles in response.

I eased the swirling sphere of water back into the coffee cup and released the air technique, a little water sluicing over the rim.

"Careful of the ledgers," Rumple cried. He'd successfully climbed into the leather rolly chair on his fourth attempt, refusing to leave his master's side when he was in such a vulnerable state. I didn't blame him; the gnomes, after helping me find a container without drainage holes to keep the goldfish in— which just happened to be one of those new coffee mugs—had started to congregate around the desk like geese around a toddler with a sack of corn. Vicious.

"Oh shush," Marigold said, kicking the ledger aside before the water could wet the pages. She used her garden hoe like a squeegee, directing the spill over the edge of the wooden counter.

"Don't forget to dry it, or it'll stain," Rumple said quickly. "You know how Master Larcen likes everything neat and tidy."

"I don't give a snail's turd for what Mr. High And Mighty wants," Marigold said, but she did sit down and scooch her fanny across the desk, mopping up the rest of the water with her little denim overalls. "But I do want this place looking nice when we take over."

Inside the mug, the goldfish swam in furious circles, spewing a whole host of bubbles that just had to be curses.

"Stop sloshing." Cornelius gave the mug a chastising tap with his trowel. The vibrations seemed to stun the goldfish, and the gnome rolled onto his tiptoes to peer over the edge of the mug. The goldfish squirted him right in the face.

Marigold threw her head back with a laugh, her brown curls bouncing under her red pointy cap. Cornelius removed his yellow one, shook the water out—sprinkling the leather ledger anew, much to Rumple's distraught whimpers—and lifted his trowel threateningly.

As much as I would've loved to see Larcen choke down his

just desserts, this dark elf was my dualcaster partner, even if he had abandoned me in the museum. And he was just a goldfish now, after all. I flicked my finger, sending a little blast of air that slid Cornelius halfway across the desk and transformed his pointy white beard into a bush of frizz. "A dead goldfish means no espresso machine."

"I wasn't gonna kill him," the gnome sulked, pawing at his beard to straighten it. "Just maybe get me a fin. That should incentivize him to make the changes we want around here."

Clustered at the base of the desk, the thirty-something other gnomes cheered.

Alder cleared his throat loudly and demanded, "What happened?"

"Oh, so many things."

"This was supposed to be something small and simple: confiscate the dagger, apprehend the thief, find out who was casting those concealment spells. How is Larcen a goldfish?"

"A shadow-walker shot him in the chest with a green arrow made of lightning."

Alder seemed like he was prepared for a snarky answer and choked on his reply when he realized I was completely serious. "Oh," was all he said.

"The thief, a human magician named Billy Macon—"

"The Las Vegas magician?"

I nodded.

"Not really a true magician, is he?" Alder swept his own comment aside with flick of his hand. "That's neither here nor there. Sorry for the interruption. Please, continue."

"He was the thief. But he wasn't working alone. We chased him down to the riverfront and found him giving the dagger to someone else. The shadow-walker."

"Are you sure it was a shadow-walker? 'Rare' still doesn't do the gift's rate of occurrence justice."

"He fell five stories down to a shadowed street, was absorbed, and appeared unharmed in the shadow of a tree. What else would you like me to call him?"

"It's just... hard to believe. Larcen's the only one who's been born with that trait in the last millennium. It could've been a very powerful necromancer or dark mage..." Alder tapped his chin and grimaced. "I might have to contact Drozvega... Go on."

"We fought, but he got away."

"With the dagger."

I lifted the dagger's bejeweled sheath from my belt. "I got the sheath," I said lamely.

"And you two didn't use your dualcaster powers or the Puddle—why?"

"Baby birds might have wings but they still need some time to learn how to fly," I said, snarling a clenched-teeth smile. And it's not like we hadn't used our own individual powers, which were nothing to sneer at. Larcen could've used his new phasing ability, but he'd been taken completely by surprise. And how was me casting an illusion going to help the situation? I glanced down at the coin that dangled from my slim pale wrist. There'd been no time to test what kind of power the Puddle granted me, plus we'd been warned to only use it in dire circumstances.

"So the dagger and the thieves are gone," Alder summarized.

"Well, just the shadow-walker. Billy's dead."

Alder pinched the bridge of his nose. "*Please* tell me you didn't just leave the body out there. What is rule one of DUO?"

"'Don't reveal the magical world.' And of course I didn't leave the body there." I turned the marble so it would spin Alder's image around and pointed. "It's right there."

Billy Macon's corpse dominated the cement aisle between the orchids and hoyas, still frozen in that twisted, upside-down-beetle posture. The purple veins under his skin had diffused, turning his whole body the mottled color of a bruised fruit.

"Out in the open?" Alder cried.

"No one's coming in here at this hour. No one—"

"Did Larcen tell you nothing? He might run a plant nursery during the day, but at night it's the finest alchemy supply store on the East Coast!"

"Larcen doesn't tell me anything. And I haven't toured the place yet because *someone* decided to give me an assignment with a partner who hates me just hours after becoming a dualcaster."

The druid glared at me, and I swear the temperature in the polytunnel dropped a few degrees. I knew he wasn't a weather druid, but he could've fooled me.

I slapped a bright smile on my face and amended hastily, "Sir."

"Get rid of that body. DUO maintains its position in the magical realm because we're discreet and discerning. We don't kill those we don't have to. But our reputation might do a tail-spin if anyone comes in there and sees we've used magic to kill a human civilian!"

"But we didn't kill him."

"They don't know that. At first glance, he looks like a customer who was given some bad herbs and died on the spot, or he could've been a test subject!"

"Oh." The smile wavered from my face. "I can see what you mean."

"Excellent." Alder threw up his hand. Then he ran that hand through his hair with a frustrated sigh. "Get rid of the body. You two are benched until we can figure out more. When the twins are free, I'll send the jet and let them to take a look at Larcen. It's definitely a curse, and they'll have the best chance of figuring out how to reverse it. Just... keep your head down and stay out of trouble, okay?"

I swallowed and bowed my head. "Okay."

Alder's eight-inch bust shrank into a thread of red light and was sucked back into the marble as the communication was cut off. I put the red marble in my sundress pocket and blinked, surprised to find a tear rolling down my cheek. I brushed it away, looking at the glistening wet on my finger with surprise. Ariels were known to be emotional, but we didn't cry. We were physically incapable. But then again, no ariel had ever had a body before, and I'd shed tears three times now.

I felt something cool touch my hand. It was Marigold, a sympathetic look on her chubby face as she patted my hand.

I gave her a watery smile and wiped my nose with the back of my hand. "I don't suppose any of you know what do with the body?"

The gnomes clustered around the desk gave each other a look, followed by a shrug.

"When in doubt, throw it down the chute," the one in the blue beret said.

I nodded. "Thank you."

The gnomes gasped.

Not knowing how to react, I just asked, "Could one of you show me how to open it, please? I don't want to break it."

Another gasp rippled through the gnomes, and they started whispering among themselves, pausing to give me wide-eyed looks of shock.

"Um..."

"We'll take care of that, dear. You've already had such a day," Marigold said. She shoved Cornelius forward with her hoe. "You go on and take her on a tour. The poor girl should get a look at her new home."

"If anyone should be giving tours around here, it should be me," Rumple said, the leather rolly chair squeaking miserably as he jumped gracelessly to the floor. "Come along, Miss Eryn."

"I'm still coming," Cornelius said, sliding down the leg of the counter like it was a fire pole. "Everything that's done around here should have a gnome present, for representation." He crawled up onto Rumple's back, holding onto the bronze collar for support, and gave the black pig a few jabs with his heels. "Mush."

"I am an Iberian pig, not a Siberian Husky," Rumple said with a lift of his snout, but he still trotted off with his little rider.

"Never heard of an Iberian pig with a Southern accent before."

"Did you know pigs can buck? Keep up that sass and you'll find out firsthand. We're also very good at eating *anything*, so if I were you, I'd mind my Ps and Qs."

"Um, Rumple?" I said. "I think the tour needs to wait."

My stomach let out such a vicious snarl that the pig reared with a squeal. Cornelius lost his grip on both collar and trowel and tumbled down the pig's back with a wail. A whoosh of air caught his fall before he could bust his lip on the cement, but then my control vanished as my stomach snarled again.

"The poor girl's hungry," Marigold called. "Go get her something to eat, Cornelius!"

"No meat," I pleaded.

"We've got nothing in the break room except Swedish Fish and cheese puffs, and whatever Rumple's got hiding in that drawer of his," Cornelius called back.

"My secret snack drawer is off limits," the pig declared. "I'm hypoglycemic!"

"Say now," a gnome said, stroking his chinstrap beard. "The boss is still a fish, yeah?"

I snatched up the coffee mug with my goldish partner in it, holding it tight to my chest. "So?"

"So that means he's not guarding the company credit card."

"Oh no you don't!" Rumple shouted.

"Pizza!" the gnomes cheered.

The next few things happened very fast: I used the last of my strength to jump onto the counter to get out of the way, half the gnomes immediately diverted from opening the compost grate to block Rumple from getting to the computer desk behind the counter, and Marigold led the charge to ransack the desk. The gnome with the blue beret was dangled upside down by his feet, each ankle held in the meaty fist of a muscular Bavarian barmaid-looking gnome, and he got to work picking the lock to the center drawer.

Inside the coffee mug, Larcen the goldfish was swirling around in angry circles, hopping up out of his container to jettison steams of water in protest. Then he squirted me right in the face, clearly demanding I intervene. And I would have, normally, except I was very hungry and very tired of getting yelled at by druids and goldfish alike, and he had just sprayed water on my only sundress. So I flashed the angry goldfish a bright smile. "Sorry, I don't speak fish."

"Got it," Blue Beret cried as the latch clicked and the drawer lurched open on hydraulic springs.

The Bavarian barmaid dropped him into the waiting mosh pit of his gnome kin, who cheered and crowd-surfed the lock picker away. Then the barmaid held Marigold's garden hoe steady and the gnome slid down it into the drawer, landing on the curvy cushion of her backside with a little "Oof!"

"Stop," Rumple cried, his black ears flapping madly as he tried to sit up. "We have a very short spending lim—Ouch!"

"Not so tight, boys," Cornelius said as his half of the gnomes hog-tied Rumple once more with garden twine. Waving his trowel, he marched up and down the pig's ribs as if he were a knight who'd felled his first dragon. "Rumple is our friend, even with his *misguided* loyalties."

"Just don't scratch my collar," the pig said with a defeated sigh, slumping against the cement and letting the gnomes finish their work. "Master Larcen already pitched a fit about the expense the first time."

"What's the collar for, anyway?" I asked. I remained perched on the counter, already having decided for my stomach's sake not to interfere.

"The glyphs are an illusion spell. They make me appear human to our human customers. It's less alarming for them that way."

"And not just any human, but a fat, sweaty human," Cornelius laughed. "Coke-bottle glasses and all. Ha!"

Then the gnome cried out as Rumple gave his wide hips a jerk and sent the gnome sliding down the pig's hairy stomach. Cornelius spilled against the cement, his pointy yellow hat spinning off his white head.

The pig immediately pinned it behind his front trotters. "Thick and proud of it, mister," Rumple said, lifting his nose as high in the air as he could while still being trussed up.

"Aw, you're getting mud on my hat..."

"Okay, everyone," Marigold cried, scrambling into view on top of the counter. "Pizza'll be here in twenty minutes. Now let's get rid of that body!"

TWENTY-TWO MINUTES LATER, a green-skinned goblin in a white chef's coat with "Omega Pizza: The Last Line of Defense Against Hunger" emblazoned across the chest arrived with a five-tiered stack of steaming cardboard boxes at the polytunnel door. He took one look at the gnomes clustered around the open compost chute—two dozen of them straining under Billy Macon's corpse like a bunch of ants struggling to make off with a picnic sausage while Marigold surveyed their progress on the orchid shelf, waving her garden hoe back and forth like a metronome and calling, "Heave! Heave!"—and shoved the boxes into my hands with a shrug. He returned to his moped as if seeing a bloated human body being tipped into a hole in the floor was the most natural thing in the world and puttered off.

I watched until his shiny red helmet rounded the corner and then pulled my head back inside with a, "Pizza's here!"

"Huzzah!" the gnomes cried as the Great Billy Macon performed his last disappearing act, the metal grate slamming back into place after his boots vanished into the chute.

"Everybody wash your hands," Rumple called, still hog-tied on the floor by the counter, though someone had wedged a patio chair cushion under his head. "And somebody save me a slice of mushroom."

I hurried back to the fountain to check on Larcen—the goldfish had squirted half of the water out of his mug before I'd thought to put him in there—and he was currently bickering with the stone frog, who apparently wasn't used to having guests. But at least he was still alive.

"I don't know if you like pizza," I told the fish, "but I'll save you some mushroom too."

Then I set the cardboard boxes on the nearby patio furniture display and lifted the lids. The heavenly scent of marinara sauce, cheese, and bread made my knees tremble. I'd never had pizza before, and if it tasted as good as it smelled, I wouldn't ever need to eat a fried tenderloin or sausage gravy and biscuits ever again.

"Where's the one with the green peppers and olives?" Cornelius asked, lifting lids with his trowel.

"Did you get one with spinach? I'm watching my figure," a French gnome said.

"Are there any pepperoncini? I like mine *muy caliente*," Roberto said.

I put two slices of mushroom pizza aside for Larcen, took another one for Rumple, and then stacked one of each kind of pizza onto my plate. No one protested my gluttony; in fact, the gnomes had encouraged me to try them all. As I fed Rumple with one hand, careful to keep my fingers away from his surprisingly strong jaws, I shoveled as much food as I could into my mouth.

My stomach happily expanded, and I could feel my strength returning to me. Satiated, I leaned against Rumple's ample belly and gave him the scraps off my plate. "Why am I so sleepy all of a sudden?"

"It's called a food coma, dear," Marigold said, sucking the cheese off her fingers with smacks of her little red lips. "Don't fight it."

With Rumple's belly warming my back, and his breathing like the bellows of a celestial silver forge, I drifted off into my very first sleep.

And I woke with a start, swearing it had only been minutes, but from gray look of the sky beyond the polytunnel plastic, it'd been hours. Dawn was approaching. And there by the fountain, the reason why I'd been roused: the heated whispers of five gnomes as they stood on the rim with makeshift fishing poles in their hands.

Cornelius smacked Blue Beret in the arm. "Don't wiggle the line like that. You'll lose the earthworm and then we'll never catch him."

"Hey!" Groggily, I yanked my bladed fan from my belt and gave it a swish, the wind crescent smacking the gnomes in the backsides and sending them howling into the fountain.

Rumple woke with a snort as I pushed off him and flew to the fountain. Four of the gnomes were already scrambling out of the fountain, mewling like wet cats. "Serves you right," I told them. But the goldfish had the fifth—Cornelius—by the pointy tip of his white beard and was dragging him down to the bottom.

"And that's enough of that." I plunged my hand into the fountain and plucked the gnome free. With a twirl of my fingers, I created a vortex that lifted the thrashing goldfish and funneled him into his oversized Grow, Dammit mug.

Sputtering, Cornelius wrung the water out of his hat and beard as he glared at the mug. The goldfish was ramming the side, inching the mug closer and closer to get at the gnome.

I put my hands on my hips and gave the gnome a frown. "I think I'll take that tour now, if only to keep you away from trying to hook my partner."

"If we're giving tours, someone needs to cut me loose," Rumple called.

A few slashes of my fan and wind crescents sliced through his garden twine bonds like they were threads.

Cornelius soon forgot how wet and grumpy he was as he climbed on top of Rumple's back and started the tour. Despite their constant bickering with Larcen, the gnomes truly took pride in growing the best and healthiest plants. I followed them through the polytunnel, trying to be attentive as they showed me the myriad plants and trees, but it was hard to focus with an angry goldfish sloshing around in his mug. I wasn't about to leave him behind and have the other gnomes try to fish for him again.

After the row of lilies, I followed the pig and gnome to a door of frosted glass in the center of the long wall of the polytunnel. Curious writing marked the doorframe, glinting with iridescence like grackle feathers if you looked at it just right. Glyphs. I didn't know how to read most of them, as ariels had no need of them, but they didn't bar us from entering.

The door opened into a greenhouse, and while as humid as the polytunnel, it was drastically cooler and dimly lit. I shivered.

"And here are the alchemical herbs," Cornelius said, gesturing with his trusty trowel.

This portion of the nursery was smaller but no less tidy and pristine, but there was something definitely different about these plants. They all seemed darker, twisted, perhaps even sinister. A lot of them had trailing vines or thorns or thistles or hundreds of small bright flowers. Most of those flowers were red or purple, some white as my hair, but they didn't smell sweet.

There was also a huge fat spider camped in the back left corner, black and hairy with iridescent blue mandibles. "Gnat farts!" I cried when I saw it.

"Oh, yes," Rumple said apologetically. "Don't go over there."

"What is that dreadful thing doing in here? Go get a broom and make it shoo!"

"It's best just to ignore it. This way."

I couldn't just ignore it. As an ariel, I was predisposed to enjoy the company of anything that found its way into the air, even little spiderlings that used their silk as sails, but *that* thing in the corner... Shuddering, I instinctively pressed my arms against my sides and held the mug close to my chest, lest I accidentally brush against anything. My hair swirled into a twist above my head, each strand giving the plants—and that spider —a wide berth.

"Well, what do you think, Miss Eryn?" the pig asked, turning around with a proud lift to his jowls. "Are you impressed?"

"I'm certainly... something." I forced a bright smile. Ariels were just as at home in a meadow of wildflowers as they were in the sky, but you couldn't trade me a year's worth of sundrop nectar to spend any more time among these plants than I already had. "Thank you for—"

The mug in my hands suddenly shattered, and a dark elf version of Larcen landed on his bare feet like a cat. He rose from his crouch, water dripping from his warrior braid and sluicing all over his *naked*—

I screamed in surprise, blasting at least his backside dry before clamping a hand over my mouth. I still held onto the mug handle in my other hand, the shattered ceramic crunching underfoot as I backed away.

"Master Larcen," Rumple cried. "Thank the slop bucket you're—"

"Nobody touches the spider," he barked.

Then Larcen lunged forward and snatched Cornelius off the pig's back. The gnome squealed, kicking with his little legs and beating his trowel against the dark elf's fingers. "Take my *fin*, will you?" the drow thundered.

CHAPTER FIFTEEN

Larcen

"MASTER LARCEN," Rumple said, trotting after me as I stormed through the polytunnel, "might I suggest some clothes? You'll scare the womenfolk!"

"I've seen bigger earthworms," a gnome—Henrietta, by the French accent—said from the ornamental ferns.

Ignoring them both, I carried the mewling, would-be-fish-fin-mangler Cornelius right into the walk-in. At the far end of the refrigerator, Drosera roused, thrashing its vines in excitement and clacking its red maw greedily.

The gnome's mews turned into squeals of terror.

Just as I was about to dangle the gnome over the slavering plant, a gust of wind slammed into my shoulder, knocking me into the metal shelves. Whirling around, I found the ariel in the doorway, the light of the polytunnel surrounding her in a humid halo. She flicked her fan once more, and the gnome's overalls were plucked from my fingers. Cornelius wailed as a corkscrew of air whirled him out of the walk-in and deposited him into the calla lilies.

When I stalked to within a foot of her, using my height advantage to loom over her, she didn't retreat or cower or avert her gaze. She just slapped one of those crazed smiles on her face and drilled into me with those jade eyes.

"You had no right to interfere," I snarled down at her.

"And you are not in Drozvega anymore," she replied, still smiling although it looked like she was baring her teeth instead. "This is Savannah, and people have manners here. Now, if you're quite finished with your little temper tantrum, we have some important matters to discuss. Like how you abandoned me in the museum!"

Her bladed fan slashed, but I had already phased. My dual-caster ability had activated instinctively, turning my body into darkness. I caught my reflection in the metallic wall of the walk-in: a drow-shaped form of black wisps, my violet eyes burning like lanterns blurred by fog. The starlight metal passed through my shadow-like throat, which felt something like silk slipping over skin, and solidified when the fan banged against the metal grate.

I caught her wrist, solid once more, and pinned her hand and blade against the shelf. "You were down. What was I supposed to do, wait around?"

"Partners don't abandon each other! If they did, you'd still be flopping around on that rooftop."

She was right, of course, but I wasn't going to admit it. I didn't remember much of my time as a goldfish, but I did remember Cornelius's threat of taking my fin, that burning sensation of not getting enough air, the relief of the water as—

"Ugh, you put me in your mouth!"

Eryn wrenched her wrist out of my grip and shoved her bladed fan into her belt. "It's not like it was a pleasurable experience for me either! It was the only way I could figure out to get you back here alive: take a big gulp of river water and plop you in. Which reminds me, the gnomes are now out of mouthwash."

I pushed past her, out of the chilling walk-in, and found Rumple had brought a canvas apron to the desk. With a curt nod, I slipped it over my head and tied the laces. Then I spied the hastily cut-open box of coffee mug merch, chopped paper strewn about like straw. I yanked one of the mugs out of its cardboard slot. "What is this?"

Rumple cleared his throat. "That's the merch—"

"I can see that. Why the hell does it say 'Grow, Dammit' on the side? It was supposed to say 'Grow Big or Go Home.' We can't sell this!"

"Well, erm, seems like the gnomes were able to hack my password to the computer..."

My stomach dropped. "They didn't."

"Well it's not like I can hide what I type with trotters as big as mine! Someone must've been watching—"

"Jasper," I hissed. That blue-beret-wearing gnome was always spying, always sneaking into places he had no business in. He had more curiosity than a cat and twice the amount of mischief as an imp.

"—and changed the order after I placed it. And, if you don't like the mugs, well, I recommend you don't check out the new website. I'm still trying to figure out how to—"

I threw myself into the leather rolly chair and clicked the mouse a dozen times before the Savannah Belle Floral Emporium website appeared on the computer screen.

The picture of the polytunnel in full bloom had been replaced by a gnome—Henrietta, the exhibitionist—posing naked in a bed of flower petals. Gerber daisies and black calla lilies covered her unmentionables as she reclined on a colorful landscape of roses, peonies, tulips, and a hydrangea whose pink petals matched her lipstick and pillowed her golden curls. She had a sultry look on her face as she blew the camera a kiss, and below her dainty feet, the new name of my plant nursery curled in gold, Gothic script: *Gnomes & Roses*. Below it, a new tagline read, "We fertilize your fantasies."

"Look at that," Eryn exclaimed. "It's like garden porn!"

"The Spider Queen sting me in the heart right now," I breathed. "How long has this been up?"

"A-a few days."

I would've raked my hands through my hair if it wasn't already plaited into a braid. I launched out of my seat, pointing at the computer screen. "Fix this! And send back those mugs."

"Yes, Master Larcen! Right away. Erm, I can only send back the unopened boxes of merchandise, especially now that you broke one, so we'll have to keep fifty— forty-nine—mugs."

I clawed my fingernails down my face and just glared at the pig. "You are supposed to be their foreman. Spider scat like this is not supposed to happen. What do I pay you for?"

Rumple's meaty jowls trembled as he tried to think up a reply, but all I got was a strained squeal of sound.

Hissing in displeasure, I turned away from the desk. "Put the website in maintenance mode and close the shop down for the day. No customers, unless they've already scheduled a pick-up. I need to... think."

"We need to do more than that," Eryn said, pointing to my chest.

I glanced down at my dark skin, my lip curling into a disdainful sneer at the sight of a green light pulsing beneath it, right above my heart. My head snapped up. "What did you tell Alder?"

"I told him everything, of course. How do I not tell him you got shot in the chest with a green arrow of lightning? He's going to send the twins to take a look at you."

I whirled to the desk, but the communication array was gone. "Where's the—"

"In my pocket, of course," she said, producing the garnet sphere. "You think I want to get yelled at again for not having —Hey!"

Snatching the array from her, I gave it a quick spin in my palm. Just before Alder's bust appeared, I gave the apron a yank, making sure the canvas covered the pulsing green light.

"Larcen," he exclaimed. "You're not a goldfish anymore."

"Just a simple transfiguration spell," I said, forcing a laugh. "No need to send the twins."

"But—"

"I've seen this magic before, and I'm fine. It's just an amateur spell to incapacitate someone's pursuers, and well, we were chasing that guy pretty hard."

"Still—"

"I'm fine." I snapped. Alder's eyebrows rose at my tone. "Seriously. It was just a lucky shot. The twins don't need to be bothered with this. If there are any side effects, I'll just go Lady Chantilly, okay? Besides, I'm a spellhunter, right? I'll just track this guy down and demand the counter curse. Before I take his head, of course."

That got a reluctant nod out of the director. "I told your partner I want a full report on my desk by end of day."

"And you'll get it," I assured him.

"Very good."

Alder's image vanished, and I slipped the array into my apron pocket.

"You're 'fine?'" the ariel asked, crossing her arms and thrusting a hip out to the side. "Your chest is still glowing from where that arrow zapped you."

"No tests," I growled, rubbing the green glow on my chest. It wasn't painful, but there was definitely something there.

"Besides, we have bigger things to worry about. We need to take a look at that body before—wait, where is it? My memory's a little hazy but I do recall a body somewhere around here."

The ariel pointed to the compost chute.

The cement around the area was still wet, freshly cleaned with the lingering scent of bleach. The gnomes had been very efficient.

In less than a blink, I shadow-walked into the basement, just in time to see Billy Macon's feet slip beneath the lip of Berthold's massive mouth. Berthold must've been digesting him for hours already. Spider scat! "Give him up," I told the plant. "At least his belongings."

The plant belched, ejecting shoes, clothes, the belt with all its pouches, and a few earrings. I caught it all and spread it out on the table beside the plant.

"Eryn, get down here!"

The ariel's face looked like a patchwork of white and russet as she bent over and peered through the metallic grate. "I have a better idea, you come up here."

"Of course. Why didn't I think of that? It makes so much more sense to rifle through a dead man's possessions out in the open where everyone can see us than down here."

"I can see just fine from up here, thank you very much. Just stay in the light."

Huffing an exasperated sigh, I turned back to the table and what remained of the magician. His clothes were nothing special, nor was his jewelry, but I wasn't surprised about that. I was most interested in his belt and the pouches it contained.

Very, very carefully, I opened each compartment and spilled, wiggled, or jiggled the contents loose into a line across the table. Vials of vampire blood for speed. The knife that had cut the ariel. Smoke powder. Basilisk bone. Mystique crystals for revealing the truth of something. Blue echeveria, red-stemmed vervain, striped henbane... These weren't the props of a Las Vegas hack. These were real alchemical ingredients, and someone had given them to him. Instructed him in their use.

With a start, I recognized the quality of the echeveria and vervain; they'd come from this very plant nursery. No one else could get their echeveria rosettes as blue as I could. Of course, it'd been processed elsewhere, as I only grew the herbs and plants used for alchemy, but I kept very detailed records. "Rumple," I called up the chute, "I need to know who purchased Sapphire echeveria and Lifeblood vervain in the last three months."

"Right away, sir!"

The echoing sound of his trotters faded as he hurried to the computer desk.

"What have you found?" the ariel asked.

"The Great Billy Macon had a master," I replied. To myself, I muttered, "And a very clever one." I lifted the blade, careful to handle it only by the hilt. It was your average, run-of-the-mill throwing knife used by circus performers and Las Vegas magicians, but its edge had a sheen to it I'd never seen before: yellow-green, like spilled oil when the sunlight catches it. Whatever this substance was had forced the ariel to phase, just like the poison on my scorpion blade. I'd never heard of anything other than a Drozvegan dart being able to do that.

I set it aside, very carefully.

The poison of the Drozvegan dart was specific to ariels alone, and I didn't know what that knife could do to another race, like me. And I had this green light pulsing beneath like my skin like a second heartbeat already.

Swallowing thickly, I pulled the collar of the apron down and touched the glowing spot on my chest. It wasn't bright, but it was persistent, and it didn't hurt, thought the memory of that lightning arrow slithering into me like an eel and diffusing into my blood stream reminded me of how much it had. What kind of curse was this? I couldn't *see* it, couldn't *see* the threads of the magic left behind. And that unnerved me more than the poisoned knife.

"How's it going down there?" the ariel called. "Find anything else?"

Nothing that mattered. I folded the magician's clothes and rolled them with his belt, boots, and jewelry into a tight bundle before placing it in one of the vacant chambers of the honeycomb lattice. The moment my hands were free, a forcefield sealed the chamber, protecting the bundle from weathering and decay.

A moment later, I was stepping out of the shadows of a dwarf bamboo palm tree and startling a yelp from the ariel.

"I don't think I'll ever get used to that," she grumbled. Then she hefted the dagger's sheath. "So what should we do with this? I don't sense anything magical about it. Should we hand it over to DUO?"

I took the bejeweled sheath and turned it over in my hands. Gold-encrusted with pea-sized rubies, emeralds, diamonds, an opalescent piece of oxhorn, nothing unusual. I didn't sense a magical signature from it, either. Without a word, I shadow-walked back into the basement and put it with Billy Macon's other possessions, reappearing behind the ariel when I was done, just to make her jump.

"Stop that," she said.

"I don't think DUO would care one way or the other. It was the actual dagger they wanted, not the sheath." Besides, if the twins didn't come to collect the sheath, then they wouldn't perform any tests on me while they were here.

"So you said Billy Macon had a master?" she prompted.

"Indeed, and one that knows how to kill ariels."

She rubbed her wrist. "I remember. But that wasn't a Drozvegan blade."

"No, it wasn't. Rumple, how's that search going?"

"Still going, sir. The echeveria and vervain are some of your bestsellers."

I turned back to the ariel. "We wait. And—"

"'We wait?' What kind of plan is that? There's an ariel-killer alchemist out there and a shadow-walker—"

I was going to say *and find the bow that cursed me*, but instead I asked sharply, "A what?"

"Oh, that's right, you were a goldfish. That archer is a shadow-walker."

"That's impossible."

"I know what I saw. In one shadow and out the other."

"Shadow-walking can oftentimes be mistaken for portaling."

"Nobody portals in the human realm. It's too dangerous."

"No one's a villain because it's a safe line of work."

"Hmph. I still think—"

"And I told you it's impossible. That bloodline ability is tested and documented with extreme prejudice. I am the only one remaining, and I certainly didn't fight you on the rooftop. I was a fish."

The ariel gave me a doubtful look.

"I can prove it to you. A shadow-walker leaves no trace behind, because there is none to leave. All other magic leaves some sort of trace. We'll go back to the riverfront and find it. Then we'll be one step closer to finding the dagger and the real thief."

The ariel let out a little huff. "Fine. But *you* aren't going anywhere until you put on some pants."

CHAPTER SIXTEEN

Eryn

THE DROW PACED over the bricks just outside the River House Restaurant, but no one was around to see it. It was a few hours past dawn, but the riverfront had yet to wake. The air was thick and heavy, beading on my white hair like dew drops on a spiderweb. Only a few gulls were around, bobbing on the gray river as they waited for the fishing boats to make their early deliveries.

Hands on his hips, he cocked his head way this way and that like a bird, his warrior braid swishing across his shoulders like the flicking tail of an irritated cat.

"So?" I prompted. "What do you so see?"

"Shh."

"What? You can't see and listen at the same time?"

The drow crouched and swept an embroidered handkerchief over the bricks. "Like I said," the drow lectured, sprinkling the handkerchief with a vial of red crystals, "all magic leaves a trace."

We watched a golden phantom of the archer disappear into the bricks and materialize on the opposite side of the street under the boughs of the crepe myrtle, the illusion lasting long enough for the archer to lift his head to glare at the rooftop before it dissolved into nothingness.

"The archer is not a shadow-walker. Mystique crystals would've revealed nothing if that were the case. You were wrong," the drow concluded.

I rolled my eyes. "Well you don't have to be so smug about it."

The dark elf just lifted his nose in the air a little higher, ever the imperious prince. "Now that we *know* it's not a drow, we can focus on finding out who the archer really is. Which would've been easier if we still had that bow."

We'd started our search that morning on the roof, searching for the bow, and had found only two piles of ash. The drow had cursed at that, kicking the piles and muttering something about incendiary glyphs.

"Even still," Larcen continued, "it must be someone with powerful magic to fool an ariel into thinking he was her natural enemy, to be sure. A grandmaster of some art."

"Well thank the stars I wasn't fooled by an amateur."

The drow gave me a narrow-eyed look as he carefully folded his handkerchief and placed it in a plastic bag. "We'll give this to Lady Chantilly to analyze and see if she can find anything."

"Look at you outsourcing your alchemy. I thought all dark elves were adepts at potions and poisons."

"I'm not an alchemist." The words almost seemed to pain him. "I just grow the plants."

"I thought you were a spellhunter. Can't you *see* something?"

"Alchemy isn't spellwork," he snapped. "It can be a component, yes, but alone, by itself... I can't see that. And I couldn't *see* the spellwork here. Which is why I used the mystique crystals."

"Someone's either very lucky or very smart," I muttered. Forcing a smile onto my face, I swept my hands down my sundress to straighten it. "Let's go see this Lady—Larcen! Why did you tell me I had pizza stains on my dress?"

He lifted an imperious eyebrow. "Do I really have to say it? That's what you get for *stealing* the company credit card."

"I didn't steal it. The gnomes did."

"And you didn't stop them, *and* you ate the pizza."

"Well you ate the two slices I saved for you on the way here!"

"Like I would let food purchased with *my* credit card go to waste? That's just bad business management."

"You're one to talk about bad business management. If you actually provided for the gnomes, they wouldn't be mutinying and hog-tying Rumple and trying to hook your lip on a fishing line." I poked him in the chest with a crystal finger. "*You* are alive because of *me*."

His violet eyes flashed at that.

"Now I want some new clothes and some hot sauce!"

Larcen grabbed my finger before I could poke him again and used it to push me aside before he started walking away. "You're in luck, little bat. Lady Chantilly has all of that at her store."

CHANTILLY BOUTIQUE WAS a hole-in-the-wall nestled between a spice shop and a small jewelry store overlooking one of Savannah's many historical squares. Metal sculptures of bronze and iron reminiscent of an abstract orrery decorated the square, the sculptures half-hidden by ornamental grasses and lemony angel's trumpet flowers.

Similar trumpet flowers had been carved into the boutique's doorframe and painted white, which was chipping. A little bell dinged as Larcen opened the door, and a tarnished candelabra burst to life in the bay window. As if triggering an unseen ward, candles burst into flame all over the store, illuminating racks of vintage clothes, wicker baskets full of seashells and bundles of dried herbs, and a long counter of worn but well-polished wood. An oversized cuckoo clock that resembled a woodland cottage dominated the wall behind the counter, its pine cone weights rising and falling in a hypnotic rhythm. The floral curtain partition at the rear of the boutique rattled on its rings, swept aside by an elegant brown hand.

"Well if it isn't my favorite dark elf," a husky voice purred.

"Lady Chantilly," the dark elf said with a nod.

A half-dryad sauntered forward, all sinuous and sultry, her elegant buttercream coiffure not swaying a hair out of place. A plunging gown of sage-colored satin hugged her body like a sheath, rippling around her gold heels like leaves in a morning breeze. Her gaze sharpened on me immediately, and I flashed her what I hoped was a charming smile and gave a little wave of my fingers. Ariels and dryads normally had a good rapport, but sometimes a dryad would leave her forest and spend too many nights in a meadow under the full moon and go rogue. By the color of the half-dryad's hair, I'd say she had had seen quite a few full moons. Lady Chantilly thrust her hip out to the side, perched her manicured fingers on it, and extended her hand.

When Larcen wasn't forthcoming, her extended arm lengthened like a growing branch, her long fingers sliding into his pocket and extracting the plastic bag with his handkerchief. I watched in awe as the candlelight shone on the striations of her skin—coffee to caramel and back again—the bands of color blending seamlessly into a smooth complexion as her arm returned to its normal size.

Lady Chantilly tapped the plastic bag against her hip. "And here I was hoping you'd come for pleasure instead of business.

Who's your little... I would say 'friend,' but drow aren't known to make nice with anyone."

"I'm Eryn," I said, forcing my voice to sound upbeat. I didn't want her to mistake my irritation with Larcen as disinterest in her store.

"And what are you, dear?"

"Oh. Right." I phased into mist and gave her a cheery wave.

Lady Chantilly was obviously too elegant and refined to startle easily, but her brown eyes did widen just a fraction. "An ariel?" She placed a hand over her heart and curtsied. "It is an honor to meet you, child of air."

She turned to Larcen, lifting her buttercream-colored eyebrows. "Looks like you and I need to have a chat."

"A short one," the dark elf said.

The half-dryad pouted. "Pity."

Larcen turned to me, taking a step forward so he loomed over me. I simply floated a little higher so he had to look up at me. *Two can play that game, you prissy prince.*

"Pick out some clothes," he growled. "And don't forget some shoes."

Without another word, he stalked off, following Lady Chantilly behind the floral curtain and yanking it shut behind him.

"'Pick out some clothes,'" I mocked as I went to the first rack.

There was an off-the-shoulder thing made out of lilac gauze and satin, a wrap-around dress in flame red, and a chiffon baby doll in pale blue. I didn't care what Maven said; I could make that baby doll look work for everyday wear. For my shoes, I found a pair of knee-high boots with a strand of white pearls fashioned around the ankle like a buckle. I put all the hangers on the counter and yelped as a squirrel poked its head out of the cuckoo clock.

"That's just Buckwheat," the half-dryad's singsong voice called through the curtain.

The gray squirrel leapt from its nest in the cuckoo clock's attic and onto the counter, sliding across the polished surface and pouncing onto the antique cash register. Chittering, the squirrel hopped from one ivory key to another, ringing up my clothes. When it was done, it gave me a flick of its bushy tail. *Is that all?*

I took a package of spiced nuts and set it on top of the clothes.

The squirrel pounced on a few more keys and gave me another flick of its tail, cocking its head to the side to eye me with a glossy black eye.

Delighted, I added a selection of hot sauce bottles, goatmilk soap flecked with lemon balm, an antique silver hairbrush, *Lady Chantilly's Forest Remedies* penned by the half-dryad herself, and half a dozen other things that sparked my fancy, and watched as the squirrel jumped from key to key.

"What are you buying out there?" Larcen's voice thundered before he slapped the curtain aside.

"Um, necessities?"

Buckwheat chattered something at Larcen—*No refunds!*— and brushed my purchases into a paper bag with a few sweeps of his bushy tail.

Lady Chantilly appeared in the doorway, leaning against the frame and tapping a white-nailed finger against her chin. "Hmm, I like your taste, child of the air. I've been trying to offload that silver hairbrush for months. A bit too expensive for me, but apparently not for the pockets of Savannah Belle Floral Emporium. Or is it Gnomes and Roses now?"

Larcen shot me a murderous look and returned to the back room. With a light laugh, Lady Chantilly followed after him. Buckwheat, after giving me a brisk nod of thanks, returned to his cuckoo clock attic.

I hadn't been barred from following my dualcaster partner, and even if I had, I would've followed them anyway. Slinging the handles over my wrist, I opened one of the hot sauce bottles, chipotle flavored, and pulled the curtain closed behind me.

Lady Chantilly's workroom was small and sparce, but what furniture it had was lavish. Her workbench was a gold dining table so intricately carved that it must've served kings once upon a time, and her work chair was a wingback of red suede. Light came from a chandelier of rose-colored crystal, and the vials on the shelves that rose from floor to ceiling were all made of porcelain.

The dark-silver knife that had cut me in the museum was on a clay plate, waiting its turn to be examined as Lady Chantilly focused her attention on Larcen's handkerchief.

The half-dryad was in her suede seat, leaning forward and letting her low-back dress reveal the provocative curve of her brown spine. A pair of long-stem tweezers were pinched between her fingers, and she was using them to swirl Larcen's handkerchief in a glass bowl of water. Her other arm lengthened and contracted as she selected vials off the shelf without ever looking up from the bowl, and little creaks like the sound of trees swaying in the breeze could be heard as she reached for the faraway vials.

"Shadow magic," Lady Chantilly muttered. "Vodou, maybe the occult. It's pure, otherwise we'd be seeing some smokey tendrils coming up from—"

The bowl shattered, sluicing boiling water and molten shards of glass onto the floor. The glass was so hot it burned its way into the floorboards.

Larcen quickly stomped on the embers, snuffing them beneath his boots.

Lady Chantilly rose, flicking the handkerchief off her satin gown with her white fingernails. "A concealment spell blended with alchemy. And a good one, too. That makes tracking this magic back to the person who cast it rather difficult."

"But not impossible," the dark elf prompted.

"Perhaps not, for my favorite customer," the dryad said, stroking the drow's chin with one white fingernail as she sauntered past and back into her store. "There are only a handful of alchemy ingredients that could mask a spell so completely, and none that you grow in your store, unfortunately for me. You said you took this sample from the riverfront?"

"Yes," Larcen and I said together.

He glared down at me, or at least, he tried to. My spirits were high now that I had some chipotle hot sauce in me and some new clothes to try on, and my feet were hovering a good twelve inches off the ground. I shrugged my shoulders at him, taking another swig from my bottle, and soared after the half-dryad.

"I can't go now, but I can take Buckwheat with me tonight," Lady Chantilly said, giving the squirrel a little head scratch. "Sometimes the first crescent after the new moon can be very revealing. In the meantime, I'll get to work on that dagger. It's clear it's been coated, but in what?"

"And the price?" Larcen prompted.

"Always business with you, my lovely. Hmm." Her eyes flicked to me as I hovered in the air, my bag of purchases dangling from my wrist as I took swigs of hot sauce. "No price. I think the cost of that silver hairbrush will cover it just fine."

The dark elf glared at me again.

I gulped down another swallow of hot sauce, my white hair swirling above my head as my feet lifted another two inches off the floor. "What? I needed it."

Larcen pointed to his own long braid of white hair. "Like I don't have hair accessories at home?"

"You'd... share with me?"

His exasperation turned to disgust. "Ugh. No."

"Then I needed it."

CHAPTER SEVENTEEN

Larcen

"YOU HAVE ANOTHER ASSIGNMENT," Alder informed us, lifting another file folder that instantly downloaded onto the marble-like communications array.

We were back at the plant nursery, the ariel floating like a cloud above the counter with a dreamy-like stupor on her face. She hiccupped occasionally, blasting chipotle-scented fumes towards the ceiling that were then dispersed by the fans. I blocked out the sound of the gnomes coming to the conclusion they they'd like tacos for lunch and focused on the file Alder had sent us. "Another artifact?"

"Apparently they're very popular."

I squinted at the provided images. "A star chart?"

"A star chart?" the ariel echoed, swirling down from the rafters and hovering above my shoulder. "Mayan, Egyptian, or Chinese?"

"Greek," Alder replied.

"Ooo, they were quite the star-mappers. What's so special about this one? Have the twins figured out what it leads to yet?"

"As you can see by the images, the star chart is a scroll, one that hasn't been unfurled in millennia. We only know it's a star chart because of the imaging the Smithsonian has been able to do. Since the scans overlay, it's impossible to tell what position the stars are in."

Indeed, the red-tinted images of the scroll revealed a fragile-looking tube of papyrus sealed by faded cords with rotting tassels. It was so ancient a sneeze would disintegrate it into ash.

"And DUO cares about a star chart why?" I asked. "There's nothing magical about them."

"Star charts are unique in the fact that they can capture a location and a specific time. It could be that it marks the location of a hidden relic. It could be that it marks an auspicious time that is returning again. We don't know. All we know is that someone wants it."

"Someone." I straightened, crossing my arms over my chest. "That 'someone' happen to be the same one we fought on a rooftop?"

"That *I* fought on a rooftop," the ariel corrected. "You were a goldfish."

"It's quite possible," Alder said with a sigh. "Like before, our information is limited because of concealment magic. Speaking of, have you two found any leads?"

"It's not a shadow-walker," I said quickly, cutting the ariel off before she could protest. "He's a grandmaster of his craft, though. And... he has a coating on his blade identical to a Drozvegan poison dart."

"Hmm." Alder rubbed his chin. "There are only a few true grandmasters out there. I can have the twins do a discreet search. Don't want to ruffle any feathers if we don't have to. And that poison... does it only affect ariels?"

"I didn't try it out on myself," I replied tartly. "Lady Chantilly is going to try to find out more tonight, while we, apparently, go to D.C."

"Can't we just tell the Smithsonian to give us the scroll and nip this in the bud before it even becomes a thing?" the ariel asked.

"Taking away a thief's target doesn't unmake a thief. A thief with powerful magic and no honor, if he's killing his own proxies," Alder said. "We still don't know *why* he wants this star chart, but you can be guaranteed he'll be able to use it with the luck he'll gain from having the Zhu dagger. That being said, this is basically a repeat performance of last night, except now you're at a disadvantage. Even so, do *not* mess this one up."

The director's voice cut off, leaving the hologram-like image of the rolled-up star chart suspended above the array. I passed my hand over it, severing a connection, and the image was sucked back into the array, the light inside the garnet sphere flickering out.

"Rumple, how is that search coming?" I barked.

"Just finished, Master Larcen, but you're not going to like it," the pig replied.

The printer started, spitting out a multipage report that made my stomach twist. "One hundred matches?"

"Echeveria and vervain are very popular, sir."

"Well that was no help." I crumpled the pages and threw them into the wastebasket. I dragged my hands down my face with an aggravated moan.

"Now, now, that'll just give you wrinkles," Rumple said. "When's the last time you got any sleep?"

"I had a food coma," the ariel piped up.

"That's not real sleep. You two need to go get some shut-eye. You've been up all night with nary a morsel to eat or wink of sleep to keep you going."

I thrust a finger at Eryn. "She ate three-quarters of a pizza. By. Herself."

"She's a growing young lady. Besides, you two can't expect to be at your best running on fumes, right? Off you go."

I glanced at the dormant communications array. "But the jet—"

"Won't be here until this afternoon at the earliest. Go on now." The pig nudged the back of my knees, herding me to the break room door.

"Rumple," I protested, my voice a low hiss. I was used to his mothering, but never in front of anyone. He was the only one who knew what Drosera hid, and had once or twice had to help me with my injections.

"Oh put the prince away and do as you're told."

I glared at him.

"S-sir," the pig amended hastily, casting an embarrassed look around at the gnomes. The ariel gazed at us curiously, her jade eyes narrowed slightly.

That was Rumple's way of telling me I was being snobbish and irritable, a term he'd overheard Timmeron use once when he'd visited me at the plant nursery. It wasn't something to be repeated in the presence of others; I *was* a prince, after all, and only deserved the rebuke of my family members.

With one final scathing look that made the pig's jowls quiver with fear, I shadow-walked to my room. It had no door, so the only way in or out was through the shadows. It was in the earth, below the training room, running parallel to Berthold's taproot so I could keep a pulse on the plant nursery even when I wasn't there. Like my room back home in Drozvega, it was fashioned out of bedrock and chiseled smooth. Air came from fine holes dug by stoneworms—the earthworm's heartier cousin with teeth —and it was just enough to keep me and the lampblossom alive.

The lampblossom unfurled in response to my body heat,

opening its fuchsia petals and revealing its angler-lure-like stamens. A soft glow illuminated my sparse haven, just bright enough to see by without causing any discomfort. Down here, I didn't need to wear my sunglasses. I left them on the ledge-like shelf by the lampblossom's pot, gave it a dribble of water from a canteen, and flopped onto the protruding lip of stone that served as my bed. The shag moss compressed to contour to my body, much like a foam mattress, sweet-smelling and reminiscent of carefree days spent in the subterranean pools catching albino lobsters. I hadn't worn an iron circlet then, and I certainly hadn't thought I'd ever be partnered with an ariel.

I threw an arm over my eyes to block out the lampblossom's light, but it was already curling its petals, no longer stimulated by my proximity. The cave became truly black, enveloping me in a darkness as deep as the shadows I walked between.

Except it wasn't the utter darkness I was accustomed to. The faintest green light emanated from my chest, pulsing in strength like a glowworm trying to attract prey. The lump felt firmer than flesh when I pressed it with two fingertips.

The memory of the hooded archer firing that crackling arrow made my breath stick in my throat.

I was the only shadow-walker left, wasn't I?

I FOUND the ariel reclining in the rafters of the polytunnel, stroking the air with her fingers and creating illusionary butter-flies. They were gray-and-red phantoms of Monarch butterflies, and I watched as she focused on adjusting their colors as they flapped against the ceiling like birds trapped in a net. I assumed after she got the color right she'd work on making their move-ments more realistic. For now they looked like sketches taken from an artist's notebook and transplanted against the fabric of the real world.

The drow in me reached for the scorpion blade at my hip at the sight of my natural enemy, and I had to hook my thumbs into my belt so I wouldn't throw the poisoned chain dart into her side. I'd been free of Drozvega for ten years, had immersed myself in human culture and those of the various races one could find at DUO, but centuries-old habits die hard.

"Those are looking a lot better this time, Miss Eryn," Rumple called from the counter. "Practice makes perfect, you know."

My eye twitched at the pig's encouraging words. Practice did make perfect, and I should be training, not watching a girl with her butterflies. As I was about to disappear into the shadows, Rumple caught sight of me and squealed, "Master Larcen! FedEx came and picked up all the unopened merch, and while I can't seem to figure out how to change the website back to normal, it's, erm, led to some interesting developments."

From the rafters, a chime-like giggle emanated from the ariel.

Ignoring her, I stalked to the counter and the pig. He sat in the leather rolly chair, his massive gut spilling over his trotters and a pair of wire-rim glasses poised precariously on the ridges of his snout. His thick ears slapped against his head as he jerked his chin at the computer screen.

Just as I was bending down to get a good look at the newest catastrophe in my life, the bell at the opposite end of the poly-tunnel chimed. Whatever rustling that had filled the plant nursery as the gnomes went about their work ceased. The bell was spelled to only ring when a *human* customer crossed the threshold.

"I thought I told you to close the shop," I told Rumple through the corner of my mouth.

"And I thought you were just making angry announcements," the pig whispered back. "Do you know how much money we'd lose if we ever closed? You wouldn't have the funds to continue your little—" He abandoned that line of reasoning after my cutting glare and hastily amended, "And the gnomes would never get their espresso machine."

"They were never getting it in the first place. They're impossible to please, remember?" I shot a glance into the rafters, motioning for the ariel to get down. She wasn't wearing a bronze collar to give the illusion she was just a bird sitting up there, and the last thing we needed was a customer to casually look upward and find a young woman reclining on a joist. The ariel just rolled onto her stomach, her butterflies vanishing, pillowing her hands under her chin to watch as her white hair wafted like a cloud above her head.

"Not to mention the damage to our reputation," Rumple continued as if he hadn't heard me. "You can't claim to be the purveyor of the finest alchemical ingredients on the East Coast 'day and night and every hour in between' if you're closed. That's just poor business management."

It seemed a lot of people had a lot of things to say about my business managing techniques recently, but I swallowed whatever scathing retort I would've made and turned my attention to the customer strutting down center aisle. I lifted my hand in greeting. "Good aftern..."

I'd seen a lot in the ten short years I'd spent in the human realm, but apparently I could still be surprised. The man wore a sleeveless net shirt fashioned from hemp rope and garden twine, like something out of a sustainably sourced BDSM clothing catalog. His frosted hair was gelled to look like he'd been caught outside in a windstorm, and white knee-high go-go boots gave him an extra two or three inches of height. Aviator sunglasses and linen short-shorts with a bouquet of embroidered flowers bursting from the crotch completed the look that my supermodel cousin would've called "garden kink."

He sauntered right up to the counter, hips swishing from left to right so violently it would've given a metronome a heart attack just to keep up. Then he gave his sunglasses a little flick so they slid down his nose to reveal his honey-brown eyes. "Ooo. And don't you just complete the whole *Midnight in the Garden of Good and Evil* vibe?"

My violet eyes narrowed as my arms crossed over my chest. If he thought I was going to bend my arms into the famous pose of that statue, he was dead wrong.

"Strong and silent. I'm a fan." Crotch Flowers winked.

"And how can we help you today, erm, sir?" Rumple asked. The script on his bronze collar glowed faintly, which meant the illusion spell was working and I wouldn't have to wring that fae calligrapher's neck. And since the customer hadn't screamed in fright at the sight of a talking pig, he must be seeing Rumple as the pot-bellied and sweaty individual that the spell presented him as.

"I'm here for some of those sassy gnomes," he said quietly, lasciviously, as if he were propositioning us for an illegal substance. Or porn.

I raised my eyebrows in mute question.

"You know, the ones on your website? The ones that are"— he bit his lower lip as he wagged his eyebrows—"taking the flowers for a ride."

"O-oh my," Rumple said, "well let me just pull up our online merch store and—Oh my truffles."

Obviously there were too many different species of plants to list them all on the website, but we had a link to the special merch you could find only at my establishment, such as those spider-cursed Grow, Dammit mugs. Apparently the gnomes' subterfuge had penetrated deeper than the home screen.

Rumple flinched as I gripped the back of the rolly chair, the leather squeaking in protest as my fingers clenched.

Henrietta and—was that Roberto?—had clearly positioned themselves in risqué poses, which apparently would be fashioned by a professional potter, glazed in the colors of your choice, and available for pick-up two to three business days after purchase. Rumple and I stared dumbfounded at the screen, and then the squeak of the rolly chair shattered the silence as Rumple turned slowly to face me. His beady dark eyes pleaded for mercy.

"Yes! That one." Crotch Flowers pointed excitedly to the icon of Roberto humping a mushroom. "He looks so vigorous. I want him in the cappuccino glaze and the mushroom bright red. The brightest red you've got."

"Our potter's got a sprained hand," I said flatly. "No gnomes for the foreseeable future."

Crotch Flowers's face fell. "But your website says satisfaction isn't just guaranteed, it's orgasmic."

My fingers jumped into my palms, the muscles in my arms tightening as I pressed my fists against my thighs. I didn't necessary want to hit *him*, but I definitely wanted to hit something.

"We can put you on layaway," Rumple said quickly. He pushed a pad and pen forward with his trotters. "If I can get your name and number and your exact order specifications, we can get you taken care of as soon as the potter, erm, gets his cast off."

Crotch Flowers let out a world-weary sigh. "Fine, I suppose."

While Rumple assured the customer that all would be resolved in a timely fashion, I went up and down the aisles in the polytunnel, smacking aside the leaves and flowers and looking for the ringleaders. They were frozen for as long as there was a human around, which meant they couldn't run away from me. "Where are you, you little spider scats?"

"Um, like, is he okay?" I heard Crotch Flowers murmur to Rumple. "Why is he talking about spider poo?"

"He's in anger management. Is there anything else we can help you with today?"

I ignored the rest of their conversation as I finally spotted the yellow tip of Cornelius's hat half-hidden among the peace lilies. "*There* you are."

Since I couldn't very well shadow-walk in front of a human, I had to walk down the aisle I was in, move over two, and go halfway down the third to get at that yellow-hat-wearing bastard. Behind me, the clip-clop of knee-high go-go boots made their way towards the exit. I picked up my pace, knowing I had to get to the peace lilies before the human exited the plant nursery.

Clip-clop. Clip-clop.

I rounded the end of my aisle and speed-walked past the pink-leafed caladiums and the striped peperomia.

Clip-clop. Clip-clop.

Above me, I sensed movement as the ariel shifted, but she couldn't very well intervene without being discovered. As a former guardian, it had been her job to protect and assist lesser magical creatures, and in the human realm, that meant not exposing our realm to them. So she wouldn't interfere so long as the human was still inside. I was almost there—

Ding!

I snatched at the peace lilies just as the pointy yellow hat slipped below the leaves. "You son of a—*get back here!*"

"We will not be censored!" Cornelius's voice was already farther down the aisle, the yellow tip of his hat bobbing amongst the orange daylilies. "The smutty website stays until our demands are met."

"I'll break that potter's wheel!"

"Ha! Shows what you know about pottery. Those figurines are slip cast and you'll never find the molds."

"Do you have any idea what you've done?" I roared. "You brought into this store an entirely new customer base that we are not equipped to handle."

"Oh, don't put yourself down, *monsieur*," Henrietta purred from the violas. "The gentleman clearly thought you could handle his equipment."

"I am not adding pornographic gnomes to the merch store!"

"Give the customers what they want!"

"Yeah, sex sells!"

"They're not wrong, sir," Rumple said meekly from the computer. "We're getting a lot of orders in for those, erm, sassy gnomes. Oh! And look at that. Apparently we have phallic-like ceramic mushrooms for sale too. Oh my truffles."

"Gah!"

"Larcen?"

"*What?*"

The ariel floated down from the rafters, the communications array blinking in her palm. "The jet's here."

CHAPTER EIGHTEEN

Eryn

"I COULD USE A LITTLE HELP HERE!"

The ogre sailed over the third-floor balcony with a roar, hands clamped together in a wrecking-ball-shaped fist over his head.

I flew under the stuffed elephant's tusks and swooped around its side, phasing to mist in the hopes I would camouflage against its wrinkly skin. The tile floor cratered as the ogre landed, and the windows in their metal frames rattled from the impact.

We were in the Smithsonian National Museum of Natural History—after hours, of course—and that archer-dark-mage-alchemist-whoever-he-was had upped his magic game and had swapped out a grizzly bear in the Mammals exhibit for an ogre heavily cloaked in a concealment spell. Mixed with alchemy of course, so our spellhunter dark elf had walked right past the display case without a second glance.

The thing had burst out of its display case at the first stroke of midnight, clearly pissed that he'd had to watch humans pass by within arm's reach all day without being able to eat any of them. After rampaging up to the second floor to help himself to all the sparklies he wanted from the Gems and Minerals exhibit, he'd burst through the concrete wall into the research wing on the third floor, and the rest, as the humans say, is history.

This time, I hadn't waited for the thief to put his hands on the target artifact. Ogres weren't known for their delicate touch, and I wasn't about to have a star chart dating back to when Zeus was overthrowing the Titans squeezed into a mound of ash. So I did as any good guardian would do: I kidnapped the star chart and made a fly for it. Now we were in the rotunda, shored up against the hide of a stuffed African elephant.

The scroll was so delicate, its faded cords so frail, I cradled it with the lightest touch against my chest like I would a baby bird. The papyrus was as soft as linen, and a wax seal, impossibly not broken, kept the parchment rolled and the braided red cord tight.

I held my breath as the ogre stomped a circle around the plinth. He smelled strongly of bear, though I couldn't tell if it was because of the pelt he wore around his hips or because he'd been disguised as one all day. An iron ring dangled from his nose and even larger ones from his pointy ears, and the rings on his leather boots jingled with every step. A tight-fitting chainmail shirt protected his core from my bladed fans, so I would have to go for his arms. Or his head.

"Give scroll now, fly!" he bellowed.

Fly? Sprite was bad enough, but fly? I didn't even buzz!

Scowling, I slid around the elephant's hindquarters as the ogre jumped around the corner, the entire statue shivering as he landed.

"Scroll not yours!"

It's not yours either, dum-dum. And where in the Underrealm is Larcen? I swear, if he's abandoned me again, I'm going to braid his hair into the headboard of his bed and light his feet on fire! After I found wherever his bedroom was, of course. And I didn't know much about the sleeping habits of drow, so he might not sleep in a bed at all but rather upside down like a bat for all I knew.

Then the shadows shifted.

Larcen glided out into the ambient light as if he was made out of liquid, lifting a finger to his lips for silence.

Like I was going to suddenly shout for joy? As if.

He motioned for the scroll.

I don't know why he thought it would be safer in his hands instead of mine, and there was half a rotunda separating us, so it wasn't like I was going to throw it to him or anything. I shook my head.

His violet eyes narrowed into a glare, and he jabbed a finger at his chest. *To me.*

I threw up my hand. *No.*

"Got you!"

Two massive gray hands the size of frying pans slapped my head and would've squashed my brain into paste had I not already been mist. I zipped into the air, my head reforming instantly.

"No get away," the ogre shouted. He leapt off the back of the elephant, his tree-trunk-size legs propelling him like a cannon-ball after me.

I yelped, tucking my feet up into my chest as I put on another burst of speed.

The ogre shouted in pain as my misty body caught the ambient light streaming in from the arched windows and turned into a thousand twinkling sparks.

Shiiing.

The ogre's shout turned into a gurgle as the chain dart wrapped around his throat.

Larcen gave vicious yank, and the ogre returned to earth with a decisive thud. With impossible strength, the wiry drow reeled the ogre across the tiled floor like he was hauling a baby humpback whale onto the beach. The ogre clawed at the chain with stubby fingers, gargling obscenities, but he never once took his silver eyes off me.

I sank through the air back to the elephant, my feet coming to a halt on its haunches and causing a ripple effect up the entire length of me until I stood in my pale body like a circus performer on the back of her trusty pachyderm partner. The ogre twisted around onto his hands and knees, scrambling against the tiles as he fought against the drow, one hand on the chain at his throat to keep from choking.

Slowly, he dragged the dark elf forward.

Larcen's bare feet—the drow *insisted* on going nude foot whenever we were on assignment—screeched as they lost traction, and the ogre sprang forward like a charging pit bull. Instead of whipping around and attacking the drow, who was a much closer target, the ogre scrambled to his feet and charged after me.

"Well keep pulling!" I shrieked at Larcen, springing into the air again and drawing one of my bladed fans. I didn't have the strength to remain mist forever, and I would be more effective in hand-to-hand combat if I had the hardiness of crystal anyway.

"Fly!" the ogre roared.

"What did you do to piss him off so much?" Larcen grunted as he yanked on the ogre's chain.

"Who cares? Put him down already!"

We needed him alive, and Larcen was the one with the sedative dart. Maven had left another case of assorted tech and goodies for our particular use on the jet, plus a black romper for me that her note said "would look just darling" on me.

The ogre spun and snatched the chain strangling him. With a flick of his thick wrist, he snapped the chain like a whip. Larcen landed on his back with a loud thud, and another jerk of the ogre's arm slid the dark elf across the rotunda to shore up against his boots. One stomp of those leather boots would've turned Larcen's head into a Jackson Pollock painting, and for a moment he seemed to seriously consider it, before he howled and clawed at his throat.

Something flashed molten red as he shucked the chain from his neck and then with a vicious snarl, he abandoned the stunned dark elf. He launched himself at me, his broken teeth bared in another bellow.

My bladed fan smacked him across his jaw, snapping those caterwauling lips closed. He fell, catching my foot and dragging me down to the floor with him. I threw the scroll into the air and drew my second bladed fan as I landed, kicking like a hare caught in a snare until the ogre released my foot.

A dark shadow passed overhead, and Larcen caught the scroll as delicately as if it were an egg. The moment it was in his hands I screamed, blasting the ogre with a storm wind that sent him cracking into the elephant's plinth. Then I was on my feet, slashing my bladed fans in a swirling pattern and bombarding him with incessant wind. His cheeks rippled like a pond after a stone has broken its surface, his silver eyes slitted against the assault. He pressed his hands into the plinth, angling forward, and tried to take a step forward.

"What are you waiting for?" I shouted at the dark elf. "Dart him!"

Larcen slunk to the side, outside the range of my perpetual storm wind, the red dart in his hand and the star chart in the other. When he was in position, he gave me a nod, and I dropped my fans.

The dart emptied into the ogre's thigh just as his gray hand snatched Larcen by the neck. Red script flared on the ogre's throat as he lifted Larcen off the ground. The dark elf dropped the star chart to claw at the thick fingers that crushed his airway, remembering belatedly to phase.

"No!" I cried.

Larcen became shadow, only his violet eyes glowing like smokey coals, and the star chart shattered into dust.

I flung out a hand as the wax seal and faded red tassels landed in a soft heap, the dust of the star chart suspended in midair. It may have shattered, but I'd caught it exactly at that moment of impact. It was still intact, after a fashion. If I could just hold every dust mote in place, maybe I could eventually unwind it and see what stars it had mapped all those years ago.

I didn't dare move, I didn't dare breathe, I didn't dare flick my eyes or break my concentration away from the yellowish-gray haze of the star map to the ogre who was stomping in my direction. I had to rely on my partner to intervene, to save me.

Trust a dark elf? A drow? A cobweb-munching caveman? Maybe I'd hit my head when the ogre had dragged me out of the air.

The ogre howled, and black blood sprayed the pale gray tiles as his hamstrings were cut. No sooner did he drop to his knees than Larcen appeared from behind, no longer shadow, and slid his curved dagger under the ogre's fat chin. "Who is your master?"

The ogre ignored him, silver eyes bulging as he strained forward despite the blade pressing against his throat. Red script flared on his throat one more time, and Larcen let his dagger go slack as he stared in shock as the ogre crawled forward, desperate to get at me.

My focus remained on the star chart, but it was starting to waver. "Larcen," I hissed through gritted teeth. "Why isn't he sleeping yet?"

"He got the full dose, I don't—"

"I can't move, and he's coming closer."

The ogre was growling now, like a trapped animal, dragging himself on his forearms as his useless legs leaked black blood over the tiles. There was something manic about his resolve, battling through his own excruciating pain to get at me. I didn't even have the star chart anymore. He'd already passed by its dusty image suspended in the air, and he'd paid no never mind to the wax seal and its tassels.

"Spider bites," Larcen cursed, "we were supposed to take him in alive."

He spun his scorpion blade in his hand for an overhand grip and positioned himself by the ogre's shoulder, poised to plunge the blade into the back of the brute's neck. The ogre didn't even acknowledge him.

Just as the ogre shot out a hand, straining to grasp my ankle, his body went limp. His silver eyes rolled back into his head as he landed with a ground-trembling thump. A tremendous snore echoed throughout the rotunda. I kept my focus on the scroll, seeing the edges waver just a bit, but I breathed an internal sigh of relief.

"Finally," Larcen muttered. "It only took—Ah!"

He jumped back as the red script on the ogre's throat flared. A ring of fire sprang to life, showering the tiles with sparks and eating through the ogre's thick skin. It was all over in a matter of heartbeats, and the ogre's cauterized head rolled a few inches away from his still-smoking neck.

"What the...?"

I ignored the dead ogre; that part of the mission had obviously been a bust, but we still had the star chart. If we could figure out what stars they mapped, maybe Alder would still call his mission an overall success. Very, very carefully, keeping every dust mote locked in position relative to the next one, I unfurled the scroll.

"Orion," I whispered. "Canis Major, the Hare—"

A sudden gust of air as someone threw open the double doors swept the dust into a cloud that collapsed like spilled sand across the tiles. "Freeze," a policeman shouted.

"Silent alarm?" Larcen hissed. He dropped, grabbing the ogre and its head, and disappeared into the shadows on the floor.

I soared to the wax seal and its tassels, scooping them against my stomach before I phased to mist. Coiling around a pillar to the ceiling, I poured down the wall and slipped through the open door right over the policeman's head. I kept to the dark as red-and-blue lights flashed against the building, disappearing quickly into the night.

This was two failed missions in as many days. I hadn't failed this much in my life.

I hadn't started to fail until I'd met that Underrealm-cursed drow.

CHAPTER NINETEEN

Larcen

"So how did it go?" Alder asked.

Slapping a smile on her face, as if that would make our failure any better, the ariel lifted the dead ogre's head by his iron nose ring in one hand and the wax seal with its faded cord that had once encircled the start chart in the other.

"I see."

"I did manage to get a look at the star chart before it turned to dust," she offered.

"How good a look?"

"Well, better than nothing but probably not as detailed as we'd like." She snatched a piece of paper from the printer and a pen, drawing the constellations she'd seen before the police had arrived. She lifted the chart for Alder's inspection. "This is part of what I saw. I wasn't able to catch it all, but if we could put it in one of those databases, or maybe ask the Temple for access to their sky maps—"

"Star charts are precise captures of the sky. No database, if they can go back that far, would be able to find anything based off a quick freehand sketch."

The ariel bared her teeth into a smile. "I'm an ariel, druid. Any *freehand* sketch I do of the stars is more accurate than any conjured by a computer. *This* is perfect. Well, a perfect piece, anyway."

"Uh-huh. Larcen? Where are you? Care to weigh in?"

"Oh, um..."

The ariel's fingers were gentle as she pinched me on either side of my chest and picked me up into view of the red, eight-inch-tall bust of Alder Shaw. Any hope he had in his face drained away faster than a flash flood in a desert canyon. "Larcen's a cricket now?"

That stupid green light embedded in my skin had just flashed without warning right before take-off, and it'd been a mercy that the ariel hadn't stepped on me on her way up the steps. After her initial fright, she'd picked me up and set me on my own cream leather seat in the jet, and I had yet to change back.

I waved my arms at him and flicked my antennae. My dual-caster coin hung from my neck like some hip-hop artist's vanity bling.

"Had it all under control, did you?" With a heavy sigh, Alder placed his hands on his hips. "You two are benched. That's it. No ifs, ands, or buts. Your case load will be diverted to someone else who has some sort of expertise in these artifacts. Which don't have. Nor do we have the true thief." He pinched the bridge of his nose as he took another deep breath. "I'm sending the twins out first thing. No discussion, this time. They'll be at the plant nursery at daybreak."

"We look forward to seeing them!"

"This won't be a social call, Eryn," Alder snapped.

"I-I know that. I *know* that."

"Be prepared to hand over whatever you have on your cases, including that ogre head. Maybe they can figure out what kind of magic killed him."

I clacked my mandibles even more. I knew what had killed him, I just needed a voice box to convey it. The ariel set me down on the counter as Alder's image disappeared. My barbed feet clicked against the wood as I hopped over to the only thing we'd salvaged from the mission: the wax seal with the frayed cord. I gave it a tap-tap with my antennae.

"Oh no, I'm not taking that to your freaky little dungeon," the ariel said, backing away.

I clacked my mandibles at her and tap-tapped the heap again.

"I said no. Underground, me—we don't mix. And *you* aren't able to stab me with your Drozvegan dart so I guess we'll just have to wait until you're you again." She glanced around the plant nursery. It was quiet in the wee hours of the morning. Most fascinari did their dealings between eleven and three, except vampires, of course, and it was almost four. The ariel yawned. "Bedtime, I think."

She slipped the seal and communication array into her pockets, picked me up, and floated to the rafters. Settling on her back, her white hair pooling like a cloud under her head like an undulating cushion, she settled me on her stomach, corralling me with her hands. "Don't want the gnomes feeding you to the stone frog," she muttered as her eyes flickered closed.

My beady cricket eyes narrowed. I didn't need her protection, an *ariel*. I was a prince of Drozvega—trained since birth to fight. Just because I was a cricket didn't mean I was any less deadly. Her misguided concern was as helpful as a pile of spider scat.

I waited until she was asleep, which took all of two minutes, before climbing over her fingers and into her pocket. Just because I was a cricket didn't mean I had an excuse not to follow my own protocols. Nothing from a job was left out in the open. It was secured in its own private cubby in the honeycomb lattice beneath the plant nursery. It was respect, pure and simple. Besides, the moment you got sloppy was the moment you got caught.

After looping the cords around my thorax, I dragged the wax seal out of her pocket and climbed down into the crook of her elbow where I paused, examining the drop to the plants below. A hard exoskeleton like mine could withstand such a fall, and I had wings, after all, but I wasn't sure it could survive a stab of Cornelius's trowel or Marigold's hoe.

The gnomes had gathered en masse directly below us and had their heads craned back as they stared upward, silent as the statues they mimicked. Their beady eyes shone like the copper pennies given to the dead to pay the Ferryman. Still watching me, Cornelius tapped the shoulder of the gnome in the Bavarian barmaid dress next to him. Trudy, the muscle of this gnome posse, clenched her fingers into a fist and rammed it into her palm.

Rattling my wing covers, I leaned down and hissed at them. It came out a vicious chirp.

They weren't the only ones who weren't going to be intimidated.

But I wasn't stupid either, so I returned to the safety of the ariel's hand-corral and settled in to wait out the duration of my curse. I had to use this time wisely, to think of a solution. The twins were going to draw my blood, and I couldn't let that happen.

CHAPTER TWENTY

Eryn

"Yoo-hoo! Anyone home?" a singsong voice called.

"Why hello there, Miss Maven, Miss Moxie," Rumple said. "Come on in."

I groaned, feeling heavier than I ever had since gaining this new body. I hadn't missed a dawn in over two hundred years, but when my eyes finally slitted against the morning light, I could tell it was a few hours past sunrise. Exhaustion could have that effect, but as far as I knew it didn't make your muscles feel like cement.

But a drow resting his head on my stomach and pinning my legs to the joist certainly would.

The braided cord with its wax seal dangled from the tip of his nose. Clearly he'd transformed sometime between four and eight in the morning, and he woke at the sound of my stomach snarling for food. I really had to eat more frequently than once a day.

"Ah!" Despite my hunger, I phased, misting through the gaps in the joist.

The drow fell against the metal supports with a clang, and if he hadn't been fully awake before, he certainly was now. "Ow."

"Serves you right." I straightened my romper with a few flicks of my fingers and floated down to where the magitech twins were. "Morning!"

Moxie just nodded, her eyes half-lidded, and took a fortifying sip from her thermos. I could smell the rooibos tea as she exhaled. Maven gave me a wave with her can of Java Monster, yelping as the energy drink sluiced over her hand.

The garden gnomes, who froze in place at the presence of humans, clearly had no misgivings about the magitech twins. They gathered around their ankles like ducks awaiting a special treat.

"Good morning, Cornelius, Marigold, Trudy, Henrietta..." Maven listed them off name by name until she was blue in the face. Then she wiped her forehead of the sweat beading there with a "Whoo! Talk about a wet heat."

"Give us the goods, sister!" a bucktooth gnome with a purple hat said.

Marigold whacked him on the backside with her garden hoe. "You'll keep a civil tongue in your head or I'll sic Leroy on you."

The giant snail beside Marigold let out a decisive snarl.

"I won't keep you in suspense any longer," Maven said, withdrawing an oversized box from her metallic case.

"Fruit snacks," the gnomes cheered.

It took six of them to carry the box, but they carted it off like it was the prized pig for a luau, the other gnomes whooping and waving around their garden tools.

"And don't think I forgot about you, Rumple." Maven bent down with a jar in her hand.

"Is that"—the pig smacked his lips—"prickly pear jam? Oh, this will go so well on my morning croissant. Thank you!"

He gently took the jar into his mouth and trotted off to the break room.

"You spoil them," Larcen said from above, slipping his hand into his pocket.

"Like you or me telling her that is gonna make her stop?" Moxie asked.

Maven ignored them both and pointed her finger at me with a little up-down flick. "Ooo! That romper looks killer on you." She nudged Moxie with her elbow. "See? Told you."

"Yes, yes. Your talents extend beyond the lab. Oh! And look at that serendipitous and not at all manufactured segue into why we're here. Larcen, we need to examine you." She clicked open the chrome briefcase she'd heaved onto the patio display table and pulled out a syringe.

The drow dropped down from the rafters, landing with hardly a sound. He straightened slowly, giving Moxie a wary look.

"We'll start with the basics." Moxie tossed him a plastic cup. "Fill that up."

"In the meantime, I brought *tostones*!" Maven said, hefting a greasy paper bag. "Not quite Bajan bakes, but they're pretty popular in the Hub."

Moxie rolled her eyes and took another long draft of her tea.

I floated over to Maven and helped myself to some of those crispy-chewy-salty starch rounds as she set up her laptop. She plugged in a few wires and held up a slim cylinder that glowed with a faint blue light. After clicking a few keys, she turned to me. "Alder said something about a star chart?"

I soared to the counter and retrieved the paper, careful to pinch just the edge with my greasy fingers. Moxie waved her little blue-glowing wand down it, and an image appeared on her laptop screen. Another few key taps and the program whirled to life, flashing hundreds of star charts per second. After a few minutes, Maven gave me a small, kind smile. "Looks like this might take a while."

Grinning, I helped myself to some more *tostones*. I knew a patronizing look when I saw one. Granted, I hadn't seen one since I was a child, but they were pretty easy to recognize. People made the wrong assumption that a cheerful disposition was the side effect of a vapid brain, that social butterflies had no capacity for complex thought, and while we ariels didn't go around correcting people—rude—it couldn't be further from the truth. You think centaurs are the go-to experts on the stars? Who do you think they learned it from? And if you're under the impression that dwarves are the best metal-smiths in all the fascinari realms, then you clearly haven't seen the star forges that refine sun gold or celestial silver. We were our own best-kept secrets, but I'd thought the people at DUO would've been a little more open-minded.

I stayed by the laptop, watching it with one eye as the twins gave Larcen a thorough examination. When they'd asked for a private place, he said there wasn't one and shucked his clothes right there in the middle of the aisle. Guess he didn't want them snooping around in his training-room-man-eating-plant dungeon.

The twins were immediately drawn to the pulsing green light under the skin of his left pectoral, but they were careful not to touch it. Working together, they splashed him with potions and powders and pressed crystals again the green light. They sprinkled a circle of salt around him; burnt herbs and wafted him with smoke; they made him hold the skull of a bird in one hand and a white stone in the other while he held up his right foot; brewed a tea that smelled of bergamot and grapefruit and somehow stewed cabbage and made him drink it.

After an hour or so, the laptop hadn't yielded a result on my star chart, and the twins were out of options.

"You're cursed," Moxie said.

Otherwise expressionless, Larcen lifted one white eyebrow. "You don't say."

Maven scrubbed her face with her hands. "Transfiguration curse, just like you said, but we don't know what's activating it. Let's draw some blood."

Try as they might, the needle couldn't penetrate his veins. It slid into his skin easily enough, but they sucked up nothing but air.

"Stab me again, and I might just stab you back this time," Larcen said in a low voice after the twelfth try.

"This is unheard of," Moxie said, wiping her glasses from the polytunnel's humidity and bringing Larcen's arm up to her face. She poked the crook of his arm. "Seems solid, but then the needle passes right through you."

"Maybe it's not just a transfiguration curse," Maven said, popping open another Java Monster. "I wonder if it's coupled with concealment magic. And why not? This dark mage or whoever he is seems very proficient in it. Larcen couldn't even see it, could you?"

Larcen gave an angry shake of his head.

"Spells are simple," Moxie countered. "They have one job, one purpose. Multi-layered spells are nearly impossible to get right."

"'Nearly' being the operative word. We're dealing with a grandmaster, Mox. Who knows what he's capable of?"

"This curse is clever, but it's still simple at its root," her twin said stubbornly. "Obviously it has something to do with his blood, or we'd be able to get a sample."

"The next time I cut myself on a rose thorn, I'll make sure to blot it and send it to you right away," Larcen said.

"Thank you," Maven said happily.

"He was being sarcastic," Moxie said, ripping her gloves off with a sigh. "Well, we'll sort through the meager results we got and see what we can dig up." She checked her watch. "Where's the stuff from your cases?"

"It's already been sent through Pegasus Express." The lie slipped easily from his lips.

"Oh," Maven said, glancing at me.

I turned the brightness up on my smile and stuffed another *tostone* into my mouth. The bag was nearly gone.

"Why would you do that if you knew we were coming?" Moxie asked irritably. "Now we'll have to sanitize the shipping bay. You never know where they've been."

"I didn't think they'd be safe here," he said. "And an emergency could've happened that would've sent you elsewhere this morning."

Another lie. Well, at least the first bit.

Moxie grumbled a thank-you and snapped her metallic case closed. "You can put your clothes back on, you exhibitionist."

"You're welcome."

Moxie snorted and headed for the door.

"Can you tell me what the computer finds, whenever it's done?" I asked Maven. The star charts were still whizzing by at a dizzying pace.

"Sure will." Maven gave me a quick air-kiss on each cheek and waved cheerily to Larcen as he was pulling on his leather trousers. Then she hurried after her sister, her cork sandals slapping against her brown feet. Thinking of something, she lurched to a halt and whipped around. "Larcen, my goldfish plant—"

"Morning light and keep it moist without flooding it."

"Gotcha. Thanks!"

When they were gone, and Larcen was buttoning up his vest,

I let the smile drop and crossed my arms over my chest. "Looks like you've really got a handle on that phasing ability."

"Drow learn fast or they die."

"Why didn't you want them to take your blood?"

"Because it's mine and it has nothing to do with the curse."

"Oh, so you're an expert on curses now, are you?"

"Moxie is right. Spells are simple. This curse has everything to do with this," he said, pointing to his chest, "and not anything else. That arrow was aimed at you originally, or have you forgotten? If it was a blood curse he wouldn't have fired at me."

"Fine, so it's a transfiguration curse. It's still a curse, and while you might be happy changing into freaky little unhelpful creatures at random times, I'm very much not. How will you be able to flip your coin to activate the Puddle if you don't have hands?"

"Didn't you hear Alder? We're benched. We're not activating the Puddle anytime soon."

"So you're content to sit on the sidelines and just watch?"

"Of course not." He lunged forward and seized my hand.

We slid out of the shadows next to Berthold, and the massive pitcher plant burped a greeting.

"May you be turned into stone and smashed into sand," I screeched.

I launched into the air, but the drow grabbed my leg. His grip faltered as I phased into mist, but then he turned into shadow and jumped into the air after me, blocking the nearest exit up the shoot. His violet eyes glowed warningly.

"I'm claustrophobic," I screeched again.

His shadowy form pointed to the honeycomb-lattice wall.

"Pointing doesn't make me any less claustrophobic!"

Shadow-Larcen zoomed around in the darkness, only his violet eyes glowing, and suddenly those weird flowers with their angler-lure stamens illuminated. Now I could see, the darkness wasn't so nearly crushing, but I didn't care. I zoomed up the chute before he could block me again, and Shadow-Larcen gave chase. The moment I was topside in the poly-tunnel I solidified into crystal. Shadow-Larcen puffed into smoke as he collided into me, reforming behind me and solidifying.

"Ugh," the drow shouted. "That was disgusting."

"I only felt a tickle." Then, before he could phase again, I reached out and slapped him. "Don't ever do that again!"

He rubbed his face as if I'd really hurt him and snapped, "And you need to get over it."

"Ariels and the underground don't mix. Never have. Never will."

"You are ridiculous." Larcen stormed to the counter and snatched something out of a drawer. Then he swiped Rumple's cell phone out of his trotters. "I need to borrow this."

"You could *ask* next time," the pig grumbled, munching on the last bits of his jam-slathered croissant.

Larcen tossed Rumple's sticky cell phone at me. A moment later it rang, and I quickly put it to my ear as I'd seen the humans do. "Hello?"

"It's me, you idiot. And press the video button."

"I'm not an idiot," I snapped, jamming my finger against the pulsing blue icon. A moment later, Larcen's face appeared on the screen.

"Since you can't get over yourself and go downstairs, I'll just have to show you with this."

"There, was that so hard? I didn't have to go down into your little dungeon with its freaky plants after all."

"They're called lampblossoms."

"Not that massive thing that eats people."

The dark elf huffed and disappeared into the shadows once again. I watched the screen, the image lightening as he reappeared in his creepy flower-illuminated dungeon of crushing darkness.

"So what did you need to show me instead of telling me with your words?" I asked. The honeycomb lattice loomed closer on the screen as Larcen approached. "Oh yeah, and remind me again why you lied about sending all this stuff through Pegasus Express? And what *is* Pegasus Express?"

"A shipping service."

"You don't say."

"Imagine a pegasus—you *do* know what a pegasus is, right? —the largest you've ever seen with the nastiest disposition you've never encountered."

"I know pegasuses—pegasusi?—are kind of aloof, but I never thought they were mean."

"These ones have to be, otherwise how else are they going to protect their cargo? They have spurs on their hooves and can breathe fire, not to mention turn their manes and tails into flame if they have to."

"You're talking about nightmares."

"No, I'm talking about the creatures that inspired that myth. Anyway, slap a sticker on whatever you want to transport, and they come and pick it up."

"What's the sticker look like?"

"Their black pegasus logo, of course."

I rolled my eyes. "Oh, of course. And why did you lie again?"

"Because as far as DUO is concerned, we're a pair of failures. I don't know about you, but I've never failed in my life—"

"The night wisp valley. That was my first failure. Seems I've been failing ever since I met you, actually."

Larcen was silent for moment, the video frozen on the honeycomb wall of cubbies. "Well, I could say the same ever since I partnered with you. And it's not a feeling I'd like to become accustomed to. So what better way to repair our reputations than to find whatever clues have been left behind and take down this thief ourselves?"

"If we couldn't do it with DUO's resources, what makes you think we can do it by ourselves?"

"Because now we need to really act like a team."

"Did you hit your head or something?"

"Or something." Larcen's hand extended to place the star chart's wax seal and faded cord into a vacant cubby. He withdrew and the video panned to the left as he turned to go to the worktable, sweeping past the adjacent cubby where Billy Macon's possessions were stored.

"Wait, go back," I cried, squinting at the screen.

"What?"

The image widened so I could see both cubbies at the same time. "There was a silver glow. The wax seal—"

"Is red. Look." The video did a patronizing circle around the wax seal so I could view it from all angles.

"I know what I saw."

"You said the same thing about the archer being a shadow-walker. It was just a trick of the light. Now, if you'll stop interrupting me, I'll show you why *I* am down here. All by myself. Without my partner."

"Some team player you are. Don't you find it exhausting to be so condescending all the time?"

"Not in the least. It's my birthright. Now pay attention."

As he turned I saw that silver flash again, from both cubbies, but I kept my mouth shut. He approached the table beside Berthold where the ogre's body, and his head, were growing stiffer and colder with every moment.

"Do you remember what happened to the ogre's neck?" Larcen asked.

"A bunch of pretty lights and a pop," I said, doing my best to sound cheerful as I delivered my snark.

The video panned until Larcen's angular face consumed the screen. "I need you to take this seriously."

I held up my little finger like I'd seen the humans do. "Pinky swear."

The video zoomed in on the ogre's neck. "Look, you can still see some of the runes."

Larcen was right. There was curling script just barely visible at the cauterized edge of the ogre's fleshy stump, on both the body and the head.

I'd seen it before.

Frowning, I floated over to where Rumple sat in his rolly chair, tapping away at the oversized keys of the keyboard as he tried—yet again—to undo the damage the gnomes had done to the plant nursery's website. The bronze collar around his neck gleamed under the grime. "It looks like the script on Rumple's collar."

"Exactly. And all inscription artists have their own personal flair." Larcen's sharp teeth flashed white as he smiled. "Let's go say hello to a particular fae."

CHAPTER TWENTY-ONE

Larcen

Fae in the human realm were often crepuscular creatures, the better to obscure their true nature, so we spent the day getting the ariel fed, actually working in the plant nursery, fending off the latest "garden kink" customers wanting pole-dancing garden gnome figurines, and I even found a little time to retreat to my private mushroom haven.

I didn't need an injection, but the new mushrooms Malcan had given me needed tending. Drozvegan mushrooms matured from their spores in forty-eight hours, so small black inkcaps with silver gills greeted me when I stooped down to inspect the trays.

"Silver?" I muttered. I'd never seen that color in a Drozvegan mushroom before. But my home caves were a vast network, some of them not wholly explored due to the other creatures that lurked in the dark. Uncle Malcan's second love was exploring, so it made sense he'd stumbled upon this rare find. Maybe it was the ingredient my elixir had been missing all this time.

I exhaled on the mushrooms, giving them a taste of the world they'd left behind. They visibly swelled, growing from pea-sized caps to buttons. "Grow, dammit," I muttered, a wry smile twisting my lips. The sooner their caps resembled tangerines in size, the sooner I could harvest them.

Moving to the workbench, I sank onto the stool and removed the trays with the dehydrated mushrooms. An oversized spice blender turned the shriveled slivers into powder finer than flour. I might've given up distributing this Night Dust, especially after the topiary incident, but it still had its uses. I slipped a vial into my pocket and stored the rest of them away, retrieving a frozen chicken for Drosera on the way out.

There were even more customers in the plant nursery when I exited the walk-in, but apparently the ariel had it all in hand. Her feet were on the ground, so her white hair hung like fine thread to her hips instead of swirling around her head as it did when she was in the air. Her jade-green eyes were bright as she explained this or that about a plant. For a moment I was surprised at her knowledge, but then I remembered she was a creature of the air. The wind was a pollinator, and she'd said herself that she'd used to sustain herself on celestial dew and pollen. She would know a thing or two about plants as instinctively as a bee knew which ones to get the most nectar from.

Even with my enhanced hearing, I couldn't determine what she specifically was saying over the droning of half a dozen other conversations. Whatever it was had the customers snatching up plants and lining up at the counter in droves. Rumple had to abbreviate his Southern greetings and small talk to "hey there" and "thank y'all so much for visiting" just to get through the line in a timely fashion. I left them to work—the ariel had to earn her upkeep somehow—and put on an apron to go hose down the mulch piles and package the compost that Berthold created.

When I came back from fertilizing the alchemical herbs— they were ravenous for Berthold's compost—the gnomes were in full swing rearranging and restocking the shelves. They were actually whistling, and the ariel soared over the plants, the wind of her passage rustling their leaves and flowers and filling the air with pollen. No wonder they were thriving.

The gnomes nearest to the alchemy herb garden yelped at my appearance and scattered, tooting kazoos like they were war horns announcing the presence of an invading army.

"Since when do they have kazoos?" I shouted at Rumple.

"Dollar General was having an end-of-summer sale," the pig replied. "It's their money, sir. What they choose to spend it on is their business."

"We will continue to toot until there's an espresso machine in the break room and strawberries for our yogurt bowls," Cornelius announced from somewhere on my right.

"And Miss Eryn gets her own room," Marigold said. "She can't possibly expect to sleep in the rafters every night!"

"Oh, I don't mind," she said.

"See?" I gloated. "She said she doesn't mind."

"Yes she does!" Unlike Cornelius, who hid to deliver his demands and insults, Marigold stood on an overturned terra-cotta pot in full view so she could swing her garden hoe. The gnome pointed at the ariel, who was tending to a pitiful-looking cherry tree, and declared, "Yes, you do. That body can't be comfortable on metal joists all night."

"It's not so bad. I'm closer to the stars that way."

"See? She's a simple girl with simple needs," I said.

Marigold thrust her garden hoe into my face. At least, she would've had I been three feet shorter. "She is your partner. That should mean something to you, especially since she's the only one keeping us from coming after you when you're having a physical identity crisis."

I glared down at the gnome. "About that. You can't demand a less-hostile work environment and then create one yourself."

"I thought drow only responded to strength."

Hn. Perhaps I'd been wrong all along by treating Cornelius as the gnomes' ringleader instead of this little thing with her button nose and brown curls peeking out of her red pointy hat. "Indeed."

A swirl of wind diverted my attention, and I turned to the find the ariel right behind me, pulling the communications array out of her pocket. It was flashing like a deranged firefly. "Somehow I think this is for you."

She dropped it into my palm and crossed her arms over her chest. No doubt she was still miffed at me for lying about Pegasus Express.

Scowling, I passed my hand over the array and an irritated eight-inch bust of Moxie appeared. Somehow her wire-rim glasses made the scowl on her face even more severe. "Well?" she demanded.

"Perhaps if I knew the question?"

"Where is it? Where's the Zhu dagger sheath, the wax seal, the—"

"The pegasus didn't exactly give us his flight itinerary."

"Pegasus Express has no record of you using a stamp. No carrier was sent to your location. Do you have any idea the hassle it is to contact them and ask where a delivery is and inadvertently accuse them of negligence? Because that's how they're interpreting this and you know they don't like anyone besmirching their reputation. Alder is still on the call with them doing damage control so DUO doesn't lose its shipping license!"

I feigned surprise. "I instructed Eryn very thoroughly on the usage of the stamps, Moxie."

Eryn's eyebrows nearly flew off her face, and her smile certainly did. Her lips became as puckered as if she'd just sucked on a pickle.

"You had Eryn do it?" Moxie's irritation only grew. "She's been in this realm for less than three days and you had *her* deal with Pegasus Express?"

"I was a little busy. And how hard is it to place a stamp? She's childish, sure, but she's not an idiot. I think."

Eryn's hands clenched into fists, but she remained silent, her outrage clear on her face.

"True," Moxie admitted begrudgingly. "Inside that bimbo exterior is a thoughtful and meticulous person. So what happened then?"

"Do you think it went rogue?"

Moxie's frown deepened. "A pegasus go rogue? It's unthinkable."

"If we're dealing with dark mage that can cast such powerful concealment spells that the Council and the director of DUO himself don't know who their target is, don't you think they could sabotage a pegasus?"

Her frown deepened, but it had turned thoughtful. "It's... unheard of, but so is everything the first time. Send an itemized list of what you gave the pegasus immediately. We'll see if we can run our own tracking spells."

"Will do. Happy to help."

She gave me one of her skeptical up-down assessments. "Uh-huh. Oh, and your test results came back. Other than a calcium deficiency, there's apparently nothing wrong with you."

"Calcium deficiency?"

"Go take a vitamin. And send me that list in the next fifteen minutes."

Her image disappeared, and I shoved the array into my pocket.

The ariel finally popped like a burst balloon. "Well someone call the fire department."

"Why?" I glanced around the nursery, wondering what could've caught fire in such a humid environment. I'd already hosed down the mulch, so—

"Because we're going to need a firehose to put out the fire in your pants from all those lies."

"No one over the age of twelve uses that expression."

"Well they should. And how dare you—what do the humans say?—throw me under the bus like that?"

"You didn't correct me, so that makes you an accomplice."

"You're my partner; I'm not supposed to rat you out. But that doesn't make it okay, either." She huffed a sigh that redirected her swirling hair from its clockwise swirling to counterclockwise. Then her face brightened with one of her smiles, the kind that masked her true feelings. "It's almost sunset. Let's get this thing with the fae over with. If we can get a credible lead, we can set this whole mess to rights. *Including* that rubbish with Pegasus Express. Otherwise... Well, I guess they'll imprison you or something equally reprimanding and I'll become the sole heir of this lovely flora establishment and the gnomes can finally get all the foamed milk they want."

"And the strawberries!" a voice added.

"And the strawberries," she amended.

"You'd... usurp me?" I snarled, feeling for my scorpion blade. This plant nursery was as much a pain in the ass as it was a golden goose, but it was *mine*. And we drow had very strong feelings about hierarchy and possessions. You respected it, or you fought to increase your social standing and holdings. This wasn't just a floral emporium. This was my refuge. Despite the cursed gnomes that came with it.

The ariel flew right into my face, her finger an inch away from my nose. "You'll be your own downfall, caveman. You need to trust me, *partner*. You chose this, remember?" She lifted her slim wrist where the dualcaster coin dangled. "You chose me. So trust me. We need to work as a team, especially with your new habit of shapeshifting at the most inconvenient times ever."

I fought to keep from baring my sharp teeth at the invasion of my personal space. Any other drow would've considered it a challenge, and I fought through instinct to *hear* her. I had to play nicely until it was time to use her power, and that meant... compromise. I nearly gagged at the word.

My upper lip still twitched, readying a snarl, but then movement beyond the ariel caught my attention. It was Marigold, scowling as fiercely as her chubby little cheeks would let her. Then she mimed a cricket hopping across her palm only to be squashed like, well, a bug.

I glanced back at the ariel. She had taken her finger out of my face and had planted her hands on her hips, hovering in the air in front of me as she awaited my response. She wasn't wrong, though I was loath to admit it. I had chosen her, in a way, when I'd accepted the Puddle's power. And... she *had* protected me from the gnomes when I'd been a cricket, and a goldfish. I'd been vulnerable, and while she could've left me—a drow, her enemy—to their mercy, she had taken me to safety. Twice. I... *owed* her.

I swallowed my revulsion and gave a brief nod. "You're right. We need to act like a team."

The ariel smiled, genuinely this time. "So what's the plan?"

"Raphael is throwing one of his notorious parties, and anyone who's anyone will be there. That's where we'll find the fae calligrapher. Faelen can't ever say no to an opportunity to be admired. No one shows up before midnight, so we have plenty of time for me to get Moxie off our backs and for you to... Henrietta! I need you. And your makeup kit."

The gnome let out a little squeal of delight. With a quick

"*Oui, monsieur!*" she was off running, her red heels click-clacking across the cement floor as she rushed to the dormitory to retrieve her supplies.

"Makeup?" the ariel asked, puzzled.

"And much more. Rumple, you have the floor. I'm going to deal with Moxie, and you, *partner*, are going to practice your illusions. Your skin needs to resemble white gold."

"Like this?"

For a moment, it was like I was looking at the moon goddess murals in my mother's grotto. Not just Selena this time, but her sister, the one whose skin looked like the night sky covered in stars...

The illusion faltered, and the goddess was replaced by the ariel.

I cleared my throat. "You'll have to maintain it. But... yes. Go practice. I'll be back."

Stepping into the shadows, I disappeared from the emporium and reappeared in my bedroom. The lampblossom immediately illuminated, washing everything in a pale-pink light. Lifting the pot, I moved it to the side and dipped my hand into the depression it hid. My fingers closed on the moonstone locket. Mother had given it to me whenever I'd left for battle, pleading to the moon goddesses to watch over her only son. She'd gifted it to me when I'd left Drozvega for the human realm, and I hadn't had any reason to look at it.

Until now.

I flicked open the clasp with my fingernail, and the locket opened. Two pictures of the same woman, one light and one dark, depicted the twin goddesses. My thumb traced the face of Selena, the goddess of moonlight. This wasn't the first time I'd seen her likeness on the ariel. But the way her skin had sparkled just now, illusion or not, it was like Lena, the Dark Moon goddess. Eryn was Steorra, the essence of stars and Ancient kings. Could she possibly have the sisters' favor as well?

Snapping the locket closed, I shoved it back in its hiding place and shoved the lampblossom's pot back in place.

"It doesn't matter," I growled, gripping the ledge. "They left us to the mercy of the Spider Queen. And I'm going to use their favored one to free us."

CHAPTER TWENTY-TWO

Eryn

"WHAT IS THIS PLACE?" I kept my hands clasped together and pressed against my chest. I wanted to float up this brick walkway, but the dark elf said it was imperative I keep my feet on the ground. Ahead of us loomed an old Southern house of wrought iron, pale stone, and tall windows. Off to the right was a paved path that must've led to a garden of night-blooming flowers, judging by the smell. The moss dripping from the trees that lined the brick walk positively pulsed with the bass of the music. "It's so loud. Any why did we have to go shopping again? You didn't have to buy me more clothes."

Larcen moved behind me, looming like a shadow, and pinched the jacket he'd lent to me at the shoulders. Leaning down so his mouth was at ear-level, he said, "Because not only is this an exclusive soiree, it is your introduction to the magical society here in Savannah and you need to make a statement." With a yank, he shucked the jacket away.

Underneath I was wearing a sparkling dress with a deep V-neck and a plunging back, reminiscent of Lady Chantilly's sage sheath. Mine had more slink and sway and seemed entirely composed of little crystals. I was wearing starlight, and I loved it. The dress and the matching heels had cost more than that silver hairbrush, but Larcen hadn't said a word about the price. He'd merely handed the cashier a plastic card and the outfit was mine. He'd even treated me to dinner tonight. Why was he being so nice? Was I finally starting to win him over?

His theatrics didn't intimidate me; they made me suspicious. Spinning around, I put my hands on my hips. "What statement?"

"You'll know soon enough." The dark elf's eyes looked me over from head to toe, looking for something.

"What? Is my makeup okay?" I had held Henrietta in my flattened palms for an hour as she had sprinkled and smeared this and that all over my face. When she was done, I had recoiled at my reflection with its shimmers and rosy red lip, but Henrietta and the other lady gnomes had said I was a "heartbreaker," which I had been assured was a good thing.

"It's..." Larcen cleared his throat and reached out with his thumb.

I smacked his hand away on instinct.

"You smudged your lipstick! Keep still." He put two fingers under my chin and tilted it up into the light coming from the windows.

"What do you know about lipstick?" I asked as he drew a small makeup kit out of his vest pocket.

"I can't fix it if you're talking. Shut up." His violet eyes narrowed as he concentrated on what he was doing. The flecks of gold in them gleamed. "All drow are either mercenaries, alchemists, or fashion models. When they're not fighting for Drozvega, that is. So I know a thing or two. There. You're done."

I couldn't wiggle out of his hands fast enough. Ariels were impervious to temperature—how else could we survive in the Temple of the Sky with its sun-warmed days and moon-cooled nights?—but ever since I'd been saddled with this *body*, I could *feel*. I could feel the heat and humidity of this place, the wind on my skin, the warmth of his thumb as he'd straightened the line of lipstick under my lower lip. It had felt... I wasn't going to say *nice*, because gross, but the sensation hadn't been unpleasant.

Larcen stepped away from me, towards the door. "Did you bring your fans?"

"What kind of guardian do you think I am?"

"I'm just curious as to where you put them."

"Then you'll stay curious," I said, giving my crystal dress a little flick to straighten it. Then I put on a demure smile—Henrietta had insisted on nothing but coyness tonight—and climbed the stoop, my silver heels clicking with every step.

Larcen knocked on the door. "Illusion time."

After practicing all afternoon, the illusion came easily. It lengthened my ears to points, far sharper and pointier than an elf's, and added a shimmering effect to my skin. Whenever my crystal dress caught the light and glittered, so would my skin.

"Remember, be aloof," Larcen said. "But enjoy yourself. Fae delight in being the center of attention."

"You know it's impossible for an ariel to both be aloof and enjoy herself, right?"

A slot slid away in the door, and a pair of green eyes with cat-like pupils filled the void. "Who is—oh! Your Highness. *Do* come in."

Larcen gave me a superior look and stepped over the threshold. Apparently the smug prince wasn't bereft of all manners, for he held out his hand to me. I didn't want to touch him, but this dress was long and slinky and I wasn't used to the heels. Keeping the smile plastered on my face, I took his hand, lifted the hem of the crystal dress, and gracefully crossed the threshold. I may or may not have cheated and floated into the house, hovering less than an inch above the ground.

"We haven't seen you in so long, Prin—"

"No introduction, Raphael," the drow interrupted. "I'm not on the best terms with some of your other guests, and I'm sure you like your house just as it is."

Raphael, a changeling, altered his cat eyes to resemble an owl's. Changelings, fae children who had grown up in the human realm, rarely manifested all the powers of their fae kin, but they often had the ability to change their features to suit their mood. "Very perceptive, Larcen," he said, whispering the drow's name. In a normal tone, he said, "I had it renovated to resemble the South during the twenties. I believe the décor was Greco-Roman the last time you graced one of my soirees."

The changeling's entire face took on a lynx-like visage, complete with whiskers and tufted ears, as he turned his attention to me. "Me-rawr. And who is this dazzling creature?"

"Eryana of Lux Argentum," Larcen answered.

Somehow his voice magnified and echoed through the entire house like a gentle roll of thunder. I gave the ceiling a bewildered look before remembering I needed to appear aloof.

Raphael gestured to the glyphs glowing on the doorframe. "I had Faelen put in a herald script for me. Saves my voice for conversation rather than the constant introductions." He waved us further into the foyer with his martini glass. "This way, darlings. Make yourselves at home."

When Raphael turned and sauntered away, Larcen gave me a knowing look. I nodded, and we parted ways. He'd given me a description of Faelen—black hair, gold skin, tall, most likely in a tailored black suit—and we were to divide and conquer. Find the fae. Then find his alchemist-dark mage employer and eliminate him, retrieve the artifacts, get back in Alder's good graces. Easy breezy.

The house was decorated in the grandeur of a bygone era, and completely packed with fascinari. Fae, shifters, satyrs, nymphs, necromancers, more than I could count. Humans referred to our collective species—those born with magic—as mythical creatures, but there was nothing mythical about us. We were just hidden way.

I drew more than a few looks, but Larcen had coached me to be as aloof as possible. I was an *aurum blanc* fae from Lux Argentum, whatever that meant—because no, not all us fascinari knew each other—so I channeled my inner Shara and tried to be as cold and withering as the north wind.

When a dwarf with glitter in his beard and black kohl around his eyes offered me a tiny quiche from a silver platter, it was all I could do to not break character and say thank you. I stuffed the morsel into my mouth to smother the words and moved on from what I assumed was the salon to the library. There was a centaur in here, and it took everything in me not to rush over and introduce myself. Ariels and centaurs, both stargazers, got on famously well. I didn't recognize this particular mare with the dappled gray flanks and yellow plume in her tail, but I was sure we had a shared friend or acquaintance. No fae with black hair and gold-colored skin in here, so I moved on to the next room.

It must've been a greenhouse at some point, for the walls from the waist up were made entirely of glass, as was the ceiling. The ceiling stretched at least two stories tall, giving the room an airiness I hadn't experienced since entering the house. A sigh of relief drained the tension I hadn't known was in my shoulders, and I relaxed.

Any plants that had once called this place home had been removed, except for the ceramic urns with the bamboo palms in them, and replaced with embroidered sofas and a piano. A nymph sat at the piano and sang as she played, her six-fingered hands gliding over the keys.

Though I know I needed to move on and find Faelen, I lingered here. The nymph's music was mournful, of summer days bleeding into autumn, and it pulled at me. A satyr with a tray of yellow wine passed by, and it smelled so much like sundrop nectar I couldn't help myself. I snatched a flute and held it between both hands. It was too sweet for the new me to drink, but the smell of it was enough. I clenched my teeth as a swell of homesickness choked my throat.

The nymph finished her song, and I struggled figure out a way to hold the wine flute steady and clap at the same time. Then I remembered I was supposed to be like Shara, and just lifted my chin a little higher. Which was a good choice, since it kept the tears that had formed in my eyes from streaking my mascara, something Henrietta had threatened me with bodily harm if I ruined her "masterpiece."

"Reminds me of home," a baritone voice said from my left. "Long sunsets and even longer twilights."

I fought the urge to spin around. I'd been so mesmerized by the music, I hadn't even heard anyone sneak up on me. Pretending I'd known he was there all along, I turned slowly, as if I was doing this stranger a favor by giving him my attention. "Indeed," I replied loftily.

Any other words I might've said lodged in my throat.

Ariels didn't put much stock into physical appearance—we were mist, after all—but even in my uneducated opinion, the male who stood before me was *handsome*. Black hair, a jaw so sharp it could cut glass, the most luscious honey-colored eyes I'd ever seen. And gold skin, golden as the sunrise with the most intricate black swirls over every inch of it except his face. Pointy ears speared through his black hair, each one adorned with a fat round diamond.

"F-Faelen," I sputtered. Then I remembered I was supposed to be a haughty fae from Lux Argentum and arched my eyebrow. "I presume."

"You presume correctly. Not many of us from Lux Argentum in this human realm. And you must be Eryana. The *aurum blanc*." He lifted my hand and kissed it with those golden lips. Instead of freeing me, he pulled me closer, stroking the back of my hand with his thumb. "What brings you to Savannah?"

Just because an ariel could sense a lie didn't mean we were very good at telling them, so I stuck to the truth. "Business. But tonight, I'm just here to enjoy myself."

"As you should." His honey eyes bored into me as he lifted my hand for another unhurried kiss.

"Speaking of"—I plucked my hand away before I gagged and he left another moist trail on my knuckles—"I think I'll go outside and—"

"Get some fresh air under the stars?" He tucked my hand into the crook of his arm. "Yes, you *aurum blanc* do love your starlight. Where's your chaperone?"

"My what?"

"You have none? Then that settles it. I'll accompany you, cousin."

Cousin? Since when we were so familiar? Just as I was about to pluck my hand free for a second time, I remembered we were here for this schmoozing fae. I'd just wanted to get away from this handsy womanizer, but now it seemed my suggestion to go outside was working in my favor. No one would be able to hear his screams when I pinned him up against a tree with my bladed fans and demand to know who'd paid him to make the ogre's script. In theory. Hmm, maybe it would be better to lead him away from the house, phase, and bring him back to the plant nursery. Larcen and I hadn't worked that bit of the plan out—note to self, *communicate*—and I couldn't sense the dark elf anywhere.

The greenhouse had a glass door that opened onto the rear patio, and Faelen pulled me beyond the rose hedges down a path to a cozy clearing in the azaleas with a stone bench by a little koi pond. White carp, as ethereal-looking as me, broke the black surface of the pond like specters through shadow. This part of the garden wasn't shaded by tall trees, so we had an unbroken view of the stars. The crescent moon was just a sickle of light, and the water constellations were arcing through the southern sky. I made sure to enhance my illusion under the celestial light, for Larcen had told me *aurum blanc* had a tendency to shimmer in the starlight.

"Better?" Faelen asked, pulling me down on the bench beside him. He flashed me a smile full of sharp white teeth.

Stars above, this guy was pushier than Larcen. At least when I was with the dark elf, I wasn't creeped out.

"Yes," I answered, shifting on the bench so I could access my bladed fan with better ease.

Marigold had made a slit in the dress's seam so I could slip my hand inside for the fan strapped to my thigh without having to lift my dress. As I moved, the illusion adjusted flawlessly, and I started to feel very proud of myself. I was getting the hang of this new magical ability! My skin was as radiant as my crystal dress, glittering like crushed diamond. Beside me, Faelen sucked in his breath. I glanced at him from the corner of my eye, feeling very smug at how I was fooling this fae, but then my confidence faltered. The genteel smile on his face had turned into something sinister.

"You must be young," he said softly, but there was nothing affectionate in his voice. "An *aurum blanc* beyond the veil and without a bodyguard. Surely you must've known someone like me would find you... irresistible."

The fae lunged, seizing me by the shoulders and smothering my yelp with his golden lips. I yanked my bladed fan out of my dress at the same time the fae was yanked off me by his hair. Screeching, Faelen tumbled off the stone bench as Larcen dragged him backwards.

"Evening, Faelen," the drow greeted. "I think you know why I'm here."

"Oh fu—"

"Uh-uh, Faelen. There's a lady present." Larcen, one hand clamped on the fae's hair and the other gripping his scorpion blade, gave me brief up-down assessment. "You certainly made the right statement."

"He—You—*I was bait?*" I screeched, dropping the illusion.

"Shh. Not so loud."

"This dress... the shoes... that nice tofu pot pie you bought me so I wouldn't stuff my face here... it was all so I could be a honeytrap?"

"Yes."

"You mean you're not an *aurum blanc*?" Faelen whined. "Oh, the deception!"

Larcen gave him a little shake to shut him up. "And I lied about it being tofu. It was a chicken pot pie. This is the South, Eryn. I don't think you can even purchase tofu legally down here."

My old hatred resurfaced, and I struggled to suppress it. We had the fae calligrapher, and that was all that mattered. At least, it should've been.

I snapped open my fan and swung it so hard Larcen ripped a fistful of hair out of Faelen's scalp as he was blown into the trunk of a magnolia tree. The fae's scream was silenced when I pounced on his chest, squashing the air from his lungs. I phased into my crystal form, catching the moonlight and scattering it into a hundred tiny rainbows. Faelen's eyes bulged, but it had nothing to do with me sitting on his chest. Well, maybe it did, since I weighed as much as the average human now, but I think it was more due to my fist hovering over his mouth. I'd robbed him of his breath.

"What? Now that you've seen my personality, you don't like me anymore?" I jabbed my bladed fan under his chin. "An ogre with very pretty glyphs around his neck attacked me in a museum last night. Glyphs with *your* handwriting. Explain."

I released my fist, and the fae gasped. Coughing, he glared at me with those pretty honey eyes. "I don't know what you're talking about, you crazy b—"

My fingers clenched again, seizing his breath. Ariels were the masters of air: storms, winds, and breath alike.

"*Eryn*," Larcen seethed, smacking his way through the azalea bushes. Guess he'd been too stunned to shadow-walk. Served him right.

"You can go to the Underrealm for all I care, caveman," I said, baring my teeth at him. I turned that manic smile down at the fae, who flinched. "I thought fae had better manners. Well, maybe not *you*, but in general." I watched Faelen claw at his throat as his face took on a lovely rose-gold hue. I relaxed my grip. "Care to try again?"

Faelen wheezed and held up his hand in surrender. "What... What are you?"

"That is not an answer to my question, Faelen. I thought we had an understanding here, but apparently not. Say bye-bye to your air again."

"*Wait*. Wait." The fae cleared his throat. "Yes, yes *I* was the one who wrote on the ogre's neck, but I didn't know he was going to attack you specifically. He said I was to use his special ink and mix it with fresh vampire blood—"

"Vampire blood?" Larcen said.

Faelen nodded. "I don't know why. The glyphs he wanted were just for an illusion, the same I made for your pig's collar. Except it was to disguise the ogre as a grizzly bear instead of a fat sweaty human."

I gave Larcen a disgusted look.

Larcen shrugged. "Illusions work better if they don't have to work as hard. Rumple's a pig. It fits." Then he turned his attention back to the fae. "And who is this 'he?'"

"I don't know, I swear. I just got a fire scroll with the job request and it said the ogre would be there with the ink and the blood."

"Then how do you know it was a 'he?'"

"I don't know! The email was brief. To the point. Females are typically more wordy and prone to use emojis. I *assumed* it was a male who hired me."

Larcen glanced at me for confirmation, and I nodded. The fae was telling the truth. Reluctantly, I got off of him, and while the fae sat up, he wasn't stupid enough to make a run for it.

Faelen's eyes darted to my bladed fan as I tapped it against my thigh. "You're not telling us everything," I said. "Why would he give you specialty ink and vampire blood?" When he hesitated, I huffed an exasperated sigh and made a show of lifting my hand into the moonlight, ready to clamp it into a fist.

"He made me add two more glyphs," Faelen blurted out.

"*And?*" Larcen prompted. "By the Spider Queen, it's like pulling teeth with you, Faelen. Speaking of." The drow seized what remained of Faelen's hair and wrenched his head back, his scorpion blade poised above the fae's mouth. "I know how important your looks are to you, and while you can grow hair back, it's a lot more difficult with teeth."

"It was an incendiary glyph and a compulsion glyph! The vampire blood was to make the compulsion glyph unbreakable."

"I thought you said you didn't know what the vampire blood was for," I said, wagging my bladed fan.

Faelen just garbled a helpless sound.

"Hn. Clever." The scorpion blade lowered until the point indented against the fae's bottom lip. "And whose vampire blood did you use?"

"It was given to me!"

"Got any more?"

I gasped. Ariels didn't consort with vampires, but even we knew that vampire blood was never to be sold or used, let alone recreationally. It was sacred to them, and its distribution would incur the wrath of their covens. That Billy Macon and this calligrapher had both been given some was unheard of.

Wincing, Faelen slipped a hand into his suit pocket and withdrew a small vial. It was half full.

"You should be ashamed of yourself," I told him sternly.

The fae just glared at me.

Larcen plucked the vial from the fae's fingers and slipped it into his own pocket. Then he crouched down in front of Faelen, tapping his scorpion blade against the fae's crotch. "I don't have to tell you what will happen if you breathe a word of this to anyone, do I, Faelen?"

"N-no."

Larcen gave a little jab of his blade.

The fae yelped. "No, Prince Larcen!"

"That's what I thought." He straightened and held out his hand. He was already half in the shadows. "Let's go."

"I'll walk, thank you very much," I snapped, storming away and back to the party. There was mushroom quiche in there, and I wanted to be able to fly home with a full stomach.

CHAPTER TWENTY-THREE

Larcen

THE ARIEL HAD DOWNED seven mini mushroom quiches, three blue crab coquettes, four cheese-and-nut stuffed dates, and didn't look likely to stop as she double-fisted raw oysters on the half shell. Apparently her aversion to meat didn't extend to seafood. The girl seriously needed pockets to keep snacks in as she figured out that whole metabolism thing.

"Eryn," I hissed, snatching her arm.

My hand clutched nothing but air. I tried to grab her again, but my fingers swept right through her shoulder. This was an illusion!

"Spider bites!"

The real Eryn was somewhere else. I scanned the greenhouse and moved briskly into the parlor where the string quartet was. She'd seemed drawn to the music the nymph had played, so she might be in here. When she'd been looking for Faelen, I'd been watching her. Faelen would've heard the introduction and would've sought her out, which he had. All I had to do was make sure the shifty fae calligrapher didn't see me, otherwise he'd run, *aurum blanc* bait or not. Then it was easy to follow them outside and interfere before Faelen could do more than kiss her.

But she wasn't in the parlor. I wove through the crowd, ignoring the greetings, to the palm-bordered archway leading to the dining room. Those pitiful plants needed a good watering and some sunlight. A flash of white swept across my peripheral vision, and there was Eryn, perusing the buffet table. She'd almost blended in with the marble statues of oceanids that framed the long walls.

"*There* you are."

She glanced up, startled, and the smile that seemed a permanent fixture on her face turned down into a judgmental frown.

"What did I tell you?" I said, storming into the room. "We need to g—"

I'd taken no more than two steps before something pulsed in my chest like a second heartbeat. A moment later I saw the world grow very large as I grew very small. The light of the rose-crystal chandelier vanished as my clothes swallowed me. Panicked, I kicked free of my vest and hopped onto my shark-skin trousers.

The ariel's face looked just as panicked as I felt.

Hearing a thunderous noise behind me, I hopped out of the way as a sea witch sauntered into the dining room. Enormously fat, she teetered on tiny feet in purple stiletto heels to the side of the table with the bacon-wrapped scallops.

"Ooo!" she exclaimed, catching sight of me. "What a beautiful black rabbit. Raphael, handsome, is this one of those Wild Hunt parties where we chase a piglet around? It *is* approaching the right time of the year for that sort of thing."

"A piglet?" the changeling called from the study. "In *this* house?"

"Not a piglet," a shifter said, bending down to give me a sniff. I chattered my teeth at him. "A rabbit. With a gold necklace." The shifter's eyes turned red with delight.

"I didn't—" Raphael cut himself off as he entered the dining room, then rolled his eyes at the sight of me. "That's not a rabbit, that's—"

"Mine!" the shifter cried, lunging.

With a squeak, I hopped out of the way of his clawed hands and under the dining room table.

"Now see here, Rufus," the sea witch cried, setting her plate down with a loud clatter. "I saw that necklace first."

"Necklace?" A goblin poked his head out of the kitchen, smearing his hands on his apron. "Is it gold?"

"Ugh, you hired goblins to cater this party?" a nagini whined. The half-snake, half-woman immediately dropped the sparerib she'd been eating and spat the morsel in her mouth into a napkin. "You know they never pass the health inspection tests!"

"My bouillabaisse and croquembouche are the best in the city," another goblin in a toge snapped back, waving a wire whisk. "And my brother's pizzeria has the highest Yelp ratings in Savannah! Now where is the gold?"

"On the rabbit's neck," the shifter said, though it came out more as a growl as he completed his transformation into a wolf.

"Larcen," the ariel whispered, crouching down and holding her hands out to me.

I was just a hop or two away from her when the sea witch barreled into her, knocking her aside. "I don't think so, Little Miss Gorgeous. It's not like you need gold anyway!"

"Ladies and gentlemen, *please*," Raphael cried, tapping a spoon against his sorbet glass to get their attention. The glass shattered on the fourth *ting*. "This is not one of those *lowcountry* parties where we give way to our baser natures under the full moon and just—"

"One ssside, Rafe," said a dragonet, joining the fray.

Under the dining room table was getting pretty crowded with both the wolf shifter and the dragonet, plus an opportunistic dwarf who had gold glitter in his beard, so I made a literal leap of faith and jumped to where I'd seen the ariel last. The sea witch caught my foot, but a vicious kick sliced open her blubbery fingers and had me free again. Landing on the table, I dodged goblin claws and satyr fingers and tureens of crawfish boils. Everything became a blur in the frenzy, and I couldn't distinguish the white of the statues from the white of the ariel while I had the whole room chasing me.

Suddenly there was a shout, and a blood-curdling scream made the rose-crystal chandelier clatter above my head.

I had to pick a direction and get off this table. *There*. There was the doorway to the parlor. Beyond that was the greenhouse and the garden. If I could get outside, I could hide in the hedges. I dodged to the right just as a tentacle came slapping down, instantly transforming the suckling pig into pulled pork and flipping a bowl of spinach-and-artichoke dip into the air. The sea witch howled as hot cheese splashed onto the front of her dress and oozed between her cleavage. I put on a burst of speed, bounding between loaves of bread and ice sculptures and candelabras, the end of the table and the parlor beyond coming up fast—

A rabbit-sized screech left me as someone snatched my ears. Twisting around, I swiped with my foot in a move that would've decapitated my enemy had I been a drow. Instead my foot bounced aside from the scaled arm. Who had an invited a marsh troll to this party?

"Hu-hu-hu," the troll laughed, opening wide. "Snacky time."

I thrashed until my ears threatened to rip off my head. Of

course it'd be a troll who'd eat me. Drow hated trolls second only to ariels, and fate curse me to an eternity of servitude to the Spider Queen if I was about to die at the hands of a troll.

"Aw, no fair," the dwarf pouted.

"Get back to work, Joachim," Raphael barked.

"At least let me have the necklace," the sea witch screeched.

"Why should you get the gold?" the goblin chef demanded.

"Why should *you*?" the nagini hissed.

A fight broke out as the troll hu-hu laughed and lowered me to his gaping mouth.

"And *this* is why I don't have Wild Hunt parties," Raphael shouted at no one in particular. "It's just asking for trouble!"

Heart beating rapidly, I realized I had only one shot to get away from the troll. I stopped struggling, reserving my energy to shadow-walk. A big mouth like his cast a big shadow. Just as my left foot disappeared into the darkness, I relaxed, as if sinking below the surface of still water. Moving through shadows was like slipping through water, but much quicker. But then the troll's stubby, hippo-like teeth grazed my backside. It hadn't worked!

"*Eryn!*" I yelped, my plea coming out a shriek.

I gave one final twist, kicking my back feet out of the way and biting the troll on his slug-like tongue with all the fury my little rabbit self could muster. Black blood spurted over my face as the troll howled, flinging me into the air. I sailed cottontail over button nose, arcing over the banquet table.

"I've got it!" the nagini shouted, unhinging her jaw. Fangs as sharp as needles spread wide to welcome me.

Shiiing.

A chain linked around my middle just as a gust of air blew the nagini onto her backside. The storm wind blew her straight out of the dining room and into the foyer, scrunching up the ornate rug into an accordion under her serpent tail before she banged into the grandfather clock.

"That rug is from the Ottoman Empire," Rafael wailed, rushing from the room.

The wind vanished, and I was yanked across the dining room table, narrowly missing the fish-shaped ice sculpture. Then I was in a pair of pale arms, and pale fingers carefully unwound the chain from my middle.

"The rabbit is mine," the ariel declared. "*And* the necklace."

The wolf shifter seemed doubtful and took a step forward. Eryn lashed out with my scorpion blade, the dart slicing a thin red line across his wolfish face. Snarling, the wolf transformed back into his human form. "Ow. I was just... checking."

Eryn leveled my scorpion blade at the crowd. "Anyone else want to *check*?"

Mutterings filled the air—except for the sea witch, who was sobbing at the loss of the necklace.

"What kind of Lux Argentum fae are you?" someone wanted to know. "They're not fighters."

"That's not an *aurum blanc*, you idiot," the dragonet snarled, cupping his mouth as blood dripped from his lips. "Just look at that blood. She's... something else."

"She is the victor, and that is all that matters," a majestic voice declared. It was the centaur, a short bow in her hand and a disapproving frown on her regal face. "We must honor the hunt."

The mutterings turned to grumbles, and the crowd dispersed. The goblins made a fuss carting off the ruined dishes to the kitchen, and a bunch of brownies seemed to appear from nowhere to clean the room. The centaur stamped her foot and turned around to return to the library, giving her yellow-plumed tail a dismissive flick.

Eryn set the scorpion blade on the table where the spinach-

and-artichoke dip had been and started rubbing the scruff between my ears. "Oh your little heart. It's beating so fast."

"*You think?*" I squeaked at her, not that she could understand me. "*I was nearly eaten by a troll! Where were you?*"

Then my little rabbit nose picked up on a familiar scent. I looked up from the cradle of her arms and saw a gash on the side of her head that matched her lipstick. So that's what the dragonet had been referring to. She must've gotten that when the sea witch had body-checked her. She'd been too focused on me to phase into her crystal form. There were also half a dozen scratches raking from her shoulder down her left bicep. She'd fought something off with claws. She had bled... for me.

"Ah, there you go," she said, continuing to rub my scruff between thumb and forefinger. It felt incredible. Despite myself, I settled into a more comfortable position in the safety of her arms, eyes drooping at that marvelous sensation. "Your heartbeat's almost normal now."

Familiar footsteps marched into the room. "Miss Eryana of..." Raphael cut himself off. "Well, we both know you're not from Lux Argentum, so I won't cringe when I ask you politely to leave."

She nodded. "I apologize for any offense. Is the nagini...?"

"Oh," Raphael snorted, flapping his hand, "she'll be pissing vinegar when she comes to. But what nagini wouldn't be, right? And no offense taken, darling. It's just not safe for you both here anymore." He leaned down until he was eye-level with me. "Isn't that right, Larcen?"

The ariel's arms tightened around me.

Raphael tittered, heading to where my dark elf clothes lay in a heap on the floor. He picked them up, folded them as smartly as if he were a butler, and layered them carefully into the purple gift bag he had slung on his arm. He picked up the vial of vampire blood and gave it a long look before dropping it in with the clothes. There was another vial there full of black powder than he didn't even glance at. "Changelings can see what others cannot. That is Prince Larcen of Drozvega, plain as day."

The ariel stiffened.

Raphael gave her a genteel smile and lifted his hands as if in surrender. "Don't worry, your secret is safe with me. And here's your gift bag. Thank you for joining us this evening, Miss...?"

"Eryn."

Raphael had an expectant look on his face, waiting for her to elaborate with either her surname or realm of origin, but the ariel gave him a closed-lipped smile instead.

"Ah, Miss Eryn." Raphael's eyes changed to those of a wolf, yellow and narrowed.

"And thank you," she said, slipping the scorpion blade into the bag, "for your kindness and discretion."

"Kindness?" Raphael tittered again, his eyes returning to his favorite lynx-like look. "Oh no, darling, that's you owing me a favor. But not to worry, I'm not the depraved sort. I'll be in touch. Too-da-loo."

CHAPTER TWENTY-FOUR

Eryn

THE GNOMES WERE STACKED one on top of the other into two gnome ladders so Marigold and Henrietta could peek out the window in the door. The excitement of their faces turned to dread as I soared up the brick walk to the emporium. A gust of wind yanked open the door to the polytunnel, the sudden change in air pressure causing the gnome ladders to collapse. A second swipe of my fan made a cushion, so the terrified shrieks of the gnomes falling to their deaths three feet down to the cement floor were replaced with delightful "oohs" and "ahhhs" and "this is what it must feel like to ride on a cloud!"

"*Ma cherie*," Henrietta began, "you simply must tell me— Blight me! What happened to your makeup?"

"Where is the oppressor?" Cornelius wanted to know.

"Oh my truffles, did something happen to Master Larcen?" Rumple squealed.

"Miss Eryn?" Marigold said. "What happened, honey?"

"Larcen used me as bait," I shouted, bursting into tears.

"Rumple," Cornelius shouted, "get the brandy. The girl's in hysterics!"

"He got me this beautiful dress and these sparkly shoes and took me to dinner and had Henrietta make me all pretty so I could *seduce* a fae from Lux Argentum! He put his tongue in my mouth!"

"Ooh la la," Henrietta purred. "So it was a passionate kiss. My makeup has that effect on men."

Marigold swatted her arm. "That is *not* the point."

"Here, girl," Cornelius said, standing on tiptoe to offer me a snifter of brandy. "That'll calm your nerves."

It tasted of fermented apricots and burned all the way down. I took one sip and had to put it aside with a gasp.

"She's had a body for what, three days, and you're giving her alcohol?" Marigold shooed Cornelius away. "Where's Larcen now, honey? Did you leave him behind? Serves him right if you did."

"No," I said with a watery sniffle.

My feet touched the ground and I upended the purple gift bag. A black rabbit wiggled out from underneath the clothes and the plethora of party gifts. Larcen twitched his nose.

"Get him!" Cornelius shouted.

With a squeak the rabbit took off running as the gnomes chased him with tiny pitchforks and garden shovels. I crouched down and starting putting all the swag and clothes back into the bag. Marigold had stayed behind, collecting the lighter items like the butterfly-shaped hair stick and the vial of vampire blood. Then she offered me a stamp-sized hand-kerchief.

"Thank you," I said, using it to soak up one tear.

"You're very welcome. Now, if you'll excuse me, it sounds like they trapped the boss and I need to make sure my kin don't do anything drastic." She hurried off, her rubber galoshes squelching against the floor. "Don't kill him!"

"If you want Master Larcen, you'll have to go through me," Rumple snorted, standing with his legs braced. The black rabbit huddled under his drooping belly. "Come any closer and I'll squash you into jelly!"

"Give him up, pig," someone shouted.

Marigold whacked that someone on the head. "You do *not* speak to Rumple that way. Now, let's settle this like civilized people."

With a heavy sigh, I linked the handles of the swag bag over my wrist and took to the air. For all his faults, Larcen didn't deserve to be tortured. Besides, the more I saved him, the more he might feel indebted to me. Which meant I could guilt him into a confession that would restore my guardianship. I came to a halt by Rumple's flank and bent down to retrieve the rabbit.

"He doesn't deserve your pity," Cornelius cried.

"No, but he's going to get it anyway," I muttered, nestling the rabbit into the crook of my arm and rising into the air again.

I was halfway to my roost in the rafters—I'd accessorized it with a pillow and a small wooden crate of my meager belongings—when the polytunnel door opened. The chime above the door let out a soft melody, and Lady Chantilly sauntered into the floral emporium in a pastel-pink dress. The mermaid cut accentuated every movement with each slinking step.

"Miss Eryn, lovely to see you again, child of air," she said. "I simply *must* speak with Larcen. Where is he?"

I pointed to the rabbit in the crook of my arm.

Her green eyes widened. "Oh my."

I put the bag of swag into my wooden crate and drifted back down to her, offering the rabbit. He didn't want to go, and she didn't want to take him. He squeaked something, and she arched an eyebrow.

"Hmm," she said. "If only Buckwheat were with me. He could've translated."

"I can translate, my lady," Rumple said, knuckling one trotter and lowering his jowls in his best approximation of a bow. "I *am* a talking pig, after all."

Lady Chantilly smiled slowly, and the pig nearly swooned.

"Well, I'll start by saying I do not appreciate having to leave my store to come down here," she told the rabbit sternly. "This is twice you've blown me off, Larcen, and I am not a woman used to rejection."

The rabbit wisely said nothing.

Lady Chantilly straightened, touching her hair to make sure none of those buttercream curls had slipped out of place as she'd reprimanded him. "My tests are complete. The coating on that dagger is spider venom."

The rabbit squeaked.

"Spider venom?" Rumple translated. "Are you sure?"

"Yes. The markers are all there, though I can't tell you from what spider. Nothing from Earth or the Fae Realms or the Elven Woods, but it's a spider with yellow-green venom. Unlike the handkerchief, this had no remnants of concealment spells on them, so the tests were straightforward and nothing exploded in my face. Oh, and the pavement by the waterfront? Nothing. Our business is concluded now, so I'll be on my way." Then she turned to me and gave me a slow up-down assessment. "*Amazing* dress, Miss Eryn. Pity about the blood."

I clamped down on my bottom lip so I wouldn't cry again. I'd really loved that dress. Lady Chantilly raised a buttercream eyebrow, expecting an explanation. "We were at Raphael's party—"

"Ugh," she said immediately. "The changeling has taste, but that nymph Isadora does not. Tell me, was she there playing that piano?"

"It was the most beautiful song I'd ever heard."

"And you didn't even hear the lyrics. Did you cry?"

"No, but I wanted to."

The half-dryad looked smug. "They never do anymore, not since I left our little band. And how did you enjoy Raphael's little soiree?"

"I didn't. I got accosted by a fae and then got all this"—I gestured to the wounds on my face and arm—"defending that rodent."

"He's technically a lagomorph," Rumple interjected.

Lady Chantilly and I both sent him an unappreciative look. He withered, backing away and mumbling, and the half-dryad turned back to me.

"You bled for a dark elf?" Lady Chantilly actually sounded surprised. "How quickly you've bonded with him."

"I haven't bonded with him," I protested, but our matching dualcaster coins would say different. "It was just... Kindness goes a long way is all."

"Indeed it does. Well, enjoy the rest of your night. And it really is a pity about the dress." With all the grace of a swaying sapling, she turned on her heel and left.

"I know a thing or two about getting bloodstains out of clothing, Miss Eryn," Trudy said, cracking her meaty knuckles. "Rose thorns be nasty sometimes."

"Just rose thorns?" Henrietta quipped.

"Why don't you go and shower off, honey?" Marigold said. "Nothing a stream of hot water can't fix."

I nodded numbly, setting the swag bag and the rabbit on the counter as I moved towards the barracks. "Nobody touch him."

"But," Cornelius began.

"Nobody. Touch. Him."

Marigold smacked Cornelius on the back of the head, making his pointy yellow hat slide into his eyes. "You heard her."

"You can count on me, Miss Eryn," Rumple said, climbing awkwardly into his rolly chair. "He won't be missing one whisker while you're gone."

"Maybe he should," Marigold said as I pushed open the break room door. "Maybe losing a whisker will teach him to show that girl at the very minimum some civility. She is a rose you're shoving away into a dark corner, Mr. Larcen. One day she'll lose her blooms and become all thorns and then you'll get a taste of your own medicine. Only it won't be indifference pricking you. It'll be wrath."

ALL THAT FOOD I'd scarfed down at the buffet, before getting barreled over by a sea witch and wrangling a dragonet, had given me plenty of energy. Under the water, I phased into my crystal form and let the blood sluice away and stain the water red. The crystal form also sealed my wounds, so when I returned to the shape of a woman, fine silver scars were the only remainder of my tussle. I was ravenous again, but I didn't have time to think about food. Larcen's curse was starting to become *very* inconvenient.

It had a rhythm to it too: in the wee hours of the night—2:32 a.m., if I'd gauged the position of the stars correctly, and I always did—and always a small animal. So far. I couldn't pick out the similarities between a goldfish, a cricket, and a rabbit, but there had to be one. Curses, while horrible, were still elegant in their design, and often simpler than one originally thought. The timing and the shapeshifting were connected, I just didn't know *how* yet.

The curse also cut into the time we could spend actively trying to pursue the dark mage. Whenever Larcen turned, we always retreated to the emporium to wait until he changed back, and then we had to wait on customers—which were coming in droves, thanks to that new website and its risqué garden figurines—before we could pursue our next lead. I couldn't do anything about that spider venom coating on Billy Macon's knife, but I could do something about that vampire blood.

I turned off the water with an angry jerk. Well, I was tired of getting my butt handed to me. I was tired of following Larcen around like a wind-swept butterfly. I was a guardian and I didn't need permission from anyone to get a job done.

A quick phase into my mist form dispelled the water from my skin, and then I donned that flame-red wrap dress, tying it shut with an intricate knot. The color emboldened me, just like my feather armor had, and I stalked back into the polytunnel in my knee-high black heels, my white hair streaming like a cloud behind me.

"Ooo, slay it, queen!" Roberto crowed.

"I like the boots," Trudy said. "You could kick some serious fanny in those boots."

"Oh, *ma cherie*," Henrietta said, "you simply must let me redo your makeup. A flame lip is required to complete this marvelous ensemble."

The rabbit gave a hop and reared back on his hind legs.

"Um, Miss Eryn, Master Larcen wants to know why you look like you're going back out again," Rumple said.

"Because we are." I dug around in the swag bag and yanked out the vial of vampire blood. "What were you going to do with this?"

The rabbit chattered something resentfully.

"No, Master Larcen," Rumple gasped. "That blood mage is trouble. You don't want anything to do with her!"

"What did he say?" I demanded.

Rumple looked uncomfortable, but he answered, "Larcen said he was going to take it the Bonekeeper."

"Good. Then that's who we'll go see."

Steeling my courage, I phased into mist and disappeared down the compost chute, careful not to touch the sides. Berthold's mouth opened eagerly at my approach, but I whizzed past the pitcher plant. "Easy breezy, this is all easy breezy," I repeated to myself as the lampblossoms illuminated with my passage. I headed straight to the honeycomb shelves, looking neither up nor down, left or right. The walls couldn't close in on me if I didn't see them. I stopped at the shelf that held Billy Macon's belongings and plucked the vial of vampire blood from his utility belt. If we were going to see a blood mage, I wanted to be *very* sure.

As I turned to fly back up the chute and get back into that sweet fresh air of the polytunnel, there was that silver glint again, flashing across my periphery and disappearing just as quickly.

I *knew* I'd seen something before. I looked again at the shelves from the corner of my eye, and there was the silver flash again, one in each cubby. It was near impossible to pick out what it was, what with that bejeweled dagger in one cubby and the jewels the ogre had looted from the Smithsonian in the other, including that massive blue diamond that must cost a fortune. Larcen would just tell me it was the light reflecting off a facet, but I'd seen the star forge smithies as a child. I knew what celestial silver looked like.

My smile turned smug. What would Larcen have to say now?

"Miss Eryn, are you alright down there?" Rumple called. "Do you need a Xanax?"

The pig's voice plucked me from my thoughts of belts woven from celestial silver and bladed fans beaten from starlight metal. Feeling the panic of being underground starting to set in, I hurried back up the chute. The gnomes had crowded around the counter, eyeing the rabbit, but no one had made a move. I tossed both vials into the swag bag, slung it over my wrist, and scooped up the rabbit.

I wouldn't tell him now. I wanted to see his face when I told him we needed to take another look at those possessions and he realized I was right.

The rabbit chittered as we reached the door, but I didn't need Rumple to translate.

"No time like the present. Your curse may hinder you, but it doesn't have to hinder *us*." I turned to Rumple. "Where can I find this Bonekeeper?"

"The cemetery, of course."

CHAPTER TWENTY-FIVE

Eryn

BONAVENTURE CEMETERY WAS by the water on the eastern part of the city, and a fog lifted off the Wilmington River that seemed to shroud everything in gray gauze.

Silent as the fog, I soared over the iron gate, thinking belatedly that maybe the black romper Maven had given me would've been a better choice than the flame-red wrap dress. But the wrap dress had pockets, which I had filled with snacks. Peanut butter crackers and fruit leathers were there if I needed them, courtesy of Rumple's snack drawer behind the counter.

The rabbit poked his head out of the purple swag bag, his ears swaying in the wind, as I soared down one of the paved paths. There was a somber feeling here, deepened in the dark. Rhododendrons, ferns, and azaleas formed niches where tombs could lay silent, and sprawling live oaks with their tendrils of moss shaded everything else. Statues loomed in night, standing vigil over the fallen.

Under Larcen-via-Rumple's instructions, I followed the path along the river. I continued my course even when the path turned inward, entering Greenwich Cemetery—the overlooked cemetery in Savannah, according to the guidebooks. It had more lawns and less-intimate places, spotted here and there with trees, but the walk by the river was well-shaded and kept me away from anyone who might be out at this hour. Even if they did see a woman with a cloud of white hair dressed in red and flying six feet off the ground, they would never believe it.

Like Bonaventure Cemetery, the path turned inward, away from the river, but the rabbit squeaked, urging me to continue straight down a dirt path. It opened into a clearing, which wasn't marked by any tombs, and still the rabbit urged me onward. I broke through the trees and onto marshland. And there, looming like a bristly thistle, was a coppice of trees at the end of the marshes.

The hollow reeds clacked against each other, sending a warning as the river wind stirred them. Night herons ducked as I flew over them, and snakes slithered in the water. Frogs, normally dormant at this hour, jumped away as my wake rustled the reeds. I had to fly low here for cover, and though every instinct in me told me to phase into mist or crystal, I resisted. My Steorra bloodline made the transition seamless, but now that I had a body that needed food to fuel it instead of celestial dew and pollen—so inefficient!—it took more energy to change. I might need that when I met the Bonekeeper.

The coppice of trees loomed high, so thick it blotted out the horizon behind it. The marsh gave way to sawgrass once more, but I didn't touch down. This was an eerie place, and I didn't want to give it a hold on me more than it already had, and that included its dirt on the soles of my boots.

Carefully, I extracted one of the bladed fans from my belt and entered the forest.

I followed the lone dirt path through the winding trees until it emptied into the heart of this forbidden place. The lawn here was overgrown and trampled, but the trees weren't overgrown, instinctually knowing not to crowd the crypt of dark gray stone. Brown leaves smothered the flat top and crowded around the edges, as if trying to sink it down into the earth where it belonged. It had no door that I could see, just a statue on the south-facing side.

It was a woman with short curling hair that clustered around her head like snail shells. She leaned over a scallop-shaped basin, her pitcher tipped, but the waterworks must've been broken because both were empty. The statue didn't look perturbed at the fact, just patient and serene. She seemed quite out of place here, trapped in a forest surrounded by river and marsh.

Carefully, I set the swag bag down on the flattened grass and gave the statue a closer inspection. Dark lichen seemed to be growing on the spout of the pitcher, but other than that, nothing seemed out of place.

"Are you sure this is the right place?"

The rabbit nodded.

"So... what now?"

Rumple had only told me where to go, not what to do when I got there. I'd never met a blood mage before, but I had imagined her quite like a witch, skulking in a crypt instead of a cottage. There was a crypt here, sure, but no skulking blood mage or a way to summon her.

The rabbit squeaked and rubbed its paws together. No, not rubbing. *Slicing.* He wanted me to cut myself.

I put my hands on my hips as I hovered. "And then what?"

The rabbit extended his paw and mimed a drip.

I looked back at the pitcher. That wasn't lichen on its spout at all.

I shuddered inwardly and pressed one of the points of my bladed fan into my thumb. Hovering my thumb over the pitcher's spout, I squeezed out a fat red drop. It splattered silently, absorbing into the stone. Phasing into crystal, I sealed the wound and waited.

There was a gurgling of water from within the pitcher, and suddenly red liquid sluiced over the spout and poured into the scallop-shaped basin. I flew back, aghast, and watched with both fans flared as the statue's plinth began to move. It was attached to the crypt's south-facing wall, and the entire thing—statue, plinth, and door, apparently—moved as one unit on an unseen mechanism. No wonder the grass was trampled here. The red water petered out to a drip just as the door finished opening with a light *foom*. An exhale of the underground crypt greeted us, and sconces along the left wall burst into flames. Stairs led down, lit by the flickering red light.

"Nope!"

The rabbit chattered his teeth at me. He grabbed the swag bag in his teeth and hopped awkwardly to the mouth of the crypt. Then he waited, impatiently tapping one of his large hind feet.

Well, you went into Larcen's freaky underground dungeon-training room all by yourself just an hour ago. This is just the freaky underground home of a blood mage. What could possibly go wrong?

Swallowing the hard lump that had lodged in my throat, I phased into crystal and followed the rabbit as he hopped down the stairs into the crypt.

RED LIGHT LED the way to a burial chamber. My skin crawled at the sight of all those shelves cut into the stone walls, mounds of ash in every one of them and shrouded by cobwebs for as far as I could see. Though the room was wide and very, very long—disappearing into the darkness where I'm sure it extended in a network of tunnels and other burial chambers underneath the entirety of both Bonaventure and Greenwich Cemeteries—the ceiling was far too low. Surely the earth above us would collapse in on us at any second, so I lingered by the stairway, where it was a short twelve feet up to the surface above. Thank Selena for that steady breeze that reminded me that an endless sky awaited me.

Not too far from the stairs was a slab of limestone, as long as a coffin and just as wide, like a plinth with no statue. The humming stone seemed to absorb the light around it, glowing with a muted white shimmer. Beyond it were rectangular recesses in the floor where dark liquid lay stagnant. Pools of... I didn't want to think about it. And bones. Bones everywhere in heaps like swept-up rubbish. They weren't sorted, skulls and thigh bones and ribs all jumbled together, and unlike the ashes in the shelves, these were cobweb free. Shiny, even. Cared for.

And that caretaker loomed at the far end of the burial chamber, just within the light of the sconces.

I gasped when I realized she was there, and then she wasn't. A blur of black-and-red shadows charged down the stone aisle between the pools, black nails manifesting first as the blood mage gripped the limestone slab before the rest of her body materialized. Whereas my skin was the healthy pale of moonlight, hers was the ash-white pallor of death. Her slim forearms disappeared into a tattered black robe full of holes, and her long hair, black and lank, hung like withered reeds. Red eyes like pinpricks of light bored out of her hood. I couldn't see her face, and I was very happy about that.

"Mmm," the blood mage purred, raising her chin and sniffing, though I couldn't see her face. "Haven't seen you around these parts before. But there's something familiar about that rabbit."

The rabbit stood his ground, but his back legs were trembling.

I had to swallow a few times before my throat would work. I wasn't afraid of this creature, but experience told me to be cautious. If anything I was more worried about the crypt door closing suddenly and trapping me instead. "I've come here for your help."

"Your name, child," the blood mage hissed. "Introductions. The niceties must be observed."

"I am Eryn." I gave her a bright smile.

"Agatha. The Bonekeeper."

She kept a lot more than bones, it would seem, but I wasn't about to contradict how she introduced herself. The blood mage swept her hand, palm up, across the shimmering limestone slab. "Why have you come here?"

I retrieved the vials of vampire blood from the swag bag and set them on the center of the limestone slab. The one from Billy Macon's utility belt was black with artistic gold script and a gold cap, and then one we'd taken from Faelen was simple glass. "This is vampire blood. I need you to tell me whose, and where I can find them, if that's possible. Please."

The blood mage didn't touch them. "And payment?"

"I have a credit card." I pulled the piece of plastic out of my pocket. Rumple had given me the company card, imploring me not max it out since he still had to order a case of whole frozen chickens next week. I didn't know why a plant nursery needed frozen chickens, but I hadn't had the time to ask.

Agatha threw her head back with a laugh that shook stone dust from the ceiling. I swear the ashes in their shelves shifted back from the sound.

"I need something of sustenance, child." The blood mage gestured behind her to the piles of bones and the dark pools.

Carefully, I put the package of peanut butter crackers Rumple had given me onto the limestone slab.

"Something with a little more *life*, Eryn."

The rabbit kicked when I picked him up and set him on the humming limestone slab. Instead of hopping off and running for the nearest shadow, the rabbit froze to the spot, ears plastered against his head.

"Two vials, two payments."

I didn't have another rabbit, and she didn't want my peanut butter crackers, so what else did I have to offer beside myself? Well, she *was* a self-professed bonekeeper, so maybe she'd take something that had been attached to something alive not a few hours ago.

I rooted around in the swag bag and produced the dragonet's canine tooth. I'd ripped it out of the creature's head after it had raked its claws down my arm. Or maybe it had raked its claws down my arm because I'd ripped the tooth out of its head. The series of events were a little fuzzy—it was a brawl, after all—but it served him right for trying to eat Larcen.

"Ooo." The blood mage smacked her lips and plucked the tooth from me before I could set it down beside the frozen rabbit. "My, my. Where did you get this?"

"Battle."

"Mmm. Even better." The tooth disappeared into the hood. There was a sucking sound, and when the hand pulled back the tooth was cleaner than when it had still been attached to the dragonet's head. "Delicious." The blood mage threw the bone over her shoulder, the nearest pile rattling with its newest member.

Agatha turned back to the vials. "Vampire blood, you say? How naughty."

She uncapped Billy Macon's vial and a long pale-pink tongue snaked out of her hood to catch a gelatinous drop. The blood sat in a syrupy pool for a moment or two before dissolving into her tongue, much like my blood had been absorbed by the statue's stone pillar. The long tongue hung suspended in the air as the blood mage repeated the process with the ogre's vial. This blood was fresher and dissolved almost instantly. Then, like a retractable measuring tape, the long tongue zipped away into the hood.

"It is not two vampires you seek, but one," the blood mage intoned. "This blood is identical."

She slung the uncapped vials across the limestone slab, and the blood hit with a wet slap. Then the blood splatter slithered and rolled to a sphere and lifted off the slab. The sphere twisted, lengthening itself into a leech. It twisted away from its mistress and hissed at us. While I recoiled, the rabbit did nothing, not even twitching his nose.

"Follow the leech. It will bring you back to its master," the blood mage said. "Keep it away from sunlight, if you can, otherwise it will burn like its master would."

"Um, thank you."

The blood mage snickered. "Such manners."

"Well... I'll just go now and follow the leech. Bye." With a gust of air, I retrieved the vials, capped them, and gathered the swag bag. When I reached for the rabbit, the blood mage's hand shot out, hovering above the rabbit's head.

"What life is offered to the feasting stone must stay," she snarled. "That is the price."

"Oh." I glanced at all the shelves with their ashes and then back to this feasting stone. "I see."

"I hope it was worth it, Eryn," she cackled.

Clutching the swag bag to my chest, I floated back to the staircase, eyes never wavering from the Bonekeeper. The leech was already in the stairwell, slithering through the air like a loyal hound intent on returning to its master. The moment the light of the torches stretched my shadow across the burial chamber floor, I spun and flew up the steps.

It took less than two seconds, but it had felt like an eternity. The moment I was clear, the crypt door started to shut behind me. The leech was slithering away, expecting me to follow it, but I just couldn't until I knew that crypt was sealed. It closed with a resounding boom that shook the layer of leaves from its roof, adding to the leaf litter that shored up against its walls.

Then an enraged scream echoed up from the ground, and I knew it was time to follow the leech and get the Underrealm out of there. Cradling the swag bag close as I flew over the marsh, I peered down at the quivering rabbit inside, the *real* rabbit. "Guess the blood mage doesn't find illusionary rabbits very filling, does she?"

CHAPTER TWENTY-SIX

Larcen

ONE MOMENT I had the wind blowing in my long rabbit ears and the next it whipped my long warrior braid out behind me like the business end of a chimera's tail.

The ariel yelped as the swag bag ripped apart and I, a dark elf once more, tumbled to the ground. I landed in a crouch on a tombstone as a circle of swag rained around me. A butterfly hair stick, nail polish that made the wearer more attractive, a makeup compact, seeds that if you planted them would grow flowers that would sing to you, a handful of mixed jewels, assorted candies, and... a coffee mug with "Grow, Dammit" written next to the image of a sprouting pea shoot.

We were donating these to be used in swag bags now?

I dropped the mug when a pair of sharkskin trousers hit me in the face.

"Get dressed," the ariel urged, lobbing my vest and then my scorpion blade at me. "You're going to make us lose the leech!"

"I can't believe you made us go to the Bonekeeper when I was still a rabbit!" I yanked on my trousers and buttoned on the damask vest as the ariel collected the swag into the coffee mug.

"Well at least I had the good sense to put a fake rabbit on the that offering slab," she snapped back at me. Straightening, she swiped the hair away from her face and gave me a dazzling, unhinged smile. "You're welcome!"

That had been a clever idea. She'd only had her illusion-creating powers for a few days, and she was already swindling fae and blood mages alike.

"You shouldn't have given her your name," I chastised. "Now she knows who to seek revenge on."

"With you pissing off Pegasus Express and lying to DUO, I was starting to feel left out."

I caught her wrist as she floated by. "That is what *I* do. Not you. You're... kind."

Kind to protect me from the gnomes, noble to fight off a room full of fascinari, brave to come to the blood mage alone.

Her white eyebrows flew upwards like cranes taking flight. "Did you just... compliment me?"

I dropped her wrist. "It was an observation only."

"Here's another observation. The leech is getting away. And the dawn is here!" She flew after the bloody thing, leaving me to catch up. Since when had she become such a go-getter?

Elves of any kind could run fast, but that leech was on a mission and that ariel was not waiting for me. I shadow-walked to keep up, resurfacing only to pick out my next shadow down the street as we chased the leech all the way to the copper-green fountain on Lafayette Square. The twin steeples of the Cathedral of St. John the Baptist rose above the trees, watching over the little park with its brick walks and wrought iron lampposts. The fountain gurgled away even at night, and I snatched the leech before it could dive into the basin.

"Why would its master be in a water fountain?" the ariel asked. "Is the leech broken? Did that blood mage swindle me?"

"Says the girl who just swindled a blood mage." I tightened my hand on the leech before it could it could wiggle away. The slow dawn of the new morning was already making the leech sizzle. We had to get it out of the sunlight. "And it's not broken. This is the entryway to Midnight Crossings. At least in Savannah."

The ariel stilled. She'd heard of it, then. Good.

"But we can only access it around midnight, so the way is closed until tonight." The leech hissed as steam lifted from its red skin. "Come on. We need to get this leech out of the light until tonight. Hopefully the spell won't expire and you haven't swindled a blood mage for nothing."

I left the ariel to follow at her own pace, shadow-walking back to the emporium in record time. The leech was starting to leave a smear of red on my fingers that made holding it even more difficult.

"Blight me," Marigold cried. "What is that?"

I hurried past the gnomes and seized the first container I could find that wasn't transparent or had any holes. Another oversized Grow, Dammit mug slammed against the potting station, trapping the leech in darkness. It didn't like that and started thrashing to get out.

I pressed both hands on the top and struggled to keep the mug from jerking off the potting station and shattering against the floor. "I need something heavy, quick!"

As a handful of gnomes rushed to find something, Marigold jerked them to a stop with an "Uh-uh!" Then she turned back to me. "What's in it for us?"

"I have a blood magic spell under here that'll expire if the sunlight hits it—our only lead into finding the dark mage—and you're using this time now to extort me?"

Marigold nodded. "Uh-huh. What's it to ya?"

"If this leech dies, Eryn would've tricked a blood mage for nothing," I said, hoping to appeal to the gnome's fondness for the ariel.

It worked. "Eryn tricked the Bonekeeper? Blight me, if she ever gets out of her crypt, she'll come straight for her!"

"This is not a time for sentiment," Cornelius said, climbing the leg of the potting station and shooing the other gnome aside. "Don't let your tender female sensibilities obscure our mission for equal rights!"

"Tender female—that's Eryn we're talking about!" Marigold brandished her garden hoe.

"I can't hold this forever," I shouted.

"I'm coming, Master Larcen," Rumple said in a muffled voice, dragging a bag of pea gravel between his teeth.

"Boys," Cornelius thundered. "Stop that pig!"

The gnomes hurried to obey.

"But I shared my prickly pear jam with you," Rumple wailed.

The talking pig successfully blockaded, Cornelius pulled a piece of paper from his overalls and made a deliberate show of unfolding it. He followed it up by producing a miniature pair of wire-rimmed glasses that he settled on the end of his nose. "Let's see what's at the top of the list. Oh yes, the espresso machine. Followed by—"

Marigold whacked him in the back of the knees with her hoe, and Cornelius crumpled in a heap with a yelp. Then she sprinted to the edge of the table and gave a sharp whistle. "Trudy! And someone get Leroy!"

As I struggled to contain the mug—the leech was impossibly strong—the ariel finally appeared in the doorway, her own oversized mug clutched in her hands. "Is the leech okay?"

"It will be, eventually," I ground out. "If I can just weigh this down with something."

The Bavarian barmaid joined us on the table and hoisted the enormous garden snail up behind her with a rope wrapped around its shell.

Marigold whacked Cornelius in the gut with her garden hoe to keep him down and then shoved it into my face. "Strawberries *and* peaches in the morning. We don't even care if they're previously frozen."

"We prefer fresh," Cornelius sulked, rubbing his midsection.

"Deal," I barked.

Marigold whistled again, and Leroy zoomed a slime trail around the edge of the mug that looked and smelled like rubber cement. Trudy clambered on top of the mug, smacked my hands out of the way, and plunked her muscled backside down. Then her countenance shifted, turning into stone.

The leech inside still thrashed, but the mug itself didn't move an inch.

"That's... incredible."

"That's gnome power for ya," Marigold said proudly. "We're like little lead weights when we wanna be."

"Now what?" the ariel asked.

"Now we wait until midnight."

ERYN STARED AT THE GROW, Dammit mug, a bag of Ruffles potato chips in her hand. She lifted cheddar-and-sour-cream chips to her mouth in a monotonous rhythm, her jade eyes never wavering from the mug and the little *tink-tink-tink* noises that emanated from within. It'd been like that all day, and now that the sun had set, the leech had resumed its thrashing with renewed vigor. "That is so freaky."

"Yeah," I said. We'd had to deter garden kink customers all day, thinking it was some interactive display.

235

Still riveted on the mug, she offered me the bag. "Chip?"
"Yeah."

JUST BEFORE MIDNIGHT found us back at the fountain in Lafayette Square, the leech struggling to get loose from my hand. I had its tail pinched between two fingers and more than once it had tried to whip around and nip me.

"Let's do this fast," the ariel said. She had her Grow, Dammit mug of swag from Raphael's party clutched between both hands, insisting that *something* inside might prove useful on our little quest. "Before you turn into a grub or something. In, out, easy breezy."

"Midnight Crossings is not a place to get lost in, though many do," I told her. "Stay close."

For once, she didn't argue.

CHAPTER TWENTY-SEVEN

Larcen

An INCANTATION LATER, we emerged perfectly dry on the other side of the entryway in a field of darkness. There was only one thing in this pocket 'verse and that was the city of Midnight Crossing, an oasis of light in an otherwise perpetual darkness. Its Baroque architecture was startling against the vast blackness, every decoration standing out in stark relief as the city and the torches on the battlements of the wall that encased it threw their light into nothingness. Well, it wasn't exactly nothingness, more like the grassy parking lot you see around traveling carnivals, except this was peat moss. And the darkness snapped and popped with bits of light, like cameras in a darkened concert hall, as fascinari from all over the globe and beyond entered the parking lot.

The visitors traipsed over the peat moss to the city's sole entrance, a massive gate guarded by two of the largest ogres I'd ever seen. They made the one we'd battled in the Smithsonian look like a toddler. Each gripped a club the size of a man in a meaty fist, scanning and grunting at the visitors like guard dogs at an airport terminal. Frankly, I think Hades copied the whole idea when he made Cerberus for his Underworld.

"Ooo," the ariel whispered. "It's so pretty."

I would've used the terms "grand" or "imposing," and her word choice made me realize that though she had heard of Midnight Crossings, she was not prepared for this visit at all. That look of childlike wonder on her face would have to go, otherwise her innocence might as well be a signal flare to the criminals that infested this place that we were here to be targeted, attacked, robbed, and otherwise manhandled in a most unpleasant manner.

While I doubted she could sustain an illusion for the length of time we'd be here—because who knew how long that was going to be—I knew we could do one thing, and that was change her outfit. She was still in last night's clothes—the red wrap dress and black high-heel boots—so there was definitely something to work with. "Take off your clothes," I said.

She answered by slapping me across the face.

I gritted my teeth against the sting. "I'll rephrase. Take off your top."

Jade eyes blazing, she swung at me again, this time with her bladed fan. I caught her wrist mid-swing and barked, "They see you dressed like that and you might as well be serving yourself up on a silver platter. Take off your top, and you'll wear my vest."

"*This* is a dress. I can't just 'take off my top.'"

I released her with a little shove and started unbuttoning my vest. "That leech is getting away. Make it work."

Eryn yanked the vest from my hands and waited until I'd turned around to change. She was quick, quicker than even my sisters when they were readying for battle. She practically jabbed me in the kidney to tell me she was done. "There. Happy now?"

I turned and found that she'd kept the dress knotted at her waist and had just shrugged out of the top part. It layered her bottom half very much like a gypsy skirt, and the black damask vest offset her luminous white skin and hair. Combined with the black books she already wore, she looked like she could walk into any criminal underground and immediately become its queen.

"Acceptable," I said.

"And what about you?"

"Drow are barbarians, don't you remember? I'll be just fine."

"I meant your chest, caveman."

I looked down at the pulsing green light just above my heart. Spider bites, I hadn't thought of that.

The ariel rooted around in her Grow, Dammit mug and pulled out a compact. On the top was a gilded black rose, and on the bottom, the ariel read, "'New Moon Rose, for those blacker-than-midnight looks.' Think this'll work?"

"Do it."

The ariel quickly dabbed some of the gel-like makeup on my chest, smothering the green glow. "There. Now you don't look so cursed. Smile a bit and maybe you'll actually convince people you aren't."

"Drow don't smile."

"Oh right, I forgot you lot are emotionally stunted creatures. Shall we?"

The crowd had more or less dispersed by the time we caught up to the leech, and the ogres grunted as we passed through the archway. In addition to actual gates, above us dangled a thick metal door, more like a guillotine than a portcullis, ready to drop and seal the city away from any attack, crushing anyone who dawdled in the threshold. The ariel gave the ogre nearest her a friendly wave and was in the middle of saying thank-you when I grabbed her like she was my halfwit sister and hurried us across.

"It's bad enough I have to wear this vest, which *reeks* of mildew, but do you *have* to touch me?" she demanded.

"That's mushroom musk, thank you very much."

Suddenly she seized my arm and pointed. "The leech. It's getting away!"

The bloody thing had indeed put on a burst of speed, eagerly thrashing its tail back and forth as it slithered through the air. Lurching forward, I caught the thing by the tail. It would not do for us to be seen actively using a tracking spell. The leech whipped around and hissed at me.

"If you didn't like that, you're not going to like this." I adjusted my hand to hold the leech like I would a snake, right behind the head. The thing wriggled, hissing, but then it calmed as I began moving again. It could still go to its master, but I was going to keep it on a very tight leash.

Eryn wisely kept her feet on the ground as the leech guided us farther into the city. It was clearly taking us to the Market, and soon the nicer and well-lit avenues and shops gave way to dark, uneven flagstones and as much grime on the stone walls as there was rubbish in the streets. Not even torchlight seemed to penetrate very far in this gloom. The transition was fully made with the appearance of the pubs and taverns, which weren't the ones you entered just for a pint.

"Stars above," the ariel exclaimed, rushing to the alley between pubs.

"Eryn, we do not have time for one of your little crusades. Get back here!"

Between stacked barrels of ale and bales of hay there was a pen for keeping pigs... and apparently anyone who couldn't pay their bar tab. Inside with rooting pigs were a couple of trolls snoring off their last few pints, a merman singing sea shanties, a human sorcerer sitting on an overturned bucket and drooling into his robes, and the filthiest unicorn I'd ever seen. The orc guard leaning against the pen yanked his pipe from his mouth and threw a burly arm across the gate as the ariel rushed forward. "Nobody leaves without paying what they owe to Shots and Chops. You a relative?"

"How dare you cage a unicorn," the ariel seethed.

"Wha? That old blighter?"

The unicorn lifted his head and gave an indignant whinny.

"I demand you release him at once," she said. "Clearly there's been some sort of mistake. Either that or you plan to eat him, in which case I'll alert the authorities at once."

The orc looked over her shoulder at me and lifted his bushy eyebrows. *Is she for real?*

"Don't look at him! I'm the one talking to you. Now I demand you release him! Just look at his coat, all black and grimy and covered in—I don't even want to think about it. Even his horn has lost its luster!"

The unicorn lowered his head with its dark horn and let out a dejected snort, scraping a hoof through the slop.

"Look how you've broken his spirits. Shame on you."

"You gonna pay or yell at me all night?" the orc barked back.

"This is extortion!"

"This is Midnight Crossings." The orc held out his hand, flapping his fingers. "Money."

"I don't have money—"

"Bah." The orc returned to his lean against the fence, replacing the pipe between his teeth and then pulling his sword free of its scabbard. He put the point in the dirt and twirled the hilt, making the metal flash. "Then go."

"—but I do have this." The ariel pulled an emerald the size of her thumb out of her mug. "Is this enough?"

The orc made a hasty grab for the emerald, but the ariel blocked his hand with her bladed fan. Then she put the emerald on the gate post opposite of the orc and shielded it with her fan. "The unicorn first."

The pen was hastily unlocked and the unicorn staggered out, making sure to step on both of the orc's feet on his way to freedom. The orc howled, staggering against the fence, and the emerald rattled on its post before dropping into the slop. Then the drunkards lunged for the emerald, and the orc had to beat them off with his fists. Soon the orc was as filthy as they were, and the ariel turned back to the street with her nose in the air. "Serves him right."

In the street, the unicorn seemed worse in the better light than he had in the murk of the pig pen. He stank of sour mash and smoke and mud, his mane and tail tangled. There also may or may not have been a rat clinging to his mane.

"Oh you poor thing," the ariel cooed, "you've probably gone lame in there or have hoof rot for you troubles."

The unicorn bobbed his head and staggered again.

"Eryn," I hissed, "we don't have time for this." The leech was really struggling now, so close to its master yet so far away. And the fewer who knew we had a tracking spell the better, even if it was just this disgusting nag of a unicorn.

"Here. Can you hold this?" She fitted a marble-sized ruby between his lips. "We passed by an apothecary on Belladonna Avenue."

The unicorn sucked the ruby behind his teeth and lipped at her hand for more.

"Oh, you don't think that'll cover it?" she asked, fishing around in her mug. "You're such a mess, you're probably right. Here's another one."

"Come *on*."

She flashed me a close-lipped smile, her eyes sharper than

cut glass. Then she turned back to the unicorn and was about to give his neck a pat when she thought better of it. "Surely that will set you straight. And then get out here. This is no place for a unicorn."

The unicorn bobbed his head in brisk agreement.

"That's it," I told her, turning on my heel. "I'm going."

"Okay, well, bye now." She gave the unicorn a little wave and hurried after me.

"This leech is about to sink its teeth into my fingers. I am *not* getting blood poisoning."

"You get back from this world what you put out," she said, a bright, cutting smile on her face. "Just think how much happier you'd be if you weren't so nasty all the time. That unicorn needed our help!"

"Fine, I'll work on being not so nasty if you promise to keep *up*."

She smiled again, this time genuinely at the thought of me improving my manners. The girl had yet to grasp sarcasm, apparently. She was just an innocent-eyed calf, and I was leading her straight into the slaughterhouse.

Whereas the city was run by Forge, an actual sprite, the Market was controlled by the succubus, Tiana. She had a cut of every operation, thugs to enforce the law—or break it, as she saw fit—and nothing was off limits. You wanted rare, exotic ingredients for your banquet table that may or may not have been an endangered species and unethically sourced, you came to the Market. You wanted to bind someone to indentured servitude for a couple of generations, you went to the calligraphers like Faelen in the Market. You wanted to buy vampire blood, you apparently came to Acquiesce.

The leech writhed in my hand as we entered the club.

It was the place to go when nowhere else in the Market could meet your particular need. It was classified a club for business purposes, but it was much more than that. At the kitchen door you could order "the special" and leave with a produce crate of baby kitsune foxes to sell for their tails or a Styrofoam container of baby krakens. At the bar, when you were ordering your Midnight Drop or Centaur Kick, you could ask for the bartender to make it "strong" and get a sachet of powered fairy wings to snort for an immediate lift. I know because I may or may not have used to sell Night Dust as a medicinal compound for overcoming anxiety. It certainly did that, lowering your inhibitions and making the world come alive with pretty-pretty lights. And in the back of the club, guarded by two burly minotaurs, was Baguette, the only place to offer fresh-baked pastries to their female patrons to devour unashamedly as they watched men with only 8 percent body fat or less strip.

One of the minotaurs chuckled as we walked past, skirting around the dance floor for the shadowy booths and tables. "Never thought to see you back here, drow. You took it pretty hard when we clocked you in at a chubby eight-point-one-five percent."

"Your calipers were rigged," I hissed.

The thunderous rumble of their chuckles faded away as we moved towards the booths. The leech was thrashing like a fire-hose, and I was surprised at how much strength I needed to prevent it from slipping loose. I tried to act nonchalant as I struggled to control this tracking spell, but I wasn't doing a very good job.

The cool touch of the ariel almost made me jump as she slid her hand into the crook of my elbow. That was the second time she'd touched me tonight without revulsion, or hostility. It gave me the excuse I needed to clamp the fist I had holding the leech to my chest for added support. The ariel lent her strength, keeping my shoulders from jerking, and to the outside eye it looked like I was simply escorting an ethereal fae gypsy queen to her table.

Impossibly, the leech's thrashings increased when we approached the corner booth, and by the way it was tugging, it wanted to arrow directly into the male's chest.

The vampire lounged with a woman under each arm and a few bottles of whatever the ladies were drinking in ice buckets on the table in front of him. Fresh fang marks dotted the brunette's neck, and from the looks of it, he was letting the redheaded nymph work herself up into an anticipatory frenzy before he deigned to pierce her flesh.

I recognized this ancient vampire immediately, though he looked no more than forty. A chiseled, perfectly-stubbled, blue-eyed devil of a forty-year-old. With his charcoal-colored hair slicked back and his silk shirt unbuttoned to his navel, he looked every inch of a cartel boss, but I knew his roots were even older. "Wilhelm."

"Oh please," the vampire purred, all trace of his Germanic accent gone. "Anyone who brings such a morsel to me as this moonlit beauty here can call me Bob." Then he actually *looked* at me, and his cavalier attitude disappeared. "Drain me. It's *you*."

The ariel's hand slipped from my elbow and I released the leech in my hand. It hit the vampire straight in the sternum, burrowing into his chest. Wilhelm lurched upright, clutching at his chest and gasping, and then he raised those bewildered blue eyes in disbelief.

The ariel gave him a little wave and a brilliant smile. "Hi, Bob."

I slipped my hands into my pockets. "Let's chat."

Vampires, especially the old ones, were incredibly fast, but no one out-ran a shadow-walker. I materialized out of the shadows by the front door and caught the vampire by the throat just as he sprang over the threshold. With my scorpion blade in his back, I marched him back to his corner booth.

The ariel was making shooing motions with one hand as she gripped her mug in the other. The vampire's guests were scooching out of the booth. "...can take the bottles with you, yes, yes," the ariel was saying, "Now be a couple of good girls and *shoo* already. Thank you!"

I threw the vampire down onto the leather seat. The scorpion blade clicked, disengaging the dagger from the dart, and I forced Wilhelm's hands into his lap and draped the silver chain over his forearms and thighs, pinning him in place.

Then I dropped down into the seat next to him, gestured for the ariel to do the same, and signaled a waitress. "Clear this swill and bring us a bottle of Tartarus Pomegranate."

The ariel kicked me under the table.

"P-Please." It almost hurt to say the foreign word.

When the waitress was gone, I turned my attention to the table.

The tables in these booths had glyphs on them, glyphs that could obscure their occupants' physical features or prevent their voices from being overheard. I touched the glyph for silence, and the throbbing bass of the club vanished.

"If this is about the greenhouse—" the vampire began.

"Floral emporium," I corrected. "And it's not. You've been selling your blood."

Wilhelm immediately relaxed and the smugness returned. He didn't even bother lying. "I have."

"Stars above, why?" the ariel blurted out.

She definitely would need to work on controlling her emotions the next time we interrogated someone.

Wilhelm gave her a patronizing smile. "Because I can."

"You've been sanctioned by your Council to sell blood?" I asked.

"Of course not. But I'm old. Very old. And when you're as old as me, you can do what you want." He gave a world-weary sigh. "Nothing thrills the way it once did. This little act, illegal as it may be, brings a spark to my life."

"But it hurts people," the ariel protested. "Vampire blood can cause cardiac arrest and agonizing mutations and—"

"But the rush is amazing. Or so I'm told." The bliss left Wilhelm's face as he frowned at us. "And who are you to lecture me? A drow partnered with a... whatever the hell you are. You're DUO, plain as daylight. You're *assassins*."

"Not yet," the ariel muttered. "And only the bad ones."

"'Not yet?'" Wilhelm laughed. "Oh my, so this is amateur hour. You don't even know what you're doing or who you're up against, do you?"

"And who is that?" I asked.

The vampire shook his head, grinning. "Tsk, tsk, little darkling. If you knew, you never would've set foot in this booth. Now release me at once and maybe I'll forget this incident and you both won't die horrible deaths. At least, not at my hands."

His patronizing tone was beginning to grate. I hadn't been called a darkling since my one hundredth birthday. My left eye twitched.

"You're out of your league, little ones. And why are you busting my chops, drow?" Wilhelm asked. "We are both creatures of the dark."

"No," I said, shaking my head. "*You* are a creature of the night, vampire. Let me show you what true darkness looks like."

I put my hand on his shoulder and melted into the shadows.

CHAPTER TWENTY-EIGHT

Eryn

I DIDN'T PARTICULARLY CARE for this Tartarus Pomegranate drink, which was so dark a red it was almost black, but Larcen and Bob had been gone for quite a few minutes, and I had nothing better to do but sip it from a narrow flute and watch the people dance. The social butterfly in me wanted to go out on the dance floor and swirl around—walking in high heels S-U-C-K-E-D—but the guardian in me told me to stay in my seat.

Giving the Tartarus Pomegranate another sip, I second-guessed my initial opinion. It was tart, which I sort of liked, with a tiny bit of sweetness on the back end that didn't activate my gag reflex. And it gave my head a delightful buzzing sensation. Maybe I'd grow to like it after all. I finished my flute and poured another one, tapping my bladed fan against my thigh in time to the music.

I was just sloshing a third—or fourth?—helping into my

flute when Larcen and Bob reappeared, the vampire whiter than new-fallen snow and screaming like a banshee.

"Gnat farts," I cursed, flipping over my flute as I covered my ears. "What did you do to him?"

Larcen casually leaned over and snapped the vampire's neck, and the screaming abruptly stopped. The vampire slumped in the booth, chin resting on his shoulder. Larcen touched the obscure glyph before picking up his own flute and sinking back into the leather seat with a sigh. A film like frosted glass radiated out from the table like a bubble. He took a sip of that dark-red liquid and cleared his throat. "I shadow-walked until he got the message."

"And just now?" I shouted, pointing to the vampire whose head no longer faced forward.

The dark elf shrugged. "It wasn't a stake to the heart, so he'll snap out of it. Get it?"

"Ugh."

"I got his employer's address, so that's something. Right here in Midnight Crossings no less. Eighty-eight Allemande Steet. No name, but I'll still call this a win."

He wasn't wrong, but it didn't seem right, either. His tactics were... brutal. But we were DUO assassins, weren't we? Well, sort of, since Alder Shaw had put us on indeterminate leave. It was in the job description, but so was protecting the magical realm from discovery. Just because we had to kill sometimes to maintain that fragile peace didn't mean we had to *enjoy* it. But Larcen was a drow. It's what they did.

The Tartarus Pomegranate suddenly didn't feel too happy in my stomach. I snatched up the mug of swag and scooted out of the booth. There was no more reason to stay here—we'd gotten the information we'd come for—and I couldn't spend one more minute in that silent booth with that vampire. His bones had already started to reset, clicking as they slowly turned his head back into the correct position.

The dance music hit me like a sledgehammer to the face, and I staggered from the aural assault until a warm hand snatched my elbow and steadied me. I ripped away from Larcen's grip, threw caution to the wind, and lifted off my feet. I'd been smothered for too long, and I needed to feel the wind in my hair again. The white strands floated above me in a swirl, and the dancers eagerly accepted this strange flying girl as one of their own. I was twirled about, tossed from one to another, and the Tartarus Pomegranate bubbled up inside of me. I felt warm and fuzzy and happy, and my vision blurred like that time I'd been dared to ride a hurricane.

Though I had nothing to drink, I cheered everyone with my mug, sprinkling the air with jewels. The dancers shrieked with delight and clapped and scrambled to catch the sapphires and amethysts before some other lucky individual could. Pulsing lights glinted on the jewels as they seemed to float over their heads, and suddenly they weren't hard little gems anymore, but soft, glowing wisps. Nef, Kin, little Lox... They were plucked out of sky by greedy dark hands, trapping them in the net of their fingers and crushing until there was no light left.

With a screech, I ripped the bladed fan from my belt. "Don't you take them! Leave them alone."

Starlight metal slashed in an arc of blinding white. Screams filled my ears, but I couldn't tell if they were mine or theirs. Murderers, all of them. Night wisps were one of the purest beings in any realm, born of the moon to guide wayward travelers to safe paths when the moon could not. They were safeguards, and these people were killing them!

Something coiled around my wrist, halting the slash that would've decapitated some sniveling thief. I strained against it, determined to avenge the wisp caught in that thief's hands.

Instead I was pulled away, and two iron bands trapped my arms against my sides. Thrashing, I phased to mist and arrowed straight back to that wisp-snatching thief, bladed fan closed and poised to skewer right through that neck, until something stabbed me in the back of the thigh. I stumbled to the floor as I fell out of flight, catching myself in a crouch as my head swam and my body tingled. Frozen into crystal against my will, I screamed at the floor in rage, but no sound came out.

"...had a bad drink," someone said, but it sounded like they were talking underwater.

I was lifted, balanced between two arms, and carried away. The pulsing thrum and swirling lights were replaced by a starless sky and the drone of far-off conversations. Yet I still felt the pulse of a rhythm: the cadence of a walking stride. As my Steorra-forged body relaxed, my stomach was the first to respond to that incessant rhythm.

"Spider bites," a faraway voice cursed as I retched.

My whole body shook as I vomited, crouched down on the flagstones beside a gutter. Brisk hands swept the cloud of hair away from my face, and the cool night air on the back of my neck felt divine. I could *feel* again. The poison of the Drozvega dart had been burned off, and I was back in my body.

I rose on shaky legs and looked down at my hands, wondering why they hurt so much. They were clamped around a bladed fan and a coffee mug. Groaning, I slipped my fan into my belt and clutched my throbbing head. "Ouch."

"Seriously? That's all you have to say right now?"

I spat the rest of that Tartarus Pomegranate out of my mouth and floated into the air. The dark elf released my hair, no longer needing to hold it out of my face as it swirled above my head. "In my defense," I slurred, "I was left unattended. That stuff tasted like tart fruit juice."

"Why would I order fruit juice in a bar? That was fortified

wine!"

"And now we know." Now that my stomach was no longer roiling, I was feeling a lot better. The anger was gone, like it had never been, and the fuzzy buzzing in my head made it feel like I had a thousand tiny bubbles trapped inside. I giggled.

The dark elf groaned and yanked the coffee mug out of my hand.

"Hey!"

"There's got to be something in here," he muttered. "Raphael's parties can be intense, so he likes to send home—ah. Here, take this." He ripped open a plastic package and fished out a blue ball the size of a large grape.

"What is it?"

"A gumball. Bubble gum with a kick. Blue raspberry, by the looks of it."

I plopped it into my mouth and swallowed.

"You're supposed to chew it, not swallow it!"

"Well that would've been nice to know before you gave it to me. I've only been eating food for three days or something! How was I supposed to know this food was not food and chew-only?" I snatched the mug back, not because I wanted the swag, but because I was tired of him treating me like an ignorant child who couldn't be trusted with the simplest things. Gnat farts, I could hold a coffee mug! "And you know what? You're the worst partner ever. You just love putting me into situations and watching them implode so you can blame me instead of your own incompetence. Well I've had enough. Eighty-eight Allemande Street, is that right? Breezy."

I soared into the air, making sure to weave around so he'd have a harder time hitting me with that poison dart. It was a lot easier to do with the remnants of Tartarus Pomegranate bubbling in my bloodstream.

"You can't go there by yourself!"

"And you can't tell me what to do!"

I'd never flown drunk before, but I was determined to do this, so I kept the fingertips of my left hand against the Baroque façade for balance as I flew down the street. They skimmed over stone walls and wrought iron balconies that overlooked the brick-paved streets, decorative carvings, and sculptures of sultry nymphs and stoic warriors. A nice fairy on one of those balconies paused in her vicious beating of a throw rug to give me directions to Allemande Street, which I would know on sight by all the trailing yellow flowers. Someone back in the day had planted allamanda in a window box and then a year later every window box on the entire street had been overrun. That someone had certainly had a punny sense of humor.

I smelled Allemande Street before I actually saw it, and sure enough, those plant-strangled balconies were everywhere, dripping jewel-green foliage and soft yellow flowers over the street. Streetlamps blazed along the sidewalks, brighter here than in the human realm, and gave the street the appearance of midday. Those little lights very well may have been miniature suns, shrunk to size by an enchantment so the flowers could get the entire UV spectrum they needed to thrive. I got momentarily distracted smelling the flowers and giving them a little spruce-up with a finger flick here and a gentle wind there, and nearly flew past the townhouse with the big "88" in iron numbers above the door. A light was on in the third-story window, glowing softly behind red curtains.

With a gasp, I quickly retreated to 86 Allemande Street, just next door, pooling into the third-story balcony and hiding behind the allamanda. Peering out from behind the floral screen, I watched the next house, but no one came out onto the balcony for a breath of fresh air. Was anyone home?

I couldn't very well knock on the door *or* the window, as this dark mage might know my face. He was probably very cautious, too, and would have boobytrapped every entrance, just in case. There was only one safe way to enter the house.

Each of these townhouses were equipped with a chimney, and no one had any business messing around in them other than the occasional bat or soot pixie. Phasing, I turned to mist and slipped down the chimney. It was very black in here, but I found an open flue on the first floor and slipped out. There was a mirror suspended over the fireplace mantel, and I caught my misty reflection, somewhat less transparent now that I was covered in a fine layer of black dust. If anything I looked like a piece of fabric torn from the night sky: all black and glitter.

I wagged a finger gun at my reflection. "Looking good, Star Girl. Shh!"

I clamped a hand over my mouth to stifle the snicker. "Shh, shh, shh. It's serious time."

The Tartarus Pomegranate bubbles disagreed.

But we both decided it would be best if I didn't touch anything. Clutching the mug to my chest, I floated up the stairs to the second floor, rounded the bend, got lost on the second floor with a momentary case of the swirlies, then took the next flight up to the third floor. I stopped just as my eyes became level with the hallway, looking left and right and finding nothing but a window at the end of the hall with a long red runner down its length. There were four doors, two on each side of the hallway, and one of them was opening.

CHAPTER TWENTY-NINE

Larcen

I STEPPED out into the hallway, my bare feet making no noise on the polished hardwood. Closing the door behind me, I turned to the ariel who "hid" on the stairs. If you really could call it hiding when her white hair floated in a cloud three feet above her head. Besides her hair, only her forehead and jade eyes could be seen above the first step, and that forehead crinkled while those eyes narrowed as she frowned at me.

"How did you get in here?" she whispered.

I threw my finger against my lips.

"Oh, shadow-walking," she giggled. "Duh."

I glared at her and gestured even more vehemently for her to be silent. Spider bites, this was literally the worst idea ever, going after a dark mage when the ariel was drunk. And in Midnight Crossings no less. Things here were already tense with Forge trying to run a clean city and Tiana encouraging her rats' nest of a Market. Forge had been looking for an excuse to oust Tiana from this place for years, and if this job went sideways, it could be the spark to start the war everyone knew was coming. We'd been seen in Acquiesce—the ariel had made damn sure of that with her alcohol-induced freakout—and now we were on one of the nicer streets in the middle of a home invasion. That damn Steorra bloodline of hers made it impossible for me to dart her and get her out of the city without her recovering within seconds and coming right back here. Maybe she'd be content to stay out here in the hall while I handled this. I motioned for her to stay put.

She flew up the stairs and right into my face. Smirking, she flicked me in the nose, turned, and kicked open the dark mage's door.

His back to the door, he lurched out of his chair and snatched for something on his desk, but my chain dart was faster. It coiled around his torso three times, pinning his arms against his sides, before the dart whipped up and slashed him across the cheek. The *alchemist* had been at his secretary desk with its hurricane lamp and writing in his notebook before we'd so rudely interrupted him, and his red eyes blazed like freshly fanned coals.

A djinn, he appeared remarkably human, but he was far stronger. I struggled to keep the chain steady.

This wasn't the dark mage who had shot me in the chest with a cursed arrow.

Meanwhile, the ariel floated around me and into the room, squealing with delight. "Look at all the goodies!" Then she proceeded to loot the room, dropping bits and bobs into her oversized mug. "This isn't a dark mage's den at all but an alchemist's lair."

I didn't take my eyes off the struggling djinn for a second, but the haze in my periphery confirmed she was right. To the right by the window was a little portable stove and a cauldron emitting something noxious: the glow I'd seen behind the curtains. To the left was a long workbench against a tower of shelves stuffed with old books and chipping scrolls and mortars and pestles and flasks and everything else needed to concoct various potions.

And there, on the workbench beside an open atlas, was a Drozvegan ceremonial knife. It was the only weapon of ours that had a hollow point, designed to inject the venom of the Spider Queen into the back of a drow initiate's neck when they turned fifteen and bind them to the false deity forever. Unless I had a breakthrough in my mushroom elixir.

What had Lady Chantilly said? *The coating on that dagger is spider venom.*

"Eryn," I hissed, "get that knife!"

"Ooo!" the ariel exclaimed, completely distracted. "Is this a scrying glass? It *is*. I'll just take this crystal and that little shiny piece over there—like mother-of-pearl that is—and just look at that—"

"I should've never listened to him," the alchemist snarled. "I should've let that ogre kill you when I had the chance."

Jerking forward, he put slack on the chain. I stumbled back into the hallway, immediately yanking to tighten the chain, but the alchemist had already turned. His hand smacked the hurricane lamp onto the floorboards, the glass shattering and releasing a swirl of fireflies. Sparking, angry fireflies whose blinking lights snapped from demure yellow to flame red in less than a heartbeat.

With a sinister smile, the djinn snatched the Drozvegan ceremonial knife in one hand, pinched a firefly with the other, and vanished. The remaining fireflies swirled madly, igniting into sparks and then cinders.

"Eryn!" I shouted.

She sent me a horrified look and whipped her fan out of her belt. With one flick she slammed the door shut and a second later, the door blew off its hinges as a conflagration roared into the hallway. I dove out of the way, rolling onto my feet by the stairs. The entire house shook from the explosion, cracks like spiderwebs lacing through the wooden walls and up to the plaster in the ceiling. Glass shattered as the windows blew into the street, the roar of flames chasing after the fresh air.

Running back down the hall, I skidded to a stop by the smoking door and shielded my eyes with a hand. "Eryn!" Recalling my chain dart, I used the scorpion blade to cut away the burning pieces of doorframe and dashed into the room.

Flames devoured everything in that room, the fireflies more potent than kerosene. Fire clawed at the drapes and chewed on the secretary desk and melted the cauldron. There was no sign of the ariel, just a massive hole in the wall where the shelves had been.

Coughing, I stumbled back into the hallway and ripped open the adjacent room's door. It was the alchemist's bedroom, and the ariel lay in a smoking heap on the four-poster bed. She must've phased into crystal to protect herself from the explosion, but the alcohol in her system hadn't allowed her to keep the change. Cuts crosshatched her pale arms, and her face and hair were absolutely covered in black soot.

Against all odds, she'd kept a grip on that damn swag mug and her fan, her second one secure in her belt. A groggy moan confirmed she was alive, and I hoisted her into my arms. She weighed close to nothing, slim as a waif she was, and suddenly I wished I'd fed her more. Like the weight would've reassured me she could pull through this. Gripping her tightly, I shadow-walked onto the street. Yellow-and-orange flames clawed at the night sky, darkening the street lamps with billowing black smoke. The yellow flowers dripping from the nearest balconies had already shriveled, and the alarms were already blaring.

There was a thunderous crack, like a redwood tree shattering from the inside, and then half of the third story buckled and sloughed off into the street. Flaming debris rolled down the bricks like infernal tumbleweeds and choked the air with smoke.

It took only a few shadow-steps to reach the front gate of the city. Crowds of fascinari rushed to see what had happened at Allemande Street, but there were plenty of us just trying to leave the city. Attacks weren't uncommon here, but Midnight Crossings hadn't seen an explosion that had taken out the top story of a townhouse in some time. The ogre guards had shifted their attention inward, scanning the crowd for the culprits, but so far, Forge had yet to order them to close that horrid guillotine-like portcullis.

Ancient magic at the gate prevented me from shadow-walking, so the ariel and I were forced to pass under the ogres' inspections. But carrying her in my arms while she was covered in cuts and reeking of fire would certainly attract the ogres' attention. Then we'd be taken to Forge for a little chat, and we seriously didn't have time for that. That djinn alchemist had escaped, the ceremonial knife was buried in flaming debris, and without DUO to back us up—Alder had basically disowned us for the time being—if Forge threw us in prison, who knew how long we'd be there? Before I shadow-walked us free, of course, but then we'd still have to get through the front gate somehow. And the dark mage, whoever he was, would be one step closer to stealing yet another random artifact and we would be two steps behind restoring our names.

We had to get out of here. Now.

Diverting to the shadows of a pillar, I eased the ariel down to the ground and dumped the contents of her mug into her lap. There was a fountain nearby, and I brought mug after mug of water to clean her off. Her hair was ruined if I didn't dunk it, so I did as my supermodel cousin Vander always said, "Own it and work it!"

I took the compact of New Moon Rose and smeared black streaks into her white hair to cover up the soot, as if she'd wanted a tiger-striped appearance all along, and used the butterfly hair stick to style it all into bun with lots of little black-and-white tendrils curling down her back. I added more of that black gel in a stripe across her eyes and tore strips from her dress, tying them around her upper arms to mask the cuts. When I was done, she looked like a valkyrie who'd just made some heads roll in one of the Market's fighting pits.

Still, I applied that allure-enhancing polish to her finger-nails, just in case. Now, she looked like a sexy valkyrie warrior who'd just made some heads roll in one of the Market's fighting pits.

Sexy, but still drunk. That Revital-Ball she'd swallowed hadn't released its revitalizing effects—that's why you needed to *chew* it—so I popped one into my own mouth. Watermelon. Seriously, why did Raphael always get the ones that tasted like human candy? Why couldn't we get the ones that tasted like spit-roasted boar or mulled wine?

When my tongue started to tingle as the compounds were released from the gum, I pressed my mouth against the ariel's and transferred the watermelon-flavored liquid. I could be repulsed later; she had to get on her feet so we could get out of here. Already the mood of the crowd had changed from curiosity to string-the-arsonists-up-by-their-genitals. Chewing rapidly, I extracted more of the stimulants and healing compounds and whatever else Raphael had put in these things and pressed my mouth against the ariel's a second time.

Her slap smacked the gum right out of my mouth.

She spewed pink liquid all over me and whacked my shoulders with the flat of her fan. "You despicable, mildew-encrusted *cave—*"

"Enough about the mildew!" I flicked the pink juice from my shoulders. "We need to get out of here."

She gave a bewildered look, trying to reconcile why a moment ago she'd been blown through a wall and then the next she was in the shadows of an apothecary leaning against a pillar. As she became more aware, she touched her hair and the strips of fabric on her arms and the stripe across her eyes. "I was unconscious and you decided to play dress-up?"

She really was having difficulty grasping the gravity of this situation. I snatched her face in my hand, pinching her cheeks hard. "In the next five seconds, we will be on the other side of that gate, or in the next six seconds, we will be arrested. Got it?"

The ariel nodded quickly, and I released her. Using her skirt as an apron, she poured the swag in her lap back into the mug—which I held, cursing its existence the entire time. Keeping her feet on the ground, she marched towards the gates, her head held high, as if it were perfectly natural for a valkyrie to prowl around Midnight Crossings with a Grow, Dammit mug in hand.

I know I certainly wouldn't have crossed her. She looked fierce and brave and—wait a minute, was this *Eryn* I was describing?

I gagged a little and then hurried to catch up.

The ogres grunted as we passed beneath the gate, but they didn't stop us. The ariel's quick-change and burst of energy had fooled them. True to time, we were clear of the gate in five seconds, and in another two, I was saying the literal magic words to get us back to Savannah.

We emerged from the fountain in Lafayette Square just in time for me to transform into a gangly fawn. Eryn glanced at the stars, gave a weary sigh, and collected my clothes. She draped them over my back and secured my scorpion blade in her own belt. She was obviously too tired from being blown through a wall and managing her first hangover to fly us back to the floral emporium. Since it was the middle of the night, we made it back to the emporium without too many strange looks, staggering into the polytunnel to be greeted by the entire gnome population.

At least, Eryn was.

"Miss Eryn! What happened to you?"

"What is this new look, Mademoiselle Eryn? It's *très* fierce."

"Here's the brandy!"

"No alcohol," she groaned.

"See? I told you she didn't like it. I've got an Alka-Seltzer!"

"There's ginger-lemon tea with honey on the stove. And we got you some fried catfish from Magnolia's Kitchen."

The ariel moaned, only to be echoed by her stomach. She didn't want to eat meat, but her new body craved it.

"Any biscuits?" she asked, perking up at the prospect from beneath her fog.

"Double order!"

"Thank you so much." Then she clutched her head. "But I think I just need to sleep. For a minute. Or forever."

"*And what about me?*" I demanded, using the last of my energy to rustle up some outrage. Except my words came out a strangle bleat from my little fawn mouth.

"If I didn't know what he truly was, I'd say he was cute as a button," Marigold said.

"I, for one," Rumple said, "am very glad to see you, Master Larcen."

"Brown-noser."

"I heard that," the pig squealed. "And I'm pleased as punch

264

to see you, Miss Eryn. You obviously took such good care of our master—"

"He's not our master, he's our oppressor!"

"—to bring him back *alive* from Midnight Crossings looking like that. Why, the nearest troll would've snapped him up and had him on a spit faster than a grasshopper could hop. And is that Tartarus Pomegranate I smell? Why are your lips so pink?"

"Both of your lips are quite *rouge*," Henrietta purred. "Ooo la la. Have you two been... smooching?"

I quickly sucked my little fawn lips behind my teeth.

Gagging, the ariel floated away, her toes barely above the ground. "I think I'm going to go throw up again."

"I bet it was like kissing a cloud," Rumple sighed dreamily.

"*I've had better,*" I mumbled, which was immediately translated by the pig.

"Oh my truffles, I'm so sorry, Master Larcen. That wasn't for public consumption, was it?"

"But she wasn't your worst," Henrietta said, tapping her chin. "Interesting."

I stomped my little cloven feet at her, but no one was taking me seriously in this fawn getup. I still had the little white spots on my flanks. Marigold reached up and gave my velvety muzzle a pat, but it wasn't particularly friendly.

"Just because you're a fawn doesn't mean you get out of providing us strawberries and peaches for breakfast." She shoved the company credit card Jasper had obviously raided from the desk drawer between my milk teeth. "Josiah's Grits and Goods is open twenty-four seven. Off you go."

"Don't worry, sir," Rumple said. "I'll go with you. With the illusion on my collar, it'll just look like I'm taking my pet fawn for a walk."

I was a drow prince reduced to a fawn, and now a *pet*. I knew Rumple hadn't meant anything by it, but as we left the polytunnel, him waddling on his trotters as I fought to keep up on my gangly legs, I couldn't help but glance up at the ariel asleep in the rafters. Her kind was my natural enemy, and while she needled me, she'd never once made me feel any less than I was, no matter what I looked like.

Maybe we could be partners after all. For a time, anyway.

CHAPTER THIRTY

Eryn

MAYBE IT WAS because I'd already dealt with a blood mage in her creepy crypt, or maybe it was the blue-raspberry Revital-Ball in my stomach finally taking effect and releasing all its fortifying compounds, but I didn't find Larcen's underground training room nearly as smothering today. Or maybe it was the confidence this new dress gave me. My red wrap was absolutely ruined, and when Rumple woke me a few hours ago when the plant nursery opened for human business, there was a new dress on a hanger waiting for me. The A-line was the color of cranberries, so while not an exact replica, it would still go with my boots, and it even had pockets. Rumple said it was hanging there when he came in from the alchemy herb section, and the gnomes didn't make enough to pay for such expensive fabric, so it had to be from Larcen. I just hoped this wasn't another one of those gift-dresses that were just honey-trap-dresses in disguise.

As humans flooded the store for plants and for those sultry

gnome figurines—the gnomes had their slip cast station hidden so well not even their shadow-walking spellhunter boss could find it—their footsteps echoed above us. Almost mimicking them, Larcen paced back and forth across the foam mat floor, his bare feet not making even a whisper.

"That alchemist was *not* the dark mage we fought at the riverfront. So the two of them are working together, unless the human magician double-crossed the alchemist and brokered a better deal. But what would an alchemist want with a dagger and a star chart? Why would a dark mage want them, for that matter? Treasure? The Zhu dagger gives luck, the star chart is literally *X* marks the spot, and then what? What are we missing?" he muttered for tenth time.

I'd already postulated half a dozen ideas, so I kept my mouth shut and continued to sort through all the goodies I'd collected from the alchemist's lair when I was... not myself. Rumple had told me that the murky head, dry throat, and sour stomach I was experiencing was a called a "hangover" and that coffee would pretty much cure me, but since we didn't have an espresso machine in the break room—here he shot Larcen a meaningful look—then the carb- and grease-heavy biscuits and fried fish he'd gotten me from Magnolia Kitchen were the next best thing. Eating helped me not cry as I remembered the events of last night, and when the food was gone, I slapped a smile on to keep my features tight.

I'd seen visions of that night the valley was taken, then premonitions of the wisps I'd saved reliving the same fate. I would've killed everyone in that club to prevent that from happening. It'd only been the drow's poison dart that had stopped me. I'd overreacted, that was obvious—no wisps had been in danger—but the emotions had been real. The Tartarus Pomegranate might've tasted divine, but the things it had showed me were certainly not.

With the Grow, Dammit mug's swag spread out over the work bench, I found a few gems that had been left behind. I picked up the tanzanite, its blue-purple color identical to Lox. "Why did you do it?" I finally asked.

Larcen stopped pacing as he caught sight of the jewel in my hand. "Do what?"

"The night wisps. They were innocent. Why did you do it?"

The drow stiffened. "Orders."

"Why?"

"It is not my place to question my king."

There was more he wasn't telling me, more secrets. "But you still saved a pod. You knew your orders were wrong, and still you burned that valley." I threw the gem back on the table. "And you're not even sorry for it!"

"There is no word in Drozvegan for regret."

I would never understand him. The Puddle had been wrong to pair us. Day and night, yin and yang, north and south, pick your favorite opposites analogy and we were ten times that. Stars above, even our homes were on opposite sides of the planet! Drozvega and the Night Lands anchored in the Amazon and the Temple of the Sky tethered to Mount Everest.

I snatched the coin that dangled from the bracelet on my wrist, the swirl design pressing into my thumb. I was going to yank this grindstone off. Or flip it. I could flip it right now and access that deep power that had bonded us together. The Puddle would take his life if we didn't activate our coins together, and I would be free. Free of him, but stuck in the same position I'd been when I'd been forced out of the Temple of the Sky. No, I needed him. I had to bear this out. I had to win him over, otherwise I'd never get my old life back.

Forcing my lips into a smile, I dropped the coin and went back to the swag. My memory was still a little cloudy, so I was sorting them into two piles: definitely-from-Raphael's-party and unknown.

I knew Larcen watched me for another second or two before he resumed his pacing. Then the communications array at the end of the worktable started to blink, and I basically lobbed it at him. DUO didn't want to speak to *me* anyway.

"This is Larcen."

Moxie got right to the point. "I got the invoice you sent me, but Pegasus Express is *insisting*—"

"Pegasus Express didn't lose the shipment."

My hand froze, hovering above the Zippo lighter.

"They what now?" Moxie demanded.

"It was a misunderstanding. Everything's still here."

There was a pregnant pause. "You want to give me a better explanation other than it was a 'misunderstanding?'"

"I don't have a better one. It just wasn't Eryn's fault."

I blinked in surprise, thankful my back was turned to the drow and he couldn't see my expression. Unfreezing, I moved the lighter to the party pile. Larcen would never incriminate himself—ever the proud prince—but he had exonerated me. That was... nice of him. First the replacement dress and now this... Was he ill? I whipped around and gave him a shrewd look.

"Alder will know about this 'misunderstanding,' Larcen," Moxie told him. "As if he doesn't have enough on his plate already with the bombing at Midnight Crossings and—"

"Bombing? And since when does DUO have anything to do with that city?"

"We have no jurisdiction there, obviously, but we like to keep a finger on the pulse as it were. Speaking about keeping a finger on things, we still need that evidence box."

"I'll send it right away."

"No!" Moxie straightened her wire-rim glasses and said in a softer, more controlled voice, "No. They are not going anywhere except directly into our hands. You stay put. Oh, and is Eryn there?"

Larcen gave the marble a spin and Moxie's image faced me. I gave her a little wave but didn't say anything. The last time we'd talked she'd chewed me out for something I didn't do.

"Sorry about before." She cleared her throat. "Maven says her star chart analysis is complete. There were... a number of hits. She took the liberty of inverting the maps so they showed the physical locations that the charts referred to, so you'll get both sets of data. She's sending it over now."

"Thank you."

"You're welcome."

"Hey y'all," Rumple's voice filtered down the compost chute. "The printer up here is possessed or something and I could really use some help because my trotters are *not* equipped to handle this kind of thing."

Larcen disappeared into the shadows. Well look at him being all helpful and whatnot. Must've been because I saved his life quite a few times over the past few nights. He might be a snob, but at least he had a little humility. We're talking a thimbleful, here, but it still counted.

Taking a deep and determined breath, I turned back to the worktable. I *had* to have picked up something of value at the alchemist's lair in my drunken stupor. With the lair destroyed, any leads we had on who the djinn was working with and why were now gone, except for what lay in front of me.

I'd apparently been attracted to shiny things: a scrying glass, a scrying crystal on the end of a fine chain, and a silver-dollar-sized piece of mother-of-pearl. My smile flattened into a straight line as I picked up the scrying glass. It looked like your average magnifying glass, except the frame and handle were fashioned from celestial silver. The decoration was ornate, too, from the

Windswept period, when I was just a child. This had come from an ariel star forge.

What was it doing here, on Earth? When we'd traded with other realms before shutting down the smithies, we'd given such valuable gifts to our allies, but none of them would've given it to the likes of that djinn alchemist. My hand tightened on the silver handle. *He'd stolen this.* And no wonder, either. It was one of the best scrying tools ever made. With reverent care, I slipped it into my belt by my bladed fans. This would never see the inside of one of Larcen's cubbies. It belonged with its owner or those who had forged it. It belonged to an ariel.

Then I picked up the mother-of-pearl shell. The alchemist had tied the crystal to the shell and had rigged the scrying glass over it all, focusing a tracking spell on the shell and using the crystal to point out a location on the atlas. As far as I knew, mother-of-pearl wasn't very valuable, thought it had an exceptional silver sheen to it, and it wasn't used in any kind of alchemy I was aware of. Not that I was an expert. I'd have to ask Larcen when he came back.

The drow returned presently, a stack of papers in his hands. He set it down on the worktable with a considerable thump. "Maven says the top five charts have the most accuracy, but she didn't want to rule anything out, so she sent all of it."

I cringed and picked up the first chart, holding it up to the light. In the left-hand corner was a small picture of the star chart that had most matched my drawing, and the rest of the paper was the topographical depiction of the location it referred to. At the bottom of the page were more specifics, like longitude, latitude, country, and province or state. The first was of Salar de Uyuni, a salt flat in Bolivia. I set it aside and picked up the next one. An island in Malaysia.

"Any luck with your trinkets?" the drow prompted. I couldn't tell if he was asking because he was genuinely curious or if he was patronizing me. He poked around the objects with his finger. "Of all the things you could've picked up and you don't get the ceremonial dagger. Proof would've been nice."

Ignoring that barb, I set aside the third chart and picked up the fourth. I didn't know what I was looking for, but something in my gut said I would recognize it when I saw it. "That shiny piece there, the mother-of-pearl. He was using that as a scrying focus. I think the crystal's still active." Scrying crystals were typically hazy when they weren't being used, and this one was as clear as glass.

"This isn't mother-of-pearl, it's oxhorn. Next to worthless." Larcen threw up his hands. "Spider bites, I can't *believe* this. That damn alchemist blows up his own lair and gets away—"

I lifted the fifth chart into the light, and my stomach with all its biscuits and fried fish sank like a boulder into my toes.

"—and has probably told the dark mage by now that we're on their trail, not that it matters much because any clues we could've picked up were fire-bombed because a certain *someone* just had to kick open a door instead of waiting for the alchemist to leave so we could thoroughly search the place—"

I didn't need to look at the coordinates to know exactly what this map pictured. *Everyone* knew of this place in the desert, but no one ever spoke of it. The resting place of the Forsaken was forbidden to record. So why was there a star chart mapping its exact location from ten thousand years ago?

"—and now we'll never know what they were after to begin with!" Larcen hurled the piece of oxhorn at the honeycomb shelves.

It never hit.

It lurched to a halt and glowed with a silver light I'd seen twice before. The shelves shook, and there was a loud pop as the oxhorn coin freed itself from the Zhu dagger's sheath. Flying out of its cubby, it slammed against the one with the chain. Then the wax seal zipped out of its own resting place, joining the others. The red wax crumbled away from the impact, revealing yet a third piece of oxhorn. Suddenly the scrying crystal lurched upright, and the entire configuration arrowed past Larcen, snatching the start char from my hands and pinning it against the wall. The pointed end of the crystal burrowed itself straight into the burial chamber of the Forsaken.

"I think we know what they're after now," I said.

CHAPTER THIRTY-ONE

Larcen

"You knew about the oxhorn this entire time?" I shouted, belatedly remembering we had customers overhead. Hopefully they'd just think it was the pipes groaning.

"I didn't know it was the oxhorn! And I *told* you about the silver light I saw when you were doing that video call with the phone, but you didn't believe me," the ariel fired back. She soared to the wall and plucked the crystal pin out of the map, bringing both back to the work bench. The crystal had turned cloudy, its mission complete. "I saw it again before we went to the Bonekeeper, and I *was* going to tell you when we got back but then things got a little complicated with that Tartarus Pomegranate and, well, *now* you know."

She untied the chain from the center piece of oxhorn and set both scrying crystal and oxhorn cluster on the work bench. The pieces were fused together, albeit not seamlessly, little gaps here and there where the edges didn't quite meet up, like mismatched puzzle pieces.

"So he was looking for more of these pieces," I said, lifting the oxhorn into the light of a lampblossom and squinting as the pink-tinged light shone through the cracks. "Why?"

The ariel was silent.

"Come, come, ariel," I snapped. "Surely you have an opinion you'd like to share with me *now*."

She pointed to the map where the crystal's point had left a permanent hole. "I don't know why he wants them, but the next piece is there."

"By the look on your face, *there* is someplace significant." I gave the map a cursory exam. "The Western Sand Sea in Algeria. It's a wasteland."

The ariel shrugged.

"I thought you wanted to be partners, Eryn."

"I don't know anything else about the oxhorn," she snipped. She plucked the oxhorn from my fingers and turned it this way and that in front of my face. "See? There's no color variation, no carvings or etchings or discernable markings of any k—" Her jade eyes narrowed as she brought the oxhorn cluster to her face.

"What?"

We needed this. We needed something to prove to Alder that we weren't chronic screw-ups. And maybe whatever the ariel saw would tell us why that spider-cursed alchemist had had a Drozvegan ceremonial knife in his possession.

"This oxhorn has a marking here," the ariel said, pointing to a dot. "See that metallic sheen?"

"Are you kidding me?" I snatched the oxhorn from her hand and squinted at it. "That's just a chip in the surface catching the light."

"That's celestial silver metal and no mistake," she said firmly. "It's a star. A binary star system, actually."

"You've lost your mind."

"Use those elf eyes and *look*, Larcen."

Smothering a snarl, I snapped my fingers, and the lampblossoms immediately furled. The training room became black as a starless night, the only light coming from the compost chute. The ariel yelped and immediately fled for the single beam. I turned my back to the chute so the light wouldn't interfere with my night vision and peered at the oxhorn. In this gloom I could see every detail, and sure enough, there was a glittering dot of celestial silver. And when I focused on it, the shine dimmed and resolved into two distinct dots. And not just that, but an uninterrupted thread finer than spider silk spread from the cluster and terminated at the edge of this particular oxhorn piece.

My jaw dropped.

"You see it." She wasn't asking a question.

"What is this?"

"It's a binary star, but it's almost impossible to know which one without a reference. There are a few famous ones, like Antares and Sirius and even Cor Caroli, but without another star as a reference, I can't tell. Larcen, this is Ancient magic."

I wanted to scoff and tell her that she was crazy, but seeing this with my own eyes made the words lodge in my throat. The dots were definitely celestial silver, as was the line extending from them, which ran against the grain of the oxhorn. There was no denying it. But the Ancients were dead or ascended—the histories weren't clear—but they had taken their magic with them, leaving no trace of it behind.

I snapped my fingers again, and the lampblossoms filled the training room with light once again. The ariel visibly relaxed, but she remained in the light from the compost chute.

"So why would a djinn alchemist and a dark mage be

searching for the pieces of an oxhorn that have stars on them?" I asked. It was a rhetorical question of course, but it spurred me to think I needed to talk to my uncle. Arcane artifacts were one of his specialties. Maybe he'd come across the mention of such a thing during one of his travels.

I needed to report the presence of the Drozvegan ceremonial knife in the alchemist's lair anyway. I would tell Alder second, as this spider venom was lethal in the wrong hands. "I need to make a call."

"No!" The ariel seized me and shook her head, her white hair swirling around her like cream poured into coffee. "You can't mention this to anyone. I mean, not the details, not the location, because—"

"Because *why*, Eryn?"

"Because those are secrets, Larcen. Ariel secrets. Please."

I gave her an assessing look. "Please" meant very little to me, but I understood the value of secrets. Maybe this was just what I needed. Maybe I didn't need to forfeit her life to take the Spider Queen's. Threatening to reveal this secret might be enough to coerce her compliance. She could keep her life that way at least.

"Fine," I said flatly.

There were humans up in the polytunnel so we had to take the stairs into the break room. The ariel practically hurled herself through the forcefield, flew through the break room and storage room, and came to a breathless halt in the polytunnel. At least she wasn't screaming in panic like she had the first time she'd been downstairs.

Eryn took a deep gulp of air and plucked the butterfly hair stick out of her pocket to style her hair, the better to appear human. Not many humans came to purchase plants in knee-high boots with pearl accents, flashy red dresses, and fashionable hair, but then again, ever since the gnomes had sabotaged the website, the emporium had been seeing a whole new breed of customers. And not just the human ones. The fascinari foot-traffic had increased, everyone on the East Coast wanting to purchase alchemy herbs with "attitude."

With customers milling about, I couldn't just walk across the polytunnel with the oxhorn in plain view, but it didn't seem right to put the oxhorn in my pocket. It was a magical artifact that could do who knew what down there. And I didn't want to leave it downstairs, even though those cubbies were layered with anti-corrosion and protection spells. If the alchemist had set up another scrying apparatus, I wanted him to find the oxhorn on me so I could throttle him. Though it had been the dark mage that had cursed me, perhaps his alchemist partner knew the counter curse to free me, and I had excelled in my interrogation studies back in school when I was a darkling. Cautiously, I slipped the oxhorn into my vest pocket. I was already cursed, the green glow beneath my skin a constant reminder, so what other harm could the oxhorn do to me there?

Like my very own shadow or personal poltergeist, the ariel followed right behind me as I hurried to the greenhouse where I grew the alchemy herbs. Glyphs on the doorframe simultaneously disguised the entrance and filled humans with such a sense of avoidance that they never even glanced this way. I still locked the door behind us, just to be sure.

"What are we doing in here?" the ariel whispered, thought she didn't need to keep her voice down. "We could've called Alder in the break room."

"I'm not calling Alder. At least, not yet." I shadow-stepped to the corner where the echo spider camped. I felt a surge of air against my back as the ariel lurched to a halt, refusing to come any closer to "the dreadful thing."

There were two ways to use an echo spider to communicate: a spider bite, which was just as painful as it sounded but ensured a conversation that couldn't be eavesdropped upon, or a spider web. I preferred the latter, and so long as the ariel kept her mouth shut, Malcan wouldn't know she was there and get hostile. I really needed him to cooperate.

"Malcan Nightblood of Drozvega," I told the spider.

When I didn't extend my hand, the spider uncurled its hairy legs and began weaving a web in the corner. The echo spider resembled the black jumping spider of the human realm, though this one was the size of my hand instead of my thumbnail. Blue iridescent mandibles clacked as it quickly and methodically built its conical web. Finished after only a few seconds, it squatted off to the side, strumming the outermost line of the web every two seconds. *Ring... ring... ring...*

"Larcen?" The spiderweb amplified my uncle's voice like a megaphone, the individual lines vibrating with each syllable.

"Uncle Malcan, I'm here."

"You alright?" His voice was clipped, as if he was among others and couldn't speak freely.

"I'm fine. Listen, I—"

"What's that? Speak up. That damn sprite didn't leave you stranded up in a cloud somewhere, did she? Do you have your sunglasses? Cloak? I swear—"

Before the ariel could make what had to be a scathing retort, I flung up my hand to silence her. Red-faced, she snapped her mouth shut and gritted her teeth.

"I found a ceremonial knife outside the home cave," I said without preamble.

"*What?*" Then his voice sounded far away as he carried on a one-sided conversation. "You there, get to the Spider Queen's antechamber at once. I want results, darkling, not excuses. Then rouse the priestess and bring her to me!" Malcan cleared his throat and said loudly, "I'm back with you, nephew."

"You don't command the faithful," I said, mildly impressed. "Throwing your weight around?"

"Why be built like an orc if I can't flex my muscles from time to time?"

I snorted. "Maybe you can flex some more and have Father send some of his retrieval experts to Eighty-Eight Allemande Street in Midnight Crossings."

"If you wanted an invitation back to the home cave, Larcen, that would have guaranteed it."

I'd thought of that, belatedly, but my priority had been getting myself and the ariel out of that trap. "I didn't get the chance."

"Hn. Anything else, then?" Malcan gave short laugh. "I'm very busy and important, you know."

"What do you know of artifacts inscribed with constellations?" I asked.

The spiderweb was silent a moment, but the spider was still bobbing its head, which meant the communication line was still open.

"I've only heard of the Ancients doing something like that," he answered slowly. "And as you know, the histories surrounding that time when they ascended were summarily destroyed. Selfish bastards."

I gave the ariel a look. She'd been right all along. "So... you can't help?"

"Of course I can help, Larcen, I'm just not sure I want to."

I crossed my arms and frowned up at the spiderweb. "Care to elaborate?"

"You're asking after Ancient magic; magic whose records and practitioners were destroyed for a very good reason. And if you're asking about it, it means DUO wants to know something about it, which means one of their targets is very interested in something they shouldn't be. And since I know all the grandmasters who might be interested in such a subject, and none of them are—which is a very wise choice—it's logical to conclude that your target is an amateur with delusions of grandeur. It's too dangerous, Larcen."

"You've never sheltered me before, Uncle."

"We've also never had a crown prince, our last shadow-walker, outside the safety of the home cave, either."

"This is my job now."

"Yes, and your allegiance is with DUO, my dear nephew, not with Drozvega."

"You're questioning my loyalty?" I snarled.

"You and I are drow, Larcen. Our first priority should be the longevity of Drozvega and the reign of the Spider Queen."

I clenched my teeth at the sound of that false deity.

"And I can't be certain that whatever information I give you won't come back to the detriment of our race. Besides, if you knew... Give up this hunt, Larcen. Those who seek the magic of the Ancients are always doomed to the same fate, regardless of how good their intentions are."

"So you won't help."

"I *am* helping, Larcen. Hopefully one day you'll see that."

The spider's head-bobbing ceased, and it came out of its crouch and began taking down its web. Uncle Malcan had severed the call.

CHAPTER THIRTY-TWO

Eryn

I wasn't surprised Larcen's uncle hadn't been very helpful—no drow ever was—but he had given us some information: we were definitely dealing with Ancient magic.

The Ancients had existed before my time, but all ariels grew up learning about them. They had cultivated a rare sort of magic, one that took its inspiration and energy from the heavens. But such magic—wielding the power of stars and planets—was too dangerous, and one cloudless night, the stars blazed and the Ancients vanished in a pillar of moonlight, leaving the ariels, their descendants, behind. Or so the stories said. Millennia passed, and we retained only a fraction of their power—weaving starlight and smithing celestial light into metals, and the Steorra bloodline, of course. Now we were no more related to them than unicorns were to horses.

And with me forbidden from ever stepping foot onto the sacred sun-gold steps of the Temple of the Sky ever again, I doubted we could get the answers we needed. If the histories and annals even had them to begin with. That pillar of moonlight had destroyed the archives the same night.

But, it never hurt to ask.

"We need to call Alder," I told Larcen.

He was already taking the garnet marble out of his pocket. Giving it a spin, we waited for the marble to lurch to a halt as someone in DUO headquarters picked up our call. It was Maven.

Her bust projected eight inches from the marble, her pea-sized eyes going wide. "Eryn! Just look at that dress. All I can say is danger, Will Robinson, you're gonna break someone's heart wearing a thing like th—"

"This isn't a social call, Maven," Larcen interrupted.

Maven gave him a sour look. "I would've said you've broken his heart already, given what a grump his is, but he'd actually have to have one."

"Who's Will Robinson?" I asked.

She waved her hand, dismissing the subject. "So if I'm not here to have girl time with my favorite air elemental, then why'd you call? Moxie's flight says she's still en route, and I *know* Alder doesn't want to—"

"We need to speak to Alder, please," I said.

"Hmph. Well, he might talk to you, sugar, but this one"—she jerked her thumb at Larcen—"had better work on his grovel. Pegasus Express isn't happy, which means Alder isn't happy, and even though he's a nature-loving druid, he'll still skin a thing or two if needed."

Larcen just crossed his arms over his chest.

Maven rolled her eyes. "Don't say I didn't warn you. Hold, please."

"You know, she's not wrong," I whispered.

"Dark elves don't grovel," he said, lifting his nose into the air.

"Don't show any humility either, do they?"

"We don't need to make a bad situation any worse, so just stick to the relevant details, okay?"

When I didn't agree right away, he glared at me—nothing new—and then Alder's bust came into view. He looked a little sleep-deprived, and Larcen immediately adopted a neutral expression.

"We have an update," I told him. Normally I would never be so brief, but he seemed to appreciate it. "I know you told us to stay put, but we went to Midnight Crossings and confronted the alchemist who's working with the dark mage—who's actually a djinn, the alchemist, not the dark mage—and blew up a townhouse."

"That was *you*?"

Larcen slapped a hand over his eyes.

"Wha— How— Explain!"

"The short version, Eryn," Larcen said.

"Of course," I said with a brisk nod. "When Billy Macon was stealing the Zhu dagger—and it's the sheath the dark mage really wanted, by the way—he drank vampire blood in an attempt to get away. Then the ogre in the Smithsonian had glyphs on his neck written in vampire blood to ensure his cooperation. We hunted down the calligrapher—a really handsy fae named Faelen—who gave us the leftover vampire blood that we took to the blood mage—who goes by Agatha or the Bonekeeper, she didn't really tell me how she preferred to be addressed—who made this freaky leech-like tracking spell that led us to the vampire in Midnight Crossings who then Larcen tortured with his shadow-walking—but he did eventually give up the address of the alchemist who paid him for his blood—and turns out he's a djinn who made his lair blow up but not before I confiscated the scrying glass and crystal and the piece of oxhorn he was using to track down other pieces with. We just got off a web call—yuck, by the way—with Larcen's uncle, who confirmed the pieces of oxhorn actually belong to an Ancient relic, but he won't give us any more information because 'it's not safe for Larcen' or other such rubbish."

Larcen's eyes were nearly bulging out of his head. "*That* was the short version? Did you even take a breath?"

Alder pinched the bridge of his nose and held up a hand for silence. After a deep breath or three, he said, "So there's an alchemist working with a dark mage and the two of them are on some sort of Ancient-magical-relic-jigsaw-puzzle-piece scavenger hunt? That right?"

I smiled brightly. "Yep!"

He tapped his chin. "Not much on the Ancients... You're sure?"

"Like ninety percent."

"And the ogre at the Smithsonian. He was after a star chart."

"The wax seal keeping it scrolled was actually the oxhorn in disguise, although..."

"Yes?"

"The star chart did reveal the location of the next piece. I think. At least, that's what the scrying crystal pointed to when all three oxhorn pieces fused together."

Alder looked impressed. "Huh, so your memory really is that good."

I gave him a superior lift of my chin. "We want your permission to go after it."

"Normally I would grant it, but with Larcen's curse—"

"He's due to change at 2:37 a.m. this evening and will change back around dawn, give or take a few minutes."

"You figured it out?" Alder and Larcen cried.

"N-no. Not all of it. Just the timing. When Larcen was turned into a goldfish, he returned to normal sometime by dawn the next morning. Then he was a cricket from 2:34 a.m. to sometime in the morning, but we didn't know when the transformation actually took place because we were both asleep. As a rabbit, he transformed at 2:35 a.m. to dawn again. The same went for when he was a fawn last night I just extrapolated the data, and from 2:37 a.m. tonight—or tomorrow morning, however you want to look at it—to dawn, he'll be another critter."

"How... How did you know the times?" Larcen asked.

I just smiled even wider. "I'm just as accurate at drawing stars as I am telling time by them. I simply gave the stars a look every time you changed, except for that time when you woke up on my stomach."

"I'm not even going to ask you to elaborate on that," Alder said. "Even with Eryn's time table, I'm still not confident—"

"The djinn alchemist had a Drozvegan ceremonial knife," Larcen interrupted. "I told my uncle, and they had no idea one was missing. If the dark mage could infiltrate my home and leave a concealment spell in his wake, as he has been doing the entire time, then what else has he taken from Drozvega? I'm the only one in the human realm who knows what they can do and how to stop them."

"*And* they're hunting an Ancient relic. I'm probably their hundredth-great-granddaughter. If anyone has a chance of understanding whatever this relic does and how to handle it safely, it's me," I told him.

"Prepared these little speeches in advance, did you?" Alder asked wryly. He sighed. "Fine. I'll redirect the jet Moxie's on and she can take you to...?"

"Barcelona," I said firmly.

Larcen flicked his eyes from Alder to me and back again, carefully keeping his face a neutral mask.

"Very well," Alder said. "Moxie will equip you with whatever you need *and* record the precise times Larcen undergoes his next identity crisis. You two have been a little less than forthcoming, this call aside, so I'll hope you understand I'll have to take it all with a grain of salt."

"Yes, sir," I replied. Larcen just nodded.

"And, Larcen, when this mission is over, you and I are going to have a little chat on how you're going to help me repair relations with Pegasus Express."

Larcen swallowed. "Yes, sir."

The marble blinked and went dark, and the drow put it away in his pocket. Then he gave me an accusatory look. "You told him Barcelona. That star chart showed the Algerian Western Sand Sea."

"A location no one should know, not even you," I replied crisply, "so I'm politely asking you to forget it." I withdrew the map from my dress pocket and the Zippo lighter with the cigar-smoking kapre decal on it. A couple of flicks and the map was on fire. I phased into crystal to hold it until the star chart had turned into ash my palm. "Me not-so-politely asking involves my bladed fans. Or this lighter. Maybe both."

"Enough of the theatrics, I get the point. Sheesh. Besides, I already told you I would. Sort of."

"Very good." Spinning on my heel, I marched out of the greenhouse and into the polytunnel. The gnomes were back at work, which meant there were no humans in the vicinity, so I clapped my hands to get their attention. "Hello, hello! Would whoever's closest to the door please lock it?"

"Right away, Miss Eryn!"

"But, Miss Eryn," Rumple protested, "we're in the middle of business hours—"

"This'll only take a moment, Rumple. Now, would everyone come over here for minute, please?"

"Eryn, what are you doing?" Larcen rumbled behind me.

The gnomes quickly gathered, tilting their expectant faces towards me like a bunch of flowers eager for the sun.

"Thank you. Now, I know one of you is *very* good with computers, as Rumple still hasn't been able to break through the firewall and encryption codes you placed to update the website."

"You mean tamper with!"

"Who said that?" Larcen demanded.

The gnomes became as silent and still as plaster like when a human was nearby.

I waved my hands. "I don't care who it is. Anyone who can put that level of protection on a mere website can surely infiltrate DUO's computer system and delete all records of those star charts."

Larcen seized my arm. "Eryn, you're talking about—"

"I know what I'm talking about," I said, shaking him off. "I wouldn't be asking this if it weren't a life-or-death situation. Now Larcen, Rumple, and I are going to go outside and redirect any customers that come by to the grotto for the next ten minutes, and when we come back, I want to see a note on that desk that says 'Done' in big bold letters, okay?"

"But, Miss Eryn, DUO's computers are on a closed server," Roberto said. "Someone would have to be there in person to erase those files. Or at least have access to a computer that's linked in."

Larcen lunged at Roberto, snatching him up by his gold satin shirt. "Your specialty is flower arranging, Roberto, not computers. Or posing nude with Henrietta for those despicable ceramic statues. You're a *patsy*. Who are you speaking for?"

I smacked Larcen on the back of his hand with the bladed fan and caught Roberto with a gust of air, settling him gently to the ground. He quickly retreated behind Trudy, who cracked her meaty knuckles.

"Fine," I said. "Then the gnome in question will conceal themselves inside a, a..." I looked around for something suitable to hide a gnome in that wouldn't raise any suspicions. But everything in here was related to plant maintenance, and while Maven would accept my bringing an oversized potted fern onto the jet as one of my many eccentricities, it certainly wouldn't fool Moxie. "Gnat farts," I muttered.

"A suitcase?" Marigold supplied.

"What's a suitcase?"

"It holds clothes and toiletries and stuff like that. Travelers use them all the time, otherwise you'd have to buy all new things at your destination."

"Ah! Yes. A suitcase. Then the gnome in question will conceal themselves inside a suitcase—"

"You don't have a suitcase," Larcen said.

"Then I'll get one! Then the gnome in question will conceal themselves inside my newly acquired suitcase and join us on the jet. Moxie will be there with her laptop. Will that be sufficient?"

Roberto nodded quickly.

"Excellent. Thank you for your attention and assistance. Now unlock the doors. And if you'll excuse me," I said, slipping my hand into Larcen's pocket and extracting his money clip, "I'll going to see Lady Chantilly about a suitcase."

CHAPTER THIRTY-THREE

Larcen

THE ARIEL RETURNED with a vintage carpet bag and a wide smile just as the jet arrived. I didn't even want to know how much she spent, but Rumple certainly would and was already squealing for a receipt. While she'd been gone, I'd packed my own luggage: a syringe of a certain black elixir. I didn't know how long we were going to be gone, and since my window between treatments was shrinking, I didn't want to be caught without it.

Eryn pushed her thumb into the ornate clasp, opening the wooden frame as the bag collapsed, and took from her crate in the rafters her silver hairbrush, the oversized mug of swag—which I hated to admit had come in very handy lately—some snacks, and her butterfly hair stick. The items barely covered the bottom of the bag, and then she took me by the hand and Rumple by the collar and marched us into the break room. A few minutes later the traitorous floral arranger Roberto called,

"All clear," and the ariel scooped up the mystery-gnome-filled carpet bag before I could even look at it.

Moxie wasn't one to smile a lot, or show any emotion other than concentration and sedate indulgence with her hyperactive sister, so we didn't receive the warmest of welcomes at the airstrip. Eryn, however, did get a little nod from her, but when Moxie turned her angular face at me, it was like a hawk regarding a mouse it wanted to catch for its hatchlings' dinner.

"Hello, *Larcen*."

Just like there was no word for regret in Drozvegan, we drow never apologized for anything. It wasn't in our nature. Any egregious offenses were settled by combat, or if it was disadvantageous for the hierarchy to lose one or both combatants, there was a ceremony held before the elders where the offended would cut the offender across the cheek or arm, deep enough to leave a scar, and then the matter was considered settled.

I doubted Moxie wanted to take me in a fight, and there was no way I was going to submit myself to a cutting. So I gave her a nod of acknowledgement, trotted up the steps into the jet, and helped myself to the caviar and champagne.

Moxie had a word with the pilot before dropping into the leather seat opposite me, deliberately settling one hand over the other in her lap as if she was preparing herself to sit and stare daggers at me the entire flight. I spooned some more caviar onto a cracker and crunched down, staring right back at her through my sunglasses.

"Thank you so much for coming," the ariel said, her voice a little too excited, her hands a little too jittery. She clutched the carpet bag to her chest, her hands under her chin like she was a chipmunk with a prized walnut.

"I was already in the air," she answered, glaring at me.

When it was clear I wasn't going to make a sound unless specifically addressed—and human intimidation tactics were nothing compared to a drow's—Moxie flicked her attention to the ariel. "Why did you bring luggage? Everything you might need is on this plane."

"I-I like my hairbrush."

"You needed an entire suitcase for a hairbrush?"

"And some clothes. And my mug."

Moxie's left eye twitched for a fraction before she smoothed her expression. "Alder says you have a piece of an Ancient relic. I'd like to see that. Run a few diagnostics."

The ariel clutched the carpet bag tighter to her chest. Moxie's expression hardened, and she looked a second away from using vodou or one of her magitech gadgets to force the ariel to comply, so I took the oxhorn out of my vest pocket and tossed it onto the table between us.

Moxie's hand slapped over the oxhorn as if she was afraid I was going to snatch it back. Keeping her hand on it, she rustled around in the seat beside her and withdrew her laptop and a contraption of multicolored glass and wire out of her chrome suitcase.

Across the aisle, the ariel stiffened at the sight of the laptop. Her target.

I made a show of flicking my warrior braid over my shoulder, but it was to disguise my sunglasses slipping down my nose so I could glare at her. She wrinkled her nose at me and relaxed, and I pushed my sunglasses back into place so my sensitive eyes wouldn't fry in the sunlight and turned back to the caviar.

Moxie opened her laptop and settled the contraption on her head, pressing a small button on the side to link it to a program on the computer. Then she cycled through the multiple lenses of colored glass, combining some and looking solely through others, as a laser from the middle of her forehead scanned the oxhorn the entire time.

"I've never seen anything like this," she muttered. "The data is incredible. These seams... they don't quite fit and yet the oxhorn pieces are fused together. Actually, not really fused, but attracted to each other as if with strong magnets. I assume there are more pieces?"

I nodded. "That's why we're going to Barcelona."

"And how did you discover the next piece is there?"

"A scrying glass and crystal." The ariel indicated the object that resembled a magnifying glass in her belt beside her bladed fans.

"Old school, but effective."

"This is ariel-made," Eryn sniffed. "There's nothing more effective on this planet."

Moxie, her head covered in magitech gear, gave her a judgmental look and returned to examining the oxhorn. "I can't wait to discover what all these pieces make. To see an Ancient artifact in the flesh would be the find of a lifetime."

"It was broken apart for a reason," the ariel said tartly.

Moxie was forming her own tart reply when I asked, "How long will the diagnostics take?"

"Hours, probably. There's nothing to quantify it against so there'll be gigabytes of data to sort through. Perfect for going over the parameters of this mission and what is expected of you and the consequences if you don't comply."

I poured some more champagne and settled into my seat. My lips quirked up into a patronizing smile: *You know I'll just do whatever I want.*

Moxie removed her headgear, smoothed her brown hair, and returned the smile. *We'll just see about that.*

❧

SOMETIME AFTER TEN in the evening I turned into a rat, which didn't improve my standing with Moxie at all. She'd been in the middle of informing us of the DUO team stationed in Barcelona —Veronica and Darrius—who would meet us on the ground and assist us in any way we needed, and lurched out of her seat with a shriek.

That noise was very irritating, so I wiggled out of my clothes, careful to conceal my syringe, and climbed up onto the table. The reflection in the porthole window said I was indeed a very handsome black rat—the light glinted off my shiny fur in the most alluring way—so I didn't see what all the fuss was about, but my presence made Moxie stagger in the aisle.

The ariel tore away from the window and caught Moxie's arm to steady her before she could fall. "It's just Larcen."

"I thought you said he turned into a cricket!"

"That was three transformations ago. He's been a goldfish, a cricket, a rabbit, and the most adorable baby deer. Guess he's a rat now."

And as a rat, I seemed to prefer the mezze platter of edibles instead of the caviar. I snatched a soft-boiled egg off the plate and tore into it with my sharp teeth, runny yolk oozing down my chin.

"Is there any particular reason why they're all prey animals?" Moxie shuddered and straightened her glasses with a shaking hand. "Why can't he be something useful like a dog or a chimp? Ugh. Why does he have to be a rat?"

But the ariel didn't reply. She had a stunned look on her face and abandoned Moxie to look out the window again. I was about to squeak at her as to what was so engrossing out there, and then I remembered she preferred to tell the time by the stars' position.

She turned away from the window with a frown. "The change is too early. It's only 10:12 p.m. EST. He's not supposed to change until 2:47 a.m."

"Guess your *ariel* time theory isn't all you thought it was," Moxie said.

Eryn didn't seem to hear her. She just went to the windows again, on either side of the plane, trying to gauge the time.

Moxie gave me a wary look and sank back into her seat, careful to lean as far away from me as she could. "Can he still understand me?"

"I think so." Eryn returned to her seat, settling the carpet bag carefully on her lap, which had not left her hand this entire time. "I had Rumple translate for us earlier, so he must understand human speech even if he can't replicate it himself."

"Good, then I can continue updating you. Though, I'm seriously considering aborting this mission."

The ariel and I both squeaked.

"Why?" Eryn demanded.

Moxie pointed at me. "Um, hello? He's a rat? *Ahead* of schedule, too."

"So? He'll change back. He always does."

"You don't know that. Part of the reason why Alder agreed to this is because you were confident in your timing of his transformations. And yet here a rat sits across from me four hours early. Something's changed with the curse."

"Curses don't change," Eryn said firmly. "There's just some other variable we're not aware of."

"Never heard of variable being a time zone." Then she let out an irritated sigh. "*But*, we don't have much choice in the matter, do we? It's not like we can sit on this. I'm still going to update Alder about this change, *and* you'll submit yourself to more testing when you change back, Larcen. Taking your blood now as a rat might be easier, but it'll still be rat blood, which our tests aren't calibrated for."

Spider bites, I cursed, sinking into a squat and dragging a piece of salami off the platter. I made sure to stare at Moxie with my beady brown eyes the entire time I chomped into the sausage round.

I was still a rat when we were beginning our final descent into Barcelona, just a few precious moments away from dawn, and Eryn used that time to distract Moxie. Unclasping her carpet bag, she left it on the seat beside her and floated down to the rear of the plane where the closet and changing rooms were. "Um, Moxie, would you help me please?"

The magitech genius suddenly became very uncomfortable, all her previous confidence evaporating. "Uhhh... this *really* is more of Maven's thing."

"Please?" The ariel gave her a pitiful look that even had me half-convinced, and I was just a rat. "I'm still not used to this whole wearing clothes thing, and Larcen's no help right now because he's a rat. I need a female's opinion."

Moxie huffed out a sigh and stood up, giving her cardigan a small tug as if she was adjusting chainmail armor. Then she leaned over the table and slapped the laptop down, giving me a glare and hissing, "I don't want your filthy little rat feet all over my keyboard."

I squeaked a tirade at her where I called her every obscene name I could think of—not because I meant it, but because I wanted to hurry her along. The sooner she joined Eryn in the back, the sooner the gnome who had been the bane of my floral emporium website's existence would be revealed.

The gnome waited a full thirty seconds after the rear cabin's partition had slid into place before parting the frame of the carpet bag and emerging like a bee from a daffodil's horn.

"*Trudy?*" I squeaked.

The muscular gnome adjusted her Bavarian barmaid outfit, slipped down the seat, and peered down the aisle for a heartbeat before determining it was safe to scurry across. She used just her arms to hoist herself into Moxie's vacated seat, scrambled onto the armrest, and leapt across the two-foot gap to the table like an Olympian long-distance jumper. Then she opened the laptop, settling the upper rim across her shoulders like a powerlifter, and surged upward with her thick thighs. When it was open, she cracked her knuckles and finally gave me a look.

"What? I exercise my mind as much as my body," she said.

With an enraged roar, I hurled the olive I'd been eating aside. *"You ruined my reputation! My plant nursery is now a smut garden! People have been leaving comments that it's like garden porn! Savannah Belle Floral Emporium is a respectable establishment, dammit!"*

Trudy thumped her hands against her muscular bosom. "Come at me, bro!"

I charged, sharp teeth bared, and she caught me by the ears like they were the horns of a bull, twisted, and sent me flying over the table and back into my seat. I bounced off the cream leather and onto the floor, and by the time I had scurried up back to the table, still stunned, Trudy was closing the laptop and pressing down on the edge until the little latch clicked into place. Then she helped herself to a wedge of summer sausage and gave me a patronizing pat on the head as she marched back to Moxie's seat.

"Easier than chugging beer."

Then she disappeared in a flutter of maroon velvet and white lace, scurrying back to her carpet bag and closing herself back in to enjoy her spoils for the rest of the flight.

CHAPTER THIRTY-FOUR

Eryn

VERONICA AND DARRIUS really sounded like nice people, and I felt bad ditching them, but I was resolved to do it. I had to keep the number of people who truly knew where we were going to just two. Or rather, one person, one gnome in a suitcase, and one rat.

The moment the plane landed, three things happened very quickly. Dawn broke, a red marble on the horizon with an orange sky that turned the scrub flanking the tarmac from gray to yellow; Larcen transformed back into his naked drow self; and we were immediately swarmed by a flock of flying serpents. Or dragons without legs, it was hard to tell. Yellow-green and as long as my arm, they rose from the dusty scrub in a sandy plume.

"Every damn time," Moxie growled, grabbing a gauntlet from her silver case and fitting it over her wrist. "Open the door on my command."

The dark elf disappeared.

"Where are you going?" Moxie hollered.

"I'm getting dressed." Larcen's voice came from behind the curtain at the back of the jet. "You think I want one of those things nipping at my tender bits?"

Moxie rolled her eyes. "Fine. One, two—"

I yanked on the latch early. The door dropped down, and the little dragons swarmed the plane. "I'm sorry," I wailed above the flapping wings. "I thought the latch was going to be sticky!"

"This is a defibrillator net," Moxie snapped. "If I use it now, it'll fry everyone in the plane too. Oh come *on*!" She swatted a swarm away from her equipment. "Get away from my laptop you damn buzzards—*don't eat it!*"

Now that the gnome's sabotage was masked, I yanked my bladed fan out of my belt and gave it a gentle swoosh. With a cacophony of little screeches, the entire swarm was swept outside, and Moxie hurried to the door. She squeezed a trigger in her palm, and a blue net ejected from her gauntlet, spreading wide like an unfurling daisy and zapping each of the little creatures on the backside. It didn't seem to hurt them, but it certainly made them think twice of swarming the plane again.

I replaced my fan and gave Moxie a smile. "How exciting."

"Once, just *once*, I want to come to Barcelona and not almost become food for a bunch of baby amphipteres. Relocating the colony out here was a mistake and I've had it!"

I brightened my smile. "Well... good luck with that."

Larcen reappeared from the shadows, settling some sunglasses over his eyes. Then he gave Moxie a brief nod and trotted down the steps to the tarmac.

"Thank you, Moxie," I told her quickly, clutching my carpet bag close to my stomach. I gave her a big grin. "Bye now!"

The car waiting for us was one of those nice ones with the thick leather seats and cupholders in the back, which was not nearly as nice now that it was covered in globs of amphiptere droppings. While Moxie gave us a brief wave from the jet, I doubted she was sad to see us go. She didn't like rats, apparently, so she hadn't enjoyed Larcen's company, and I had pretended to be quite incompetent when choosing my outfit.

In reality, I had gotten the hang of it pretty quickly, especially if I just kept it simple—dress, boots, starlight metal belt with fans and scrying glass—but I needed clothes for the desert without making it look like that was what I was doing. I'd paired hiking boots with a crop-top, a mini-skirt with a khaki jacket, sandals with an oversized scarf that I'd attempted to use as toga. In the end, Moxie had shoved an outfit she'd snatched from the hangers into my hands with a shrill, "Wear this and *only* this!" before practically hurling herself through the curtain and back into the main cabin. Since she hadn't screamed in outrage at the sight of a gnome messing around with her laptop, I figured everything had gone according to plan and stuffed the desert gear into a bundle that I wrapped in a spare set of clothes for Larcen.

The car took us to the café where Veronica and Darrius were scheduled to meet with us. It was a bright, crisp morning here, the old city awake and bustling, the smell of coffee and pastry everywhere.

I wish we could have stayed. I hadn't eaten much on the plane, too nervous to let my guard down for an instant, and a cup of steamed milk and a chunk of buttered baguette sounded so good.

Instead, the second DUO's car turned the corner, we stepped into a taxi and took it back to the airport.

"Hold on," Larcen said.

A moment later we were in the belly of a plane headed to Algiers, and I was smacking the dark elf. "Get off, get off! You know I hate it when you do that!"

Laughing, he started shifting the luggage into the semblance of an easy chair. "And how did you expect us to cross the desert? On camelback? Where you going to fly us the entire way there?" He snorted, flopping down on the luggage and pillowing his head against his interlaced fingers. "Not with your metabolism."

I glared at him as I pulled a package of peanut butter crackers out from my pocket.

"We're going to have to shadow-walk, and you're just going to have to like it."

"I'll endure it, but I won't like it one minute," I huffed, sinking down onto a leather trunk and stuffing a cracker into my mouth.

As the plane took off, the temperature in the cargo bay dropped dramatically.

I was already swathed in my toga-like shawl, my head and shoulders completed covered in off-white linen. Larcen sat up, fidgeting.

"Got anything else in that carpet bag of yours? A jacket or something?"

"But won't that hide your muscles?"

His violet eyes sharpened into slits. "It's kinda cold in here, and unless you want me rampaging through everyone else's property for a sweater, then—"

"Wait a minute! This is just a ploy to get me to open the bag so you can see what gnome is in here, isn't it? Well it's not going to work, caveman. He or she has immunity, sanctuary, protect—"

The carpet bag clasp clicked free, a gnome pushing aside the wooden frame and popping out like a gopher from its hole.

"Trudy!" I cried, both surprised and delighted that it was her and that she was okay. "I... never would've guessed it was you."

"Neither did he," she said, jerking her thumb at Larcen. Then she gave him a bold up-down look. "I think you were more manly as a rat."

"Why you—"

"I found a hat in here, stuffed into one of those hiking boots." She threw it at Larcen. "Maybe he'll stop whining now."

~

IN ALGIERS, WHICH WAS "BLISSFULLY HOT" according to Larcen, we shared a hearty meal of heavily spiced couscous and lamb—which I let Larcen eat—and double-checked the scrying crystal. It pointed to the same spot on the map as it had the last four times I'd checked it, so the alchemist and the dark mage hadn't found it yet. We didn't know how many pieces they already had, but each piece in our possession meant one less in theirs and one step closer to actually figuring out what this Ancient relic was. After purchasing some gallons of water and flatbread stuffed with bean paste from a market stall, we started our trek into the desert where the Atlas Mountains disappeared beneath the wasteland dunes of the Western Sand Sea.

As much as I loathed being in the shadows—the all-consuming dark was worse than any claustrophobia I had ever experienced—it was an incredibly fast way to travel long distances. Larcen merely had to see a shadow, no matter how far away, to step out of it. Constantly using his bloodline ability eventually wore him down, and then I took over. Ariels might be made of mist, but that had no effect on our grip strength. He held the suitcase while I held him, and I soared over the desert thermals easier than a falcon.

We reached the X on the scrying crystal's map in the middle of a cloudless afternoon.

Great cliffs rose in the distance, mountains behind them on the horizon, and here, in the middle of a red waste, was a ksar. The massive chunk of stone was the bone of a mountain before the sand sea had whittled it away to almost nothing and the wind had pitted it with countless holes and caves. The locals called it a castle, or a place where one could find refuge from the sandstorms and the oppressive desert heat.

Though I had never seen it before, I knew it was the entrance to the Windless Place. The prison of the Forsaken. Why would there be an Ancient relic hidden among the greatest criminals the ariels had ever known?

CHAPTER THIRTY-FIVE

Larcen

I STEPPED out of the shadows and into the cooler caves of the ksar, as the ariel had called it, pulling the ariel and her carpet bag out of the darkness behind me. She sagged against the stone, in the light, of course, and fought to find her breath. You couldn't breathe in the shadow realm, but we were never in it longer than it took to blink. It must've been her claustrophobia.

I took the bag from her limp fingers and opened it. A sweaty Trudy hopped out and hurried over a hyperventilating Eryn with a bottle of water.

"I wonder if Raphael put something in his swag bags that deals with anxiety," I said, rooting around. My fingers finally felt the coolness of porcelain and I pulled the oversized Grow, Dammit mug out of the nest of clothes. I still had the Night Dust in my pocket, but I didn't want to offer that if I didn't have to. It was powerful, and addicting if you took too much of it. "You'd be surprised how many fascinari get social anxiety. He usually spikes his punch with the stuff, just to make sure no fights break out at his parties... Spider bites, there's none in here. But—" I lifted a lemony-yellow candy with black striping. "Look. It's a Honey Bee Happy sucker."

The ariel gave it a doubtful look. "Is this food-food or is this like the bubblegum where it looks like food, tastes like food, but actually isn't?"

"You can actually eat this, but it's better if you just suck on it. It'll make you happy or giddy, depending on your current level of emotion."

"So... I'll still be anxious, but I'll be happy about it?"

"Precisely."

The crinkling plastic wrapper echoed through the tunnels like the crackling roar of lightning, but nothing roused. Eryn popped the candy into her mouth, made a face at its sweet taste, and waited for the happiness to take effect.

Two seconds later she was skipping down the tunnel with her scarf and her hair streaming out behind her like May Day ribbons, though she didn't stray from the sunlight. With the scrying glass and crystal in her hands, she called, "This way, this way" in a singsong voice. The gnome and I shared a look of disbelief before she dove head-first into the carpet bag and I snatched it up and raced after the ariel.

With the aid of the scrying glass, the ariel led us through a maze of tunnels, each heading deeper into the ground than the last. We bypassed caverns and so many tunnels that the drow in me couldn't help but be curious as to what untold passages and secrets we'd left behind. We might refer to Drozvega as a home cave, but it was a cave network of hundreds of miles of tunnels and arching caverns and subterranean lagoons and thousands more still unexplored.

Eryn's mood dimmed the deeper we went, and she started to hug her arms to her chest and shy away from the darkest shadows. As we took a water break, I fished around in the mug for another mood-enhancing candy.

"Ooo!" she said, plopping the red ball into her mouth. "Spicy."

The Feisty Fireball perked her right up, and after punching me squarely in the shoulder with a crystal hand, she urged us onward.

"Ow," I complained, rubbing my arm.

"Wussy," came her challenging reply.

But it did hurt, more than I thought it should. I'd actually felt something pop or crack in there, like a hairline fracture. Moxie had told me that I needed to take more calcium, but this was ridiculous.

"Hurry up, caveman," she goaded. "You should be the one leading, not me. I don't even like caves."

"Then give me the scrying glass."

Scrying glasses weren't just good for finding things; they *revealed* them, too. Using the glass in tandem with the scrying crystal, the ariel was uncovering the hidden path to the next piece more effectively than a bloodhound.

"You mean *this* scrying glass?" She held it up to her eye, peering at me as if I were a rare specimen under a microscope. "Profession opinion concludes that yep, you're a controlling asshole. And a sparkly one too!"

"Eryn, give me the—"

The ariel just flashed me the middle finger—where had she learned that in five days?—with a loud "a-ha!" and took the next tunnel to the right.

I followed, nearly crashing into her as she stood just a few feet inside the biggest cavern yet.

Beams of yellow sunlight crosshatched the vaulted space, turning the walls pale orange, as if we were trapped inside the world's largest cantaloupe. Sand rained down as scorpions and other such creatures that called this desert their home skittered over the vent holes. It was warm in here too, despite its depth below the sands, waves of heat wafting towards the ceiling.

Ledges jutted out from the striated walls, dark passageways heading deeper into the ksar and the rock below. There was a relief carving here, a mural, one that wrapped the entire circumference of the cave, or at least the bits of wall that hadn't sloughed off into piles of sand.

I recognized the twin moon goddesses immediately. Their spitting image was manifested in flesh behind me. This mural depicted the time of their ascension, when they still walked the mortal lands. It was a time when there was no balance between light and darkness, before Sol took them all into the heavens to safeguard creation with endless light. Shadowy horsemen on nightmarish steeds terrorized the land, reaping souls with bows and swords and the jaws of their great hounds. The next dozen paces' worth of mural had been worn away, the sand drifting over my feet as I hurried to the next recognizable piece.

The Night Lands, my home before the Spider Queen.

There were no drow depicted, but I knew it was our ancestral land by the oversized mushrooms and prowling shadowcats, the giant willows whose branches bowed before Selena's light. And night wisps. The gift to her sister, Lena. There was no sign of the horsemen nor their hounds, though I suspected their demise had once been told in this next swath that lay in heaps of sand on the ground.

I followed the rest of the coarse wall back to the entrance, where only the carving of a sun and moon marked the stone above the tunnel. The ariel hadn't moved from her spot, her eyes riveted on something behind me.

In the center of the cave, illuminated by a single shaft of sunlight, was an inverted bowl of obsidian glass. Spanning over six feet across, it was entirely peppered with shallow depressions, a collection of white marbles at the bottom of the basin.

"What is this place?" I whispered, my voice echoing like the roar of a crashing wave against the ceiling.

"It's a door," the ariel said flatly.

"I've never seen a door like this before."

"You've never seen an inverted planetarium display?" she snarked, the Feisty Fireball apparently still alive and well in her system.

Of course she'd recognize it for what it was, and now that she'd said something, so did I. "So the obsidian is the night sky and the white marbles are the stars. But how do we know what sky to map?" No sooner had I said it did it dawn on me.

"The star chart," we said in unison.

I shook my head. "Too bad you burned the map and destroyed all copies of it."

"Good thing I have an eidetic memory," she snapped back.

Smirking, she tossed me the scrying crystal and put the glass into her belt next to her fans. Then she scooped all the marbles out of the basin, swept the sand aside with a puff of her cheeks, and got to work systematically placing the marbles in the depressions. I recognized most of the constellations and noticed she was leaving a few out. When I asked about it, her reply was,

"This was made in ancient times. Back then, there were only forty-eight named constellations. Of course ariels knew them all, but they had to make it difficult for everyone else, no matter the era."

"This is ariel-made?" I sputtered.

Her expression darkened. Apparently I wasn't supposed to know that, or mention it.

"What is this place?" I asked again. Why would ariels carve the history of my mother's faith into a place like this?

She didn't reply, pursing her lips and placing the last marble in its depression.

Instantly there was hiss, and the marbles sprang into the air, whizzing round and round the planetarium until the air was white. We retreated a few steps at the sound of a loud crack, and the planetarium split in half. Sand poured into a pit as the halves spread apart, revealing a black hole that no light seemed to penetrate.

The ariel turned into mist and approached the edge of the pit, visibly trembling.

In my hand, the scrying crystal tugged persistently, clearly indicating just where we should go.

"'And beneath the sands in the heart of a mountain you shall be buried, never to feel the air again. You will be known as Forsaken, your true name forgotten,'" she intoned, and dropped into the pit.

CHAPTER THIRTY-SIX

Eryn

Sand as fine as flour cushioned my feet. It was so still here; there was not even a waft of air from the surface far above. If I raised my hand I could block out the light of the tunnel, and though I stood in its circle, its strength was so feeble down here it did little combat the suffocating blackness.

The effects of the Feisty Fireball were starting to fade—rapidly—as my pulse spiked, and I yanked my starlight metal fan and scrying glass from my belt. Reflecting the light off the fan and watching it through the glass, it illuminated the star-shaped mound of starlight metal on the wall. I slammed my palm against it, desperation flooding through me.

But starlight metal never failed.

A shock of white-gold light rippled down the tunnel and arched over the exit, crackling and sparkling like lightning caught in a bottle. I didn't wait for Larcen. I had to get out of there.

Phasing into crystal, I arrowed down the tunnel, slamming my hand into the next star-shaped mound of metal and illuminating another cavern larger than the one hundreds of feet above my head.

"No," I whispered, "don't think of it that way." If I thought of just how deep I was below the desert surface, not only would I break out into a flood-like sweat, I'd probably lose myself to hysteria and pee myself. I hadn't had a body for very long, and even I knew that was shameful.

Instead I forced my gaze upward to the cavern that crackled with veins of white-gold light. This place was much less refined than the orange-colored one that housed the planetarium: stone black as a starless night and chunks that had fallen from the ceiling and walls over time strewn about the place like a baby giant's building blocks.

I jumped when Larcen appeared at my side, stepping out of the shadows in that eerie way of his. He had a brown, barrel-shaped sweet wrapped in cellophane in his hand. "I've got a Sweet Sassy Molassy right here."

"No more candy!" I shrilled, though the less-hysterical part of me appreciated the gesture. "Let's just d-d-d—" I couldn't get the words out.

"Do what we need to do and get out here?"

"*Yes!*"

Larcen gave me a sharp nod, set the carpet bag down by my feet, and unhooked his scorpion blade from his hip. Moving around me, he let the scrying crystal tug him further into the cavern.

I couldn't seem to get my legs to move, but I could still get my shaking arms to function. Lifting the scrying glass to my eye, I scanned the cavern and found exactly what I didn't want to find.

"The scrying crystal looks like it's taking me to a well?" the dark elf called. "I think there are statues—"

"Don't touch them!"

"Alright, alright, Miss Bossy. I won't touch them."

Cautious so he wouldn't accidentally knock one of the statues, he leaned over the rim and visibly started. "Hey, this well, it actually has water in it. White water. It should be drier than bleached bone in the middle of this desert. Uh, Eryn? The water, it's... glowing."

I didn't have to be close to know exactly what he was looking at. A well hewn from a single stone, seamless and perfectly smooth, its rim dotted with seven statues. The statues were no taller than Trudy, and while they all had a general likeness in sinuous shape, there were no defining facial features. But it was clear they yearned for the well. It was almost like they were leaning inward.

I had to swallow a few times before I could say, "It's a moon well."

"What is this place?" Larcen muttered for the third time.

"The Windless Place," I whispered. The prison of the Forsaken.

"Hey, the crystal just turned dark. This is it." He put it in his pocket and pulled out the oxhorn, carefully passing it over the surface of the water, trying to attract its kin.

"W-well?" I asked.

"It's not working. The pieces aren't even glowing like they did before."

"Did you break it?" I shrilled.

"Of course not."

"Maybe it's dirty. Rub it on your pants."

"My trousers have seen enough wrinkles to last a drow's lifetime, thank you very much. I'm not adding insult to injury."

"I don't give a gnat's fart about your trousers!"

With a scoff, he rubbed the oxhorn on his trousers. "There. Nothing. See? Maybe it needs an ariel's touch."

"A what?"

"You *are* a descendant of the Ancients, and a powerful one at that. Maybe it really is connected to you. Come here. You need to hold it."

"But I don't want to come over there."

"The sooner you get your skinny butt over here the sooner we can leave. Don't make me shadow-walk you over here."

"No shadow-walking! This place is bad enough." Shuddering, I forced my eyes upward and focused on the crackling starlight metal that illuminated the room. It seemed so high above me, yet not high enough. "Easy breezy, this is all easy breezy," I muttered, taking my first step forward. Then I rammed my toes into a boulder. "Larcen! You have to guide me."

"Just look—"

"I'm looking at the ceiling and all that glorious air up there! It's the only thing keeping me sane right now, so tell me if I need to go left or right or so help me I will take a pair of pruning shears to every pair of sharkskin trousers you own and set fire to every plant in your floral emporium and then get Trudy to advertise on that damn website that you're hosting garden-themed stripteases every Friday n—"

"Alright, alright! Go right."

Sticking my hands straight out in front of me, I floated to the right.

"Forward. And you know you look like the walking dead with your arms out like that, right? Why don't you just phase into mist?"

"And waste energy?"

"Spider bites, this is going to take forever. I'm shadow-walking y—"

"Don't you dare! Stripteases, Larcen, the risqué kind with

naked gnome backup dancers and where the patrons get to slap you on the fanny and ask you what you're doing later. Now which way?"

"Still straight. Go right. Spider bites, your left. Left!"

"I'm lefting!"

I strafed and crept forward little by little, and eventually I felt his cool fingers curl around mine. I clamped down so hard he hissed in pain, and then I was yanked forward until my knees knocked against the moon well. The white water inside rippled with the impact, but the statues along the rim did not.

"Now that you're *finally* here, take this." Larcen shoved the oxhorn into my hands.

I had to grip it with both hands I was shaking so bad.

A heartbeat later, the edges glowed silver and the oxhorn trembled in my hands.

"See? I told you s—"

"It's not me!"

The oxhorn jerked out of my hands and flashed across the room, back the way I had come.

A tall and lean hooded figure stood in the entrance of the tunnel, arms braced in front of his stomach as the oxhorn clanged against the writhing silver mass in his hands. Hundreds of oxhorn fragments whirled around each other in a swirl of pearlescent gray and shining silver, sorting and shuffling themselves until they resembled a long horn.

A hunting horn.

The seams spiderwebbing across the hunting horn still glowed with a silver light, but fainter now, as the dark mage stepped into the cavern of the Forsaken.

And disappeared.

He stepped out of the shadows on the opposite side of the moon well, the glowing light of the water revealing a familiar face as he swept back his hood. There was a flare of green light from his palm, and instantly his towering stature shortened and his musculature thickened, the concealment spell broken.

"Uncle Malcan?" Larcen whispered.

"You're crowding the moonlight, nephew."

He thrust out a hand, a glyph on his palm flaring to life with green light. Filaments as fine as spun silver ejected, weaving into a web and blasting us clear across the cavern. Terrified as I was underground, my guardian instinct always prevailed and I caught myself, phasing into mist. The web slipped harmlessly down my body as I banked upward towards the ceiling. Larcen phased into shadow, buffeting against the far wall and slipping through the mesh.

With us out of the way, Malcan dropped the horn into the moon well. A pillar of light erupted towards the ceiling, the horn suspended within. Malcan put on a pair of sunglasses and watched as the silvery edges of the individual pieces fused and disappeared until only a flawless piece of pearlescent oxhorn remained, its surface dappled in celestial silver with the constellations of Canis Major, Canis Minor, and Canes Venatici.

The Hunting Dogs.

I yanked the bladed fans from my belt and dove with a scream just as he placed the horn against his lips and blew.

CHAPTER THIRTY-SEVEN

Larcen

I APPEARED RIGHT BEHIND HIM, scorpion blade poised to stab Malcan between the shoulder blades. I didn't want to kill him, just incapacitate him long enough to figure out what in the spider-cursed hell was going on. This was my mentor, my favorite relative—which meant something among us quarrelsome drow—the one who had been the most supportive of my new life in DUO. And had made himself one of DUO's targets, apparently.

Malcan spun just as I lunged, smacking my arm wide and blasting me again with that damn glyph. "You always breathed too loud, Larcen."

Phasing into shadow, I let the web pass through me before solidifying into my drow self once more. "You're a shadowwalker?"

"Ha! I've just reformed an Ancient summoning relic and

that's what you have to say? Drow are vain creatures, nephew, but you take it to a whole new level."

Malcan pivoted, thrusting his glyph palm at the diving ariel, who sliced the web in half with her bladed fans. She careened into him with the scream of an eagle, driving her bladed fans into his chest.

Or she would have, had he not melted into the shadows.

He appeared half a cavern away, raising the horn to his mouth and blowing a second time.

"Don't let him sound the horn again!" she shrieked.

I lashed out with my chain dart, but Malcan had already disappeared into the shadows of the tunnel. "Why?" I recalled the dart and raced after him.

"Just a wild guess from all those constellations on the side of the horn that it summons dogs," she hollered, her crazed smile and misty form speeding past me. "Three constellations, three blasts, it makes sense, don't you think? Or are you still hung up on the fact that the dark mage who happens to be your uncle is a shadow-walker *just like I said he was*?"

"You were right, I was wrong, do you want a trophy or something?" I snarled, diving head-first into a shadow and leaping out into the planetarium cavern above.

The ariel was right behind me, glittering like diamond. "We can't let him escape!"

She soared up to the ceiling, the very opposite direction of where Malcan was headed. Thrusting her arms out wide, she seemingly multiplied until a dozen more crystal ariels floated in the cavern, catching the sunlight and reflecting it until there were no more shadows to be found.

I couldn't use my bloodline ability to catch up to Malcan, but then again, he couldn't use his to escape.

"Damn sprite," he snarled up at the ariel, flinging half a dozen poisoned knives into the air at random. They passed through the illusions and clattered against the orange stone walls.

"Ha!" Eryn crowed. "Missed me, you cobweb-munching caveman!"

As Malcan barked out a curse, I lashed out with my chain dart again.

Just as he disappeared, the point buried itself into its target.

Malcan reappeared a second later, yellow-green ooze dripping from the ruined glyph as he plucked the dart from his palm. I recalled the dart with a hasty jerk.

"You let her *bite* you," I spat. No wonder he had been wearing that bandage on his hand when last we met.

His own violet eyes narrowed at me. "It was the only thing that could blind that damn sight of yours. Blind you all, in fact. Not to mention it has the added benefit of casting actual webs, not just the concealment kind."

"Why are you doing this?" I shouted.

"I'm doing this for the glory of Drozvega. Our legacy that you've forgotten!" He made a dash for one of the tunnels, but a blast from the ariel's fan swept him aside. Regaining his footing, he lifted his palm to use the glyph, but the marking was ruined. He would need to heal and have the glyph redrawn before using the Spider Queen's poison against us again. Snarling, he moved his scimitar into his wounded hand and held the hunting horn with the other.

"You cursed me." I slapped the chain dart against the sand as he tried to retreat another way. "I've been a goldfish, a cricket, even a rabbit. And nearly everyone has tried to eat me at some point! How does that bring glory to Drozvega?"

"That arrow was never meant for you. It was supposed to free you from that damn sprite up there and bring you back to us. To me. You were supposed to help me, Larcen. Us, the two shadow-born sons destined to fulfill the Spider Queen's vision."

"And what's that?"

"Restore us to the Night Lands." He gestured with the hunting horn. "And this is how we do it."

I stumbled. If we returned to the surface, it would not be just the drow leaving their caves. *She* would come too, and destroy what little there was left. The Spider Queen enslaved everything she touched with her venom, indoctrinating us to fight in her name as she consumed all and gave nothing in return.

I should never have waited. I should have returned to Drozvega the moment I had partnered with that ariel and called the power of the Puddle and eradicated that cancerous blight from our lives once and for all. The drow of this generation might not survive without her venom, but it would free all generations to come. "And how does a hunting horn do that?"

Malcan pointed to the ariel with his scimitar. "Why don't you ask her?"

I risked a glance at Eryn, whose dozen images frowned in confusion.

"Me?" she asked. "But I don't know anything about a hunting horn."

"And yet you wear one on your belt, *guardian*."

We both looked at her belt buckle where the horn, sword, and bow images were all intertwined in celestial silver. She ran her hand over the raised design, her frown deepening.

Malcan laughed. "You don't even know what you were guarding, did you?"

"The night wisps," she snapped.

"Didn't you ever wonder why?"

"They are innocence, pure and untainted, and you killed them!"

"Bah, *innocence*. The fawns of the forests are innocent. A unicorn is pure. Virgins are untainted. What makes the night wisps so special?"

The ariel didn't have a reply for that, and neither did I.

"Are you blind to the history around you?" Malcan demanded, sweeping an arm at the mural surrounding us. "It was only after the creation of the night wisps that the Wild Hunt was curbed, forbidden to enter the mortal realms until the rise of the Hunter's Moon, when the veil between our worlds thins. The veil of the night wisps, almost destroyed in full that night. The Wild Hunt yearns to be set free once again, and they've been calling, if you've had ears to listen. With this horn, I can summon their dogs whenever I want. The Spider Queen will rise and we will reclaim what was taken from us!"

He lifted the horn again, but my chain dart slashed. Malcan either had to parry the attack or blow the horn and get a dart buried in his eye. He dodged, sweeping his scimitar under the chain and pinning it in his armpit. Spinning, he tried to jerk me off balance, but I just leapt, whipping the chain midair and shaking him loose.

I rolled my landing and lashed with the dart again and again, trying to close the distance between us. I had to get that horn.

"Why are you fighting me?" Malcan shouted. "Surely your five-day alliance with DUO cannot eclipse centuries of devotion—"

"Because it cannot be done! It shouldn't. The Night Lands are lost to us. To take them back, to resurface with *her*, would cause side effects we cannot imagine, in the realms of the fascinari and humans alike. It would be catastrophic!"

"Where is your faith? The Spider Queen will lead us—"

"We already wage her wars on the surface for scraps. We are scavengers, Uncle, and she made us that way!"

His face darkened. "Careful, nephew. Our queen has given you a great gift."

"That overgrown arachnid is not my queen."

"You bear her blessing and yet still blaspheme her name?" Malcan glared up at the ariel. "You have corrupted him, you infernal—"

"That is my partner," I roared. "A union you only have yourself to blame for from ordering the slaughter of the night wisps. They were innocent! They are Lena's—"

"You are forbidden to say that name," Malcan thundered.

"It wasn't a raid for resources at all." I'd gotten close now, able to fight with the long, curved dagger as well as the dart.

My uncle swept his scimitar so fast it left flashes of phantom silver in the air as he blocked both dagger and dart. "You've been outside the home cave for too long, Larcen. You've lost your perspective."

"I've *gained* it now that I'm free of her poison!"

"Are you? Truly now, is that little elixir you inject yourself still working, or are you having to take it more and more frequently?" Malcan shoved me back and tapped the back of his neck, where a raised scar identical to mine marked the skin. "We're hers, always."

"*No*," I hissed.

It wasn't the Spider Queen who had seen me through the Trials, that twisting network of caves that culled one out of every three six-year-olds, but a wisp. A wisp who had found me lost and starving and disappearing into the shadows with no control. A wisp who had led me to the fresh air of the surface, to the feet of a lady whose skin was like the star-studded mantle of the night sky. It was *she* who had given me heart plums and shown me where the scorpions prowled so I could hunt and eat, to thrive, *not* the Spider Queen.

"Then you are no blood of mine," my uncle hissed.

The chain wrapped around the scimitar, preventing his upward cut. My dagger clanged against his heavier sword, and the two of us strained against each other, Malcan using his greater weight to force me back. My feet slid back in the sand as I gritted my teeth, muscles straining to keep his scimitar from coming any closer and cutting into my shoulder. The chain dart dragged in the sand as I kept two hands on the dagger, and Malcan sneered at me, "For the sake of your mother, I will tell her you died with honor, but the Spider Queen will not mourn your loss. She despises weakness, and so do I."

His forehead came crashing into my face.

"Larcen!" Eryn cried.

It was like getting hit with a cinder block. I staggered back, barely cognizant enough to kick the chain as it slid off the scimitar.

Malcan blew the horn a third time, the stars on the horn finally flaring to life, and then my dart buried into his stomach.

CHAPTER THIRTY-EIGHT

Eryn

My illusion failed as the cavern ceiling above me exploded. I swerved as chunks of orange stone pelted the ground from the newly formed gap, a bolt of crackling lightning as thick as a tree trunk snaking through and burning the sand below into glass.

Four dogs, each as large as a pony and composed entirely of star fire, stepped out of the lightning. Their hides crackled with white, sparking light, their eyes and maws as blue as the stars. Everywhere they stepped, the sand turned to glass beneath their paws. As one, they lifted their heads to the sky and howled.

Malcan tugged the dart out of his gut and thrust a bloodied hand at Larcen. "Destroy them!"

The star hounds leapt to do his bidding.

The dark elf became shadow, expecting the nearest dog to pass right through him, but these dogs hunted *souls*, not bodies. It pinned him to the sand like a writhing black ribbon, rearing its slavering jaws back to strike at his neck.

I screamed, blasting the hound off its prey, and swooped low just as Larcen returned to his elfin self with a gasp. Then he was in my arms and we were sky-bound.

The hunting dogs bayed and gave chase, leaping from one boulder to the next to the ledges and working their way up to the ceiling at a frightening speed.

"*Nein!*" a little voice shouted. "Go away!"

"Gnat farts! Trudy!" Without thinking, I dropped Larcen and spun around to help the gnome, who was currently battering a dog across the muzzle with the carpet bag. The fabric smoked with every hit.

"Hey!" Larcen cried, dropping to the ground and rolling onto his knees. He raked his dagger against the snapping jaws of the dog who lunged at him, kicking it in the head as he backflipped onto his feet.

A sweep of my bladed fan sent the dog crashing to its side, and a kick of my crystal foot made it yelp before it scrambled to its feet with a snarl. Trudy sprinted out of the way, velvet-and-lace barmaid skirt flying, finding refuge in a fissure and tugging the carpet bag in after her. The star hound forgot about the gnome and stalked forward, blue eyes blazing at me.

I yanked my second fan out of my belt and snapped it open with a flick of my wrist. It snarled at the challenge and lunged.

Something hit me from behind. Sand coated my mouth, smothering my surprised cry, and claws as hot as molten sun gold dug into my back. The dog that had ambushed me snapped forward, seized my crystal head in its jaws, and lifted me onto my knees. Blue teeth lunged for my throat.

A chain dart wrapped around the dog's muzzle and yanked just I slashed with my fan. *The chain dart? Did Larcen just... help me?*

The bladed tips missed the dog in front of me, now that it was leashed, but I let my arm go wide, snapping the fan shut so it was just a cluster of barbs. The points rammed into the eye of the dog squeezing my head. The teeth snapped free as the dog howled, and I rolled out of the way, phasing into mist and springing into the air.

The dog pawed the fan from its face with a whine, snarling up at me even as its leaking socket cauterized and healed. The scab cracked like an eggshell before fluttering away and revealing a perfectly blazing blue star of an eye all within a few heartbeats. Then it had the audacity to use the back of its nearby kin as a springboard and leap into the air after me.

A vicious swipe of my fan brought it low to the earth.

Larcen danced out of the way as the dog crashed, his attention already split two ways as he wrangled the dog he had muzzled while defending himself with his dagger against the attacks of a second. The crackling white hide turned away the scorpion blade at every turn, growing so hot in the drow's hand he had to drop it with a hiss. He snatched up my discarded fan and raked its points against the dog's snapping jaws.

Swooping out of the air, I phased into crystal and body-slammed the dog mid-leap, sending it careening across the sand and into a boulder. The stone split with a thunderous crack, and the dog shook off the sand and loped straight back at us.

Larcen tossed me my fan as I gave his dagger an underhand throw. I pressed my back against his, and Larcen wrapped the chain of the muzzled star hound one more time around his forearm before the remaining three descended upon us.

Over the past five days, I'd learned what it truly was to have a body. To feel the muscles stretch and contract, to feel hot and cold against my skin, to the feel the solidity of the earth beneath my feet. As much as I had complained, I'd relished these new sensations. But the only sensations I focused on right now were the shifting of the drow's back against mine and the sound of his harsh breathing as he fought against the star hounds. An ariel and a drow fighting literally back-to-back. Who would've thought?

"Watch your left," Larcen barked.

"You mean the dog with all the nasty teeth?" I snarked. A sweep of my fan and a silent scream from my throat shot the hound straight into the wall, burying it beneath a rockslide. "Handled!"

Larcen jerked as the muzzled dog slammed a paw down on the chain and used the claws of the other to rip half its muzzle off to get itself free of the chain. Star fire blazed as the wound healed itself, and the angry dog leapt with a snarl.

"Drop!" I seized Larcen's braid and yanked, dropping us onto our backs as two star hounds collided in the air above us. We rolled out of the way, Larcen slashing with his dagger and me with my twin fans.

"That is a warrior's braid," he shouted, kicking off the shoulder of a dog to put some distance between them before he spun with his chain dart. "Not a rein to pull my head wherever you want."

"You can just say 'you're welcome' and get over it." I slapped both fans together, the shockwave crippling the two hounds rushing me. They face-planted into the sand and slid under my feet as I sprang into the air. "Or are there no words for that in Drozvegan?"

Larcen phased into shadow and joined me in the air, his lantern-like eyes flashing. Below us, the four dogs circled and snapped, taking turns lunging into the sky and missing our feet by inches. Malcan was nowhere to be found, but there was a thick blood trail across the sands leading into a tunnel. Gnome-sized footprints followed it.

"We can't kill them," I panted. Wincing, I gripped my stomach as I involuntarily phased from crystal to human form. I needed peanut butter crackers, fruit leather, a bottle of hot sauce, *something*. "And I'm starving. Exhausted. I can't keep this up."

Shadow-Larcen nodded, somewhat less transparent now and more opaque. He was tired too. Violet eyes flaring, he lifted his wrist. The dualcaster coin glittered like a little golden sun.

"But we haven't tested it yet." The warning Alder had given us of the devastation we could wreak if we didn't learn how to control it made me shiver. I had joined DUO to protect the innocent, not bring about another massacre. "Alder told us to try it first in a controlled environment—"

Larcen's violet eyes blazed, and though he had no voice in this form, his message was clear: *We're in the middle of the desert! We're in as controlled an environment as we're gonna get.*

I couldn't argue with that, but I still didn't like the idea of activating an unknown magic source while we were trapped inside. I was still an ariel underground, though there was a big gaping hole in the cavern ceiling above us.

"Let's get outside." I grabbed his hand, as he was becoming more solid by the second. "Maybe we can bury them—"

Larcen bellowed, no longer a shadow, as a dog clamped onto his foot. His hand was plucked from mine, and as he plummeted out of the air into the pack of writhing dogs, he shouted, "Flip your damn coin!"

I seized the golden coin at my wrist, clamped my eyes shut, and gave it a flick.

WIND PULLED AT ME. But not on the outside. No, the storm was inside me, and it was begging to be let loose. The power of the old gods surged into my veins, and I pulled at it like it was a mooring line. I—we—needed this to survive. And the storm inside me needed release, or I would explode with it.

My head snapped back with a scream.

Overhead, the flawless blue sky darkened. Storm clouds built from nothing, boiling black and crackling with lightning. Waiting for instruction. I had conjured storm winds before, but I had never controlled the storm itself.

With my bladed fan, I directed the storm at the pack of hunting dogs. The storm funneled from the sky like a tornado, swirling with lightning and black clouds and the force of a hurricane. It speared the sand, scattering the dogs like freshly threshed chaff. Lightning caught one in the flank, actually singeing it, and another was thrown aside so forcefully it cratered into the cavern wall, triggering an avalanche that destroyed yet another part of that timeless mural and burying it beneath tons of stone.

Yipping, the other two bounded away.

I yanked my fans back, ready to give chase, but they had only gone two paces before two shadowy tentacles shot out of the storm and wrapped around their rear legs. The dogs howled as they were dragged back into the darkness, paws scrambling at the sand and teeth biting at the tentacles. With each bite, the tentacle dissolves into mist, only to resolidify a second later, and the dogs were relentlessly pulled back.

The dogs I had stunned had recovered and emerged from the stone, barking and racing towards their captive kin. I swept my fans to the side, and the storm followed, churning stone into sand and sand into atoms as it clawed after them.

A shadowy figure was left in its wake.

Larcen's eyes were black, and a sleeveless robe of inky black-ness covered him from neck to foot and spread out in all direc-tions, rippling across the ground in thousands of smokey tendrils. Two of the largest had leashed the dogs, dragging them back to the darkness that emanated from the dark elf. If I had found shadow-walking horrifying, then I could only imagine what being smothered and choked with all-consuming darkness would be like.

Like he was conducting a symphony, Larcen controlled the movement of his shadows like they were tangible things. Secondary tendrils joined the first, but this time wrapping around the star hounds' throats instead of their rear legs. Tightening his fist, he began to choke them.

Whining and thrashing, they fought... and were brought to a stalemate.

It was the same for my pair of hounds. No matter how much my storm pounded them into the stone with wind, or drowned them with rain, or lashed them with lightning, they gritted their teeth and endured.

The power of the Ancients was too much, even for us.

CHAPTER THIRTY-NINE

Larcen

"LARCEN!"

My fingernails sliced into my palms, blood squeezing into the seams between my fingers, and still the dogs' throats wouldn't break. My shadows wanted to feast, and I was trying to let them, but their quarry had this annoying habit of being able to bite through them, their crackling lightning hides impervious to the utter blackness that enveloped them. And if that frustration wasn't enough, the ariel was shouting my name again, cracking my concentration.

"What?" I roared.

"It's not working!"

I strained, lashing the star hounds down with even more shadowy ropes, but it didn't seem to matter. "Suggestions?"

"Where's Malcan?"

The hunting horn. What had called these creatures could send them back. But when the ariel had dropped her illusions, shadows had come back into the sunlit cavern. Any thousands of avenues from which to escape. He could be anywhere.

Blood.

My gaze arrowed in on the thick smear across the sand. This was old, congealed, but I could still smell its freshness farther away.

"Hold these." I twisted, flinging my dogs into her storm.

Her storm caught them, pinning them against the wall with their kin and lashing them with lightning and fierce rain. Their howls raged over the storm, but so long as the ariel's strength and the Puddle's power held, they would be trapped in that maelstrom hell.

The shadows swarmed around me in my own tornado, launching me out of the gap in the cavern ceiling. The ksar exploded as I rocketed into the sky, stone and sand spraying across the desert. The evening sun was harsh, and I immediately shaded my eyes as I scanned the sand sea for any sign of Malcan.

The wind swept across the dunes, lifting reddish plumes into the air, and I smelled blood. Twisting to the right, I spied the depressions of footsteps and a carpet bag discarded halfway up a dune. A few feet later, a pair of sunglasses was already sinking into the shifting sand.

The shadows I commanded swallowed my arms and spread, giving me wings. A trail of smoke followed me as I soared over the dune, landing on the opposite side of the crest in a cloud of darkness. I stepped out, the shadows flattening against my body like a rippling robe once more.

Amidst the scattered swag of the Grow, Dammit mug, Trudy was gnawing on Malcan's leg, dodging the blows of his scimitar with the agility of a crazed squirrel. A lucky shot with the rounded butt of the hilt cracked Trudy in the side of the head, and the gnome went limp, sloughing away into the sand. He then caught sight of me, violet eyes widening as he clenched one hand over his seeping gut and used the other to help him sidle backwards towards the next dune. The hunting horn dangled from a strap on his neck, the constellations still twinkling like little diamonds.

"You were a shadow-walker all this time?" I snarled. "Why didn't you tell me? Do you know what it was like to grow up like that for years and not realize what I was?"

"We thought it better no one knew."

"Who? Father?" That made no sense. According to our laws, a shadow-walker had more claim to the throne than a royal. Malcan could've taken the throne any time he'd wished, yet he'd chosen to be Drozvega's ambassador, free to roam and... collect the oxhorn pieces of the hunting horn.

"The Spider Queen, of course."

"Her venom has made you mad."

"I prefer the term 'inspired.' The Night Lands *will* be ours again, Larcen."

"Never. The Spider Queen will never rise from her pit."

Malcan swung his scimitar as I lunged, but the shadows caught his sword arm and then the one pressed into his gut, wrenching them straight out and pinning them against the sand. Malcan grunted in pain, struggling even as dark blood continued to seep through his clothes. Seizing the hunting horn, I yanked it off his neck, the chain breaking free with a loud *snap!*

It hummed in my hand. The celestial silver stars adorning its smooth surface beckoned me, urging me to lift the horn to my lips and command the dogs to my own will.

I could kill the Spider Queen right now. I didn't need to use the ariel at all. One horn blast, and the star dogs with their coats of rippling white lightning would flood the tunnels of Drozvega and find that Spider Queen in her pit and rip into her. They would tear into her striped legs and rip into her abdomen, seize her neck in their jaws and burn her with every touch. Her screams would echo in the halls... and summon thousands to her aid. Those still enthralled to her venom. Seasoned warriors, the elders, the newly initiated fifteen-year-olds with their spider bites on the backs of their necks not yet fully healed. Mother, and Elvera, despite their faith. Thousands would come to her aid, and thousands would be slaughtered. No one would survive to teach the next generation, and my people would die as slaves.

Something inside me contracted.

The shadows pinning Malcan to the sand convulsed and retreated, writhing around my ankles like a pool of eels. The golden glow emanating from my dualcaster coin flashed.

The Puddle was giving me a warning. Its primordial desire for balance was at its tipping point. It had given me the good, these tangible shadows that obeyed my every thought, and if I continued, it would give me the bad. If I'd been a fire mage, maybe it would slowly burn me from the inside out. But I was a shadow-walker. A spellhunter. Would my own shadows consume me?

My elf ears heard the ariel shout, but she wasn't in trouble. Yet.

I had a decision to make.

Malcan's face was sour as I flicked my violet gaze from the horn back to him. He'd started crawling away from me again, clutching his wound and digging into the sand with his scimitar. I squinted into the setting sun, my expression hardening.

I could end my uncle's crazed crusade right now, and I didn't need the hunting dogs to do it. My scorpion blade felt cool against my thigh. One stab to the heart, and it would all be over. I'd still have the Spider Queen to deal with, but I could be patient a while longer. I could still use the ariel's power. I had her secret, so she wouldn't have to die. But if she didn't come willingly... we were barely partners anyway.

As he crawled away, Malcan started to laugh. "You know what you need to do, and yet you still don't have the strength to do it. A real drow wouldn't hesitate. And now you've lost everything."

That same power inside me contracted again and I released my hold on the Puddle. I needed to be alive to kill the Spider Queen. The shadows shed their robe-like form to swirl in a fog around my ankles before disappearing with a single *poof*. The ariel shouted again, this time in panic.

"I have the hunting horn in my fist and you on your back," I snarled. "I haven't lost anything."

"You lost track of time, nephew."

And just like that, the setting sun dipped below the dune. Malcan had crawled high enough that he was immediately swathed in shadow, meager as it was. He smiled, baring purple-stained teeth at me, and spat. A wad of gum—grape flavored, by the smell—tumbled down the sand. A Revital-Ball.

My chain dart buried itself into the sand just as Malcan disappeared with a wink.

Dart still buried in the dune, I stared at the spot as the shadows deepened, the power of the Puddle gone, my best chance at striking a devastating blow into the Spider Queen's plans gone.

"Larcen," the ariel shrilled, skimming low over the sands like a crazed phantom, her white hair whipping like a whitecap behind her. She slashed wildly with her fans, blasting crescents of wind and sand with little thought as to where they went. "Larcen! I let go of the Puddle and I'm—just look behind me!"

Four star dogs loped behind her like they were pursuing a hare, barking and snapping at her heels with their sparking teeth.

I lifted the hunting horn to my lips and blew.

The dogs broke off their attack immediately, which was a

good thing because Eryn whizzed behind me, using me as a shield. Her breath blasted hot against my neck as she panted.

The star hounds stood, tails lowered and ears pricked, awaiting my command. I could still send them after Malcan, but if he had returned to Drozvega, he would have no qualms about sacrificing his kin for the sake of his holy mission.

"Go back to the stars," I spat.

The dogs' forms fizzled, transforming into shapeless clusters of lightning. A second later, four white streaks blazed into the sky, disappearing into the darkening heavens. The constellations on the hunting horn dimmed, and the humming vibration in my hand stilled.

It was done.

CHAPTER FORTY

Eryn

As much as the ariel in me still protested being transported by jet—it was the principle of it all—I was too tired to care. And ravenous. I was also too tired and ravenous to care that when we landed at DUO headquarters, we would get the "ass-chewing," as Moxie called it, of a lifetime. *I'm over three hundred years old, lady. You think I've never been reprimanded before? Now pass the butter.*

I ate everything the jet's kitchen had to offer, slept, and ate some more. Somewhere over the Atlantic, Larcen turned into a rooster—the fancy English kind with all the colors—but I only looked out the window to confirm my suspicions, not the time. Time was subjective, I had to remind myself, but the stars were not. I'd seen the truth of his curse while I'd been having an attitude adjustment with that Feisty Fireball in the planetarium cavern.

Lifting the scrying glass from my belt, I examined the rooster through the lens. Just as I'd seen in the cavern, thin threads of starlight emanated from where the green glow would've been on his chest. They stretched towards the heavens, each of the eight strands connecting to a specific star in the constellation Lepus, the Hare. As long as all eight of those stars were in the sky, Larcen would turn into another prey animal, until the curse could be broken.

Larcen hadn't said much after he'd sent the star hounds back into the sky, and as a rooster, he said nothing at all. Instead he tucked his spindly legs under his feathers and brooded on his cream leather seat, his clothes a nest around him. After he'd transformed, I'd swept up his clothes into the carpet bag—birds seemed to have no control over their bowels, having been splattered by only a thousand of them in my lifetime. No doubt Larcen would find a reason to blame me for soiling his own clothes. Something cold brushed against my fingers as I wedged his sharkskin trousers under Trudy's bandaged head. A syringe? The black liquid caught the fluorescence of the interior lights and glittered at me. I hastily wedged it in the crook of Trudy's arm and layered Larcen's damask vest over it all, quickly clicking the clasp shut.

I didn't know why Larcen had kept this strange syringe a secret from me, but he was keeping mine about the Windless Place, and he was my partner. He'd proven that to me in that fight against the star dogs. When that one had had me by the head and the other ready to rip my throat out, he hadn't abandoned me this time. We had actually worked as a team, a true duo, and had it been anything other than a primordial power we had been fighting against, no doubt we would've won.

I offered the rooster some salad greens. When he didn't take them, I ruffled the feathers on his neck. Despite himself, the rooster leaned into my scratching fingers, eyelids drooping. Why was he so much easier to get along with when he was an animal?

In Alder's office, an uncomfortable silence hung in the air as Alder, Maven, Moxie, and I waited for Larcen to change back into a dark elf. Other than telling them what I had discovered about his star curse, I hadn't said a word of what had transpired in the desert.

"Do you know how to break it?" Alder had asked.

"Just because I lived in the sky for a few centuries doesn't mean I know *everything* about the stars. And we don't go around cursing people, so it's not like we're familiar with counter-curses."

Presently, Alder pruned his bonsai plant with little snips of his tiny iron shears; Maven tinkered with her newest gadget; Moxie complained about how those insufferable Spanish amphipteres had deleted all copies of the star charts I had asked for plus half a dozen files of low-priority data, citing it the last straw and that they needed to relocate the private airstrip away from the amphipteres' breeding ground. I just kept a smile on my face and clutched the carpet bag tighter to my chest.

Maven shrieked as the rooster seemed to explode and Larcen appeared in the leather chair beside me. He nonchalantly crossed his legs and ran a hand over his warrior braid with a sigh. "Who knew feathers could be so itchy?"

"Is it always like this?" Maven demanded.

I nodded. "Pretty much."

"How about some clothes, Larcen?" Alder asked, setting his shears aside.

I fished them out of the carpet bag, joining the others in looking at the ceiling while Larcen dressed. When he was done, he dropped back into the chair as the leather exhaled with a faint *foom*. "So... do you want a written report or should we just debrief now?"

"Yes," said Alder, securing his bonsai into the same cabinet as before, now that Larcen was a drow again.

"The thief you had us pursuing is not a dark mage at all, but my uncle, Malcan. A shadow-walker."

Maven gasped like some juicy morsel had just been revealed on her favorite soap opera and Alder's eyebrows flashed upward, but only for a moment.

"Well. That was... unexpected," Alder said. "And makes relations with Drozvega an absolute beast now."

"But that doesn't explain the concealment spells," Moxie said suspiciously. I wondered if she'd ever trust us again.

"No." Larcen shook his head. "He has the Spider Queen to thank for that. She... blessed him. She gave him the power to weave concealment webs. They can cover anything, even intent, if woven correctly."

"You said your uncle *is* a shadow-walker. Not wasn't," Alder said, leaning his elbows on his desk and steepling his fingers.

"He escaped," Larcen explained.

"Just like his alchemist partner, the djinn," I reminded them. I didn't want them to forget about that guy. He'd blown me through a wall after all. I needed to at least repay the favor sometime in the future.

Alder let out a long sigh. "So you flew to Barcelona with a few pieces of oxhorn and blew off Veronica and Darrius only for us to receive a strange request for a pick-up in Algiers, and folks in El Kasdir reported seeing the largest dirt devil in history somewhere on the southwestern horizon. I've looked at a map; there's nothing out there. And a shadow-walking drow and djinn alchemist escaped."

"In our defense, we lost track of the djinn after that explosion in Midnight Crossings," Larcen clarified. "Haven't seen him since."

"What were you *doing* out there?"

"Getting this." I extracted the hunting horn from the carpet bag and placed it on the desk.

"You had this the entire time?" Moxie demanded. "I could've been running diagnostics on the plane!"

Larcen and I had agreed before the jet had picked us up in Algiers that no one would see the hunting horn until we were safely back in DUO headquarters. I gave Moxie a bright smile. "I didn't want it getting lost. We've had a lot of lost shipments lately."

"I wouldn't have *lost* it," she huffed.

"Would someone please tell me what I'm looking at?" Alder asked the room.

"The horn of the Wild Hunt," I said.

The magitech twins froze, and Alder turned thoughtful.

"You mean," Maven asked slowly, "the primordial hunters who cull the souls of the living? The army that portends coming wars, famines, and natural catastrophes? *That* Wild Hunt?"

"I don't know the lore of humans," I said, "but I know this. That horn is Ancient magic, and when blown, it summons dogs from the stars that we cannot stop. Even when we flipped our coins, our power could only reach a stalemate against them. Larcen sent them back to the stars after he took the horn from Malcan."

I could tell the magitech twins were itching to examine the artifact, but Alder was the one who picked it up and turned it over in his hands. The smooth, pearlescent surface glinted in the morning light. He traced a finger over the Canis Major constellation, bringing it closer to his face to peer at the celestial silver.

"That's not all." I unclasped my belt and laid it carefully on the desk, the starlight metal glowing even in the sunlight. "Malcan seemed convinced that I should know more than I obviously do and referenced my belt. Every guardian wears one like this, and each has the same buckle. We were taught these were the tools most sacred to the Ancients: the horn, the bow, and the sword. Since we ariels don't even fight with such weapons, nor smith them, I started to wonder if we were guarding *against* them."

I leaned back in my seat. "I've had a lot of time to think on the plane ride here. To remember. Centuries ago, I was charged with protecting the valley of the night wisps, but I never asked why. All I knew was that only those who have the Steorra bloodline are chosen for that task. Ten years ago, they were massacred by the drow of Drozvega."

Larcen, who had been looking down at the carpet, seemed to be trying to drill a hole into it with his eyes.

"That night, when all was lost, something shifted. It was like I'd seen the air become tangibly thinner. And then when we confronted Malcan, he said the Wild Hunt had been curbed by the night wisps. That the *veil* had been created to keep them from running rampant. And Larcen told me that the raid on the valley had been a lie—they had taken no resources. What if the purpose had been to weaken the veil between our realm and that of the Wild Hunt?"

"And then use the hunting horn to call them the rest of the way," Alder said. He frowned. "But you said only dogs answered this call."

Swallowing, I pointed to the insignia on my belt, at the three interlocking pieces that formed one design. "I think there are more artifacts needed to finish the summoning."

Alder sucked in his breath, set the hunting horn down next to my belt, and leaned back in his chair.

Nobody moved, and if anyone was breathing, they kept it to themselves. Larcen finally looked up from the carpet and met my gaze. Drow might not be able to express regret, but they certainly were able to show resolve.

"If Eryn is right, all three will be needed to summon the Hunt," he said. "We have one. That means there are two more out there that we need to find before Malcan does. And he already has the advantage. He's had centuries to plan this, and with the Spider Queen's help, too. Malcan will not stop until he restores us to the Night Lands."

"That's what this is about?" Alder asked.

"But there are thousands of fascinari living there now," Maven exclaimed. "Maybe millions."

"Have you ever met a drow who was afraid of battle?" Larcen asked. "And with the Wild Hunt as his command, Malcan can take whatever he wants. Even expand. Our numbers have only multiplied underground."

"And the ariels will be called to protect those who can't protect themselves," I said. "The People of the Toadstools, the flower fairies. It will be another Fields of Avalor."

Larcen grimaced at the mention of that infamous battle. It had been a draw between our two peoples, the fields littered with so many of the dead that the grass had yet to grow back, even three centuries later.

"Except this time it will spill over into the human realm," Alder said gravely. "The Night Lands are anchored in the Amazon rainforest. A war on that scale would not be able to stay hidden for very long, not even there.

"Moxie, Maven, it's time you analyze this horn," he announced. "Perhaps your analysis will give us insight into finding the other two relics."

"Yes, sir," the twins said in unison.

Moxie reverently picked up the horn, and Maven was already examining it with her gadget as they left the office. I closed the door behind them with a flick of my fingers.

"And us?" I prompted.

"Larcen's still cursed, but I think it's manageable in the meantime until we find a way to break it, don't you agree?" Alder asked.

Larcen nodded. "The sooner I get my hands on Malcan, the sooner I can wring the counter curse from his neck."

"Indeed. In the meantime, you will speak of this Wild Hunt to no one. I'll not have a multi-realm panic on my hands making our jobs that much more difficult. We will handle this surgically." He leaned forward and tapped my belt buckle. "It seems King Erysson might be inclined to help us, but I doubt Drozvega will give up the king's brother."

"Not a chance. Though... we might have an ally." Larcen shifted in his seat. "My mother."

I leaned forward in my seat. I hated sitting still. "What should we do in the meantime?"

"Go back to Savannah. Train. Learn all you can about the Wild Hunt. Contact your people, if you can, and I will do the same. I'll keep you updated on the twins' progress. You're dismissed."

Larcen and I nodded and stood at the same time.

"You did good, team," Alder said, going over to the cabinet and extracting his bonsai. "It took you a while, but you did good. Keep it up."

"THANK the slop bucket you're back," Rumple cried. "Master Larcen—"

"Let me guess," the dark elf said, giving me a sideways glance, "they've threatened to turn this place into a strip club every Friday night if their demands aren't met?"

"That's a brilliant idea," Cornelius crowed from the bamboo ferns.

"I'll get my fishnets," Henrietta called.

Rumple shuddered. "They've added flamingo lawn ornaments with studded collars and leather bridles to the website, sir. I've had that computer on lockdown this entire time, sir. I have no idea how it happened."

Larcen eyed the carpet bag in my hands. Apparently Trudy had found other things to do on Moxie's laptop than just delete star charts and other low-level programs.

"Spider bites." He pinched the bridge of his nose and let out a sigh. "I suppose it could be worse. How are our sales?"

"Through the roof, sir."

"I guess I can't argue with that."

"And where is the gnome we sent with you?" Marigold demanded, brandishing her garden hoe like it was a spear.

"Trudy's just fine," I said, setting the heavy carpet bag on the ground and releasing the clasp. "See for yourself."

The fabric slid down, revealing a triumphant Bavarian barmaid of a gnome, her head still bandaged and her smile missing a tooth, sitting atop the box of a brand-new espresso machine.

Silence blanketed the collected gnomes, and one by one, each set of eyes widened in delight.

Larcen crossed his arms over his chest and growled, "Consider this recompense for above-and-beyond service. But I do *not* want to smell any milk going rancid because you all got crazy with the foamer and didn't clean up aft—"

His reprimand was drowned out as the gnomes cheered, swarming the box like ants and lifting it, and a triumphant Trudy, onto their shoulders to cart it off into the break room. Larcen rolled his eyes and let out a little huff.

I floated into the air, swirling around him as I bit back a knowing smile. "You didn't tell them that we spent over an hour going to three different stores so you could buy the *deluxe* model. You big softie."

He swatted at me like he would a fly. "Away, little bat. And I

347

was doing what you said. I was practicing being"—he grimaced—"*nice*."

"Careful, or you'll get better at it."

"Feh. Not likely." He glanced at the clock on the wall above the desk. "I shouldn't contact my mother until later, after nightfall, and I don't turn into a guinea pig or something for another ten hours or so. Do you... want to spar?"

I flashed him a delighted smile. "Sure, just let me put my stuff away, *partner*."

Larcen shuddered. "Ugh. Don't say that. We're not there yet."

"Oh, I think we are, *partner*."

"Stop saying that!"

"I'll say it and you'll like it," I said as I floated up to my bed in the rafters. "Especially if you want me to keep protecting you when you turn into a nice fat grub or a cute little frog."

"Fiiine. I'll see you on the roof, *partner*."

I smacked my floating hair out of the way so I could look down at him. "The roof? Not your creepy little dungeon?"

"Don't make me change my mind." And then he stepped into the shadows.

I quickly unloaded my carpet bag into my crate and kept my desert clothes on—the linen trousers and cotton shirt really had a delightful breathability about them. On top of my meager possessions, I placed the scrying glass, the lens catching the afternoon light and lancing me across the eyes.

I blinked away the resulting tears. Served me right for lying. Of course I knew how to break a star curse, but I wasn't about to tell the drow that. It was the only curse that could kill an ariel, which would explain why Malcan had wanted to fire that arrow at me. The pull of the stars as they wheeled through the sky would've torn me apart that first night. The curse had hit the drow instead, mutating it, but the method to break it was still the same.

And I needed to keep that card up my sleeve, as the human saying went, until I could use it to gain my guardianship back. And if Alder Shaw was successful in securing us entrance to the Temple of the Sky, I would be playing that card very soon. That dark elf would confess, or be cursed to transform every night Lepus was in the sky, and that's if the ariels chose to let the drow who had led the attack on the valley of the night wisps live.

Still, guilt chewed on me like the perpetual hunger that gnawed on my stomach. Larcen and I had fought with each other, saved each other, even—stars above, we were even bonded by the Puddle—and here I was with a knife poised above his back. But he had killed my charges, the innocent night wisps. I could never forgive that.

A shadow passed over me, and I whirled around to see Larcen's blurred image as he stood on the polytunnel, hands on his hips. "Coming, little bat?"

"Get ready to eat my bladed fan," I fired back with a fierce smile, phasing into mist. *Now, and again when the ariels take their vengeance.*

The End of Book I

CONTINUE THE ADVENTURE

Eryn and Larcen aren't done yet! Click here to sign up for a BONUS SCENE as well as chapters 1-3 of the (currently unnamed) sequel.

"Would you like to know more?" — *Starship Troopers*

Join me online! Lurkers welcome!

Author Website:kattasticreads.com
  Follow on Facebook: Kat of Kattastic Reads (page)
  Kat Healy's Magical Book Café (reader group aka the fun zone)
  Delta Underground Operatives (page)
  Follow on Instagram: @thekatwithblueeyes

ACKNOWLEDGMENTS

At the beginning of 2022, I declared, "Lord, let this be my Year of Opportunity. Whatever comes my way, let me say yes—to the best of my sanity and ability, of course."

Then along came Nicole Grotepas, an author I knew nothing of, with an offer: join her in writing Delta Underground Operatives.

Yes.

A special thanks to Jenn Mitchell (J Lee Mitchell to some) and Shavonne Clarke (SW Clarke to some others) for advocating me to Nicole for her consideration. Your support and belief in my abilities means the world.

To Scott Walker, who quickly adopted me in this group. I call him my mentor. He insists on calling me his peer. We've may or may not have settled on Menteer...

To my fellow dualcaster authors: you guys and gals are great. You all accepted this greenhorn without a second thought, which was a huge boost in my confidence. We had some great laughs (still do) and you've been instrumental in not just making me a more thoughtful series writer, but a more purposeful indie publisher/marketer/swag-slinger. I'm so happy I got to meet a lot of you at the 20BooksTo50K Vegas 2022 conference!

And to my family, particularly that handsome man I married: you're the bestest sounding board ever. Whenever I need an uncouth comment, you're right there. Whenever I need to make a scene more bizarre, your ideas never fail. And to my Wagtail Collective for all the snuggles and walks we went on to clear my head.

Lastly, but certainly not least, to you, my reader. You bought this book, you read it to the end, and hopefully it meant something to you. Maybe it was all the feats of derring-do? The snappy dialogue? The intrigue? A lovable sidekick? (I love me some Rumple.) Whatever it was, I appreciate your time and enthusiasm. Stay tuned for the sequel! Larcen and Eryn aren't done yet!

CREDITS

Editor:
Motif Edits

Cover:
JoY Author Design Studio

Formatting:
Crimson Sun Graphics

ABOUT THE AUTHOR

Kat Healy is an urban fantasy author living in the Midwest with her Wagtail Collective: an adorable black cat named Nefertiti, a goofy hound dog named Griffin, and a spiteful-yet-affectionate cat named Turtledove Warpaint (she insisted Kat publish her full name, because the world needs to know what a boss she is).

She also has a sass-mouthing writing partner named Olive. You can learn more about her and her antics online.

When not writing, she tries her best at turning her yard into an orchard, because this lady has a thing about fruit. And pastries, particularly the flaky kind. Or just food in general. And since those calories won't burn themselves off (pity), she enjoys outdoor adventures, particularly snorkeling, hiking, and kayaking. Oh, and cage fighting. Not particularly an outdoor adventure, but it's a real rush.

UPCOMING DUO TITLES:

Hunter's Curse - Kat Healy
Consuming Wind - Kimbra Swain
Revenant's Brigade - Jenn Mitchell
Cloak and Dagger - Scott Walker
Split Infinity - Jamie Davis
Whisper and Blade - S. W. Clarke
Halo of Light - N. A. Grotepas
Unholy Deuce - Ben Zackheim
Puppet Master - Mel Todd

Visit the Delta Underground Operatives Facebook Page for updates and information.

Made in United States
North Haven, CT
03 July 2024

54379081R00219